A double graduate in engineering
much of his early working life in
the attractions of the City of Lonc
He plied his developing investment
marketplace from Milan to Stockhc
most of his time in the German- and I ...-speaking business world before moving gently into semi-retirement. Then he started to write, drawing on a great wealth of personal, political and business experiences, which he hopes lend richness and credibility to his tales.

He remains passionate about many things, including but not limited to culture and language, travel, geography, food, fitness (cycling, rowing and rugby specifically), politics, economics and the arts. One day he will get back to those oils and acrylics of his youth, but not yet. There are still a few more books in his head, each one jostling for his attention.

Oliver lives with his wife in Suffolk, England. Their adult children are spread conveniently about the globe, offering useful stopovers for the next big trip!

Find out more at www.oliverecadam.com

MEN ON THE HILL

Also by Oliver E Cadam

Once Too Many Times

A lifelong love affair 'out of Africa' is cruelly invaded by a devious fraud whose charade carries him through twenty years of wistful scheming to the point of no return. But how quickly even the best-laid plans can unravel! Was he overreacting? Was she really pushing him away, and so soon? But why...what did she know?

Idle Deceptions

The first in the DCI David Lehrer series

Surely it had been a contract killing...such a clean despatch...and to DCI Lehrer's experienced eye, not unlike recent calculated assaults in and around the ports. But his investigation struggles to establish links to those who value firearms, drugs and illegal migrants as assets to be defended at all costs. How could a very ordinary life produce such a confusing list of suspects?

THE SECOND IN THE DCI DAVID LEHRER SERIES

MEN ON THE HILL

OLIVER E CADAM

SilverWood

Published in 2017 by SilverWood Books

SilverWood Books Ltd
14 Small Street, Bristol, BS1 1DE, United Kingdom
www.silverwoodbooks.co.uk

ISBN 978-1-78132-641-1 (paperback)
ISBN 978-1-78132-642-8 (ebook)

British Library Cataloguing in Publication Data
A CIP catalogue record for this book is available from the British Library

Page design and typesetting by SilverWood Books
Printed on responsibly sourced paper

1

a question of priorities

There was nothing quite like English rain, she thought. In fact, there was nothing like Lake District rain at all. It had that peculiarly soporific quality when, on still airless days in spring or early summer, it would fall vertically from the grey clouds with such intensity that it became a series of signature sounds upon reaching the earth below. Above her a steady dull thrumming indicated a torrential deluge. Its impact vibrated through the heavy roof slates and conveyed a subtle muted resonance in the beautiful wooden trusses still exposed within the bedroom. The gutters and spouts gushed and spluttered as gravity drew the flow inexorably earthward, and as the downpour smacked onto the cobbled yard outside a sibilant hypnosis teased her wandering mind.

She felt a little dreamy as she lay there assimilating the familiar soundtrack. Her eyelids fought reluctantly against her natural inclination to drift off. But in the shallows of her somnolence, her mind hurried this way and that as she sought to order some of the more chaotic features of the unsettling life she had built around herself.

It wasn't just how she spent her time or what attracted her attention from one day to the next. It wasn't her location either. She liked living in the grand house up on the hill. She especially enjoyed the apparently elevated status she had been accorded in the local community by virtue of their impressive property and enviable surroundings. Well anyway, she thought the place to be splendid, and she was not alone, or so it appeared.

She didn't think her disquiet had much to do with their few neighbours either, but she readily conceded that they were all seemingly pressed quite close together within the layout of their shared, remote settlement. The farm next door was probably more accurately described as semi-detached, bearing in mind the original Victorian model-farm concept. It even facilitated a joining door from the farm kitchen through into her old scullery, which, these days, served as a wood store for the modern kitchen range. They really should have closed that off when they'd spent all that money on the refurbishment project. Ah well, too late now!

With that reference to money, she remembered the roof leak in the largest guest room – the damp stain above the door to the en suite bathroom would again be absorbing the wet in weather like this. Oh yes, and that reminded her of the drainage problem below the restored Lakeland cottage out the back. Their elderly tenants were so lovely, gentle souls both. But they baulked at every need to ask for something to be repaired or replaced when failure of service or supply had brought them to a standstill. No, they kept themselves very much to themselves and she only ever saw them as they headed off for their regular constitutional hikes out onto the fells.

No, it was more than that. It was something else...something about relationships, so many tangled liaisons. Was it about managing things a little more carefully, or was it more to do with the toll it had taken on her in recent years as she'd juggled her priorities in an ever more frantic schedule? Would she want to change things? Was it really so bad? Would she miss the excitement if her life were to become suddenly more conventional? Oh yes, for sure, she knew without a moment's hesitation that she couldn't jettison the thrill of it all.

As she lay there supine, naked, her arms locked together over her midriff, constraining her fulsome breasts, she perceived the external cascade as a background rush as her mind skipped through these, her own flailing concerns. She was disconcerted and sufficiently perturbed to want, need even, to find the source of her anxiety. She realised that it wasn't even about her own immediate family. Well, at least not entirely. That had its problems, of course, but didn't all families? It was certainly more to do with the men in her life, all of them, and seemingly so many. Indeed, how had she reached this point? How had she worked her way into such a consistently stressful existence, a rigmarole which demanded so much forward planning and yet still introduced so many risks in its execution? Even accounting for the fun of it all, was it really worth it...really...seriously?

Gilly thought about her husband, Keith. She smiled. She raised her hands and clasped them behind her head and squashed them into her pillow. Her heavy breasts sagged to either side and she felt them pressing on her ribcage.

He'd always wanted to come back home to Cumbria. Even from their earliest dates together in Manchester, she'd known that he was never likely to stray far from the northwest. South Lakeland would consume him once again just as soon as he felt he'd made something of himself; enough at least to allow himself to hold his head up high.

He came from humble origins. Humility came quickly in Barrow-in-Furness! As a Grange-over-Sands girl she could say that, and she smiled again at the point scored. Ironically though, she considered, he hadn't really tamed that ego. He could be a bit up himself, as the modern vernacular might put it. Yes he'd done pretty well for an ordinary northern lad, and he'd furnished the family with a decent standard of living, but the pinnacle of his career achievement so far had been the finance director's job at a run-down local quarry. The owner, his old school mucker, Austen, had promised him the earth. Well…not the earth exactly, but local prestige at least and significant earnings. But that great gaping pit in the ground had seen its best days fully ten years before they were persuaded by Austen to move back up so that Keith could take over the effective running of the business. Of course it had been a con trick of the most slippery kind – and between mates as well – but they'd muddled through it. Keith had latched on to Austen's hallowed reputation among the great and the philanthropic good of the elevated echelons of Cumbrian country society…if indeed such social climbing was possible or even relevant in Cumbria. The clincher had been this house. In the end it had been the real sweetener in the deal that had made it palatable for Keith.

But what about her own view? Yes, she could tell herself that she was happy. She knew that they could never have afforded such a spacious and well-appointed home of this calibre without Austen's assistance – guilt money she had always tagged it. But their diverse and fascinating relationships with Austen had brought a variety of unexpected rewards which she could never have predicted or rejected.

In any event, Keith's often-sullen moods had picked up of late.

He seemed more buoyant, more optimistic perhaps than he had for a long time. They'd even gathered enough cash together to have the entire premises rather lavishly redecorated, and to quite some standard too. He'd muttered something the other day about sending the lads a slightly bigger stipend while they were still at university, so the old quarry must still have a bit of slate in it yet. Yes, whatever the reason or reasons, Keith had recovered some of that jaunty swagger she remembered from twenty years ago. Okay, at forty-seven he was a lot thicker round the middle than he'd ever been, and he really did need to address that fairly soon and fairly seriously, but it was nice to see a spring in that albeit laboured step. Maybe she should get him a pair of walking boots and push him out onto the fells at weekends to encourage some kind of cardiovascular exercise programme. But then she frowned. That just wouldn't be him. In fact neither of them had any real interest in the great outdoors despite living on the top of a hill at the end of a two-mile track in the middle of nowhere surrounded by some of Britain's wildest and most rugged countryside.

Still, she mused, at least his amorous attentions towards her hadn't shown any aggravated inclinations of late, and for that she was grateful. She managed his expectations carefully in that regard. She tried to keep their assignations to something approximating a six-week cycle, and even then she cleverly seduced him when he was inebriated, or at least pretty well oiled, because she knew his staying power then to be worse than unreliable.

She grinned to herself. She wondered how often he had seen his little winky in recent years other than in the full-length bathroom mirror, hiding as it did beneath that sagging pot-belly. Anyway, it was hardly impressive, and she hated the way that his belly slapped against her bottom as he tried to jam the little thing into her from behind. She refused to take him on top anymore; it was just too grotesque, especially now that she had better physical encounters to look forward to and to relish.

The rain still pummelled the rooftops and the trickling water in the gutters subdued her thought processes temporarily. She turned her head slightly to one side and watched him as he slept. He nearly always fell into a soft sublime sleep immediately after he'd exploded inside her and rolled away in complete exhaustion. She looked at him now. One arm was thrown above and behind his gorgeous pre-Raphaelite curls and the other lay wide to the far side of her bed. His bristly boyish shadow reached down towards his bulging Adam's apple. His lips, slightly parted, snored a gentle quiet rhythm as his impressive pectorals rose in synchronised time. She counted the ribs she could see down his near flank. She marvelled at the rippling abdominals, which led her admiring assessment to the fine pubic line running south to his manhood. There it lay, his flaccid member, sticky with her wetness, bloated like a great wet shiny slug, brown and wrinkled and thoroughly ugly. She knew just how easily she could transform that despicable creature into the rampant bulging totem she had come to want and need with such ill-disciplined regularity. And boy oh boy did he know how to use it! He lay there relaxed and supple, her own Adonis, a young man not much older than her own sons. He had learned so many deft and skilful pleasures during the last couple of years purely, and probably exclusively, through her thorough instruction. This beautiful boy knew how to make love, and he certainly knew how to fuck! A pounding heart inside his magnificent corporeal frame; the engine he relied upon to drive his awesome erection to her heart's selfish desires. She loved him, but more obviously, she knew, she lusted after him and those climactic highs only he could craft for her.

They had played their clandestine game for more than two years. Through careful and yet simplistic planning they had so far gone undetected, even at festive times and holidays when there were usually so many more people about. He kept himself busy on the farm whenever her own boys came home from university. He maintained a certain distance, a deliberate sense of the aloof, so as not to encourage any great time-share with the teenagers.

They had never worried about Keith turning up unexpectedly: for one thing it was impossible to navigate the long stony driveway undetected, and they both knew that Keith worked long hours at the quarry and almost never took any time off in a typical working week.

But even then, at those domestically fraught times of year, she had still managed the odd riotous tryst with him in the most outrageous of places and she had been so grateful for the sexual release. In that specific regard their clever little signalling system had worked a treat on more occasions than she dared to recall. Seeing him out on the farm, hefting bales or wrestling sheep for the shearing, she had found herself so stimulated by the mere sight of his sweating muscular body that she found herself just needing him right there and then. How wonderful then for him to trundle out into the fields in the pickup or on the quad bike ostensibly to check on the ewes or their lambs, only to take a very short stop behind the drystone wall at the end of their extensive plot and a quick detour through the old gate shrouded in wisteria – just a few strides to the potting shed where they thrashed together standing up for no more than a minute or two before he zipped up and disappeared back on his tour of duty.

She contemplated the notion that she might be some kind of predatory pervert, or perhaps just over-sexed, but no…it wasn't like that at all. This was a young man, but a man not a boy like her sons. This was a man who knew how to satisfy a demanding woman. Did it matter that he was more than fifteen years her junior? Whether he plied his passionate trades elsewhere, among younger women, she couldn't tell, but she instinctively doubted that.

How his mother might react if she were ever to discover their secret would be an altogether different prospect, but could she honestly say she cared? Old Ruby hadn't exactly unfurled the red carpet when they had eventually moved into the big house next door. After all the problems Ruby had endured with the previous owners of Rowan House you'd have thought a fresh start might have appealed in many ways to her and her grumpy old husband, Eric. Some neighbours they had turned out to be! They were always harping on about something or other, but the root cause of their disenchantment had been envy. They had coveted the house for themselves, but their scruffy sheep farm hadn't been able to support the outlay until their son, and only son, had come of age. He'd smartened the place up, delved deep into the cosy government grant system and opened up the old dying business to several new outlets: holiday cottages, wood supply and timber, pheasant rearing and shooting, and *green guardianship* – whatever the liberal do-gooders believed that to be. Their boy, her lover, had come of age in more ways than they had realised, and Gilly had no intentions of giving up on him for the foreseeable future.

She watched him as he snoozed quietly. She wanted to touch him. She'd have to wake him soon. His miserable old dad had driven off to

Newby Bridge an hour ago and he'd be back soon enough.

"No point in being caught out by your father when he comes looking for you to ask why that fence hasn't been fixed," she said softly to him. But in his slumber she knew he'd not registered the remark, and so what if she wanted just a few more precious moments with him, just to watch him, just to enjoy him?

She smiled again and almost dissolved into a fit of giggles when she noticed, as if for the very first time, his enormous feet. She snorted as she quelled her humour and he rustled a little before rolling over with a grunt, thus exposing his firm taut buttocks and broad powerful shoulders. She gave a plaintive gasp of admiration. God, how Keith and Austen just couldn't get near, by comparison, to this specimen of chiselled masculinity.

She reclined full-length again, looked at the beams above her, and reflected on Austen, her other *sometimes* casual lover. She dreaded to think how Keith would react if he ever found out. Then she recoiled from that idea in favour of which would be worse: Austen, his boss and lifelong friend, or young Ben, the sex machine lying comatose beside her? But Austen was indeed a very casual acquaintance, at least of the sexual kind. More often than not he was a friendly visitor, dinner guest or drinking buddy for Keith. He'd treated them to some wonderful holiday experiences and fascinating trips, but she could never quite escape the nagging irritation that all of it had been some form of apology for having stitched up Keith's last and most pivotal career move.

Having said that, she hadn't turned him down when, in a fairly drunken stupor, he'd propositioned her in the basement whilst hunting down a Château Lafite. He'd humped her right there and then. It had been a non-event by her demanding standards, but they'd reconvened on the odd occasion since then and he'd not let her down.

She knew she was no looker, and perhaps her acceptance of that had led her to get married too early to a man she had once loved and now simply tolerated. However, she also knew that she had great tits! Men looked at her or, more accurately, at *them* wherever she went, and she could see their appreciation telegraphed across their unguarded faces. Ben had been no different, but at least he had chosen to look away when her eyes had held his gaze and challenged him. She'd known then that she would have him, and thank the dear Lord for the encounter.

She tilted her head forward and stared down the length of her naked form. She wasn't too unhappy with the outcome. She would never like her stretch marks, obviously. She was a bit loose around the tummy, and her bottom too for that matter, but in her early forties, she really didn't think she looked too bad. Hey, she counselled herself silently, if a twenty-five-year-old stallion couldn't get enough of her, why should she complain? She followed her line of sight down to her dark blonde pubis, recognising a recent trim perhaps just a fraction too close. Then she alighted upon a ruffled plume of Kleenex tissue which she'd stuffed between her legs to prevent any leakage of his warm gooey mess. Her heavy thighs ran away to slender lower limbs and quite delicate feet. She looked again at those thighs and sighed in frustration.

She leaned over and prodded him with a stiff finger, saying, "Time to get up and get out, lover boy." He groaned and twitched, but only when she reminded him about his father returning shortly did he sit up and look around for his shabby working clothes.

She swung her legs off the bed and sat up with her back to his on the other side of the bed. Then she stood, careful not to lose her tissue, and waddled around the bed straight past him and into the bathroom. She knew he would be transfixed by her pendulous boobs and so he was, but she ignored him, locked the door behind her and by the time she emerged he'd disappeared just as stealthily as he'd arrived an hour earlier.

The rain had stopped. She wouldn't have noticed but for a shaft of early-afternoon springtime sunlight that bounced off the wet tiles of an adjacent gable and illuminated the bedroom just as if someone had flicked a switch.

She parked herself on the corner of the bed as she towelled her hair dry. The lads would be back from uni in a few weeks and she was looking forward to that. They both had short summer jobs – short in the context of going travelling from the back end of July well into September. Evan wouldn't be back at Lancaster for his final year until October, and he planned to put in a few weeks at the cattle mart in Ulverston before heading off to South America with his girlfriend. Will had opted for shelf stacking at the Farm Store in Grange, but he too would ditch that after about six weeks in favour of another six weeks in Toulouse on a business-French course with Airbus. That had been a prestigious scoop for him, and he didn't need to return to Stirling until the very last week in October. She felt a sudden pang of anxiety for them. Was it Evan backpacking in Argentina, which hardly filled her with glee, or was it just her understanding that they needed to do well in order to escape this hilltop life which offered them absolutely nothing in terms of career development? Didn't all mothers fret about their kids? She guessed so.

Rummaging around again with the towel, she decided it was time for the drier, but something had thrown an emotional trip and she recognised the downward spiral to her little girl lost. She wondered about the boys and just how much they could really remember. They'd been just six and seven when Alice had eventually succumbed to the ravaging tumour at the age of five. In these moments of despair, which Gilly shunned as best she could whenever they crept up on her, she could never determine whether or not it would be best for the boys to have retained nothing of it, or, conversely, that they might still remember their cute little sister and much that she had brought into their household. She often wanted to talk to them about it, but Keith had sternly counselled against it lest it should prove unsettling and disruptive to them as they were growing up. She now felt less and less inclined to follow his lead however, arguing to herself that they were surely old enough to discuss the trauma, if in fact it remained traumatic for them. On the other hand it never quite seemed right, and they never broached the subject unprompted, so she carried on with a certain reluctance to engage with them from the heart, her forever-to-be-broken heart.

Alice had indeed been a bright, interesting and excitable little thing who had rounded off the family unit perfectly; that much Gilly held as incontrovertible. How many times had she projected that forlorn hope for a long-term mother-and-daughter relationship? How different might life have been? Where would they have ended up – still here on their Lakeland hilltop or somewhere very different? Would her own relationships have developed along very different lines suspecting, as she did, that young women are very much more perceptive than most men, even grown men? All of these questions and a myriad of applicable responses swirled around in her head, and she knew from long experience that there was no profit in this morose train of thought. She bit her lip and smeared an unwelcome tear across her cheek with the back of a forefinger. Despite so many distractions she would always fall foul of these brittle moments when she couldn't banish the anguish of their very own tragedy. She chided herself as she remembered that she hadn't been down to Alice's grave in South Manchester for quite some months. She promised herself and Alice that she would put that right soon.

Then she heard a bit of a commotion outside and she crept, still naked and not wishing to expose herself, towards the window. She peeped out to see the girls from the Lodge House apparently running across the lane and dipping in and out of their own gate. A strange couple, she thought, as she peeked past the edge of the curtain. Obviously *girly* girls, she acknowledged to herself flippantly. Helen was clearly the bloke in the relationship, she argued with equally unabashed candour, but they were amicable and chatty whenever she met them out there by the gates and she really couldn't fault them. She and Keith had even been invited round for drinks and the whole thing had been so much fun that they had reciprocated. It had been a huge success except for the smirks of their own sons, who had struggled in their immaturity to accept the status quo. Never mind – the girls had handled the whole thing quite superbly. No...that wasn't why she often felt in a way confused about those girls; it was their astonishing fitness regime matched only by their burning commitment to all things environmental. Their green credentials seemed to consume them and they appeared less than comfortable with the National Park Authority for some reason to which Gilly had simply never paid enough attention to understand. Certainly they were often out on the high tops in all weathers and their cross-country running and cycling endeavours had become legendary in just the couple of years since their arrival. In fact, hadn't someone mentioned that they'd been wetsuit swim training in Coniston Water last winter? Something to do with those three-way races...what were they called, triathlons or some such? Bizarre!

But what are they doing? she asked herself mutely. Oh...ha! It's a runaway sheep. Poor thing must have barged its way through one of Ben's makeshift fences – where the drystone walls had collapsed here and there – and shot off down the lane. It looked like they were trying to coral it inside their gate at the old lodge. She laughed out loud as she spotted the animal bolt past the girls and make a break for freedom. But sure enough one of them took off at a formidable lick and overhauled it quite quickly, ushering it back up the track and eventually in through their own yawning gate which was then hurriedly closed and secured. They'd summon Ben, she knew that, and he'd run down with the quad bike and the short trailer attached to collect the woolly prisoner. She honestly didn't know whether or not they too would admire his sturdy frame. Perhaps they would, at least from an athletic perspective, but surely not with any form of sexual appreciation. Either way, she felt no pangs of jealousy.

She retreated from the window, threw the wardrobe doors open and flicked through her casual gear. She thought she might take a run into the village. She reminded herself that there remained a lot of heavy grey cloud around and she should be prepared for more rain. She also warned herself to make the damned bed before she left.

2

dyed in the wool

Ruby Meaner (née Greenmoor) had lived in the Lakes area all her life. Her parents had owned a sheep farm over Kentmere way, just above the village of the same name. She'd gone to school there, and later in Staveley in her teens. She'd not been a great scholar, but her days in the classroom had been tolerable. She'd loved the wild hillsides and fells up above her father's small enclosures. Her favourite escape was always to hurry aloft on sunny afternoons after school, so long as she'd finished her chores of course, to sit in the protective lee of gorse or broom and look down upon the loose collection of small stone buildings. There she would watch the slow progression of the flock of Herdwicks as they chewed the short grass, periodically raising a head here and there to locate wayward lambs or to anticipate dangerous intruders – foxes were particularly prevalent in that valley, despite the very active local hunt. Her father's cold commercial assessment would have suggested that once the summer sun warmed the slopes the lambs would be simply too daunting a prospect even for a rogue dog or a determined vixen. But in the early spring, when snow could still fall regularly, the tiny newborns offered a welcome kill to experienced hunters who had hungry cubs to feed.

The celebrated Herdwicks were a tough lot. They were associated with the southern and western sectors originally, but their hardy resilience and pleasant nature had made them popular in many parts of the region. Their weakness was simply that their lambs were small by the standards of other breeds and they grew slowly. Such basic factors would always test the viability of a small herd.

Times had always been tough for Ruby and her family, but that didn't divert her attentions elsewhere when seeking a role in adult life.

During her formative years she had travelled little, having waited several decades before she made her first and only trip to London. She had never travelled abroad – well, if she excluded that holiday in the Isle of Man – and even Manchester, Leeds and Liverpool counted as great adventures. Nevertheless she had been happy as a youngster and never imagined moving away from either farming or the Lake District itself; God's own back yard, as she liked to call it.

She had met Eric in a pub in Windermere. In so many ways he wasn't a great catch, but his enthusiasm for farming, despite his *towny* background, had captured her imagination. With a small contribution from his father (an office manager in Penrith), together with a terrifying bank loan from Lloyds in Ambleside, they'd pitched themselves into sheep farming. It had been a prospect so daunting that it took Eric three lambing seasons before he fully realised what they'd done. Ruby had been only twenty years of age and Eric just twenty-five, and yet they had bought Rowan Tree Farm near Satterthwaite, just below Grizedale Forest and high above the silvery sheen of Coniston Water.

As she sat alone in her farmhouse kitchen, she cupped her hands around her coffee mug. She looked through the narrow window, without focus, at the distant slopes beyond her small walled garden. She was miles away, both in distance and time, as she reflected on so many events from those early days; the thrill and the hardship, the joy and the bitter taste of so many disappointments.

They had bought the place at auction in 1970 – could that really be thirty-seven years ago? Fortunately its dilapidated state had engendered little local interest so their hastily gathered finances were not totally swamped by the purchase. Their own land comprised just a little over two hundred acres of rough stony territory with a couple of local water courses, a holding pond in one stream and a natural water source pumped from below the heights up behind the main farm itself. In addition, and so typical of many Lakeland livestock farms, they also had grazing rights of access to a vast area of open fell pushing right up to the boundaries of Grizedale Forest itself. They shared this territory with several other farmers, but that wasn't unusual, and under normal circumstances it might have encouraged a greater sense of community with others of the same vocation. However, Eric had always viewed his neighbours as competitors rather than collaborators despite a great deal of help and assistance they'd enjoyed in their earliest travails.

The farm was reached by a narrow but metalled one-way road (with passing places) which meandered for nearly two miles up from the lower road at High Ickenthwaite. For most of its length it was bordered by a dense swathe of trees, evergreen and deciduous, which kept the westerlies at bay in the winter and thus gave the animals some shelter in the worst of the weather. Ruby conceded in her reflections of those days that they had seen the woods as something of a limited resource until quite recently when her son, Ben, had initiated a small and growing timber business of sorts. For decades the wooded areas had been merely a source of firewood for their own home – a trick missed for sure – but she knew that only when government grants became available for business diversification had they started in earnest to siphon available funds.

It had been the European Union that had really made the difference. She shook her head gently in amused dismay at how much money was being thrown around for fallow fields, clean drains, sewage treatment, water purification and an extensive list of environmental and commercial causes that neither she nor Eric could ever have predicted way back then in the early seventies. Then, with barely two pennies to rub together, they had worked themselves to sleep many a night, fixing fences and drystone walls, lambing in the early hours by jeep headlight out there in the driving rain; the lambing ewes would take themselves off to the far corners to lie down and so were often still out there instead of back in the birthing pens in the barn. Even so, that had certainly been the time of their lives, and she nodded gently as if to affirm her recollections in her own mind.

As the years had ticked along they'd done alright, but their concentration on just sheep and a few cattle had constrained their growth for too long. Yes, they'd got up to six hundred head of sheep, mainly Swaledales and Herdwicks, but the farm had remained tatty and cluttered as they'd focused more on livestock than on property. In defence of themselves they'd had little time for anything else, but when grants were offered for holiday cottages they were already well behind the curve in terms of prettifying their immediate surroundings conducive to taking in holidaymakers. Of course they had then put some extra muscle into that aspect of diversification. They'd borrowed a few times to accelerate those changes deemed necessary by England's Heritage and Cumbria Lakes Cottages in order to achieve their ridiculous ratings and endorsements. She'd soon learned how to cut some of those corners. They were able to get a couple of carefully secluded caravans plus their first rented cottage into the holiday magazines in time for the Easter break of 1990. The demands made of them by the planning department at South Lakeland's County Council had been onerous bordering on hysterical, but they'd installed a small additional septic tank and promised to treat their groundswell water even though it looked as clear as melted snow.

All the while they'd worked around their various neighbours next door at Rowan House. The old place, in fact the entire settlement, had been developed as a Victorian model-farm late in the nineteenth century. Many of the features of the original layout were still clearly evident even to any present-day hiker who might wander through the yard on his way to Grizedale via the public footpath which drew walkers up from the lower levels. The house wasn't so grand really – better now after Keith and Gilly had put some cash into the fabric of the buildings, and into the gardens, but a country manor it certainly was not. A big house tacked onto their own would have been a better description, and Ruby grudgingly acknowledged that they should have secured it for themselves when that outdoor activities business had gone bust and vacated the premises almost overnight. It hadn't even been expensive! They'd worried about the flooded basement and that bit of structural cracking in the gable end, but it had been a short-sighted mistake and now they had *Her Ladyship* lording it over them from her gazebo while taking tea in the sun. They hadn't been in there that long...what, about...well, actually it must be about ten years now. Mid-nineties, she reckoned, so yes, a little longer than she had thought, but what a miserable cow that Gilly had turned out to be. And Keith...well, he fancied himself as some sort of bigwig – got himself on the local parish council for a while before he realised how tedious that could be. Then he seemed to disappear off the map in favour of that old quarry.

They'd seen Austen Smiley up close quite a few times in recent years. He was worth knowing, for sure. His reputation had stretched right across the Lakes with his good deeds, good works and quite a lot of funding here and there – he could give the EU a run for its very considerable money, and presumably he didn't ask for quite so many boxes to be ticked and files to be stacked. Those very careful bureaucrats in Brussels always made sure that backsides were safely covered. Anyway, she mused, whose money was it that they were doling out if not British taxpayers' in the first place?

She took a last slurp of her fast-cooling coffee, before moving over to the sink to leave the mug in the washing-up bowl. Just then she recognised the distant rumble of a vehicle approaching up the rutted track – not much tarmac left these days, she thought. Hardly surprising, she countered silently, after all those trucks and vans had been bashing their way up to Rowan House to facilitate their extensive works in recent years. Had their Lord and Ladyship offered to chip in for some repairs to the surface of the drive? Well of course not! Even those pen pushers at the development grants office wouldn't consider something as basic as vehicular access as a qualifying factor in their need to do something with the lane. After weeks of heavy rain it seemed like they were driving home up a riverbed. Sometimes the torrent gushed up to the middle of the hubcaps in places. No wonder they all had four-wheel drives and pickups! Sometimes, in a few inches of winter snow, only tractors could make it up the steeper sections. The gouged and worn bends were especially treacherous for normal everyday cars.

It was Eric, back from Newby Bridge. She could tell it was him from the familiar rumble of the pickup. He'd been to get a few extra lengths of portable fencing for the temporary pens Ben wanted to set up for the sheep dosing procedures in a week or so. They could do that job in a day each in three of the main fields so long as they got themselves organised and the dogs were on form. They'd been promised a bit of help from the local vets practice in Haverthwaite, but she knew it was only because the young trainee there had taken a shine to Ben. He had shrugged his shoulders when he'd heard, but he couldn't fool his old ma who, at this moment and for the first time in over an hour, wondered where he could be. At least the rain had eased. She could see a touch of blue sky out the back. Maybe she should nip round the cottages and check they were all tidy before their holiday lodgers got back from mountain biking up in the forest. Apparently those colour-coded runs were quite something – just like skiing they said, although what that meant she couldn't hope to guess.

By the time she'd pulled her boots on Eric had parked the Toyota and jumped straight into the John Deere bubble car: a two-seater, Perspex-covered rock-hopper that he used to run around the outer reaches in wet weather. She shuffled out into the yard having flicked the kettle on hoping he'd take a short break and a mug of tea, but as she opened the door she heard the buggy start up.

"Eric wait...what about a cuppa...Eric?" she shouted, but the din of the motor masked her call and she only just caught a glimpse of his hunched shoulders and silver hair as he chugged round the bend in the lane and out of sight.

"Oh, Eric," she protested out loud as she watched him go, "you shouldn't be working this hard at your age, you daft ha'porth. There's always time for a cuppa...well, almost always," she added ruefully.

She changed tack and padded over to the five static caravans in the dell, but no sooner had she stuck her head in through the doors of the first two did she abandon the examination. Katarina had them looking spotlessly clean, and she marvelled yet again at the industry and reliability of their Polish cleaning girl who seemed to come and go exactly as required, with minimum fuss, producing outstanding results.

Ruby's features crinkled into a little grin as she backtracked to the yard, remembering meeting Katarina and her gorgeous little girl in Hawkshead just a couple of days earlier – what a photogenic pair, mum and daughter; fit to break into modelling contracts surely, she assumed. It had been Ruby's first encounter with Tanya, despite her mother's two years of skivvying part-time up at Rowan Tree Farm. Ruby had laughed at the girl's thickening Lakeland twang. She wondered if it carried over into her Polish. It must do, surely, she imagined; not that she could tell when she'd heard them babbling away together. She wondered what it might be like – Poland that is – and what it must be like living not just away from home but abroad in a foreign land. That wasn't something she herself could ever have attempted. The language alone...but then she reminded herself that apparently everyone just about anywhere spoke English, so perhaps it wouldn't be such a test after all. Shame about Katarina's boyfriend though; he'd decided to return to Poland for reasons Katarina seemed unable to explain to Ruby. So, no man about the house down there in Satterthwaite and no father figure for Tanya – not for long,

Ruby surmised. A young woman that pretty would have the dogs sniffing round the doors in no time!

She thumbed through her heavy bunch of keys and opened up the first of her three holiday lodges. Again, it looked immaculate. She tarried awhile, admiring the makeover. They really had done a very tasteful renovation of what had been the old workshop. Then she locked up again, crossed the cobbled reach and entered another similarly rescued apartment-style rental. She lingered there too, popped into the main bedroom just to check that Ben had fixed the wardrobe hinge, and then vacated the premises in favour of the older cottage next door and closest to the gate out onto the fell. As before, Katarina had spruced the place up beautifully. She guessed the couple who were currently renting would be back quite soon. They'd gone scorching off on mountain bikes up towards the forest some hours ago and they'd be in need of a hot bath and feet up by now.

With the keys at her disposal she then popped round the back of the covered tractor shed and peeped into her kids' own billets. Ben's older sister Rhona lived and worked in Newcastle. She had gone into law, and after qualifying she'd joined a solicitor firm in Jesmond. She seemed happy, although her mother wondered when she would find a steady partner and produce some grandkids – she was already thirty-two years of age after all, and the clock was ticking. Rhona came home at irregular intervals and had only twice brought a boyfriend to stay, but those relationships simply hadn't lasted. She was due home in a couple of weeks, but Ruby had warned her that she might have to donate her apartment to a holiday booking and come back to a spare room in the farmhouse. As Ruby gave Rhona's pad the once-over she sighed in exasperation as she realised her tangential mistake. Forewarning her daughter of the need to take a farmhouse bedroom would almost certainly determine that the current man in Rhona's life would not accompany her across to the Lakes.

In Ben's flat...well, what a chaotic mess. What was it about lads and keeping their own bivouac in some sort of tidy functional order? What if he ever brought a girl back home, for this was his real home. He worked in the business and, she quickly conceded, he had become the main driving force within their modern farming enterprise. This was where he lived, independent of the main house as befitted a self-driven young man with serious commercial responsibilities. But how on earth could he live in this squalor? No wonder she'd rarely seen girls coming back after Friday nights at Young Farmers in Graythwaite. She made a mental note to tackle him about it. It wouldn't be the first time, but she needed to make some impact because his place might also be needed soon for another booking that was likely to be confirmed in the next day or two. She knew he'd complain. He saw it as too invasive, as if he really didn't have his own place after all. He'd even threatened to move out during the previous summer, but upon reflection over a beer or two with his father at the White Horse in Bouth he'd come to his senses. Farming, especially with livestock of just about any kind, would always be a twenty-four-hour job. You were always either working or on-call. The notion of living off campus, so to speak, and commuting to work every day and at every moment's notice just didn't fit. So he'd caved in and taken the hump for a week or more.

From Ruby's perspective, she not only needed him around and at hand with some reliability, but hiring out his digs to an extra couple of hikers for a week or two only helped to take the edge off the scam they'd pulled to secure that business development grant. Converting old barns and outhouses into holiday lets was one thing, but not when your kids were allocated two of the new dwellings as permanent residences thereafter. Wow, the number of times she'd had to blag her way through visits from Lakeland Holiday Homes and their like she couldn't count. If the soppy beggars ever turned up unannounced and found Ben's pit looking like that, well...that might prove even more testing than having to go and live in Poland!

She emerged from his door with a determined look across her wrinkled brow. After locking up, she proceeded back to the main yard. With times and dates running through her head it suddenly occurred to her that Gilly's two lads must be due back from university in the next week or so. Nice boys, she thought; well mannered and courteous for two little rascals who may have grown up in physical terms, but who, like most men, still had some way to go to maturity. She admonished herself for being so judgemental. She had enjoyed having them around when they'd been younger, just pushing into their teens. They'd helped out on the farm quite a bit, especially at lambing time, but she giggled again at the memory of them watching the tups going at the ewes in the autumn. The boys had been really embarrassed, but Ben had taken them off and had delivered a fatherly word to them. God only knows what he said – he was only a lad himself – but from then on they just seemed to idolise him and the die for that relationship had been well and truly cast.

Then she heard a shriek and a call from beyond the curve in the lane and she immediately thought it must be her mountain bikers returning, as expected, from those colour-coded runs up in the forest. But when they didn't appear in the farmyard she became curious. Stepping out towards the noises she could hear, Ruby passed the end of the high wall which flanked the approach to the yard, and then she saw them. The girls who lived in the old gatehouse, formerly the Lodge House to Rowan House, appeared to be running about in a perfectly random fashion in the lane. Only when she crested the slightly elevated mound in the road did she see the ewe, the subject of their attention. Ruby watched with some amusement as they darted back and forth in an attempt to hem the poor thing in and cajole it into their own small garden, presumably to recapture it so that Ben could reclaim it. The daft sheep must have squeezed out from behind that temporary post-and-wire arrangement a little further down.

"Watch out, Lucy... Grab it, get a hold of it," she heard Helen yell at her partner, as the two of them side-stepped in the lane, arms held wide as they attempted to deter the poor creature from making a run for it.

"I'm not touching the thing," Lucy shouted back. "It might bite me!"

"It's a bloody sheep, girl, not a crocodile," came the agitated retort.

Ruby chuckled as she looked on down the lane.

"And it stinks...smelly old thing," Lucy pleaded, willing Helen to perform the physical capture herself.

"Will you just listen to yourself... Whoa, watch it, she nearly squeezed through by the wall there!"

"I mean...just look at all that dried poo clinging to her back end," added Lucy in despair.

"No chance of you becoming a nice young farmer's wife by the sounds of it. I wonder how our resident young farmer would react if he heard you?" Helen posed.

Lucy stood still momentarily, head tilted slightly askew, and looked at her girlfriend with a whimsical expression, as if to question the validity of the prompt. As she did so the ewe bolted past her and Helen cursed as she lurched after it with an impressive sprint.

Ruby wondered about those two. Perhaps she was as old-fashioned as her very old-fashioned name – as her identifying label in society, Ruby had never been pleased with her own name, even as a child, or most especially as a child – but two grown women living together in every sense of that term was something she struggled to comprehend and to accept. Lesbians they may be, she told herself...oh give over, lesbians they so obviously are... but that really didn't have anything to do with her. How they chose to live their lives in their own home was their business. But there was something else more disconcerting, somehow more challenging, confrontational even, and she couldn't quite put her finger on it...and she laughed behind her raised hand at the unintended suggestion and coloured a profuse pink. She thought maybe it was the confidence – bravado was perhaps a better word – with which they outwardly flaunted their shared sexuality before the surprised and often shocked rural community. Or maybe it was their overt physical fitness and their excessive sporting exploits, uphill and down dale or even in freezing cold winter waters, which had become well known and surprisingly often talked about in some very unexpected places. The Helen girl was stocky and very solid, and remarkably quick on her feet, whereas Lucy was a little slimmer, but lithe and athletic. They'd lived at Rowan Lodge for a few years now and yet still she didn't know what either of them did for a living. She saw them running and biking all over the place, and they would be away for lengthy spells too and for what reason again she was at a loss, but they didn't appear to have ordinary jobs.

As for confrontation, they weren't short of the direct approach either. They'd given her some serious lip when they'd discovered that the shared water supply was being *contaminated*, as they had put it, by a bit of sheep poo. The old concrete tank in the top field had been built into a bank. It had been cracked for decades, and on warm days the sheep would scale the bank and venture out onto the flat surface of the lid and lie there in the sun. Their natural discharges would fall and leak through the cracks and into the water beneath them. The tank had been the main water source for all the properties up there on the hill. It had been fine. She and Eric had been drinking the stuff since the day they'd bought the place, way back, but oh no! The girls had contacted the local authorities and all sorts of tests were taken. Before she could say 'couple o' dykes' she found herself installing new ultraviolet filters and all sorts of new pipework and fittings for the holiday lets. Then the bitches had dobbed her in it for a new septic tank because the old one was leaking down the hill and into the lower stream. What a palaver all that had been, and thank the Lord for EU environmental grants for good clean causes! Fair enough; that old septic was indeed caving in and it had leaked for a long time, but it had been there since before the First World War by all accounts.

She watched them a while longer. Ah well...at least the ewe was trapped in behind their nice new wrought-iron gates. Ben could get the little trailer down there when he had a minute. Where was he anyway?

3

breaking rocks

Keith stood on the edge of the great chasm and pulled the hood of his works cagoule up and over his head against the depressing downpour. It wasn't that he was worried about getting his hair wet. He didn't have much, for a forty-seven-year-old. No, it was simply experience working in his favour. He knew just how quickly one could get thoroughly soaked when hanging about in mucky Lakeland weather.

He peered through the rain as it descended below his level, falling effortlessly into the great hole in the ground below him. He was searching for his assistant who had apparently driven the old jeep down the spiralling perimeter dirt-track in search of the foreman on duty somewhere down there among the mighty machines. Despite the deluge and its naturally deadening effect on the noises from below, he could still hear the muffled whining and clanking of heavy equipment as the team busied itself before the vast open seam of Lakeland green slate. He knew they'd soon be setting the charges, having already undercut the next section of the rock to be dislodged. He knew too that they would soon vacate the immediate vicinity prior to detonation, and that would be the signal for his right-hand man to return whence he'd come to seek refuge back in the office.

Christ, he thought, it's bloody miserable out here, and so it was. His wellies squelched and sucked at the green-grey mud and he fumbled with the front zipper of his coat in a late attempt to repel the damp. But then he saw the jeep starting back up the service road, accompanied by a clutch of blokes in the old on-site minibus. He realised at once that they would only retire to a higher tier, perhaps two levels up in the great graduated excavation. From there they'd watch the controlled explosion on the other side of the quarry. By the time Justin came slithering to a halt in the slime beside him, the two of them had barely enough time to nod to each other before a sharp crack erupted from far below, and a precisely cut ledge of heavy slate toppled onto its side with minimum fuss. There appeared to be little dust created by the explosion, despite the rapid redistribution of many tons of rock, such was the dampening effect of the incessant deluge.

The minibus revved and choked as it began the journey back down to the fallen mass of beautiful green slate, etched in milky turquoise veins and slightly darker aquamarine streaks. The team would soon have it sectioned and on its way to the cutting sheds back up at the top level. As he stood in front of a gaggle of prefabs which masqueraded as the office complex, Keith looked down into the depths again. Although he never ceased to marvel at the natural beauty of the slate, especially in its raw form, on this occasion he simply couldn't see the stuff clearly enough through the near-opaque rain filter before him.

Keith Salcombe turned to his younger subordinate and, by way of silent instruction, flicked a thumb in the direction of the admin block behind them. As the two of them splashed and slopped their way back to the office, Keith identified their immediate priority.

"I'm getting grief, Jason," he complained from under his hood.

"How d'you mean?" his junior queried.

"Just had the accountant on the blower – the tax man is still sniffing around those heavy equipment purchases from the year before last."

"What? Still? Those guys must be short of things to do."

"That's for sure, but we need to get a few spread sheets up on screen so I can conference-call the accountant pretty smartish. I'd said we'd be back to him within the half-hour and we're pushing that already."

"Is it the capital allowances?" Justin asked.

"Oh no…it's the tax relief we claimed, at a guess. It's always the tax relief – something for nothing is how they see it."

Justin found himself quickly despatched to his own tiny room in order to retrieve a particular accounting file and to send it promptly across to Keith next door in more spacious but only marginally more comfortable surroundings. The file hit Keith's screen a few minutes later. He clicked it open and cast a wary though experienced eye across the rolling data on display. There were no surprises. Everything looked much as he'd expected. The conference call was a formality, as it turned out. The accountant knew precisely how to play the next step in the obfuscation process.

Keith closed the file down, saved it under encryption and leaned slowly back in his super-modern, super-comfy Herman Miller office chair. He looked out of the window at the greyness beyond and wondered if a real summer would ever come this year. He thought about it for no more than a passing moment, but in that time he readily acknowledged that his new chair was the only truly modern piece of kit anywhere on-site at ground level. That thought drew a slow sigh of disappointment and frustration.

Rusland Quarry & Slate Mine had been a going concern for over a hundred years. For many decades it had supplied builders and architects, both national and international, with some of the Lake District's finest materials. The business had developed a prestigious reputation as far afield as the United States, South Africa and India. Among its most appreciative clients, the firm had revelled in the attentions of the Italians for whom special building stone of such exquisite quality had matched even their own world famous marbles and alabasters. The business had mushroomed from its earliest beginnings. Despite the enforced downturns associated with two world wars it had succeeded in employing hundreds of local men until the demands for efficiency in the extended post-war era had necessitated improved levels of mechanisation. The company had gone through various changes of ownership. Different owners had reported differing degrees of success, but in the face of growing overseas competition the quarry had succumbed to closure in the early sixties, and had lain dormant for some years thereafter.

In the flush of Thatcherite recovery during the eighties the old place had been taken on again and had enjoyed some considerable capital input on new equipment, new vehicles, new transport processes for the stone, and new cutting sheds and tools. The old mining tunnels had been abandoned and closed up, but the open-cast mine was successfully reactivated and the business had progressed very nicely. A consortium of northern businessmen together with some venture capital from an unseen City source had been responsible for the reinvigoration of the site. A late joiner to that group was a local-lad-made-good by the name of Austen Smiley, who had committed himself to the team in 1990 at the remarkably young age of just thirty. He hadn't joined to share his mining expertise – that would have been a very short discussion – but as the pilot investor of considerable funds from London, his seat on the board had been effectively reserved until such times as he could extricate himself from the big city. He also brought with him considerable private wealth.

Like Keith, Austen had been born and raised in the old industrial town of Barrow-in-Furness on the south-westernmost tip of Cumbria (Lancashire then). In fact there the two of them had gone to school together and become close pals at an early age. Austen had excelled at school and gone off to university in Oxford to study business and economics. In his early twenties, and having been snapped up by an ambitious hedge fund operation in the West End, Austen had soon found himself managing sizeable investment funds and enjoying a not inconsiderable salary. He also took significant performance-related management fees on those assets. Then, having joined the board and properly participated in the growing wealth of the firm for some years, he and his colleagues cashed in their chips. They sold the assets on to new managers and effectively retired when all of them were close to just thirty years of age. Their accumulated wealth would have staggered just about anyone back in the far northwest. He had always hankered after a return to his native patch – perhaps not to Barrow itself, a living example of the deprivations of regional industrial policies practised for too long at Westminster, but to the Lake District, the countryside playground of his teenage youth.

And so, having helped to fund the Rusland Quarry Consortium from afar, he couldn't fault their invitation for him to join the board and thus to secure his return home to the stunning hills and fells of Cumbria.

What he missed in his haste to head north proved to be a fundamental error in the research due diligence he was expected to perform on the business at that important juncture. Perhaps he just skimmed over the accounts. Perhaps he thought he already knew the profitability of the firm well enough. As an experienced business analyst he would later claim that the impact of foreign imports on a wide range of commercial stone and slate had simply been imperceptible at that time.

The early nineties had continued well for Rusland, but already the invasion of cheap Chinese product had begun to nibble away at profit margins. By the mid-nineties, when he encouraged his lifelong friend to come and join him at the quarry and thus to complete his own planned return to the region, it could have been demonstrated that the future of the business was looking far less assured.

And now, just over ten years later, as Keith looked forlornly out at the torrential rain, he ground his teeth and tapped his fingers angrily on the desk as all manner of disheartening recollections of those early discussions coursed through his memory.

Keith Salcombe too had left his beloved Lake District to seek preferred employment away from the struggling ship-building industries of Barrow. Just like his best mate Austen, he too had done very well academically. Within the Victorian red-brick confines of their grammar school he had demonstrated an exceptional aptitude for mathematics and business studies. Not surprisingly then, he took himself off to Warwick University to read maths and business administration. He then quickly headed back north as far as Manchester where he joined a fast-growing accountancy and business consultancy practice. His career had progressed quite satisfactorily from there, as indeed had his personal life. He had met Gilly, his wife, during that early phase in Manchester and they were soon married and moved quickly into the family environment while the two of them were in their twenties.

Keith and Austen had remained casually in touch throughout, and each had wondered periodically just how well the other was really doing. It hadn't taken them long for each to recognise that Austen's independent City-based bachelor lifestyle had quickly left his good friend's more cumbersome and much more demanding domestic menagerie far behind. Austen had become very wealthy in a remarkably short space of time. Nevertheless, and despite considerable success within his own career, when the call came from his good friend to go home and settle back into their beloved region of origin, Keith responded eagerly.

It hadn't been easy to give up an established and lucrative post as senior partner. That very same consultancy had, for the best part of twelve years, grown not just the man but also his own professional standing in the great northern metropolis. It had been even more challenging, and so many times since then it had seemed cold and treacherous to have left behind the grave of their youngest child who had succumbed to a malignant cancer when just a sweet little girl. He knew he would never rid himself of that sense of guilt, but he knew too that Gilly would continue to make her regular pilgrimages back there to lay flowers and toys and to keep the headstone neat and tidy. It could never assuage his own remorse, but he hoped at least that the little mite would be able to look down and see the love she was missing.

As for Gilly, well…Keith was not at all sure about her true thoughts and feelings beyond those for Alice and the boys. She had talked interminably in recent years about discussing their loss of Alice with their sons now that they were of an age to engage on such potentially torturous matters. He'd counselled her to leave well alone. He wasn't really sure that his reluctance could be accurately placed against concern for them or, more likely, selfish concern for himself and his wife. In short, he just wasn't sure they all could cope with revisiting all of that heart-wrenching torment. Besides, she seemed to have dropped it of late and that, he believed, could only be a good thing.

In terms of their move up to the Lakes and indeed into Rowan House, he remained unconvinced of her essential happiness and he fretted about that on occasions. He wondered what she did all day. She hadn't worked since they'd moved up. Twelve years of day-to-day independence – no commuting out to that school in Cheshire had to be a good thing – but stuck up on that hill all day next to those miserable sods next door at the farm, well…life could be difficult sometimes. To that he could readily attest. Apart from the odd shopping trip to Kendal or Manchester, she must be bored witless. But then again, she had her committees. Two of them shared the same platform as Austen, no less, and she'd also given a great deal of time to planning and management for the recent refit at Rowan House, so perhaps he shouldn't be so harshly judgemental.

And their relationship – how did that stack up? Again, he really couldn't say with any certainty. They seemed to be bumping along together pretty well, but the spark had long gone. It appeared that they only strayed into anything approximating lusty liaisons after hosting a decent evening with friends or business acquaintances at home, or whenever they were away on a trip and staying in expensive hotel suites. That was the way it looked and he had adapted to it quite well, or so he thought. At least that kind of excursion was well within their financial scope. Whatever the truth of it, he clearly wasn't getting enough. She may not have been the prettiest girl he had bedded during the frenzied escapades of youth, but who was he to complain now? Looking down at his bulging stomach and running his fingers through his thinning hair, he recoiled from his own self-assessment. In addition, he conceded, time had treated Gilly very well despite bearing three kids, and he would jump at every opportunity, however rare, to get his hands on her magnificent frontal elevation. He realised that other men appreciated her greatest assets simply because they couldn't keep their eyes off her whenever they were in company or in public together.

He looked out of the window again, attracted by an abrupt end to the pummelling of his Portakabin roof. A sympathetic easing of the cloud cover suggested something a little brighter in the offing. He thought again about Austen and involuntarily frowned in concentration.

Austen had spent much of the last five years, maybe a little more, very much detached from the regular running of the quarry business. Of the original consortium he was the last remaining shareholder and a majority shareholder at that. He still chaired the board and effectively owned the organisation, although Keith smirked at that vague description of the rather run-down operation for which he and his engineering manager took full operational responsibility. These were the three main owners of the business, Keith and his on-site colleague enjoying only minority participations.

As a very wealthy man, still only in his late forties, as was Keith himself, Austen Smiley had rather backed out of the declining stone and slate enterprise in favour of grand philanthropic designs, enterprise projects and a murky mix of Lakeland politics. He had even flirted with the idea of going into politics full-on before common sense had reined in his developing ambitions – who needed to be back in London only to miss the many pleasures of Britain's once finest national park? He found himself on working parties, involved in local action groups and dabbling in parish and county council affairs. He also crossed swords often with the Cumbrian Lakes National Park Authority, an organisation he considered much too comfortable, remiss in many of its coordinating functions and falling short of some of its core targets and key obligations. He had developed a close connection to the chief of police and was thought by many a committee member to enjoy considerably more influence in that quarter than he should. Keith believed that the truth was a long way from popular perception.

Such activities had steadily won more and more of Austen's attention as the nineties elapsed. It had become clear to Keith, quite quickly after he'd joined, that he had been installed purely to take over the running of the dying beast that was the enormous great hollow in the ground just beyond his window. By the end of the millennium, just seven years ago, it was still making money, but a paltry return when compared with just ten or fifteen years earlier. Did it matter? They were still well off by the standards of most. Did he care? Was it what he wanted to do day after day? Actually, he mused, it wasn't uninteresting work, and with his fellow on-site director, Brian, looking after the mechanics of production, he could see the thing running until his retirement in, say, another ten years.

If he were honest with himself he would admit that he enjoyed the prestige, admiration even, afforded him by many of the locals. They had known the quarry all their lives and many still looked upon it as a noble example of the region's industrial capabilities. Few appreciated that the place looked so dilapidated today, or that it only employed barely thirty men and women. However, if he could stomach his own treadmill existence, sitting daily above an ancient and massive open-cast pit, he could much more easily bask in the perceived cachet of near-celebrity as the proud owner of Rowan House. As far as fine country residences were concerned, he genuinely believed that theirs was one of the grandest and most sought after piles in the entire South Lakes swathe. That he couldn't have afforded it without Austen's financial assistance had long since ceased to irritate him. Like Gilly, Keith viewed that support as a form of just compensation for Austen's earlier and potentially cataclysmic chicanery. After all, if Austen could spend his time and considerable resources re-roofing local churches, funding drystone walling projects or installing new playgrounds and picnic sites in the national park, then why shouldn't he cough up a balance of payments to put them, the Salcombes, in their wonderful home on the hill?

Keith looked at his watch – only a couple of hours more. By then the flat-loader would have left with those two five-ton blocks bound for

Birmingham, and then the guys would be clocking off. No night shift to consider any more: the place would be locked up and the site gates chained.

Then he remembered that his little sister Henrietta was due over again for some dinner. Henri was always a welcome face. He loved her dearly, and the very idea of her being up at Rowan House when he got back warmed his heart. But he quickly registered that Gilly might be less than ecstatic – another of her whinges, and no mistake. Henri tried so hard to accommodate his wife's variable moods, and yet so often, and so easily, she appeared to disappoint. Keith had lost his rag on a few memorable occasions and had torn into Gilly for her short temper and her apparent lack of understanding. What would it take for her to realise that it was always going to be hard for Henri now that Mum had gone? Henri was seventeen years his junior and she'd taken Mum's passing very badly. He was determined to keep her close, to protect her as best he could, and Gilly simply had to accept that reality. Christ, how tough must it be for a thirty-year-old woman working in an estate agency in Ambleside: no man in her life, years given up to caring for her own dying mother, and nothing exciting on the horizon? What was so damned difficult about sympathising with someone, especially your own sister-in-law, in a tight corner quite so horrible?

His train of thought was interrupted by the aggressive whine of a trail bike as it raced up the long smooth curve of the tree-lined approach to the quarry. He guessed that Morgan, one of their own working lads, had arranged a summer evening out on the fells with his squad of fellow motor-bikers. Keith checked his watch a second time and shook his head ruefully – no way was he getting off this early! He pulled himself up and onto his feet and made for the door. As soon as he stepped out onto the scaffold-walkway of his first-floor pre-fab he saw Morgan chatting to a leather-clad co-conspirator and Keith hesitated. He decided to leave them to their own devices. He rattled down the open steps heading towards the old buildings towards the back of the site, but as he hit the ground and pushed on he heard Morgan shout out in his direction.

"Hiya, boss, how's it hangin'?"

Keith waved casually at the two young men without looking back. He sensed the sarcasm, the potential intimidation in the younger man's voice, and after their little tête-à-tête the previous week he wanted to avoid any fractious exchanges in the public environment of the open site. He stomped away through the mud, and proceeded to where the old offices hid behind one of the earlier warehouses, both buildings a mix of brick and metal cladding, now looking thoroughly derelict. The former office section was still used for storage and he wanted to check something there anyway, so he stepped out at a reasonable pace and hoped that Morgan wouldn't follow.

4

stick in the mud

"Skip!" he cried. "Skip…c'mon, boy."

He looked across the yard towards the corner of the old barn expecting to see his Border Collie come racing out from his favourite lair under the cover of the lean-to wood store. The warm summer breeze ruffled his silver hair and he cast a hand across his brow to push a few windswept strands back from his eyes. The dog remained unseen. He guessed that his faithful old companion simply hadn't heard his call. Perhaps the whispering tussocks had masked his appeal, so he curled his tongue under his palate and projected a piercing whistle in the same direction. Sure enough, Skip appeared in a flash and raced across the short run to his master. He wagged his tail furiously and skittered back and forth in anticipation of the imminent excursion.

"Yes, yes, alright," Patrick said, as he bent to ruffle Skip's gleaming coat. Then he lowered himself to one knee, captured the excited creature under one arm, and gave him a good old scratch under his muzzle and around his ears, taking care to relieve any irritation under his prominent red leather collar.

Patrick deftly attached the long lead to the collar ring and then, pushing himself up with hand on bended knee, he stepped out toward the five-bar gate and the open fell beyond. Skip was already straining at the leash. He'd let the dog run freely as soon as he got over the adjacent track – no point leaving himself open to the critical scrutiny of his local sheep-farming neighbours, or for that matter any passing hikers who would surely be thoroughly familiar with the country code. It wasn't that Patrick was either careless or cavalier with the rules of engagement expected by responsible dog owners out in the country; he just knew his dog and he knew in his heart that Skip was as reliable as he was loyal. Every spring and summer season Patrick would pick up the gossip at the Black Cock in Broughton, or sometimes at the White Horse in Bouth, that a wandering stray or even the unruly household pet of a visiting family on holiday had been despatched by an irate farmer's shotgun. Dog owners, he thought, had a real obligation to protect both livestock and their own animals. It could never be the farmer's fault – no, their responsibilities would always lie with their stock. It was their business, after all. However, in their remote patch up by Tipple Bank, and not forgetting Skip's exemplary discipline, Patrick knew they'd only rarely come across another soul up on the tops during their daily outings.

Patrick Lawner was remarkably fit and agile by the standards of most octogenarians. He'd lived with his wife Milly in their remote whitewashed farmhouse for more than thirty years. He'd retired early from full-time employment within the depths of the civil service in Whitehall in favour of the great outdoors and a very different lifestyle. They had renovated the ancient stone structure with a chunk of savings which had been put by for just such a purpose, although they had completed much of the arduous physical graft themselves in order to keep their contractors' fees to a minimum. In executing their plan they'd kitted the main homestead and connected outhouses into a 'bed and breakfast' home-from-home. Then they'd worked just as hard seasonally, over many years, as they'd entertained visiting holidaymakers who yearned for their own slice of the same wilderness their hosts had quickly come to love and respect.

Winters could be severe: often the long exposed track which brought them home from the outside world would be snowed in. They'd learned quite quickly that their stock of firewood needed to be fully replenished as they moved into the autumn if they were to avoid going cold by late February. Power outages were frequent at the wrong time of year, their electricity and telephone supply cables stretching precariously across the open moor and fell, and remaining vulnerable at all times to high winds. They had decided to close to visitors during these periods; demand was minimal, although they usually had several enquiries each year for Christmas breaks which they had not been persuaded by. As spring arrived each year their guest numbers would usually pick up quickly and then the school summer holiday stretch would push them quite hard, especially if the weather remained inhospitable and their guests were forced to loiter on the premises for days at a time.

In all this endeavour Patrick and Milly had remained busy and active, not just in the business sense, but also in their precious private time. Getting out into the wide open spaces captivated their imaginations and always released any building tension or anxiety.

Tucked away as they were just a quarter-mile off the Cumbria Way, they discovered to their glee that most hikers and fell walkers passed them closely by without interference as they pushed north towards Coniston Water and the central Lakeland village of the same name. This afforded Patrick and Milly the virtual freedom of a huge swathe of undulating hills and haws, barrows and crags, and they adopted the vast elevated tracts of Lakeland fell as their own. They had come to know the territory in intimate detail: every ridge from where they could catch the sun reflecting off the sea far off in Morecambe Bay, every lush green fern-filled hollow in spring, every ripple of purple heather in late summer, every slope of crunching rusty bracken in the early winter. This had become their own restitution, and for decades they had shared it with one another, with their much-loved canine friends of many generations, and with their own family, friends and paying guests.

Once across the rough lane the two veterans rounded the first mound and pushed on up the steady gradient of the narrow track. It was a sheep track really, one which they shared with the roaming Herdwicks that passed that way intermittently in their random perpetual drift in search of green shoots. Patrick knew that his four-legged friend could almost match his own longevity when measured in canine years, but to any would-be onlooker the pair would have appeared robust and determined as they made comfortable uphill progress.

This was a muddy ribbon they had negotiated so many times over so many years that it barely required conscious thought. Patrick had already decided to complete the 'crag loop', a familiar thirty-minute circuit that fitted his available time on the day. Skip didn't as yet know which route they'd take, but his primary objective at that moment was to get off that lead. He turned in toward his chaperone's strides as if deliberately getting in the way of Patrick's normal gait as he crested the top. The dog's human companion recognised the signal immediately and released him. The black and white figure shot off into the dense ferns in search of interesting scents and traces. Patrick carried on at a leisurely but steady pace. He called and whistled every so often so as to keep his charge reasonably close at hand. Thus the two of them absorbed their splendid surroundings, one welcoming the damp warmth of the very green landscape and the other sifting more exciting whiffs from the overwhelming odour of wet sheep which clung to the leaves and stalks with irritating persistence.

The sky was a bright, clear blue with white fluffy clouds that hurried high overhead. Visibility was near perfect and Patrick stopped a number of times to gaze at the distant detail of small farms and tiny hamlets. To the south the distant tide was well and truly out, evidenced by the vast expanse of mud flats running up to the ragged coastal edges. In the north he could make out Helvellyn and even Skiddaw such was the clear air at his disposal. He wished he'd insisted that Milly came along too, but she wouldn't be persuaded. It may have been some years since they'd stopped the B&B business, but she still immersed herself in all manner of projects and she'd reluctantly decided to stay at home to finish some feedback forms for one of the tourism boards.

Inevitably his mind drifted onto other themes, and as he strode along he pushed through the ferns at tight spots in the path and avoided any awkward footfalls where the ground became stony. He remembered that he had some more parish council write-ups to complete before the next fast-approaching assembly.

He also remembered that he had a few more entries to make on his website, especially those photos from Stutterthwaite Common, taken last week. They should prove very convincing for Nature England's desperate attempts to hang on to that area's SSSI classification. Sites of Special Scientific Interest were under just as much threat as the national park itself, despite the enhanced protection they were supposed to enjoy. Bandit incursions were very definitely on the rise again and he really should make sure that the action group maintained a state of high alert and a readiness to confront the motorbike problem wherever and whenever possible.

Of course there was the book to get back to. It had slipped from the radar screen of late, he knew that, but if he wanted to bring it to a close after all these years of careful research and planning then he really would have to knuckle down. He chided himself, as he rounded another gentle curve in the track, for his itinerant attention of late. It was important – he wasn't the only one to think so or say so – but it had proven a monumental task to collate that long list of examples and case points which cemented the arguments so firmly, and he felt a sense of exhaustion whenever his thought processes ventured that way.

Then he saw it – crowning another hillock, and turning his head to whistle for Skip, he looked ahead and into the distance as, step by step, a distant view of Woodstone Fell was revealed. There could be no mistaking it, even from roughly three miles away – a dark muddy sinew that stretched and wound itself up the leading edge of the distant escarpment, right up and over the top of the fell and out of sight. He didn't have the time to walk over there, and anyway, he'd forgotten to bring his camera. He knew from bitter, embattled experience that the heavily etched mark on the hillside had been gouged and ripped into the earth by the passage of nine or ten high-powered trail bikes. They hadn't passed his way. He'd certainly have heard the racket created by that many scramblers tearing by at speed. They were always travelling at pace simply because it made any attempts at identification very difficult indeed. They knew only too well – no longer any room for ignorance among the petrol-heads – that their activities were strictly illegal.

He felt as if the disfigured landscape somehow cowered in fear and shame, the victim of a violent personal attack. He realised that desecration on such a scale would equate to a two-metre-wide rut of gouged soil and spewed stones, sufficiently deep, loose and treacherous on such a gradient as to be threatening underfoot. Fifty or sixty horsepower transmitted directly into the soft ground through the rear driving wheel of just one Honda or Kawasaki trail bike could devastate the surface of the original track in a single pass. It would take several months for such an imprint to grow over again. However, the passage of so many machines over even virgin turf would carve out a vivid broken slur which might take two summer seasons to recover – assuming, naturally, that no more damage would be inflicted by any subsequent traffic, and so far this season the carefree yobs had just kept on coming.

The damage across the entire Lakeland region had become so visible, and so offensive to so many, that the Lakes Tourism Board had recently petitioned local MPs to bring more weight to their simple thrust that law enforcement was suffering the distraction of budget cuts and re-jigged priorities. In short, it was easier for the police to carry out a typical Friday night pub round-up in Barrow or Bowness than to apprehend a series of fast-moving targets in difficult mountainous terrain. Nevertheless, tackling the scourge had already become a real and very serious necessity.

It wasn't just that Patrick and his allies were thoroughly fed up with the regular exploitation that the countryside seemed destined to suffer, but in addition the economics of tourism, the region's biggest earner, were beginning to sag as visitor numbers steadily declined. Tourist agencies had meticulously surveyed the root causes of the gathering slump, and their results were unequivocal: speed restrictions for boats on Windermere may have been one aspect, and traffic congestion at key access points was a recognised issue, but these factors appeared irrelevant when compared to the wanton and wilful destruction of the nation's most famous national park. Bands of aggressive, often abusive motorbikers had all but seized the region for themselves. They thought nothing of driving through innocent groups of hikers at dangerous speeds, scattering them from even the most celebrated walking trails the region had to offer. In short, tourism was quite literally being driven off the Lakeland map.

Patrick cursed under his breath. Skip looked up at his leader and then lowered his head onto his paws as he recognised anger and dismay. After the recent Stutterthwaite incident, not to mention the great acreage of slimy sloppy mess to the southern approaches of Beaston Tarn (on the Cumbrian Way itself), and now this, another significant invasion involving an entire troupe of riders, Patrick found himself beginning to despair that their attempts to protect the Lakeland fells would ever prove successful. So much for the website, he frowned. So much for coordinating the various agencies across the region: the Cumbrian Lakes National Park Authority, Nature England, the Woodland Commission, the Forestry Trust, the Cumbrian Tourism Board, parish councils and the county council for heaven's sake, the Nation Trust, even Cumberland Police...the names of so many organisations trickled through his brain as he stared at the ugly scar on the far elevation of Woodstone Fell and begged of himself so many frustrating questions. What would it take to combat these mindless, selfish rural vandals?

"C'mon, lad," he announced, as he turned on his heel and headed for home. The dog tucked in behind him and the two of them padded their way downhill and back round the gorse-covered bluff towards a hot cup of tea for one and a soft lie-down in the wood store for the other.

5

brave new world

Janice Lehrer, the new Mrs Lehrer, rather liked her new office, and she liked Mr Lehrer even more. She hadn't been there very long at all, just a few weeks in fact, but she had settled into her very comfortable routine quickly and easily. She knew Windermere quite well having visited the busy lakeside town many times when she had been able to enjoy her holiday cottage over in Coniston village in years gone by. Once she'd given up that great escape she had never seriously considered returning to the Lake District, not even for a traditional British vacation. Such had been the heartfelt trauma associated with that exit that she really hadn't believed it possible to overcome her own evident reluctance to return. Odd, she thought, as she looked out onto the bustling pavement, just how quickly life can do you down or lift you up with barely a signal to register the change before the result has been achieved.

In Suffolk she had worked as the in-house manager of a sizeable retirement home, one which had catered for nearly one hundred residents, or 'inmates' as some of her more endearing charges liked to refer to themselves with a wicked twist of good humour. She had enjoyed the all-consuming intensity of the managerial role; running her own team and maintaining a good rapport with her customers, for that's what they had been, had inevitably been challenging but rewarding too. Living-in most of the time had been the only real drag. She had missed much of her children's development as they had made those tentative early steps into adult life. But circumstances had carried her away to Bedford from her home by the Suffolk coast and at the time it had appeared not only unavoidable, but in some ways desirable.

At least Laura, her daughter, had been spared the worst of it. She had already suffered her own tragedy and all the emotional upheaval that went with it. Some years earlier, she had returned from school to find her stepfather lying dead in the garden. The girl had loved that man as if he had been her own father, and Janice...Lord knows, Janice had loved him too. They would still be together as a family if fate hadn't delivered such a terminal blow, and in such a cruel fashion – a whacking great coronary that felled him while alone in his own back yard.

However, her son Josh, and later his pretty young wife, had been pressed through life's wringer and only just survived the ordeal...or should that be ordeals in the plural?

She reclined in her chair, lost in recollection as she reflected on her own turbulent history and how it had affected her kids, and many others besides. She didn't need to remind herself that this was her fourth marriage. She had never considered herself to be some kind of marital gypsy, moving from one man to another at will. She just didn't see herself in that way. After all, her first husband, Laura's father, had just gone out one day and simply never came back. Her second partner, the real and true love of her life until very recently, had given her riches beyond estimation in the love, the passion and the sense of reliability he had bestowed upon them as a family unit. He, Jeff, had shown her how wonderfully exciting shared experiences could be, and he had even completed her utopian vision by providing her with their son, Josh. But poor Jeff had been some years her senior, and it was he who Laura had discovered prostrate on the patio that fateful day.

If such a calamity could possibly have been matched or even bettered, in the entirely negative sense of course, then her next and biggest mistake fulfilled that remit many times over.

Lee had been a fabulously different character in lots and lots of ways, and their early times together had been exhilarating. However, her growing children saw through the charm offensive much sooner than their naïve, moonstruck mother. She discovered the full horror of her carefree errors only when she found herself, her life and her finances in a catastrophic tailspin. He had cleaned them out! He took just about everything they had: not just broken hearts and deeply compromised allegiances, but their small business, their assets, their cash and even their Lakeland holiday home. That rogue had even applied a financial charge to their family home, and much to her seething anger she found that she could do nothing to protect either herself or her children from his wanton excesses.

But if Janice herself had cultivated a very real, deep-seated contempt for that waster, her emotions paled into relaxed melancholy when compared with the simmering hostility he had propagated within her son. The revelation, some years later and only very recently, that Lee had been murdered should not have shocked her like that – not really. That malicious creep had given plenty of indications that they, she and her family, could not have been his only victims. Somewhere out there could have been someone with just as many, maybe even more grievances against him. Nevertheless she should not have been entirely unprepared for the earth-moving jolt that hit her next.

Josh had worn his evident disgust for and hatred of that man very publicly on his sleeve. No wonder then that he very quickly became the chief suspect in the subsequent murder investigation. She had never felt so utterly helpless at any previous time in her life, and, with a rueful smile, she conceded just how many times she had tested herself to desperate limits in the past. For some time it truly had appeared entirely possible, probable even, that Josh may have taken his version of revenge just a step too far. For weeks he had remained incarcerated, bail having been denied.

But for the accidental spillage of a vital clue by one of her own retirement home favourites, together with the dogged persistence of a smart detective who simply couldn't and wouldn't allow incomplete evidence to rest, Josh would have spent several decades behind bars for a crime he had not committed.

And that God-sent policeman had been Detective Chief Inspector David Lehrer, formerly of the Suffolk CID and now of the Cumberland force based in Kendal. Moreover, DCI David Lehrer had recently become Janice's fourth husband, a little trifle to some but one with which she was eminently delighted.

During their earliest engagements they had uncovered a mutual love of the Lake District, although at the time neither of them gave that common ground a second thought. It was only when a potential transfer had cropped up – and their relationship had surpassed mild curiosity by some margin – that David had introduced the idea of a move north and a substantial lifestyle change. He would carry on as before, but hopefully in a less demanding environment – no London overspill to worry about and nothing like the big container port at Felixstowe to regularly undermine the weekend break. She, on the other hand, would take a huge step down from the very real pace and pressure of her former role. The harrowing and often volatile circumstances of their earliest encounters and indeed of the murder case itself, with all of its unsavoury fall-out, had left them drained and mentally scarred. With such an inflamed and so very sensitive backdrop, why not make a clean break, reset the emotional clock, and withdraw to a new countryside idyll? The Lakes represented an area they had both loved all their separate lives, but together, as one partnership, they could refresh that very positive outlook and embrace a new, thrilling and stimulating life together. They were neither of them spring chickens and wasn't it about time they achieved that sense of fulfilment in life?

It had been a powerful and passionate marriage proposal, and so, yes, why shouldn't she try the traditional union just one more time? She had learned to trust this man for his innate decency and sense of responsibility, and anyway, by national standards her own two-two score line was probably a reasonable result. She may have picked a very immature first husband, and then later a malevolent cheat of the worst kind, but in Jeff and now in David she firmly believed that she had found good men and that she deserved this late unexpected walk in the sun.

In Windermere she was discovering a determined business community and a society proud of its Lakeland heritage. The people seemed friendly enough and there was always something going on down by the waterfront. She admired the town's traditional signature, with its buildings of dry-stone construction and roofs of emblematic local slate. It looked like a step back in time, but then...well, that was its charm, what the day-trippers and holidaymakers came for. In the season the lake, strictly speaking a mere, was always a tumult of water-born activity. Sails proliferated, speedboats tried not to be in deference to speed restrictions on the water, rowing boats struggled against the choppy waves and canoes flitted here and there with a sense of urgency. The ferry crossing plied its trade across to Sawrey every ten minutes or so – she and David had already taken that old trip, not for the first time, but for the first time together. It had been fun. She knew it would be a bleaker but no less beautiful scene in mid-winter as the grey waters churned in the north wind and sparse groups of visitors would appear fully fleeced and cagouled against the chill, but that was for another day.

In her new office abode she looked back to her on-screen inbox and registered a couple of recent emails.

The Cumbrian Tourism Board had offered her a senior position in recognition of her considerable managerial experience and a very impressive CV. It was a doddle! It wasn't that there weren't some important and pressing issues; it was just that the pace of things was so very pedestrian. She didn't mind. She had already adjusted. Her new responsibilities were something of a walk in the park – a walk in the national park perhaps – yes, she liked that. She got a lunch break for heaven's sake. She never worked beyond five thirty, although sometimes there were evening meetings to attend with other local groups. She'd actually managed two lunches and one evening dinner with David in town after work. Such things were unprecedented and she was doing her utmost to enjoy it.

Of course she earned much less now, but she'd understood that aspect of the plan. By selling David's house they'd been able to hang onto her own Suffolk farmhouse only through the remarkable intervention of her late and murdered husband's estranged son. He had materialised seemingly out of nowhere – another duplicity on his father's part – but he too had railed against his father's cavalier approach to life. As a gesture of settlement, after the event so to speak, he had removed the charge against the old house in order to release her and her grown-up kids from their purgatory. She had been grateful. The law had not demanded that of him and he'd attained a certain stature in the eyes of many for the nobility of his actions in that specific regard. Her own son Josh, with his wife and young daughter, had moved back into the home in which he had grown up. It had been just reward for the chaos he had witnessed as a youth and the turmoil all three of them had endured through that dreadful investigation. His sister Laura had missed most of the action as she was working in Brazil, and she'd returned home when the strain of the legal process had receded. She had been relieved that the house had been brought back within the bounds of the family, and once again she was able to adopt the place as the location to which she was rooted.

It had been a wrench for Janice to leave her former home, especially when she remembered the time and effort she, and Jeff, had given its renovation. But she knew that Josh would take its upkeep very seriously. Besides, she had an exciting new adventure before her, and at fifty-seven she was still fit, strong and eager to welcome the challenges before her.

Again a new, incoming email drew her attention back to her screen, and she sat forward at her keyboard and rattled off a very quick response.

6

more of the man

Janice kicked back in her chair again, unable and unwilling to discipline her thoughts within the confines of her comfortable office.

David was turning out to be a mercurial sort and she revelled in the process of discovering new characteristics, foibles and mannerisms of the new man in her life. His modesty and sincerity had shone through very early in their relationship, in fact before there really had been a relationship to speak of. Her own reliance on him had been absolute – only he could have rescued her son from that apparently inevitable miscarriage of justice. His professional pride and almost brooding attention to detail had saved the day. Her recognition of his quiet, almost moody submersion in the finer nuances of the case should have prepared her for some unexpected surprises later.

She had woken one morning recently to find him gone. The morning sun peeking in through the blinds had stirred her and she'd immediately seen that his side of the bed was vacant. She'd looked up to see his robe gone from the hook by the door, so she'd got up and made to follow him, stopping for a moment at the full-length window at the half-landing on the stairs to marvel at the view of the great stretch of water far below. She had sighed contentment at that captivating vista, and she reflected again just how fortunate they had been to find such a fabulous rental with so much glass, so much light and so much space. The place felt cavernous and yet homely, despite its very modern style. Carrying on down to the open-plan kitchen she'd entered the breakfast room to find him leaning over a huge ordnance survey map that covered the entire tabletop. She had stopped dead in her tracks as soon as she'd realised that he'd simply not registered her soft bare feet on the cool tiled floor. He'd taken a slurp of coffee from his left hand, and she'd shot a glance at their magnificent Sage coffee machine to see coffee grounds all over the bench next to it. The lights were still illuminated on the front console. The aroma was tantalising, but she'd not dared reveal her presence in anticipation of some form of mild entertainment unfolding before her.

He'd grumbled and muttered to himself, something about steep slopes or screes, and then a casual reference to woodland tracks being faster and more comfortable. Then he'd put his coffee mug down and collected a piece of paper and a pencil. Positioning the paper in a precise manner on the colourful contoured landscape, he'd manoeuvred it about the chart, flicking at it frequently with the pencil as he went. Then he'd reached for the scale at the bottom of the huge sheet and placed the paper against the graduations announcing softly, but with some finality, "Twelve miles. Can she do twelve miles? Yes, of course she can do twelve miles. She can even carry the rucksack some of the time as well."

"Oh can she now?" she'd interceded from somewhere behind him.

"Shit!" he'd coughed, spilling some coffee from the mug he was in the process of retrieving. "Are you looking for husband number five already?" he'd demanded. "You nearly frightened the life out of me, creeping about like that."

But she'd just giggled, and she'd stepped forward into a welcome embrace and a warm coffee-flavoured kiss.

"Mmmh," she'd drawled, "you are very tasty Mr Lehrer, and in more ways than you think. I must have some of that dark roast right now," and she'd broken away, heading towards the machine. "And what on earth are you doing? It looks like you have some kind of orienteering test arranged for us. I thought we were just getting our boots on today and going for a nice long walk."

"Oh, we are, honey. We are. But I just want to be sure of our bearings, key indicators to watch out for, tricky terrain underfoot, you know...outdoor stuff really. We don't want to get caught short, now do we?" he cajoled her with that melting smile of his.

"David, it's the Lakes in springtime – how wrong can things go?"

"Come, come, ye experienced mountain guide of Wainwright fame. I shouldn't need to entertain that question with any gravity, surely?" But at that point he'd launched into a gentle delivery explaining the route he had chosen. The landscape would be diverse. There would be some stunning lake views as the intended route meandered this way and that through the many folds of the countryside. He'd applied particular thoroughness to two carefully scrutinised stretches which, he'd assured her, traversed a clutch of tightly scrunched contours on the map. She knew without looking up, busy as she was with the coffee, that he was describing steep climbs or descents.

"You can have the backpack at those points then," she'd asserted, and he'd chuckled as if to himself as he'd pored over the plan.

Only then, sat there in her new office on autopilot, did it dawn on her: attention to detail, naturally – c'mon, you idiot, he's a detective! That's why he was such a good organiser. He didn't leave things to chance. She wondered then, whether or not that was a good thing, but of course the successful release of her son had been achieved only with this kind, lovable man's appreciation of the real importance of every pixel hidden in every picture.

Maybe that's why he was so good at chess, she mused: meticulous, intense sometimes, able to absorb multiple potential options, a natural strategic caution, but the tactical capacity to strike with devastating consequences for his opponent – and recently she'd been his only combatant in this regard, and she was getting tired of losing.

Or perhaps there was something about his Jewishness in all of that, she countered silently. Was it just a notion or had she somehow picked up a subtle understanding that the Jewish character and nature, if indeed there existed such a thing, exhibited some kind of proclivity for mental agility in all its various forms? She knew, of course, that Jewish success in business was famous – infamous, David had said – and when she'd questioned that, he'd suggested that strategic caution was a self-defence mechanism of sorts which had been developed and honed among his community over many, many generations.

Yet he'd been at pains to point out that his Jewishness was no longer especially important to him. It hadn't been since he'd rejected the formal expressions of his earlier adherence when still pushing through his teens. He remembered his bar mitzvah and one or two earlier references to the learning of his now lapsed faith, but he couldn't forget the bigoted bullying and intimidation he'd suffered as a kid. He'd argued with his immediate family that wearing the badge of Jewishness, metaphorically speaking, had in fact perpetuated the problem with some of their north London neighbours. It advertised their differences, most often with an assumed sense of condescending superiority. Religion in general, of any and all faiths, had not stood up to the incisive interrogation he had given it as he was growing up. So he had drifted away as maturity had taken hold, much to his poor mama's disappointment. However, and in great contrast to his religious apathy, he had cultivated a blooming interest in the history of his people and of his own family line in particular. In that sense his religion couldn't be entirely ignored.

Janice had learned that of his family heritage there were few living souls with whom to confer. His aged mother still lived in a Jewish retirement home near Enfield. She had been delighted to meet Janice and had thanked her for rescuing her lonely boy from the clutches of sadness and ignominy, even at their apparently late stage in life. Of course the old dear remembered her first daughter-in-law from many years earlier, and according to the old girl the younger model had been lovely, but her feckless son just hadn't been ready for her. David had later corrected his mother, when out of earshot, when he'd confessed to Janice that it had been the job and the thrill of the investigative chase that had put paid to his first marriage. He was beyond all that now, he'd assured her, and so far their new joint enterprise had proven an intoxicating carousel of warmth, passion and burgeoning mutual appreciation.

His father had died many years earlier. Their relationship had never been a good one apparently. David had consigned that to experience quite quickly. Actually, when his father realised that his only son had given up the code, he had pushed the boy away. It had been a dreadful mistake and one which broke David's mum's heart. By the time the older man had recognised his error, time had caught up with him just as it was running out.

His dear old grandmother, long gone, had been the pivot around which David's domestic life had hinged. Through her he had learned so much about the family. Through her, and quite contrary to her own daughter's pleadings, the lad had soaked up every word, every last morsel of information which would enable him later to reach back in time, right through the devastation of Germany in the thirties, through the camps, the trains, the wanton slaughter, in order to piece together his migrant lineage. It had been here, in this most sensitive arena, that Janice had begun to find his innermost self. She had learned quite quickly that he was emotionally robust and could be devoted, supportive and fervid, but finding his true heart and soul was never going to be easy. On occasions he had opened up to her with such unguarded candour that she began to wonder if she could match him or indeed adequately respond to his needs.

Her absent-minded reflections alighted upon another recent occasion when they had been dining late at home one evening and savouring a fulsome red. As they'd slouched on the couch, gazing out over the twinkling lights on the lake shore, he'd recounted the tale of his own trip to Germany not long after the Berlin Wall had been breached. In those days his German, and even his Yiddish, had been just about workable – now he regretted the loss of that linguistic capability and he put it down to lack of practice, as simple as that. He had travelled over with a small mixed group of like-minded folk who were intent on a bit of genealogy of their own. They had been driven by much the same backgrounds too, he'd discovered, but the lot of them had ended up visiting Buchenwald concentration camp, and inevitably it had turned out to be a sorry encounter.

An avid reader, David had always – and it remained true to the present day – carried a book around with him. There was one by their bedside – although she smiled knowingly at his other preoccupations in the bedroom of late – and there was another on the kitchen breakfast bar and yet another in the day room. As a younger man he had read in German, noting the likes of Böll, Schwaiger, Kafka and Zweig among his favourites. He'd argued, of course, and how could she possibly have countered, that Dürrenmatt had been essential for any budding detective. But in all this, and like most other readers, he'd surmised, he read mainly for pleasure and for the stimulation it provided.

He had always known Lehrer (teacher) to be a rather common name in the German-speaking world. Nevertheless, he had reached a stage in which he knew with some certainty that several Lehrers of his particular bloodline had been incarcerated at Buchenwald. He'd suspected, again with some certainty, that none had survived.

However, he had been shocked and overcome to discover an apparent link with one of those favourite authors.

That night, as they'd reclined on the sofa, he'd casually drifted into a segment of his past that somehow possessed a part of his subconscious, that in a way defined an important cornerstone of his character. He'd simply explained, quite naturally, the significance to him deep down inside of one of his favourite authors.

Stefan Zweig had become a true titan of the pre- and post-war literati in Europe. His iconic classic *Schachnovelle* had depicted the life-and-death struggle against Nazism in Germany by way of a fascinating story about the great pre-war chess masters who toured the civilised world at that time playing their great challenge matches before packed audiences. The well-to-do, educated businessmen, entrepreneurs and attendant intellectuals flocked to see them. Often such high-minded contests were fielded in the opulent lounges of great passenger liners as they steamed between glamorous destinations such as Hamburg and Buenos Aires, New York and London. The grand masters were gifted exponents of the greatest table game on earth and they possessed not just a complete understanding of the game's complexities, but also a raw intuition with which they would dissect the developing strategies of their opponents while wallowing in the adulation of rapt high-brow onlookers.

As he'd relayed the yarn, Janice had sensed a mounting emotional tension. The timbre of his voice had shifted. He'd looked out to the lake more frequently and had sipped tentatively at his great roundel of red wine, sloshing the silky smoothness round the periphery of the glass. At one point she'd gripped his hand as if in support. He hadn't acknowledged it, but he hadn't rejected her either.

Back on the cruise liners of the nineteen thirties, a young upstart had burst onto the chess-playing scene and had quickly taken several prestigious scalps. His reputation spread quickly and soon he was pitched against some of the greatest chess minds anywhere in the world. He had been a farmer's boy, just a labourer on the land, a crude muscular brute of a young man devoid of any understanding of manners or etiquette. Yet he appeared able to compete favourably with his betters and even gloated outlandishly over his many victories.

David had explained to her that Zweig, another Jew just like him, had used simile to denounce and to ridicule Adolf Hitler and his murderous band of trolls. In the passage of time the coarse young creature had been found out and had been sent packing. His weaknesses had been several: his lack of educational and cultural appreciation, a distinct lack of true intellect, and that critically instinctive capacity to decipher his opponents' cleverly constructed strategies had been missing all along. He had learned the game by rote and as soon as his limited tactical awareness had been exposed he'd been destined to return to his inconsequential former life. Stefan Zweig had sketched the rough, often violent oaf as the Nazis, and their vile dogma had, as in real life, proven no match for the vibrant intellectual supremacy of Europe's mature cultures.

She could tell that he was becoming slightly more agitated, but she began to wonder where the tale was leading.

"In Buchenwald I stood next to the bear pit. I knew before I got there that the commandant of the camp had built a terrifying reputation throughout the Reich as the purveyor of human skin lampshades," he'd continued quietly. "The bear pit was used for entertainment. Sometimes one or two animals would be starved for a few days and then put into the pit. They would lower into the deathly crater a screaming emaciated inmate who would then fight for his life watched by officers and guards who leaned in over the parapet and howled with laughter at the carnage below. Human skin had been in cheap and plentiful supply it seems."

He'd swallowed hard and then taken another swig of wine, and then he'd run his fingers back through his greying blond hair as if searching for a distraction. She'd held his hand a little firmer.

"Not far from there was an experimental surgery with several marble operating tables complete with drainage channels and leather restraints for arms, legs and heads. I couldn't stay in there for very long – just reading about the live experiments on child twins was enough to force me out of there, and it hadn't been part of my quest anyway. But when I stepped out into the cold fresh air I took a real mental and emotional hit when I was confronted by an enormous monochrome photograph on the outside wall of the building."

"What did it show?"

"A huge pile of skeletal bodies stacked up to a height of about...well, my height...and it was at that moment that I realised the photo had been taken right where I was standing!"

He'd exhaled slowly and shaken his head in dismay. Just as she'd been about to ask him to stop, he'd carried on.

"You see, I was looking for several of my Lehrers, and I did find them, but not before coming across yet another shocking discovery. It turned out to be my error, but I learned even more from that mistake."

"In what way?" she'd asked.

"Well, as I approached what had been the administration block I spotted a plaque on the wall which told the earliest story of none other than Stefan Zweig.

"I simply hadn't realised that he had suffered there. In fact I'd always assumed that he had managed to escape from Germany in the nick of time. I was fairly sure that he had found a way to get to South America before the Holocaust had overwhelmed him, but no, apparently not. When I saw that plaque, and read his name, I was devastated. I'd thought all along that his ability to vilify the Nazi regime in literature had been his crowning success, not the cause of his incarceration and presumably his ultimate end. I hadn't connected him with any of it, let alone the deprivations of Buchenwald."

He'd had to stop then and gather himself. She'd tugged on his arm and snuggled up closer to him. Still he'd continued.

"But I simply had to read the entire inscription..." and he'd stopped yet again, "...only to learn just another horrifying footnote among millions of equally frightful personal histories. Who would have credited the fateful coincidence of that famous name in Germanic literature and culture?"

She'd lifted her head at that intriguing question and looked at him intently. "What did you find?"

"Well, there were two Stefan Zweigs. It can't be a unique German name, I suppose, and the author whose works I had devoured in my youth was Austrian not German, but two Stefan Zweigs famous in Germanic literature is some achievement in itself. This one turned out to be a Polish Jew named Stefan Jerzy Zweig who was interned in the camp as a little boy. He had certainly been destined for Mengele – not a twin you understand, but that monster carried out such heinous experiments that children were just guinea pigs, and little Stefan was only three years old.

"However, a number of adult prisoners decided to hide him. The risks were incalculable, but they assumed they were never going to get out of there so what did it matter? They hid him between and behind hessian sacks and fed him their own scraps whenever they could. Every so often, on a regular basis, the sacks were taken out on trucks. They contained clothing, dentures, spectacles, prosthetic limbs, jewellery, watches, human hair…and at those times the lad was very exposed, but they protected him. They saved his life, and they did it successfully for several years, although some of them paid for it with their own. Minor misdemeanours were often necessary to cover for him and during that period several people were executed for related crimes, and of course they took their secrets or any potential witness statements to their shallow graves."

She'd looked up at him and into those astonishingly pale blue eyes and simply said, "I think I know what you're going to say."

"Yes…you're right, of course you are. My grandmother's mother and elder brother were shot together, side by side; two wretched washed-out souls in a long line of others just like them, the two of them holding hands as the volley sounded behind them."

A solitary tear had rolled down his cheek and he'd wiped it away with the back of his hand.

"So you see," he'd gone on, "I did find those family ties, but the whole thing was so gruelling. I could never decide, even to this day, here and now, what it really said about my people – victims of course, but why? Was it avoidable? Was there something about us, is there still, that we might have done differently? Or was it all down to those cavemen in uniforms so resplendent they almost looked admirable? And little Stefan Jerzy's tale didn't help my attempts to rationalise the whole thing one little bit."

"Why not? What happened to him?"

"He survived, that's the first thing to say, but obviously at great cost to others around him. Which of us would not try to save a little boy in great peril? I'm not a father, but I sincerely hope that I and others like me would extend a protective hand to child refugees who are in mortal danger. It's human nature, isn't it? But after the war, a rumour emerged that little Stefan had been swapped with a teenage boy in the camp. The older boy went to his death. It became the subject of a disputed book. It was said that Stefan may indeed have survived the camp during both the German and Soviet periods of its history, but that he never recovered from the later discovery that his life had been purchased in that gruesome exchange. How had that been achieved? Who had been in a position to barter such an outcome? Would I have done the same to protect someone dear to me? What would that say about me, or about us," and with that he'd waved a sweeping arm out towards the lake beyond the window as if to include every Jew in the global envelope.

"After that trip over there I used to worry my way through various analyses of those horrors, just trying to fathom the unfathomable. The propensity for human beings to abuse others when let off the leash in times of great economic hardship is something that is impossible to calibrate. The effects of such barbarity however, are there for all to see. It doesn't seem to take much to trigger depravity among humankind. But are we any better prepared for those dreadful experiences? Would we encourage those same reactions again in a different time and place, or do we inflict such horrendous crimes upon others when the jackboot is on the other foot?"

Then he'd just sighed and laid his head back in the chair, exhausted. He'd asked no more questions. He'd sought neither criticism nor reinforcement.

They'd sat there, huddled in the gathering evening gloom and had said nothing more. She was beginning to understand him. She suspected that he'd confided the experience to only a precious few individuals; not his younger wife – they had divorced before his trip to Weimar and the camp – but probably his mother and...well, just to her, just now. She found herself wanting to protect him and she instantly saw the irony of that – hadn't he been her saviour not many weeks ago? Also, she began to tie the various threads of his heritage together. Now the Germanic features, though curiously not overtly Jewish, his name, the Jewish ancestry, the craving for all things cultural, this was the man she was just beginning to see for the first time.

And she reminded herself that this morose, lachrymose state wasn't typical, not at all. Instead he'd already surprised her with the breadth of his interests and his inquisitive perception in subjects new and untried. As for that invisible stamp of Jewishness, invisible to her at least and probably to many more she imagined, there was his unbounded love of music and perhaps a characteristic leaning toward the violin and those exceptional Yiddish rhythms that surfaced every so often in modern popular refrains.

Then, still a timeframe away from the demands of her work, she recalled another evening not a week earlier when again they'd been enjoying good food at home – another of his unexpected talents. He had very pointedly seized the remote control for the Bose music system, which lay next to the wine bottle on the table. With a great flourish, he'd selected a change of track and those arresting first piano keys from Leonard Cohen's 'Dance Me to the End of Love' had immediately captivated their shared attention. He'd stood with mock theatre, stepped around the table to take her hand, raised her up and walked her extravagantly to his makeshift dining-room dance floor. There he'd pulled her close with commanding swagger and wheeled her round and round with gliding steps, rising and fading in glorious time with the passionate cadence of the lilting violin. By God – anybody's God – she had been overwhelmed, especially when he danced her all the way to bed, and she wouldn't forget that night for a long, long time.

Suddenly, through the mists of her of happy recollections there he was, standing in the doorway of the Windermere office of the Tourism Board, waving casually in her direction. She'd been lost in the comforting folds of her recent and so very exciting past and had completely overlooked her lunch date – another treat for both of them.

She closed her screen down and hurried off to catch up with him outside on the pavement in the sunshine. Her colleagues watched her go and took the opportunity to give her handsome man the once-over.

7

a moving target

He'd planned it so very carefully and in all its simplistic detail. He'd 'walked the course', as his golfing mates used to say, although he hadn't played golf for a few years. The chemotherapy had stolen that pleasure from him as well, just like everything else that had been quickly eroded when the disease had set in. He stood there stock still, looking across the open expanse of greening springtime heather toward the fringes of the forest. He grunted his discontent as he tried to recall when he had last come out to the wide open spaces without carrying with him that deep-seated anger and gnawing frustration at the hopelessness of his terminal condition. Yes, he conceded, he had been well enough to get up here several times during the last few weeks in order to assess the limits within which the task would have to be implemented. He knew however, that this last temporary remission wouldn't last much longer. He was off the infernal poisons – they hadn't worked anyway – and he wouldn't allow them to pump the toxic filth through his veins anymore. It had been his decision and his alone. He may not have had enough of life itself – seventy-one was hardly ancient these days – but he couldn't face that degrading injustice even one more time.

Still…time enough to make the ultimate statement for the cause. There would be no clues, no traces or spores, no evidential thread for those lacklustre disingenuous boys in blue to pursue. And if he himself lasted another month beyond this day he'd be very surprised, so why should he care?

It was a bit of a murky day; not as clear as he would have liked, but clear enough for his purposes. The wind had turned from a crisp north-westerly to a more favourable south-westerly, heralding the arrival of summer perhaps a little sooner than expected. No matter, he thought, he wouldn't live long enough to feel the midsummer sun on his back.

In the last two weeks he'd examined a few vantage points and made sure in each case that he'd accurately understood the physical dynamics of each potential hide. Facing the darkness of the conifers would provide him with a perfectly contrasting backdrop which would etch his target in distinct form. In addition, and knowing the intended trail to be taken, his chosen lair would give him several opportunities in relatively quick succession to achieve a precise despatch. Furthermore, the preferred spot offered him the quickest and easiest escape. His aching limbs and laboured breathing wouldn't cope with anything too dramatic. In any event, the old Forestry Trust pickup would make the short downhill sweep back to the plantation without being seen – it was private land after all, and it was also a Sunday; he already knew there would be nobody at work. From there it would be a short cross-country walk via his carefully selected exit route to his old van, and from there a short drive back to his remote cottage on the tiny back roads. He'd ditch the hardware en route – an ingenious solution which, he was confident, would never be rumbled.

It wasn't that he would mind being identified…well, not really…in fact it might set an encouraging example among other campaigners, but no, that wasn't part of it. As a dead man walking he wanted to leave the scum in fear. He wanted them and their ilk to know real gut-wrenching anxiety. He wanted them truly to believe that it could happen again, to any one of them at any time and in almost any location in the park. If he could achieve that level of disquiet among the selfish hordes he would very probably rest in peace, reassured in the knowledge that he'd made a difference at last.

He knelt between the gorse clumps and checked his surroundings again. In his camouflage combats he knew he could rely on near invisibility, certainly from range. He swung his rucksack from his back and cringed in pain before laying it carefully on the cold flat stone bed before him.

He remembered his last encounter with his intended victim. The wretch had been just a teenager then, but now he was in his mid-twenties and still inflicting his self-indulgent destruction on the landscape they had loved and cherished. The gobby little shit had thought nothing of mowing down his poor wife as she'd bravely stood in the way of their racing column. It had careered toward the two of them without a care as they were out hiking on that fateful day. She'd waved her hands wildly and gestured to them to stop, but the leading rider had actually accelerated as he got nearer. As she'd tried to evade the impending collision at the last moment, he'd coursed through her trailing leg, smashing the bones in several places. It was an incident from which she never recovered; blood poisoning had eventually carried her beyond his own loving reach.

The hospital had been about as effective as the county court. The lad's cohort, in close attendance and obviously cognisant of the truth behind the calamity, had simply colluded in their successful strategy to extricate themselves and the guilty party from a difficult position. It should have been manslaughter at least in his view, but they got away with an illegal riding conviction and a small fine as minors.

After the trauma of losing his lifelong love, he had determined to fight back, not just against the entire filthy gang of them, but especially against their leader on that day. So he'd established a deliberate plan of surveillance, secretly checking on the four of them in an attempt to bring about some kind of revenge. They were locals, all of them. On that awful day, the beginning of the end of his own life he could now claim with some surety, their thug-in-chief had even halted briefly after crashing into her, only to disgorge a stream of foul-mouthed abuse at the two of them. His caustic vitriol and utter disdain had been enough. From that moment he'd set himself the task of delivering that young man's come-uppance, and as the seven subsequent years had rolled past, he'd got to know that despicable creep's every move.

He'd also discovered, much to his eternal disgust, just how widespread the trail biking problem was and just how frequently such deplorable activities were undertaken by these delinquents and so many other gangs of young men across the region. It all helped to explain the visible proof that he had collected in the same period, until his own sickness had descended upon him, that the scale and regularity of their incursions had reached epidemic proportions. No wonder the entire national park was capitulating in the face of such a reckless onslaught. No wonder the various rambling clubs were creaking under the weight of complaint. People were giving up. Good, honest, decent people were no longer coming to the Lake District. They were afraid of confrontation, knowing through bitter experience that so many beautiful stretches of England's most prestigious countryside were being ripped up and terrorised. Mindless yobs travelled miles, from all over the north of England, North Wales and the Scottish Borders to flout the law in the pursuit of their own self-gratification.

And how had the authorities reacted to this blatant escalation of hostilities? Not at all! It was as if they just couldn't be bothered – don't rock my boat, mate, I've got a cushy job in the Lake District so let's not be upsetting any apple carts, shall we?

Well no more! It was time to kick back, time for retribution, time to stiffen the response of the timid majority and to set a new standard.

He checked his watch. The probable time zone was almost upon him. Within five and ten minutes, give or take, he would expect to hear his target's approach. Then he would have to wait, prone and ready to strike, for no more than another four minutes. His wasting body could manage little more.

He unpacked the weapon with practised swift efficiency. It was a fairly old unit, one he hadn't fired for nearly twenty years until so very recently. He smiled as he remembered how easily he had come by it – from a friend who had earlier been a regular gun club member. It had been a gift, an enticement perhaps for him to think about joining the club. It really hadn't been his scene at all. After taking it home, he'd never used it. He'd never even registered it, but he had cleaned it once or twice and kept the ammunition with it in the back of the old broom cupboard under the stairs. Mary had given up complaining about it. In the end, he thought it entirely possible that she had actually forgotten about it. He hadn't. After she'd gone he'd decided quite quickly, almost subconsciously, that he'd get it out and check it over. Then it had been a very short step to trying it out in the secluded woodland above his old place. By then the plan was already formulating in his head, although several years had then gone by as he secretly scrutinised his intended target before the curse of the cancer had accelerated his scheming.

He snapped the butt into place with a subdued click. The scope was already racked, and he twisted the barrel into place with cramped bony fingers. Then he did the same with the old silencer – *suppressor* they called them nowadays. Finally he dropped the bipod stanchion from beneath the body of the rifle to support it from the ground, and he lowered himself very gently onto his hollowed belly, looking all the while at larch, pine and cedar just three hundred yards away.

The brisk headwind was filtered by the same trees and he sanctioned himself the joy of immersion in their gentle rushing, swishing melody as he relaxed into the task ahead. Relaxation was crucial – tension in the limbs at the critical moment could ruin the exercise. He had to get this right – just one single shot. However tempting it might be to gloat over his victim, that was simply not in the plan and he would not weaken. The risks would be unthinkable. He cocked his head to one side and listened hard for that distant fretful whirring, that staccato buzzing signature not unlike a chainsaw but subtly less industrious and certainly more frivolous. Almost precisely on cue there it was, an agile and yet powerful driving engine climbing up through the lower reaches of the forest and fast approaching the clearing at the edge of the trees.

He pressed his eye to the cushioned rim of the telescopic sight. Looking beyond the cross-hairs, he focused on the trail as it widened at the tree line and burst forth onto the fell. The wind pushed at the gorse around him and the heather relented under the pressure. He knew he didn't have to worry about the wind speed. The range was too short for it to offer any meaningful deflection to the bullet's trajectory.

He heard it again, more persistent this time, nagging, irritating almost, that sickening whine which he had for so long associated with the arrogance with which these louts wilfully defiled this, his own hallowed ground.

And then he saw him racing up the last gentle slope and out into the light. It was him alright; of that he had no doubt. He released the safety catch and exhaled very slowly. The yob braked the surging Kawasaki and brought it to a halt. The brilliant white machine looked stark against the background foliage despite its mud-splattered lower chassis. He stood down on one side, and revved the engine again and again with repeated twists of his right hand on the throttle. He oozed bravado as he glanced left and right across the open reach. Those ridiculous all-white leathers identified him despite the apparent anonymity provided by the full-face blue skid lid complete with sunscreen visor. The matching blue stripes running down arms and legs, together with emblazoned names of several sponsors across chest and thighs, completed the caricature in the eyes of the waiting assailant.

Then the rider released the clutch and the scrambler lurched forward heading directly towards his unseen nemesis. Viewed through the scope, the victim advanced quickly to the first optional action point on the track, but a slight swerve to avoid a stone added a few extra seconds to his life. He dipped down into the first hollow and out of sight, and the screaming engine sounded muffled for the same few seconds, but then he reappeared at pace. Negotiating a minor dog-leg with ease he straightened up as the cross-wires located that very trendy visor. At the second optional action point precisely, the marksman gently squeezed the trigger. Simultaneously he felt the heavy recoil of the rifle at his shoulder and heard the gentle spit as the high-velocity projectile sped forth and homed on its target. He saw the visor shatter and a shocking crimson spray erupted from the back of the rider's helmet. The bike continued forward in a straight line despite the loss of its pilot who had been jettisoned backwards from his seat and lay sprawled across the pathway. He had been killed instantly. The machine eventually teetered to the left and crashed off the track and into a shallow boggy pool.

There was no need to check his results. The deed was done. He felt a warm glow inside and not the sort he'd experienced too often of late when piped up to that evil chemotherapy equipment. He dismantled the weapon calmly and quickly, repacked it into his rucksack and set off for the first stage of his exit strategy. He smiled as he walked away. They'd come for him; he knew that. They'd surely backtrack through the records and find that devastating incident seven years ago – clear motivation for anyone to see – but they'd never trace the gun, and they'd never be able to pin him down on his movements, especially if the final phase of his plan was given just an extra day or two to mature.

8

in for a penny…

Keith sat there hunched over his dark pint of bitter, drumming his fingers impatiently on the tabletop. It was a smooth draught of Timothy Taylor's, one of his favourite brews, but he would have preferred more relaxed, convivial surroundings. There was nothing wrong with the quiet snug at the Old Grenadier in Flookburgh. On the contrary, it was perfect for their hastily planned but hopefully secretive meeting. No, that wasn't the problem, not at all. His anxiety was beginning to take control despite the quiet seclusion and gentle ambience proffered by the old pub.

They tried not to meet unless absolutely necessary – less chance of being seen together – but he had identified this venue as a suitable location in moments of crisis. The entrance from the narrow end of the car park brought customers in through the little snug. But most visitors arriving by car tended to make use of the main entrance doors thus avoiding the snug, which remained untroubled and largely out of sight.

Once, a couple of months back, they'd arranged to meet at the very same table only to find a couple of young lovers tucked away in there. They were kissing and canoodling, hands all over each other and probably underage for both drinking and sexual adventure – so they'd had to work out a plan B on the hoof, and they'd reconvened just a few miles down the road in a picnic site car park; hardly ideal.

Nervously he looked again at his watch. Where the bloody hell was he? Already he was fifteen minutes overdue and he felt that developing sense of being kept waiting in order to make a point. Then he heard the raucous rage of the motor just outside as the arriving bike surged from the street through the pedestrian ginnel and came to an abrupt stop just beyond the back door to the pub.

"So much for travelling incognito," Keith announced sarcastically, as Morgan burst through the door. He was dressed in full leathers and still wore his crash hat emblazoned with a strident Welsh dragon in an intense, unavoidable scarlet.

"Aye aye, boss man," came the confident response. "Have you not got one in for me then, Butty?"

"No I sodding well haven't, at least not yet, and I'm not your sodding Butty, alright? And do please keep it down, for Chrissakes. We're trying not to get noticed, in case you'd forgotten."

At that prompt, Morgan whipped off his crash helmet and plonked it down on the table nearly sending Keith's pint glass flying. Then he took a cautious glance around the corner of the chimney breast into the wider lounge bar. "No worries, guv'nor; not a soul h'yur in the lounge and just a few bods through in the bar. Now are you gonna get me that beer or not?"

"Okay, okay," Keith answered as he shuffled out from behind the table. "What will it be? Oh, no...don't tell me, lemme guess. Er, what about a pint of that yellow piss you usually drink? What is it? Foster's? Is that the one?"

"You know full well that's the one, so stop yankin' my chain and get yourself over to that sweet young thing behind the bar. She'll most likely remember a hunk like me if she's ever asked to look at a photo-fit, but an old roly-poly granddad like you would likely test her powers of recollection to the limit."

Keith rolled his eyes and threw his head back in mock disgust, but then disappeared round the corner and into the lounge to get the golden elixir for his younger counterpart. When he returned to the table, setting the lager down next his own glass, he realised that Morgan was looking a little jumpy. He fidgeted with his long hair, seemed unsure as to the need to retain his leather jacket or to remove it, and appeared to spend some time unzipping the thing and then zipping it up again as the indecision took hold. Then Keith spotted the hooded bloodshot eyes and he guessed immediately that his opposite number was flying like a bird. He leaned forward surreptitiously and ventured his concern in subdued tones.

"Morgan...for fuck's sake...have you been at the merchandise again?"

"So what if I have? It doesn't matter – just a quick smack before I came over – it's properly cool man. Chill!"

"Are you totally out of your tree, or what? Do you realise how dangerous this is? You're riding a trail bike, doubtless way over any of the speed limits, and you say it's cool?"

"Never crashed yet, big man," Morgan retorted glibly.

"You fucking bone head," Keith hissed beneath his breath. "It's not about you killing yourself in a dope-infused blur, it's about you driving like a mad bastard and attracting the attention of that lemon-curd sandwich that normally holes up in the Backbarrow lay-by, and then we'd both be screwed."

"Relax, boyo, for Chrissakes, that's just not gonna happen. I'm too smart for that – trust me. I took the back road over – nobody anywhere to be seen."

"Trust you? Trust you? Just listen to yourself. On what basis should I trust you? From what I've seen so far, it looks to me as if you are far too flash with the cash. You are going to get the three of us in deep shit before very much longer."

"Oh please do pipe down before you give yourself a stroke or something. We're doing fine. Production is good, quality excellent, and distribution is so effective that my link has asked how quickly we can up the output."

"Oh no you don't," Keith stammered anxiously. "I called this meeting to tell you to start winding the whole thing down. I can't take the risk anymore. There is simply too much at stake. If this scam were to be uncovered we'd both be spending the next ten years in Strangeways, and for me, at my age, there would be little left to come out to after that length of time in the can."

Morgan had started to shake his head as Keith delivered his latest jitters. "Not a chance, Butt. Get this straight," he whispered forcefully, "we are not packing this in, not now at any rate. We're just beginning to make some serious dosh. Two more years like this and then we can just stop it whenever we want. I'll be wallowing in it, and you, well…you'll be even more stinking rich than you are already."

"Don't damn well kid yourself, son. I think you have some fanciful notions about my personal wealth…"

"Oh, come on now, boss, don't be shy. Living up there on that hill in that palatial mansion of yours...I mean, what am I supposed to think? I mean...isn't that the perfect camouflage? Why would one of the county's wealthiest and most respected men ever need to dabble in drugs?"

"Keep your fucking voice down, you prick," Keith commanded in a seething slur. "You're missing the bleeding obvious, as per fucking usual."

"Oh am I indeed?" Morgan challenged. "And what is the bleedin' obvious then, Mister Bigwig?"

"That reputation...all of that you've just spewed all over this pub for anyone to latch on to...that's just too much to risk. If I'm the Lake District's richest man, it's in your eyes only – I'd take a stab at our beloved chairman, Mr Austen Smiley, for that particular accolade – but you're right, there are many aspects of my life which are simply too valuable to be put in jeopardy by running a back-room narcotics factory in an old derelict warehouse."

"But we're already eighteen months in and it's just beginning to gather some momentum. I've got the process under control. We don't have to worry about discarding some of our less disposable materials because there's enough capacity in those old sheds to stash the stuff there without affecting anyone. Years from now they'll come across that waste and simply not realise the connection. It'll just look like industrial discards from way, way back. Nobody will know the difference and we'll be long gone, and—"

"Stop! Just stop. I don't want to know any of the details. That was our original agreement. You were to tell me nothing. I'd grant you space at the old railhead, in those old ruins out the back there, and you'd achieve your own access through your own clandestine means along the old railway track. I don't need to know any more. I'm not interested in how you come and go – four wheels or two wheels, on foot, I just don't care – but you were never to use the main driveway to the quarry for any of this."

"I know, I know, and I haven't. I stuck to that agreement in every aspect. I mean...I only ever come up the hill when I'm coming to work, you must have realised that?"

"Yes, yes, I know that, but..."

"But what? What the fuck is the problem? I've just got my distribution drop properly organised out by the M6, and—"

"You see, there you go again – too much information! If I ever get nicked I want to be able to say that I know nowt. That's what we agreed. If you ever get nicked you're on your own and I'm supposed to deny any knowledge of some rogue operation going on under my nose in a distant corner of the site that hasn't been used for ages and is all chained and locked up for safety reasons."

"How very supportive of you, boss."

"Oh piss off...don't gimme that. You know that's the best way to run this scam. It's your scam, let's not forget that, and you're paying me my little cut purely for making the, er...shall we call it 'factory space' available. Isn't that it?"

"Little cut? Are you pullin' my plonker, or what?"

"Alright, okay, it's not bad money, I'll grant you that, but the rewards still don't bear the risk – not by my assessment anyway. It's time to shut it all down, Morgan. Come on, you must see that?"

The younger man sat back in his chair. He shook his head in frustration as his ire steadily simmered. He took a long slow gulp of his cold beer and then placed his glass carefully back down, wiping his lips with the back of his hand.

"Listen up and listen good, boss man. We'll close this thing down when I'm good and ready and not before. In the meantime," he added with determination, "me and Stevie will continue to do the doing, so to speak, and you will simply turn a blind eye in return for your regular and rather rewarding percentage."

"But that's another loophole..." Keith pleaded, leaning low over the tabletop to press his case more forcefully. "Stevie's just another risk. He's gonna blab at some stage. I mean...how do you know he's not spilling the beans already? Is he using the stuff too? What if he just can't help gassing to his mates after a few weekend beers too many? The risks are legion. How the hell can you be sure that you have him under control?"

"Look, for fuck's sake, why do we have to go through all this again? Stevie is kosher. He's smart. He knows he's onto a life-changer, and he's smart enough to see and understand that. We don't have to do this for years and years. At this rate and with the acceleration we've created over the last six months or so, we'll be making hay on a monumental scale soon enough. A couple more years and then we just wipe it down and walk away."

"Oh grow up, Morgan, please. You're not just gonna walk away. You guys won't be able to do that. You've gotta be realistic, c'mon."

"Keith, I mean it…you are just gonna have to trust me! I need Stevie, not just because he has a good instinctive radar," and he tapped the side of his head to indicate a quick mind, "but he's our second delivery man. I can't do it all on my own, as you know…"

"You're doing it again," Keith spat back at the younger man. "I don't want to know the logistics. It's safer that way."

"And anyway," Morgan retorted, "Stevie doesn't even know that you know! He has no idea. He actually believes that the two of us are working on the quiet out there. He thinks that our secret operation is precisely and exactly that – secret! It helps a lot in terms of how we manage our own comings and goings along the old railway sidings…" But then he realised his repeat mistake and he held up a plaintive hand to halt the next barrage of abuse. "Look, we carry on. What are you gonna do, Keith, shop yourself along with the two of us? How smart would that look?"

"You shifty bastard, you'll get yours one of these days…"

"Woah, just hang on a minute. Who's a shifty bastard? You're the one who keeps on wanting to change the game plan. You're the one who keeps getting cold feet. I have stuck to our terms to the letter, and it's working a treat. Don't threaten me. You have no idea what sorts of people I'm dealing with and before you say it, you don't wanna know either. Just mind your language and we'll get through this and be much the richer for it in a very short space of time."

Keith sat back in his fixed bench seat and bit his lip in frustration. Morgan took another long draw on his lager and breathed a slow sigh of satisfaction as he again placed the pint glass back on the table and licked his lips.

Keith wondered just how he might extricate himself from his predicament. The lad was right; they had certainly been making some serious money. Hadn't Gilly been delighted with the refurbishment back at the house? He would have to carry on spinning that yarn about how well the business had been doing of late, but if she were to mention that loosely to Austen in an unguarded moment it really might get a little awkward. Unlikely though, he considered. They may do those committee meetings together, but he had the impression that Austen and Gilly were really only friends because of his own lifelong attachment to Austen.

Then he started to throw a new idea around in his head as Morgan prattled on about something unconnected – trail bikes again, was it? Who bloody well cared? No no, he mused, there are more important things in life. What about accidentally on purpose discovering the narcotics lab in the old sheds...you know, just happening upon it on-site with a carefully chosen colleague one wet, miserable morning? He could call in the police, claim complete ignorance – not to mention innocence – and the lads would be dragged off soon enough on the basis of DNA evidence available in those old warehouses. He had no doubt that Morgan would grass him up, but with what tangible proof? Every payment had been made in cash, and most of it had been retained in cash rather than putting it into a bank account, which of course would have been traceable. But then there were mobile phone records, and if pressed by the boys in blue no doubt the builders and decorators would confirm that they had been paid in cash; not insubstantial sums either.

He took another swig of his bitter, and Morgan jumped up, took the two empty glasses and headed round to the bar for refills.

Keith scratched his head and swept his thinning hair back with both hands. What a bloody awful mess. How had he allowed himself to get into such a tight corner? He thought about it for just a moment longer before alighting upon the guilty party. Austen Smiley, his boyhood pal. What a stitch-up that had turned out to be. Come and run my dying business for me while I do much more exciting and rewarding things with my much more valuable time. Bastard! It had been that sod's plan all along, and he must have known that the money would be good but not extravagant, and wasn't that where Morgan's scheme had stepped in, to fill that void? Shit, hadn't it seemed so easy?

As a frustrated and bone-idle young chemist, Morgan, who had no intentions of working a ten-hour shift at ICI for the rest of his natural, had popped up out of nowhere with a bright idea. All he'd needed had been space and discretion in return for a very nice little supplement to the somewhat mundane personal finances of a disgruntled managing director whose pride had got in the way of business sense. But now look at it...in it up to the neck with all his cards on the table – idiot!

Maybe Morgan was right. Perhaps there really was no more sensible option other than to let the lad run his course and just hope he'd stick to his stated plan. Another two years of ridiculous risk-taking during which time he would continue to put everything he owned, admired, even loved in absolute jeopardy. Anyway, he thought, he couldn't shop those lads. For one, it would be well-nigh impossible to carry off his supposed lack of involvement, and secondly, he just didn't have the guts to do it to them.

Morgan returned with two more pints. Keith signalled his reluctant commitment and the conversation drifted off to other less intimidating topics.

Ten minutes later, just as Morgan was grunting his departure and making to leave, the back door opened and in walked two young men.

"See," said one, "I told you that was Morg's bike out there."

"Hiya, Taffy," ventured the other, "leaving so soon? It's early doors just yet!"

"I know," Morgan responded in jovial fashion, "but I just popped in for a quick one, and to put down a marker with that new barmaid." And then in hushed, conspiratorial tones he added, "I wouldn't mind taking her for a ride...on the bike you understand!" The three of them laughed like the lads they were, as Morgan edged past the newcomers and headed out to the car park. He didn't look back and the two new patrons pushed on into the pub acknowledging Keith with a gentle nod as he sat there finishing his pint. They appeared quite keen to ratify Morgan's assessment of the bar staff.

Keith hoped to God that they hadn't connected him with Morgan. He sensed that not only had that link not been made, but also, and of equal importance, that his own anonymity had not been relinquished. They had no idea who he was.

9

tired and trying

As part of his own settling-in process, Lehrer hadn't considered putting their in-house liaison officers at the top of his list. Important though they undoubtedly were, he had applied a keener focus to his new team, understandably, and to getting to meet some of the leading lights from across the region. However, when PC Michael 'Mitch' Mitchell popped his head round the door to invite his new DCI to a regional planning meeting, Lehrer found himself intrigued by the proposed agenda and its unlikely list of contributors.

Apparently the meeting was due to convene just across the way at the Morley Mill HQ of the Cumbrian Lakes National Park Authority (CLNPA). That in itself was perhaps unremarkable, but when Mitch highlighted that the primary purpose of the meeting was to examine the 'motorbike problem', something chimed in Lehrer's recent memory. Hadn't Janice, his new wife no less, mentioned something about that? Wasn't it something to do with mounting agitation within the Tourism Board spawned by declining tourist numbers in the Lakes? The notion had sounded far-fetched on first pass, but perhaps there was more to this than he'd realised. He knew it was a tad off-piste, but as the new senior in the office he felt he had a degree of latitude. He looped his jacket from the back of his chair and followed Mitch down to the car park.

He knew the Lake District well enough to understand the physical, emotional and financial dynamics at play. Naturally he'd expected Cumbria, despite its unique terrain in England, to exhibit many of the same crime patterns as many other parts of the UK. Local statistics certainly supported his expectations, but when compared with the more challenging profiles of London or the big ports down south,

Lehrer was relieved to find that homicide seemed not to preoccupy Cumbrian folk.

Nevertheless, after two hours of fascinating, intimidating and thoroughly depressing presentations he discovered a sense of awe and trepidation within. This was not the Lake District he knew, or at least remembered fondly. This was a region under threat and under pressure, a region beginning to yield to the persistent and unwelcome scourge of selfishness practised to a destructive degree.

When they got to the open discussion at the end, and he was eagerly asked for his thoughts – their evident anticipation suggesting that he may have brought with him some kind of magic wand through which all their long-suffering anxieties might be purged – he really didn't know where to start. This was a beleaguered mix of caring regional custodians just about at the limit of its patience.

"Look…er, I have so many questions," he faltered, "and, at this stage, not very many answers. Some of this is familiar in the sense that I have been involved in tackling this kind of pestilence in another part of the country, in East Anglia actually. We were quite successful there. But first I have a few burning questions, if I may?"

"Please, Inspector, go ahead," responded Dan Parsons, one of the CLNPA's outdoor rangers and the person chairing the meeting.

"Well to be honest, if it hadn't been for Mitch here," he inclined his head towards the uniformed figure to his right, "I wouldn't have made it to this gathering, and I'm so glad he collared me. I had no idea of the extent of the task before us."

"Ah, but it's encouraging, Inspector, for us to hear you use the collective pronoun. It suggests that we are in this together, a far cry from reality if the past performances of the more senior authorities in the region are anything to go by," offered a silvery-haired elderly chap who sat across one corner of the select-committee-style quadrangle of desks.

"Well…yes, er…that's as may be," blustered Dan Parsons, "but I'm sure our newest recruit," and he beamed at Lehrer with a syrupy smile, "would rather not be burdened with internal politics from day one."

"On the contrary, er…Mr Parsons," Lehrer affirmed after quickly checking the list of attendees on his agenda, "is there a suggestion here that we haven't all been pulling in the same direction at the same time?"

"No, not really, Inspector," Parsons said, as he scanned the faces around him for complicity.

"Yes, Inspector, you could say that," interrupted the same elderly combatant with some determination. "It certainly has appeared to some of us for some time that the three primary forces at work in our team have not been pulling their weight in any particular direction."

"How so?" Lehrer shot back at him.

"Simply put, Inspector, without Mitch here, and one of his female counterparts from your Ulverston station, it would be fair to describe the commitment shown us by Cumberland Police over recent years as lukewarm at best. As for your hierarchy, well...there has been no serious engagement from the very top, and the same could be said of the national park and especially the county council. These bodies seem to be unaware that the entire region is under siege. We are staring at impending catastrophe. Not only is an environmental disaster unfolding before our eyes, but the economic lifeblood that is Lake District tourism is being very effectively turned away on an ever more intimidating and offensive basis. In short, we have lost so many battles that we are very close to losing the war. Our most senior, most influential people would be sat on their hands if it weren't for slapping one another on the back in celebration of a very comfortable lifestyle in one of the nation's hitherto most beautiful and most remote natural landscapes." Dan Parsons coloured an embarrassing puce and slipped slightly lower in his chair as his elderly sparring partner stared him down.

"Eloquently put, Mr...er...sorry, I didn't catch your name, sir," begged the detective.

"Lawner, Patrick Lawner. Please, Inspector, do call me Patrick."

"Thank you, Patrick, I will, and your role in all of this?"

"I represent a small bunch of local scouts; residents out there in some of the remoter parts of the territory. We keep watch and inform the network of movements at ground level. We report such activity to the police action line in Penrith, for what good that has ever done. We place data cameras and recorders out there on the fells to gather the sorts of statistical information you were presented with earlier during the PowerPoint show. We do have a very good understanding of numbers, frequencies and favoured routes associated with bandits on the move.

"We also run a live website which records photos of the damage these dreadful people leave behind. Sometimes we can even load up video footage from cameras or phones in an effort to identify the miscreants in action, but that's often futile since they carry no identifying marks, and they're gone in a flash. We try to encourage ramblers and hikers to assist us in our task, but frankly speaking, I understand their reluctance to either confront large swarms of bikers on the move, or to be caught filming or photographing them. Some of these ruffians can be violent, and out there on the fells is a very lonely place to be when reinforcements are miles away."

"Yes I can imagine, Patrick. I bet some of them don't even carry number plates when they are approaching the off-road stretches," said Lehrer.

"Correct, Inspector. Usually, if they're not local, they'll stash their number plates in a flat backpack once they know they are away from tarmac and wilfully breaking the law. A common strategy is to travel into the area from afar in inconspicuous vans. The vehicles typically carry three or four bikes and riders. They find a favoured quiet spot often well outside the national park, unload the machines and then access the park either on the main roads (with plates on show) or through a carefully plotted series of connecting lanes and tracks. They can cover fifty miles in a day very easily, most of it illegally."

"But surely, if you've got all of this fantastic data on movements, it must be a piece of cake to pinpoint some of these roaming bands, or even the location of their transports, and set the trap?" Lehrer pursued.

"Not quite so simple, Chief," Mitch chipped in. "How do I say this, er...discreetly?"

"Just say it, Mitch."

"Well...it's just that the chief constable has never been too keen on, as he puts it, flooding the fells with bobbies on the beat. He has a point, I suppose. I mean...even when we get a couple of four-wheel drives closing off two ends of the same valley these buggers just scramble up and over the nearest pass to escape into the next dale. It's hopeless. It's also very time-consuming for little return."

"So how many convictions have we had in the last five years?" asked the detective pointedly.

"Ha," came the derisory snort from Sam Bukes of the Forestry Trust.

"Well," pressed Lehrer of his adjacent colleague, "come on, how many?"

"Er...just one, Chief."

Lehrer looked truly crestfallen. "How many bikes have been crushed then?"

"Just the one, Chief."

"Only one in five years?"

"Yes, Inspector," piped up Katy Washbrook from Nature England, "and that's a time period in which the dreaded tribes have multiplied in droves. These thugs flout the restrictions posted out on the land with casual disdain. It's not just visitors either. There are many more locals coming in from the working towns round the edges of Cumbria. They seem to have taken the lead from the farming community. Most farmers use quad bikes as an essential tool of the trade and you can see why. But a lot of the younger lads get the trail bikes out for their recreational pursuit up on the high tops. A lot of working lads in Barrow or Ulverston see that kind of excitement as just as much their right as anyone else's."

"We shouldn't forget the fallout from scrambling events either," Sam Bukes added.

"Meaning what, exactly?" prompted the detective.

"It's about control before and after the event. Most of these races take place on private land through the generosity of landowners who either have an interest in the sport or who just want to help the local lads in the towns. The problem is that getting to and from an event can be a bit of a free-for-all for the youngsters – we have hundreds of bikes just ripping the countryside to shreds."

"Hey, Sam, why should they follow the rules when even seasoned professional TT riders and their ilk are known to come up here regularly for a bit of off-road scrambling? They say there's nothing like a bit of R and R on a muddy Kawasaki when the following week you're hitting speeds of two hundred on the tarmac at Oulton," Katy Washbrook asserted. "When these lads see their own real-life superheroes tearing through forest and glen with impunity, they draw the obvious conclusion – why not me too?"

"And in this age of apparent *entitlement*, Inspector, you can see how the rights and wrongs become so easily blurred," Patrick Lawner threw in.

"Yes, but there's a bigger problem there, as you know, Patrick," Katy Washbrook returned. "Many of the farms, and even some of the wealthier private estates are on land protected not just by the national park, but also by triple SI status, and the penalties for owners offending in this way in those highly sensitive areas are very severe indeed."

"So why so few prosecutions then?" pleaded Lehrer. "Why not set that example, at least in the triple SI spots?"

"To be frank, Inspector," Katy demurred, "Cumberland Police have always baulked at the CPS's stringent demands for case integrity."

"What does that mean? No, sorry…I know what that means, of course, but why? What's been missing?"

"Apparently missing is a consistent thread of misdemeanour! You know, Inspector, the idea that we should be able to track these guys along their entire route through the park such that legal *greenways* can be seen to be linked up only through illegal off-roading between these isolated old tracks."

Lehrer shook his head, confused. "Why don't we just corner them back at the vans if we know their favoured parking hideouts, and surely we can employ police trail bikes to actually chase these people across the countryside?"

"As they do in the Northumbrian National Park you mean, Inspector," asserted a bearded, leather-clad mountain of a man sat next to Patrick Lawner. "I'm Neil Fletcher from the Moto-Corps. We're keen to promote responsible motorbiking. Frankly, we've had enough of the bandit set. They are ruining the image of all bikers with their bloody-minded arrogance. They know what they're doing alright. You only have to grab a coffee at the motorcycle caff in Broughton and listen to some of these bone heads chatting as they fuel up with Red Bull before crashing through the bracken and out into the wilderness. They don't give a damn about livestock, even in lambing season. They don't seem to give a damn about much, truth be told."

"But to an extent you can understand it if they see the locals doing it," Mitch suggested. "And we can't apprehend them at the vans, Chief, because we need to witness them in the act of illegal riding."

"What, even if we've recorded their entire passage through the park and can demonstrate illegal practice by virtue of the route taken?" Lehrer pressed. "It smells a bit like a lack of will on our part, Mitch. We had none of these drawbacks down south."

"Getting back to the local offenders, that's where it comes down to education," sighed Dan Parsons, trying to ease his way back into the debate. "You know how much time and effort we've put into mailers and flyers, stops and drops, classes at local techs and affiliated clubs...you know, a lot of work and money has gone into that. Just look at all the new signage out on the land."

"Aw c'mon, Dan, we've been through this so many times. It's been a waste of time and resources. We've all seen these bastards just ride up to some of those new posts and put a stiff boot right through them. That's why the Geordie coppers took to the trails on their own bikes to run the sods down," the bearded biker insisted.

"Well that was certainly effective for us in East Anglia too," Lehrer stated.

"Yes, but all it achieved up north was a serious degree of long-distance displacement," the big leather jacket emphasised.

"In what way?"

"The Northumbrian outriders became so successful that the bandits started to come here instead."

"No way," said Lehrer, incredulous.

"Oh yes, Inspector," insisted Patrick Lawner. "I wouldn't claim that our tsunami of bandits includes those from Suffolk, that may be just too far away, but we have copious evidence to confirm regular incursions in some numbers from Manchester, Merseyside and North Wales, together with riders from the Yorkshire Dales and the Peak District National Park too. The word has long been out, Inspector: the Lake District is the easiest option. It's a soft touch. There is no fear of any form of serious retribution from the authorities. It's open season. Even our local MPs are at the end of their tethers."

"Okay, Patrick, please...let's not go overboard on this," urged Dan Parsons.

"No! Sorry, Dan, but you're wrong. That's the whole problem. Why not go overboard?" begged Felicity Frobisher from the Lake District Coalition. "We're getting nowhere with this, and it's just that sort of attitude that's responsible for a lack of bite in our attack. When are the big three going to take this seriously? There's even talk about extending the Lakes National Park to join up, across the M6, with the Dales Park in Yorkshire. How on earth can our key local authorities justify that increased expense when they can't even manage what we've got? Christ, it's like the Wild West out there. We need to turn this around."

"Hey, don't slate the county council. We've always got stuck into these difficulties as best we can, but we have a lot of other issues on our agenda. We don't have a bottomless pit," moaned a portly young man in an ill-fitting suit to Lehrer's left.

"'As best we can', please…if that's your best shot then we really are screwed," retorted Frobisher.

Lehrer quickly realised that the conference was in danger of unravelling. Tempers were fraying; anger and animosity lurked just below the surface. He held up his hands in a silent request for calm.

"Look…this is surprisingly helpful to me. Obviously Mitch and I can flesh out a lot of these issues in our own debrief, but although you may not be able to tell, I am very, very keen to respond positively to your situation in very practical terms and most certainly at ground level.

"The cry for more resources is a common one in public services and charitable organisations alike. You don't need me to tell you that nearly all of you fall into those categories, excepting of course our network of local residents like Patrick. There will also be private firms and businesses who are suffering this onslaught in different ways and I will get to them in time."

"Inspector Lehrer," came a voice from directly opposite, on the far side of the quad of tables, "I'm Nation Trust, based over at Sizergh. Oliver Stanton by the way," he added with a slight inflection in Lehrer's direction. "Would I be right in thinking that your new appointment here in Cumbria has also brought your lovely wife among us at one and the same time?"

The well-worn copper was taken aback momentarily, and then he smiled and nodded back in acknowledgement. "Yes, Mr Stanton, you are right indeed and particularly well informed, if I may say so. Dare I ask the source of your intelligence?"

"You may not, Inspector," joshed Oliver Stanton with an amused reaction plastered across his face. "An ex-journalist would never reveal his sources, but you may rest assured that she is most welcome back here in our neck of the woods. Please do pass on my sincere and warm regards, and do tell her that I will call in on her in Windermere on my next drive up there."

"Ah, so you really are informed," stammered Lehrer in surprise.

"Always, Inspector, always, and I congratulate you on your impeccable taste. I raise that good woman's profile only to point out that her new employers will be one of your best routes into that great spread of privately run businesses that are indeed feeling the pinch of falling visitor numbers. It's not just hoteliers and the B&B brigade, but farm shops, local supermarkets and post offices, outdoor equipment retailers, cycle hire, delivery firms, holiday cottages, estate agencies…you name it – everyone is feeling the squeeze. If we don't kill off this disease in the next year or so I fear the Lake District will be lost forever in a sea of mud littered with hordes of aggressive foul-mouthed thugs too ignorant to parley with. The Tourism Board has woken up to the scale of the threat, or at least I hope it has. They are not represented here today unfortunately, but if Janice is still the powerhouse I remember from her time in Coniston some years ago, then they'll get the message very soon. The private sector will be well represented there and of course via the Chambers of Commerce in Carlisle, but I have yet to see them get a grip of this debilitating reality."

"Thank you, Mr Stanton, but I can't help but ask, how do you know Janice?"

The rest of the group were completely high-jacked by such an intriguing diversion. Tensions relented momentarily.

"Ah well, I knew her late husband Jeff many, many years ago and subsequently met her through him during their many visits to Coniston village."

"Really. Well…I wonder what the odds were on the two of us making this connection here today?"

"Extremely slim, Inspector, but I look forward to seeing the two of you together for a drink or even dinner perhaps, but let us stick to the current narrative shall we? I was very keen to hear more about your successful methods for combating bandits in East Anglia. Do please give us the salient points and maybe we can adopt some of them forthwith."

Beside him Lehrer heard Mitch's phone buzz insistently on his belt clip. The younger policeman pushed his chair back and hurried out into the corridor to take the call.

The group fell into a babbling exchange before the chair brought them back to focus.

Dan Parsons ventured a sobering thought. "Inspector, you are obviously familiar with the Lakeland terrain here and the Broads down there. Do you think there is a chance that in the eyes of many riders, the elevated physical challenges of the mountains simply represent a challenge that just can't be denied?"

"You know, Dan, you might just have something there. I don't think it means—" And just then the door flew open and a rather flustered Mitch beckoned to his superior to join him in the corridor.

"Excuse me for a moment, won't you?" the detective offered, already on the move towards the door.

10

a minor inconvenience?

"Earlier today a body was recovered from an area in the southern fells. The deceased has been identified as a young local farmer who had been missing for several days. He was found in a remote spot, a favourite of his for his trail biking pursuits according to his father."

Lehrer paused and took a steadying deep breath.

"He'd been shot in the head from range – a single shot from a high-velocity weapon – and with considerable accuracy." Gasps and a rumble of serious disquiet rippled through the attentive audience. "The perpetrator shot him through the visor of his crash helmet, leaving him where he fell in his full motorbiking leathers. A Kawasaki trail bike was also recovered from the scene. The victim and the bike are undergoing forensic examination, as is a cordoned-off area at the crime scene.

"Clearly this is an extraordinary event, for which, of course, there will be an explanation, however extreme. But be in no doubt, this is murder in the coldest, most calculated and most clinical fashion imaginable. As in any homicide investigation, and as you would rightfully expect, we will leave no stone unturned. If we are to apprehend the guilty party, an assassin by any measure, we will have to be meticulous and thorough, but of course we will need help from you, the media, and from local people if we are to make progress quickly. I would like to ask any member of the public who believes they might assist us with even the smallest scrap of information pertinent to this crime to come forward as soon as possible."

The DCI then handed over to a uniformed officer who led the eager assembly through the suggested timeframe and relevant location appertaining to the crime. Then he handed back to the senior man.

"Cumberland Police is aware of elevated tensions within the local community here in Cumbria caused by a growing rift which exists between some motorbiking groups and many other sections of local society. As part of this urgent investigation we will be convening with representatives of many different parts of the community in order to better understand these frictions and, hopefully, to track down the killer. In the meantime we would ask everyone to be cautious and vigilant, and to report anything suspicious or unusual to the police.

"Thank you. There will be no questions at this time."

Lehrer's statement to the media was greeted with a barrage of shouted questions and critical comments from a bevy of largely scruffy regional journalists. He remained steadfast and left the press room quickly. He hoped to get a second bite at the cherry in a week or so, but then hopefully in front of the national media and a bigger audience altogether. He headed straight to the operations room.

He sat gingerly on the edge of the table and looked at a room full of faces. The team had gathered; uniformed staff and plain clothes, technical and administrative. They already knew the basics and they'd already grasped the difficulty and complexity of the factors swirling around in the mix of challenges before them. They knew, of course, that the motorbiking plague had rumbled on for years. Some of them wondered what all the fuss was about. Others had seen its withering effects on some elements of local life. None of them had expected a spike of such magnitude in the tensions they all recognised out in the sticks. Murder, and through such effective means, was an escalation no one had predicted, but they knew instinctively that it changed everything.

Detective Inspector Iain Young took the team through a rapid status check – largely for DCI Lehrer's benefit. The boss nodded his approval. They were as prepared as they could be, and initial enquiries were already underway.

A voice from the back of the room cut through the rising debate. "Sir, do you really think that this shooting is directly linked to our motorbike problem? I mean…is it conceivable that this is a reaction, an extreme one obviously, but a direct result of the poor lad being on a trail bike?"

Lehrer cleared his throat in a slightly nervous tone.

"For nearly three hours this morning Mitch and I discussed and examined the shocking deterioration in the condition of the once glorious Lake District landscape with a collection of action groups over at the National Park offices at Morley Mill," and he flicked a nod in the direction of that external venue close by. "The extensive damage to our landscape at the hands, or should I say wheels of a growing band of marauding louts appears irrefutable. These yobs clearly retain little or no respect for the region, its geography and its essential economy. If I, as a newcomer of sorts, had been in any doubt as to the visceral passions created and released by this...well, er...how should I put it...*unnatural disaster,* then I suspect I need doubt no longer. This is a disaster of epic proportions and one which must surely detrimentally affect lots of people across the region."

"Yes, DCI, but affect them enough for some bloke to get a rifle out from his strong box and actually shoot someone?"

"In answer to your question...yes, it's possible. It may seem barbaric to us, but with incomes, jobs and livelihoods at risk, there must be many affronted parties who take this persistent assault on much that they hold dear to their hearts very seriously indeed. Who knows what real rage will drive some people to do?"

Mitch pointed out to the team that Lehrer had endured something of a similar scourge in East Anglia, before his transfer north to the mountains. For the benefit of the group, he asked the DCI to outline his experiences there.

"The petrol-head curse looked just the same to us ten years ago as it does to you here, today. First and foremost, the good news is that East Anglia has expunged the problem. Secondly, let me say that it took us about five years in practice, but we had to build our organisational infrastructure from scratch. From this morning's meeting, I can already see that much of that is in place through the buy-in of so many concerned parties and stake holders.

"I'd like a better understanding of where the overall farming and estate-owning communities sit on this issue.

"Our strategy down south comprised two main thrusts running in tandem, side by side: we needed to take the law and the letter of the law more seriously, and we needed to divert our lawbreakers away from the national parks in favour of special facilities specifically built for the biking fraternity. There is a role for education in all of this. The educational process is costly and time-consuming, but without it you can't change the way these lads look at their sport. Equally, education without a shift of outlet is akin to herding them all into a very large cul-de-sac with nowhere to go. They'll just get angry.

"East Anglia doesn't have one big protected space as we do here within the national park. There are lots of smaller equivalents: reed beds, extensive foresting, broads, lakes, bird sanctuaries, coastal marshland… all sorts. The bikers used to infiltrate all of these reserves at different times. It looked like a really good day out to cross from one to another to create an entire racing chain at high speed out in the wild. We didn't have the mountains to contend with and I can readily appreciate the logistical difficulties involved in trying to apprehend bandits up here. You should also bear in mind that the climate there is much drier. High-speed pursuit is easier in dust than in mud, and yes, we did use our own riders just like Northumbria Police. In the last couple of years we even adopted these new drones to locate, follow and ultimately to coordinate the apprehension of the culprits."

Mitch Mitchell interrupted the flow to point out that drones had been mentioned at the Morley Mill meeting earlier in the day. Lehrer took the initiative back when he realised that Mitch was stepping into potentially delicate internal politics.

"Yes, Mitch, that chap Patrick Lawner was quite a revelation in himself." Turning to the wider assembly he continued, "He's a good example of a hardy bunch of committed campaigners who try to combat the mechanised hordes out there in the wilds of beyond, and often at great risk to themselves. Frankly, I think we owe them better support." Some in the team shuffled uncomfortably. "They track and record bike traffic movements, collate and transmit data to our operational centre in Penrith…you can imagine the sort of thing. He claimed to have already made representations to the chief constable on the use of drones. Apparently he made that approach through very supportive local MPs, but they were told that the force here in Cumbria would never be granted the appropriate licences for such emotive, high-tech machinery. Obviously military-style drones come with a certain reputation attached. They are still innovative and do not yet carry a service record of proven reliability. However, he also rather cheekily pointed out that they are cheap to purchase when compared with the recruitment of many more policemen or park rangers and they are easy to operate," a suggestion that was greeted in the room with raised eyebrows and the odd cynical smile.

"That's right, Chief," Mitch added. "He also reckons that in ten years' time you'll be able to trundle down to PC World or Jessops and just buy one for a few quid, but in any event, you've just told us that the Norfolk and Suffolk forces have been using these things for what, two or three years?"

"Correct! We'll work on that idea once I've been able to get the chief super and chief constable in closer alignment," Lehrer proposed with apparent confidence. "But right now we can work with the law as it stands."

His audience waited for the significance of that to drop. He carried on.

"With East Anglia in mind, I can assure you that the law in England and Wales is just the same there as it is here. We don't need any new powers or new legislation. We have more than enough to work with and we will have to up our game, not just in terms of applying existing laws, but also to making prosecutions stick. Down there we sequestered and trashed hundreds of trail bikes over several years. It didn't take long. The message got out very quickly – that we were serious – and it worked. At the same time the local authorities chipped in and built an extensive range of specially designed outdoor scrambling tracks in old reclaimed gravel pits and on waste industrial ground. Nowadays you can see small bands of riders out at the weekends in Suffolk. They race down the main roads and back roads and suddenly disappear through a gap in a hedge into a couple of acres of banks and berms, humps and hollows, where they zip around for ten or fifteen minutes before rejoining the road and moving on to the next pit. It works a treat, and we had great feedback from many different participants. Above all, it rescued our protected spaces from the blight you've been suffering up here for far, far too long."

"Chief, if I may?" came a call from the back of the room.

"Yes, go ahead, please."

"You're talking about the bovver boys on bikes as if they are the only problem, but in fact, one of them has just been murdered. There is clearly another side to this."

"Yes, absolutely, and in the context of murder, we could be forgiven for wishing it was the other way around. At least then we'd have a ready group of suspects to tackle. This way around that target list is almost infinite – it could be just about anyone from a vast range of potentially vengeful, hateful corners of a very diverse population. Where to start? That's the real issue."

11

not the best of starts

By the end of the week their investigation had ground to a disheartening halt. Lehrer could have done without such a challenging case to kick-start his tenure in Kendal. His immediate team quickly sensed his growing frustration as each and every line of enquiry rapidly dissipated without reward. The atmosphere in his office, as they gathered for another end-of-day review, was decidedly subdued.

"Right," he said, by way of concentrating their collective thoughts, "we've got nothing from ballistics other than a basic confirmation of bullet type and composition. Whatever he used was pretty unremarkable. We could pick up a box of the things at any rifle club in the country. We have no slug, and I guess that's hardly surprising since we have no accurate fix on the trajectory, line of sight, anticipated range...nothing! It's a bloody great big space out there and we're not going to get lucky on that score."

"And anyway, guv," added DI Young, "even if they found it, chances are it'll tell us nothing without matching it up to the weapon...and we don't have that either."

"Nothing at the boy's farm?" prodded Lehrer.

"Naw, guv," Young responded in his gentle Scottish Borderer brogue. "It was always going to be a long-shot, but..."

"Subtle. Nice try," interrupted DS Caroline Sutton with a wicked grin.

"Aw, do you ever let up?" Young retorted. "Look, we didn't expect to be that fortunate. The chances of the murder weapon actually belonging to the deceased, or at least to someone at his own farm, were always going to be slim, and in this case there seems to be no reason for us to suspect family involvement of any kind. To have found a rifle there would have been so unexpected as to have been blindingly suspicious from the off."

"Yeah, you're right," countered Sutton, "but it would have been at least something, anything...to work with I mean."

"Well that's for sure," Lehrer sighed, "but as it is we have virtually nothing. In fact, besides digging deeper into the lad's apparently combative escapades on the fells in days gone by, do we have any other leads? Caroline? Iain?"

Both detectives looked rueful, but Young reverted to the dead man's reported reputation for having been an aggressive protagonist whenever confronted by angry fell walkers who took exception to his blatantly illegal riding out in the wilds. "We had hoped to be able to build some sort of picture or timeline of his more hawkish encounters with backpackers over the years. He seems to have revelled in the strife of the face-to-face showdown from quite an early age, as bikers go. Certainly by his mid-teens many of his mates saw him as some sort of leader of the pack whenever their rites of passage were contested. There appear to have been many minor incidents over several years, but also a number of more serious clashes which we hoped would help us with our profile construction."

"And they haven't?" asked Lehrer, with a plaintive frown.

"'Fraid not, Chief," Young responded. "You see, he began to lose friends as these incidents multiplied. We're talking about teenage lads who just wanted a bit of a race out on the tops every now and again without getting noticed too easily and too often. They knew all along that their motorised hobby was perfectly illegal, but with a friend like our victim, who had his father's own acreage to enjoy, well...what could have been better? As they got older, bigger and bolder, nipping out onto common land or into the national park became not just enticing, but also more dangerous."

"Yeah I get it," chipped in DS Sutton. "The park was more exciting, but they knew they were placing themselves at greater risk of being stopped."

"That's it," DI Young confirmed, "and finding yourself at odds with the backpackers on too many occasions was too much for some of these young guys. Remember," he cautioned, "by now they're in their twenties and hopefully in full-time work. We may have a pretty poor record of arrests and convictions, but the lads would still have been anxious not to push the boundaries too far. Those who have driving jobs, either as commuters or perhaps van or truck drivers, have a real reliance on their driving licences. They'd have known since their late teens that getting done for illegal off-road riding could extract not just a meaty fine, but also whack three points on their driving licences. If they were stopped without number plates, a common tactic adopted to avoid identification at speed, they'd immediately be at risk of another three points on their licences. If they have two bad weekends in a row when our uniformed chaps managed to collar them twice, well...Bob's your uncle...driving licence completely compromised and no job to go to on Monday morning."

"So don't tell me," said Lehrer, "those you've been able to identify from way back are very thin on the ground and none of them want to talk to us because it would be potentially incriminating for misdemeanours long overlooked."

"Correct!" offered Young, bluntly.

"Is anyone talking?"

"No, guv."

"But what about the lad's parents? They must know something, at least from his earlier scrapes."

"Not really. It's plausible that they wouldn't have accompanied him on his many outings. As he grew up and took on more and more responsibility for the farm, he naturally became more and more independent and less accountable."

"But they must know a clutch of his closest mates, surely," insisted the senior man.

"Oh yes, that much we have," Young acknowledged, "but they're saying precious little. We should bear in mind that he was riding alone on that fateful day, and as for previous incidents, the only one we've been able to progress has led us to a hospital bed in Lancaster."

"The cancer patient," Lehrer affirmed with a wry shake of the head.

"There's nothing there for us in my view," insisted Caroline Sutton. "It's the only incident any of those lads would talk about, and it does seem to have been a nasty fracas to say the least."

"But we have that on file – court case, the lot – so they can hardly not talk about it."

"That's true, Chief, yes, and it goes back a few years too, but essentially that guy's wife was driven into by our victim in a fairly reckless charge on his bike. It broke several bones in her leg and her recovery developed all manner of complications, which probably led to her death. That was almost two years later after a terrible time in and out of hospital. It's the only recorded incident in our files. The boy was a juvenile at the time and he was given a severe caution, but those lads covered for him pretty well on the day."

"Clear motive though," Lehrer asserted.

"Sure, Chief, but unless our pathology people have got time of death wrong by some margin, two or three days perhaps, then our man was already piped up in Lancaster General long before the lad was killed. Even then, and having met him only two days ago, I am absolutely rock-solid certain that he would have been in no fit state to even get out there on the fells never mind to do the deed itself. We've gone through his place with a fine-toothed comb...nothing. We have no record of gun ownership, no trace of anything like that, no indication of any connection between the deceased and the dying since the altercation with his poor wife all those years ago. Forgive the horrible pun, but it's a dead end."

Iain Young raised his eyebrows in mock salute.

"And he is dying then...the chap in hospital?" probed Lehrer.

"Yes, I'm sorry to say. The doctors give him no more than three weeks," Sutton confirmed.

"How did he react when you spoke to him?"

"He was a bit groggy with all the medication running through his veins, but there was no disguising his delight at the outcome out on the fells recently. His only regret, or so he said, was that he hadn't had the courage to do the job himself years ago. I challenged him of course, but he didn't back down."

"And what about that pathology report? Could they have been so wrong?"

"Doubtful, Chief," Young suggested, "but our victim had been missing for some time, several days, and achieving accuracy is difficult because his folks were away from the farm for several days over the preceding weekend, so they really don't know how long he had been off campus, if you get my drift."

"But hang on, guys," DS Sutton said, arresting that train of suspicion, "there is no way on earth our man in Lancaster could have been out there. I think our chaps have it about right and he had already been carted off by ambulance at least two days before, perhaps more."

"No family possibilities?" Lehrer tested.

"None, Chief," she confirmed.

"So we really have nothing to work with?"

"Ah, well…it's not quite the end of the trail, Chief, but we are moving into a vast area of research which is going to require a lot of bodies. Actually, and to be precise, we need lots of fingers and good attentive eyesight."

"You mean screen work?"

"Yup…hours and hours of it would be my best guess, Chief."

"Go on," urged Lehrer.

"How familiar are you with social media, Chief," prompted Sutton with a cheeky smile which barely camouflaged her suspicions about the older man's avoidance of such outwardly frivolous means. To her surprise he countered in the affirmative.

"You're referring to this dreadful online warfare that's been rumbling on for years over this entire off-roading question, aren't you?"

"I am, Chief, yes," she said, unable to mask her curiosity.

"Don't look so shocked," he retorted with a casual grin, "I'm not drawing my pension yet and I do know how to turn on my computer. Allow me to remind you that I had the joys of a three-hour session at the National Park Head Office just over the road there with Mitch Mitchell at the start of the week. I am fully aware of the antipathy with which the green countryside lobby and the petrol-heads each hold their enemy. I have already reviewed some shocking exchanges on those new social media sites…you know…er, what are they called…Twitter and Facebook is it? Well, there's some rum stuff knocking around on there I can tell you, but it does give us some new outlets to pursue."

"There are also some very interesting websites to latch onto as well," DI Young added. "We've been out to see a canny old stick just above Greenodd. He's been running an anti-trail bike campaign for nearly ten years. He might be able to pick up on more of these hillside confrontations through his backdated records, and feedback of that sort would be incredibly helpful."

"Would that be Patrick Lawner, by chance?" enquired Lehrer.

"Yes it would. You met him at that meeting I gather."

"Yes…we spoke about him at our planning meeting too, but you were already chasing leads at the time. He's an interesting chap; quite direct, great knowledge of the background to all of this I'd wager. Not a murderer I'd say," Lehrer proposed.

"No, guv," said Young, "and a reliable alibi anyway," he noted.

"Well look," the senior man ventured as he tried to round up, "it's worth saying that these new social media sites are still new enough not to have too many players. If you were to ask me, I'd say they'll never last, but I might be wrong. However, they may prove something of a breakthrough for us if we can follow some of this antagonistic on-screen rhetoric through to some potentially conclusive personal IDs. Somebody out there has just upped the stakes considerably, but his frustrations may be evident in some of his social chatter. Let's see what we can find out, and I'll try to rustle up some extra pairs of hands for the necessary trawling exercise."

"Just one other thing, guv," insisted Young. "Patrick Lawner asserted with some confidence that *we* have been hiding the specific details of previous arrests, attempted prosecutions and so on. He maintains that when Mitch and his cohort come along to those quarterly meetings, it has appeared very obvious, his words not mine, that our uniformed colleagues have been muzzled when it comes to updating certain aspects of successful actions at ground level."

"But there is often a need for discretion in terms of the legal process. He must understand that."

"Of course, yes, he does, but he quotes several examples of failure to prosecute because of the interventions of specific high-ranking individuals," Young explained, adopting a rather vacant and questioning look.

"You've been on this beat for long enough, Iain, what would you say?"

"Allow me to dodge that missile if I may, sir, by repeating one of Patrick Lawner's accusations that the chief constable has intervened personally on more than one occasion, as has one of our local MPs. Lawner's best guess is that corporate muscle has been flexed in order to protect certain commercial interests."

"What? This is the Lake District for God's sake, not Westminster or the City of London. What can he possibly mean?"

"He proposed two potential scenarios: that the big chief chipped in to protect a personal friend who may just have been another senior ranker from another force enjoying a spin out in the wilderness, and also that a professional bike rider was once nabbed while having some fun time off. His main sponsor, a well-known Japanese bike manufacturer, was about to take on some very nasty negative headlines about deliberate environmental abuse. In that case both the big chief and said local MP worked very hard together to keep the arrest out of the courts. When you look at the global websites of these very big hitters they really do push the environmentally friendly message on a massive scale. To find one of their own superstars ripping up one of the oldest national parks in England, well…you can imagine the risk of reputational damage."

"I'm speechless! How the hell am I going to approach the big chief, as you so affectionately call him, to ask him about possible back-handers from global engineering firms with instantly recognisable household names and familiar logos? Having met Patrick Lawner, I have every respect for his opinion. Clearly we have hurdles to breach and battles to fight at many different levels, and we're going to have to be very careful."

12

a case in point

The girls slopped and splashed their way through the trickling flow that threatened to submerge the rugged pathway completely. Lucy turned her wrist inward and glanced at her waterproof chronometer. They were just about bang-on time. They would have to drop back down to Rowan Tree Farm, running right past their own front door, and then slog onward round the edge of the settlement, heading back to their van parked up by the Coniston Water shoreline. Another fifteen minutes or so would complete the trial circuit.

She looked up ahead and saw her partner Helen pushing on into the drizzle, negotiating a couple of larger rocks in her path and then bending into the murky greyness as she tackled a slight incline. Lucy could see the other girl's determination in her posture; that robust, competitive tenacity that infused everything she did. Lucy so admired that in her partner, and she gave a little start of anxiety that she might fall behind and disappoint the girl up ahead.

For her part, Helen had no such qualms. That same respect and admiration was mutual. She didn't need to look round to know that Lucy's slender elegant frame belied a fearsome commitment. She knew she'd be not ten metres behind, and sometimes she picked up the odd splash of a footfall for reassurance. They had trained together, and lived together, for three years now and she was never disappointed with her co-competitor, the true love of her life.

Their competition standings had been steadily improving and they really were beginning to look beyond the British National Championships in London the following year towards the Europeans, Worlds and hopefully then the Olympics. For now however, it was the

Scottish National Championships, which demanded an acute level of concentration. The competition was only two weeks away and the professional triathlon duo knew only too well that their swim training in Coniston Water suited the anticipated aquatic section in Loch Lomond just perfectly. The subsequent cycling element would take place on quite narrow roads very similar to those in the Lakes, and then the road-run over ten kilometres would bring them home. A cross-country out on the fells was hardly the same, but they had decided to tough it out for several good reasons: softer ground was more relenting than tarmac or concrete and they wanted to avoid any repetitive impact injuries so soon before the event, and road running was simply tedious when compared to getting out into the natural greenery of the countryside.

They forced the pace as the final kilometres began to pass them by. The drizzle turned to rain, but they told themselves that they were nearly done; almost back to the van, then the short drive home and a shared hot bath – none of that 'wheelie bin full of ice' nonsense!

Then they heard it: the unmistakable, garbled whine of a scrambler approaching fast from the lower levels, out of sight but not for long. Lucy looked up and saw Helen stop dead in the track. She surreptitiously reached for her chrono – right hand across to left – and paused the time capture, and then she raised both hands and planted them firmly on her hips, blocking the narrow track completely. Lucy raced up behind her just as the bike came into view and slithered to a hasty halt a few feet before her friend.

"Bloody hell, Ben, it's you!" Helen shouted into the driving rain. Lucy had made the same connection in the same moment. It was the crash hat with the daft sheep motif on the left side. They couldn't really see the boy's face until he flipped his visor up.

"What's up?" he shouted back in mock innocence.

"What do you mean, what's up? What do you think?"

"Oh bugger off – you're not still on that environmental high-horse of yours are you?"

"We're always on that environmental high-horse, as you call it. It's not some sort of temporary affliction you get tablets for at the doctor's you know. It's important. We care about this countryside and so should you. Christ, how many times have we had this conversation? You're a bloody farmer as well – you should know better."

"Like I keep saying – not that you ever listen – I'm up here all the time on the quad bike with the flock, so what difference does a few trips out on this monster make?" and he tapped the fuel tank of the bike with some affection.

"That's just it," Helen shot back in exasperation, "it's a sodding monster alright. Have you seen the mud bath up there at the crossover of the two tracks, just below the tree line? You people are destroying this land. What the hell is the matter with you lot?"

"Oh get over yourself, Helen. How much damage do you think you lot do with your mountain bikes, and let's not forget thousands of boot prints every year on the same worn-out paths. It's just the way it is. You can't have all the fun to yourselves. I've said that to you before. Now move aside and let me through," Ben demanded, and he revved the throttle for extra emphasis. But Helen shouted back at him through the din.

"You fucking farmers – guardians of the countryside, my arse – you're plugging every tax break and development grant going, and the best you can do is ruin this landscape for your own selfish pleasures," she yelled.

"Let's not get into selfish pleasures, not with you two," he smirked. "Like I said, you're quite happy to take a pot shot at us bikers, but the mountain bikers, fell walkers, runners like you," he added, giving them both the once-over, "even horses get out here, but all that's just fine."

"Come off it," Helen screamed, getting really agitated. "None of those types create even a fraction of the damage those bloody machines can produce," and she nodded at the motorbike. "Horses, bloody horses?" she shouted. "You've got about fifty of them under your scrawny arse gouging the hell out of the ground everywhere you go. When are you gonna show some respect, or do you need a grant for that too?"

"Oh give it a rest. C'mon, move over," Ben motioned with the flick of his head.

"As for pot shots," Helen continued, "you've surely seen the *Gazette*, you know...that young farmer who got himself shot dead just over yonder doing exactly what you're doing now?"

"What are you saying? Are you threatening me, you daft mare?"

Helen looked genuinely confused for an instant, but then replied, "No, don't be so thick. I'm suggesting that there is somebody out there who feels a lot more strongly than me about these issues, and who knows where he is and when he might strike next?"

"Oh please...look, I can look after myself and you should have better things to think about. Now just stand aside," and with that he throttled up and tore off past his persecutor, rushing into the first big puddle on the path and pluming a huge cascade to either side as he powered onward.

Helen screamed some following obscenity in his direction, but the curse was lost in the deluge. Lucy put her arms around her lover and just held her as they stood there dripping and wretched. "Come on," she said. "We're putting in a good time here. Let's trip the timers back on and get down to the lake shore. We've got about ten more minutes. Put him out of your mind. It'll be a good test of concentration."

"You're right, Luce," she agreed with a desperate shake of the head, "let's move it. But I tell you this, I am going to formally report that arrogant little shit at the first opportunity."

"Language, my girl, language," Lucy ridiculed.

They synchronised chronos, and then legged it down the hill.

13

so many distractions

It was a bizarre idea, but it sounded like a reasonable excuse for a city trip so she agreed to travel up to Edinburgh by train with Austen. Their Church Renovations Committee had agreed locally in Keswick to contribute a substantial sum to the roof refurbishment project of St Luke's Presbyterian Church. She considered that there couldn't be too many such establishments in England, it being an organisation of Scottish origins. However, having signalled such generous intentions, Austen found himself summoned to the Church of Scotland at Charis House and he thought it a possible business opportunity of wider proportions. He always said that he would never turn down a meeting with any cash-rich institution, and they didn't come much wealthier than the Church.

The journey proved tolerable – first class of course, no scrimping by Austen – and he'd secured two rooms for them at the Balmoral on Princes Street, so she knew she'd get a bit of shopping time in the next morning, and hopefully a very enjoyable dinner at one of the city's many highly rated restaurants. She liked her wine, and she knew Austen would make a fuss of the wine list before choosing something exquisite, and expensive. As the train slipped through the stunning Border region she contented herself that the excursion was certainly a step up from another evening at home with Keith's interminable sister Henrietta moping about the place.

The afternoon meeting did seem to produce a number of interesting possibilities for Austen's conniving mind, but overall Gilly came away with the impression that the church elders seemed more interested in his financial attributes than he was in theirs. Perhaps she'd misread proceedings.

They dined in style just off the Royal Mile, and probably consumed just a cocktail too many before the wine, but arm-in-arm for mutual support they later teetered down the road across North Bridge and back to the hotel.

He took her quite by surprise when he saw her back to her room, and then pushed through the door with her and threw the lock decisively. He started to undress her there and then, smothering her with misguided kisses. She could see that he was more than a little eager to expose her breasts, muttering something about how magnificent they were as he released her bra and watched them escape with boyish wonder etched into his gleeful features. Soon they stood together naked, and not for the first time, but she really wasn't sure what was supposed to happen next, or even whether or not she could be bothered. With not much happening downstairs she dragged him into the bathroom and into the fabulous walk-in shower where they enjoyed the cleansing torrent while groping each other in anticipation of something more physically demanding. Before she knew what was happening she cradled his head in her hands as he kneeled before her, his intrusive searching tongue finding her most sensitive inner warmth, and she let the waves pass through her as the cascade descended upon them from above. She threw her head back and let the hot shower blast into her face and over her breasts, and all she could think of was whether Keith would be playing his old vinyl records at home in her absence, or whether his sister Henri would be in another one of her moods requiring sympathetic attention.

When she woke the next morning Gilly had to think, just for a moment, about her precise location. The hotel room was fairly self-evident. A distant and distorted view (through the double-glazed window) of Edinburgh Castle reminded her of the previous night's frivolities. She rolled over quickly expecting to see Austen lying there, but she was alone and she realised that one half of the bed was damp. Then she remembered dragging him back from the shower, still dripping, throwing him directly onto the bed and straddling his impressive erection. She remembered that it had all ended rather abruptly and she'd bailed out by simply throwing herself toward the pillow on the far side of the bed. Her last thought had been to wonder how Ben would have performed.

She sat up in bed, looked at the bedside alarm clock, and realised she could manage a couple of hours of shopping before their departure from Waverley around lunchtime. She decided to order a light breakfast with coffee in her room, and then she padded round to the shower to begin the process of renewal.

Keith Salcombe sat in his office above the quarry. He was finding it difficult to concentrate. He'd sent word down to the cutting shed that he needed to speak to Morgan on a technical matter, but that was already half an hour ago. He sat there drumming his fingers on the desk and fiddling with his mouse as he skipped from one email to the next.

Then a rap on the door and Morgan sloped in looking filthy from the slurry he'd been wiping down the front of his overalls all morning.

"Wotcha, boss. What d'you need?" he asked.

"Sod it, Morgan, don't play games with me, mate," he hissed in evident agitation. "Shut the door," he ordered, and nodded at the gaping portal as if to emphasise the immediacy of his command.

"Not again, man. What the hell is up now for Chrissakes?" Morgan implored, as he turned back from closing the door.

"You kidding? A young bloke on a trail bike gets himself shot dead in the middle of nowhere, but just down the road from us, and all you can ask is what's up? It's all over the press and it even made the national news the other day. Isn't that just getting a little too close for comfort? Shouldn't we be calling it a day and wrapping it all up?"

"Oh shit, h'yur we go again," Morgan sighed in his dulcet Welsh twang. "How many times do I have to say this? We're in the clear. This has nothing to do with us. There are hundreds – probably thousands – of bikers like me and Stevie out there on the fells all through the year come rain or shine. This is just one completely unconnected incident."

"You mean...well, I mean...you guys don't know this poor lad?"

"No. Should we?"

"I don't fucking well know do I, but you must all rub shoulders together at some stage, don't you?"

"No. He was just some farmer's son who had apparently roughed up too many fell walkers and mountain bikers by the sounds of it. Somebody was pushed over the edge. Maybe he had it coming."

"Had it coming? He's dead, man. It's not some sort of computer game. He was shot from range and it looks like a very professional job if you care to read between the lines. Who's to say the killer didn't think he was one of you two?"

"Jesus! Look, I'm going back to work if that's okay, boss? There is absolutely nothing to worry about."

With that he turned away, resolutely pulled the door open, and headed for the stairs. Keith chewed the cuticle of his right thumb as he listened to the younger man clatter down the metal stairs outside.

14

media hype?

"There's a lot of stuff on here that just doesn't match up or fit together, Chief," claimed DS Sutton as she scrolled through pages of various websites and flicked quickly back and forth from one to the other. "Here, just pull up a chair and I'll show you what I mean."

Lehrer grabbed the nearest plastic-backed, standard-issue police station chair and lifted it into place alongside his colleague.

"You see, Chief, I've been playing around all morning with websites that I hope are relevant to our investigation. I'm on the Cumbrian Lakes National Park site and also the Cumbria County Council site. I've also been sifting through some assorted downloads from the team out there," and she nodded towards the open office next door, "from the National Park's Facebook pages and, most informative of all, from an entire raft of personal or organisational Twitter accounts. Some of that stuff is alarming, at the personal level you understand. I'll come back to that in a minute, but as an overview I think it shows us the true state of relationships at ground level in the countryside. The situation could hardly be described as pleasant or attractive.

"What's just as revealing to me, however, is the apparent lack of recognition of any problem, anything at all, from the two main managers of the region. Neither the national park nor the county council make any significant reference to the plague of motorised locusts that is destroying their greatest asset in very short order. It's all green and sunny uplands, fresh air and independence, boating, cycling, hiking and even horse-riding. You have to look very closely to spot the tiniest link, here, er…let me find it for you…there you go…this is the national park's entire engagement with the thorny problem of off-road four-wheel driving and trail biking.

"As you can see, it's just a scrappy note and a list of attached maps. If I click on a couple of those you'll quickly see the gist of the logistical problem at ground level."

She clicked through another page and then magnified an ordnance survey map upon which he could see some random coloured lines scattered very loosely across the area displayed.

Leaning closer he asked, "Are those the *green ways* we've been hearing about?"

"Yes they are."

"But there are so few of them, and they're so far apart," he stated, with a startled expression.

"Exactly, that's problem *numero uno* if you're a trail biker looking for a day's riding in open country! You can hardly go anywhere legally, and most of these ancient green ways or green lanes, as they sometimes call them, are nowhere near any regular tarmac roads."

"So even to reach one of these isolated stretches of old thoroughfare, you have to break the law?"

"Yes, Chief, these guys just can't avoid it if they want to enjoy a wild day out."

"So you're suggesting that all the key authorities, including ourselves, are playing down the whole issue of countryside vandalism, habitat destruction and all the rest of it because we simply cannot claim ignorance of persistent wilful law-breaking?"

"Absolutely! When we look at these very informative, professionally designed websites they are chock-full of useful helpful info, but the organisations choose to virtually ignore any serious attempt at crisis management through their websites.

"Compare their approach to that adopted by the Trail Bikers Fellowship," and in response to her own prompt she brought up another webpage for Lehrer to examine. "This site screams out loud and clear that this group is under siege. They talk about strength in numbers, about getting your local MP on board so that he might fight your corner for you."

"And what is it that they think they're fighting? It's clearly not the primary regional authorities, as we're beginning to understand."

"Dead on, Chief – they're fighting the many activists out there in the heather and in the woods, on the fell tops and down by the lake shores. They are, in their own minds, in some form of wilderness combat with an entire range of popular groups like the Ramblers Association, the Caravan Club, the Lakes Coalition, even the Drystone Wallers' Trust. Naturally all of these clubs and bodies have the preservation of the Lake District etched into their collective souls, but of course they consist fundamentally of private individuals who love the Lakes enough to want to save the landscape from the barbarians, as they see it."

"Ironic isn't it," Lehrer said with a gentle smile, "that it's the corner-stone upon which the national park was founded – the very first commitment written into the organisation's effective constitution."

"Sorry, what is?" she asked.

"Their primary duty: the protection and preservation of the countryside."

"Well, Chief…we can see how that's been going," she added disconsolately. "But we shouldn't overlook the obvious though unspoken message seeping out from the Trail Bikers website."

"You mean that they know they are in the wrong?"

"Yes, Chief. They haven't got a leg to stand on, and they know it. All they have is bravado and camaraderie. Stick together and we're strong!"

"And yet they appear to be just that: strong enough to hit the hills in numbers without a care in the world."

"Until now perhaps," she cautioned. "This shooting has unsettled some, and it's also clear that many from within the ranks of the opposition have been emboldened. Let me give you an outline of what's on Facebook, and then I'll show you some stunning comments on Twitter."

"That sounds a bit more entertaining," Lehrer offered.

"Well…entertaining is one way to describe it, but I have to tell you that there are some volatile participants on Twitter and together they may be presenting us with an awful lot of painstaking work over the next few weeks." With that she minimised one screen, closed another and then produced a gorgeous view of Derwent Water which quite took him by surprise.

"This is the CLNPA's site. It looks cute, but it's not all that helpful. There's nothing about bikers or anything of that sort. It's just a nice self-congratulatory view of those same sunny uplands with every implication that we should thank the Park Authority for its naturally occurring landscape.

"Interestingly, though, there was a flurry of external banter on here several months ago about speeding notices. Don't get too excited, Chief...it was about horses being brought down to a walk from a trot or canter in some remote spots where, oddly, traffic concerns seem to be sensitive. Their original post did seem a bit condescending, but it wasn't the horsey set or the farmers who reacted. It was the walkers' lobby who erupted, and only because they see the CLNPA being petty in this way while patently ignoring vast speeding hordes of rogue bikers."

"What did they have to say?" asked Lehrer, curious.

"Oh, they went at it full tilt, but the confrontation shifted when some bikers began to follow the debate live online and it really did unearth some vicious threats and insinuations. The exchange seemed to go on over several days between bikers and hikers, and we will need to contact Facebook to see whether or not they'll help us with a few IDs."

"They'd damn well better," insisted the DCI. "This is a murder investigation!"

"As for Twitter, here, have a look at this kind of thing."

> Mountain Machine @Birkenhead2005
> @FrankAD_DofE Make sure u r wearing yr incontinence pants next time out Gdad - I'm gonna ride right thru u old fossils & scare the f-ing sh*t right outta ya!

> Tree Hugger @FrankAD_DofE
> @Birkenhead2005 You're next you f-ing barbarian. No safety in #s will protect you. I can watch your every move close-up from 2 miles away. I know u!

"This kind of language and open animosity is only instructive in that it's not unusual. That's how Twitter can be, and only too often. Nothing is what it seems, however."

"How do you mean?" queried the DCI.

"Well, for us, looking for viable leads and connections, it helps to be sceptical. For example, is *Birkenhead2005* indicative of his location, or his origins, or a club he's linked to that was founded in that year, or is it just a favourite place? Here it's his Twitter address, effectively. The *Mountain Machine* is just his chosen ID. It may refer to a trail bike, but we can't tell."

"So the 'Tree Hugger' may not be elderly, as implied in the first tweet, and he's probably just leaning on recent events in the implied threat."

"Exactly! What's sometimes more revealing is the biography hidden below the little logo. These are not compulsory, and they're often left blank by those who'd rather not give anything away. Naturally they might be of more interest to us for that very reason. When we click on *Mountain Machine* it takes us to his page and we can review his tweets, as well as check his biography. Look, here it is."

> Mighty petrol-head. #TTraces #Oulton Park
> #DoningtonPark
> Hate all things PC – tell it like it is.
> #LiverpoolFC #NeverWalkAlone
> All tweets my own. RT doesn't mean I agree with you.

"So the Birkenhead link has some credibility, obviously, and he's certainly a biker," said Lehrer, nodding his head at the apparent ease of connection.

"Yeah...looks that way, Chief, but the same biog for our Tree Hugger simply tells us that he's basically an environmentalist of one sort or another. There is nothing about age, background, where he's located, even that he's a he, but what about this next exchange of ideas?"

> Scrambling Eggs @Eddie_M33
> @GooseGreen#2 Call it the 'age of entitlement' if you like, but the National Park is not just for some and not others

> Flodden Hero @GooseGreen#2
> @Eddie_M33 U & yr kind r destroying nation's natural heritage. Ppl fought wars to protect this country & its interests. U demean their sacrifices

Scrambling Eggs @Eddie_M33
@GooseGreen#2 We have every right to enjoy open road just as much as any other interest group. It is not for likes of you to decide rights and wrongs

Flodden Hero @GooseGreen#2
U r operating beyond the rule of law. Authorities choose to ignore u, & offer no chance of retribution, I shall NOT! U have been warned @Eddie_M33

"This guy 'Flodden Hero' looks for all the world like an ex-army type with a grudge. He's not uncommon on these pages, but he's also easy to copy, so we have to be circumspect. Often you'll see the use of an emblem or crest which looks vaguely militaristic. Sometimes you discover that it refers to the SAS or Royal Marines or something of that nature. The 'GooseGreen number two' address is a direct reference to the Falklands and Two Para, but can it be a realistic link? Certainly this guy is historically aware. He may be anti-Scots from the reference to Flodden Field, but his biog says virtually nothing. His tone is very measured and very threatening, but is it viable? Should we take him seriously?"

"Wow, Caroline…you were right earlier when you said there is a lot of work here. We need other forces on this job, and smartish! We must isolate realistic suspects and find them, and we have to do it quickly."

"That's for sure, Chief, and as an aside," Caroline Sutton added with a smirk, "I think our Scrambled Eggs character works for the national park in Kendal, from what pops out of his biog."

15

unexpected callers

"Oh, Hen, for goodness' sake, you've got to move on. I know you miss your mum, but it's been too long now. You have your own life to lead. You can't keep moping around like this. I know Keith understands, and I can see how that must help, but you know...he has his life to lead too. He's got a lot on his plate."

"I know, I know, and I'm sorry, Gilly. I know you don't like me being here so often..."

"No, no, it's not like that, not at all..."

"No, Gilly, please...you don't have to be so nice just for my sake. I can see the look in your eyes sometimes when I turn up, but I do understand. This is your family home, and..."

"But you're family, Henri, come on, what are you saying?"

"I'm your husband's sister, that's all. That's not like I'm real family, but he's the only real support I have. I mean...you guys have been so comforting, so sensitive to my moods...which have, let's face it, been all over the place, and I am grateful, really."

"Don't be so hard on yourself, Hen. You're depressed. You've gone through some very tough times. You've lost your mother. You've had some disappointing relationships..."

"Ha, you can say that again," Henrietta conceded sarcastically, as a single tear ran down her cheek.

"And you need to move on now before it consumes you completely," and saying this Gilly stepped across from the kitchen range to give her sister-in-law a warm embrace. "And another thing...I know you don't like that bloody boring job of yours, but now is probably not the time to uproot yourself in that regard. It's at least some stability in your life."

"But bloody boring is about right. I almost jacked it in yesterday."

"What?" said Gilly, alarmed at the prospect of mounting obligations.

"Honestly, Gilly, I did. I was that close," and she held up a narrow gap between finger and thumb. "Since they put me on the London buyers' file it's just been harrowing. Money may talk, but does it have to come with such unadulterated arrogance and rudeness? Some of those people have no idea about the benefits of a cordial business relationship."

"But, Hen, you'll meet aggressive tossers all your life. You can't let bastards like that get you down."

Henrietta recoiled from the crude language, but added, "Maybe so, Gilly, but that doesn't mean I have to bow and scrape to middle-aged retirees whose only claim to prominence is that they've bagged an offensive level of wealth through some dodgy commercial chicanery. Now they expect the perfect Lakeland property to be showcased on demand."

"Well, I can't argue with that, Hen, but I suspect you need to take one thing at a time, and chucking your job on a downer might just be the last thing you need when you're trying to get yourself out of a difficult corner."

"Yeah…I get that much," Henrietta agreed, "but hey…what if one of these blokes came in and swept me off my feet, carried me off to a palatial pad with a view of the lake, gave me babies…"

"Babies!" screeched Gilly, incredulous.

"Yeah…babies…why not? I'm thirty pushing fifty. The shelf is very dusty where I'm sitting."

"Just listen to yourself, Henrietta. Where did that come from? Bloody hell, girl, I mean… That's just it – you're just a girl. You have the best years of your life ahead of you, and all you want to do is mess it all up."

"Eh? Is that how you see your life then?"

"No, no, I didn't mean that," Gilly scrambled awkwardly.

"Well what did you mean? I mean…is a life with my big brother so awful?"

"No, no," Gilly said, defensively. "Me and Keith are fine. We get by. I mean…no, no, it's better than that, you know, every relationship has its ups and downs, but we stick together. We do the right things for the boys, you know, that's the sort of stuff that matters, and that's the sort of stuff that equates to real responsibility. You don't need that kind of load on your shoulders just now. Just remember, babies are for all the time and forever," and a pale image of her lost little girl flashed across her mind, "even when they're big, spotty and hairy…" and the two women looked at each other momentarily, and then dissolved into a fit of giggles.

Just then a smart rap on the back kitchen door arrested the hilarity, and the two of them looked up in search of the interruption. They collapsed again with howls of laughter as the large hairy frame of the young farmer from next door peered through the glass with a bemused expression.

"Ben?" Gilly asked under her breath. She moved quickly, unlocking the door with a twist of the protruding key. She eased the door ajar and carefully pushed her head out. "Not now, Ben," she whispered, "got company."

Ben smiled sardonically. "That's not why I'm here," he assured her. "I just need to get off the farm for twenty minutes or so."

"Sorry? What do you mean?"

"Can I explain inside?" he proposed, as he pushed the door back gently and moved on into the kitchen.

Gilly's tactical brain jumped rapidly through a few challenging hoops. Under no circumstances could Henrietta be given any alarming signals. Their lovers' secret simply had to remain beyond her sister-in-law's grasp. There could be no overt familiarity, no casual closeness to germinate seeds of doubt in Henri's mind. Gilly paused to gather her thoughts and then, closing the door firmly, she turned and made ready to set an appropriate tone with the young man from next door. What could be so pressing that he just had to come indoors, apparently to lie low for a little while? He must have several favoured spots tucked away on the farm for just such a hideaway exercise.

Gilly posed an outwardly obvious question, "So what's the problem, Ben? It's not like you to be skulking around my kitchen…" but she sensed immediately that something else was underway. Her normally confident, even boisterous young lover appeared overwhelmed by a bout of reticence that caught Gilly just as unprepared as Ben himself. He stood stock still in the middle of the spacious room, his dirty hands stuffed rigidly into the pockets of his scruffy jeans. He looked at Henrietta, smiled coyly and then looked down at his boots for a moment as if unable to hold her gaze.

Gilly couldn't remember ever seeing this timid version of her otherwise rampant sexual partner, and she found the contrast immediately unsettling. She watched mutely as the cameo played out before her.

The apparently apprehensive young man took a couple of steps forward and then stopped again. He nodded towards Henrietta, smiled, and tentatively held out a dirty great mitt as if to shake the girl's hand. But then he hastily withdrew the offer in order to wipe his paw roughly down his right hip, only then to re-present it with a self-conscious grin.

"Hi," he said softly, "I'm Ben...er, from the farm," and he nodded in the direction of the farmyard not far off.

"Hi," Henrietta responded, accepting his firm clasp around her own delicate hand as she sat on a high stool at the breakfast bar, "I'm Henrietta, Gilly's sister-in-law. Just call me Henri, everyone else does."

"Ah, okay," Ben nodded meekly.

And at that point Gilly realised what was happening. Was it jealousy that pricked her senses? Was he flirting with her? More importantly was she flirting with him, her own Adonis? And anyway, they were acting as if they'd only just met for the first time, but surely they must have encountered one another many times before out there in the lane or at the gate? Then she looked more scrupulously at the girl who, only moments before, had been in tears at the apparently hapless state of her uninspiring life. Now here she was fluttering her eyelashes and crossing her legs to raise her hem a little higher before her newest admirer. As she attempted to gauge the younger woman, Gilly absorbed instantly the need to recalibrate her earlier off-hand assessments. True, there wasn't much of her, and Gilly knew only too well how attracted Ben had been to her own fulsome figure. However, sitting there on that stool, long legs showcased with casual aplomb, short blond hair stylishly framing a rather plain countenance, but one illuminated by a broad fresh smile and bright blue eyes, Gilly acknowledged inwardly that Henri would not register in Ben's eager examination as the dispirited figure with which Gilly was so very familiar.

"Hang on a minute, you two," Gilly interrupted. "Are you trying to suggest that you've not actually met before now?"

"Well...er, we haven't, at least not properly, not face-to-face like this," Henri offered.

"Really?" begged Gilly in exaggerated surprise. "But, Hen, you've been up here tons of times, just as you were saying earlier, and Ben is always about. I mean…he runs the farm. He has to be here. You must have met before, surely?"

"We've passed each other in the lane," Ben threw in by way of explanation, "and I guess we've each known who the other was, but no, we've never actually spoken until now." He looked back at Henrietta and grinned. Henrietta returned the compliment with a warm smile. Gilly cringed inside. She wondered what had been triggered by such a chance encounter, and she anxiously tried to deflect the gathering glow of mutual appreciation.

"So what's going on, Ben? It's very rare to see you at my back door," she lied quite deliberately, "but your need to duck in here to avoid something out there in the yard does seem a little unusual, I must say."

"Oh it's nothing really," he shrugged. "It's just a temporary inconvenience to be honest," he suggested.

Both women looked intrigued.

"Well it's all to do with my trail biking up on the fell, or at least I suspect that's what it's about," he continued.

"How does that work?" Gilly demanded. "Don't farmers use trail bikes and quads all the time up there? Why's that a problem?"

"That's true, we do," he concurred, "but quads seem to be tolerated a little more readily than trail bikes. The scramblers are associated with leisure pursuits these days, and there has been so much land erosion inflicted on some of the popular areas by the weekend lads up from Ulverston and Grange that the authorities are trying to clamp down on the two-wheeled problem, if not the four."

The girls still looked somewhat confused. "But why are you hiding here with us now?" Gilly pressed.

"You see, the girly girls down at the lodge have been on a bit of an environmental rampage of late. I got it in the neck last time I was out on the bike. I just happened to run into them, not literally you understand, but on the same track when they were out recently doing one of their training runs. They are professional triathletes," he explained to Henrietta who again smiled warmly and tried not to reveal that she had no idea what that meant.

"So you're hiding from Helen and Lucy?" Gilly suggested with growing disbelief. "Does that mean you'll be running in here every time you see them out by their gate?"

"No, no, sorry…it's the police. There's a police car parked in the lane right outside their place. It looked like a plain clothes chap, big lanky bloke, plus a uniformed policewoman. They appeared to have a very brief exchange with Helen at the gate before heading up into the farmyard. I could see them from the old hay loft. Mum and Dad are out so they got no response from the house, and when they shouted out in the yard, you know, trying to get some attention, I just stayed put. Then they walked back down to the lodge and they're still in there now. I reckon Helen must have put in a complaint and they've decided to take it seriously for a change. They must be getting her statement or something like that. They'll be gone soon enough, I'm sure of it."

"But how serious is that?" Gilly asked.

"To be honest, I don't really know," the lad conceded. "I think there is a growing sense of frustration among the green brigades and rainbow warriors of various types, not to mention walkers and backpackers, but my status as a farmer should protect me."

"But this hasn't got anything to do with that recent report in the *Gazette*, has it?" Henrietta demanded.

"You mean the shooting?" Ben asked directly.

"Shooting?" Gilly queried in alarm.

"Yes, you must have read about it, or even seen it on the news?" urged Henrietta.

"Henri's right," Ben advised. "I first heard about it at Young Farmers. It was a young bloke just like me; a farmer over Torver way – shot dead as he rode along a track just off his own land and out on the common fell. They reckoned he'd have lost his head completely if his skid lid hadn't held it all together."

"Skid lid?" asked Gilly meekly.

"Crash hat, you know…helmet," Henrietta interpreted for her sister-in-law, and Ben warmed to the girl's obvious familiarity.

"My God," whispered Gilly, as the murderous scenario settled into her consciousness. "You're making me glad that I don't own a pair of walking boots – sounds too dangerous to contemplate taking to the hills."

"Oh no," Ben cautioned. "It isn't really like that at all. This is a one-off incident, and there is a rumour running around that the lad in question had a long history of aggravated confrontations with other fell users. It all seems a bit extreme, I grant you that, but it may be the case that old scores have been settled. I don't think the same risk exists for all of us."

"But it would explain the police car in the lane," Gilly acknowledged, "and if Helen Dyke has grassed you up, you being a farmer and all, perhaps the cops are paying her more attention than she deserves."

"Helen Dyke? Gilly Salcombe, you can't say that," Henrietta admonished, with a gently wagging finger.

"Oh yes I can," Gilly insisted. "There is no place in this house for political correctness. In my estimation it's killing off our cultural norms, and especially our sense of humour, faster than bikers are being dispersed from the fells by a madman with a gun.

"Coffee, anyone?" she asked. "We might as well be comfortable while our dyke-baiter here is keeping his head below the parapet." With that she crossed to the sink, filled the kettle with water and set it back down on its plinth. Flicking its switch at the back with a casual forefinger, Gilly returned her gaze to her visitors, only to register their closer mutual proximity, and to witness them lost in deepening conversation.

"I must ask you again, Helen, do please calm yourself," the uniformed police constable advised. "We understand your anger and frustration, but you will help us more than you know if your statement can be delivered carefully and thoroughly."

"Yes, yes, I'm sorry," Helen responded.

They sat in the cosy snug of the old Lodge House. The décor boasted bold contemporary colours and a beguiling feeling of warmth despite the limited light afforded by the traditional Edwardian window frames. The view out to the fell, and the forest fringes high to the left, accentuated the sense of prime location. What a way to view the world, was all that DI Young could think as he'd settled into a comfortable armchair and stared out at the stunning vista before them. However, the agitated mood of their complainant and chief witness had quickly taken the edge off their appreciation of the natural beauty of their surroundings.

The girl, Helen, had been barely able to marshal her disaffection during their early exchanges, and quickly the tension had crept beyond restraint and developed steadily towards outright belligerence. It appeared to have been their admission that successful police prosecutions had been very thin on the ground in recent years; quite the corollary to the growing swarm of mindless rural vandals who, in her estimation, were running amok with impunity.

The other girl, Lucy, appeared much more placid; if anything, her anxiety was for her friend and partner's volatile temperament.

Nodding at her copious notes, DI Young asked his colleague to summarise the salient points of the statement taken.

"Right then," she commenced, as she flicked several turned sheets back to the front page. "It looks like we have every required detail of the confrontational episode that took place on the track in the rain. We have all three protagonists. We have precise timings, dates, weather conditions and even a specific location on the ordnance survey map of this area. Helen and Lucy here are agreeing to be formal witnesses to any proposed prosecution, but of course we have to catch up with our perpetrator first before we can begin to put any CPS file together.

"Our witnesses identified the bike in question on the day. They recognised it as the same machine they have seen many times and we should be able to locate it on the farm and link it to our suspect fairly easily. Crucially our witnesses observed said suspect in the act of riding in an illegal fashion, that is to say riding in a designated and protected area of the national park. That illegality is, in their belief," she cautioned, "adequately signed at various access points to the specific location where the incident took place. Ignorance of illegality could not be taken as a reasonable excuse. The same area has triple SI implications and so the potential penalties attached to a successful prosecution could be quite damaging, but that is an assessment beyond our jurisdiction.

"We have a written attestation to the gist of the conversation that took place during the incident. Reference was made to a recent fatal shooting just a few miles from here, but there appears to be no connection of any sort between this encounter and that more serious incident.

"We have also registered within the statement some claims and accusations about certain financial and ecological irregularities appertaining to the running of the Rowan Tree Farm. We have already advised Helen that she should reconsider the inclusion of these details in this statement, and we have offered her some time to reassess before committing her signature to any official document. However, we can summarise these points now: dumping of waste materials, chemicals, farming equipment and general refuse on the open fell behind the farm in contravention of guardianship rules applied to government grants which are awarded to farmers for protecting the countryside; abuse of the business development grant system through the building of family lodgings on the farm using subsidies designed to support the building of holiday dwellings; bribery in connection with approval of drinking water test results from source water known to be dangerously contaminated – most particularly with E. coli associated with sheep discharge into the water supply; deliberately polluting natural water courses through the illegal discharge of untreated human sewage.

"These are all very serious accusations. They would demand an intense degree of technical investigation and some financial forensics to verify or discount such claims. Legal fees would be hideous. Local relationships, currently somewhat strained, would be terminally disrupted and the acrimony could be quite debilitating.

"That's where we are, Detective Inspector," the constable concluded.

"Alright then," he replied, "I think it's time we took another stroll up to the farm. We've been here, what…about an hour," he said as he took a brief look at his wristwatch. "Ladies, I'd like to thank you for your time and for your courage in raising these issues. I would iterate the constable's advice to you, Helen, to think long and hard about the second section of your statement. You really ought to seek proper legal advice. We cannot advise anything other than caution on your part. We apprehend lawbreakers, we can't prosecute them. The issues you have highlighted will plunge you into some difficult, challenging and costly legal affairs which you may come to regret, even if you should win through the courts. You are not seeking to gain personally, I can see that, but as a whistle blower in this regard you may still accrue some sizeable legal costs, especially if your case collapses for whatever technical or legal reasons. This is about reputational risk as much as perceived misdemeanours, and your neighbours will fight you for that.

"As for the biking incident and the implications of your primary complaint, we will pursue this further, and we will expect you to sign off at least that aspect of your statement within the next day or so. Be aware that we will be confronting your two-wheeled neighbour just as soon as we can reach him. It won't take long. Therefore, be aware too that your relationship with him and potentially with those around him too, may well deteriorate from here. Your own behaviour must remain controlled at all times irrespective of any animosity directed your way."

Helen nodded her understanding. She clasped her hands together and arched her fingers before reassuring them that she would indeed sleep on it before signing the full statement. In her heart she already felt a twinge of doubt about the broader section, but she remained steadfast in her determination to tackle the trail biking issue head-on.

The two girls showed their official visitors to the door with hesitant thanks for having been taken seriously. They hadn't really expected such a response, or indeed any response, but they guessed that since the recent shooting any incident within the biking community must be attracting careful scrutiny.

The police officers headed off to the farm once again, but within no more than five minutes the girls heard the police vehicle start up and descend down the lane. Clearly Ben had not been located yet.

In the car, the tall, handsome detective thought about the lithe and lissom frame of the Lucy girl, but he then checked that train of thought with the knowledge that she would presumably not have shown the same interest in him.

16

conspiracy theories?

Janice topped their wine glasses up and continued to take her new man through an interesting and quite revealing in-house report from the Tourism Board which had been commissioned roughly one year earlier. It was quite improper, they both knew that, but compelling subject matter all the same. It made no bones about the dramatic decline in the local economy, and in that regard the last two years appeared to exhibit a very clear acceleration from the previous three. In combination, the last five years' figures suggested an irrecoverable slide. Equally, the summary and conclusions made no pretence at hiding the root cause of the problem on the ground.

Quite specifically, and in some detail, the review considered the outcomes from a number of initiatives behind which the Tourism Board had swung considerable effort and resources in an attempt to win the attention of key motivators within the police, council and national park administrations. What struck Lehrer as particularly strange was the apparent reluctance of the primary influencers in the region to get to grips with the dilemma before them. It seemed very obvious that the most senior ranks in these organisations were not only sensitive to the idea of offending the farming community, but also that their wariness was in some way reinforced by the guidance they seemed to have received from politicians at various levels in the local hierarchy. Lehrer reflected on the huge agri-businesses in his old stomping ground in East Anglia. He knew that some of those could apply very powerful financial and political clout indeed, but he doubted, perhaps naively he wondered, that the hill farmers here could pack the same punch. What was it that held the establishment back from confronting the issues?

The next morning back in the office, his wife's rather indiscreet exposition appeared fortified by none other than the chief constable himself, who had let it be known via the chief superintendent that the farmers were not to be bullied. DI Young had reported that the official statement taken from the two girls at the lodge at Rowan House had been quietly sidelined. He had been instructed to do nothing more with it and, in particular, not to pass that on to the complainants.

DS Sutton reported that a rash of interview requests and some arrest warrants had been pumped down the pipe through other police forces from as far afield as Strathclyde in the north to Derbyshire and Staffordshire in the south. These had been triggered by their extensive trawling through social media accounts. Many more hands were turning that mill, and host companies were being surprisingly cooperative bearing in mind how jealously they guarded their relatively new gold mine services, but as yet nothing of any substance had materialised.

Their plight was beginning to look so depressingly helpless that an intervention from the Met in London, normally a worrying intrusion, suddenly offered them a degree of respite by way of distraction.

One of the Met's informants had recently fed an intriguing idea to the drug squad there. For some time they had been stalking an infamously successful dealing cell based in and around Peckham and Bermondsey, just south of the Thames. Apparently their intelligence had been steadily lining up a small but precise number of supply chains. All of these were London based bar one, and the assumption had developed that the final link in the supply chain would take them north to Birmingham. However, more recently this connection had been tested and eliminated by West Midlands' under-cover officers. The merchandise was coming from further north. Greater Manchester had been unable to corroborate any potential new producers on their patch, and so the tentacles of the London investigation reached further north still. Some interesting but as yet unanswered questions probed the M8 corridor in Scotland. Glasgow was apparently enjoying closer scrutiny, but Cumbria was being asked to examine the M6 motorway and rail corridor more carefully. Lehrer's own unit, with assistance from Greater Manchester, was asked to carry out spot checks on vans and trucks under the somewhat ambitious ruse that anti-terrorism measures demanded stop and search procedures at random in the search for arms and explosives. Such searches would be carried out at motorway truck stops at variable frequencies and, hopefully, in response to prescient intel.

Gilly headed off with a mixture of warm anticipation and doleful sadness. She drove down the long stony track in her four-wheel-drive Volvo estate having first emptied the vehicle of her usual assortment of travelling extras. Why she carried three umbrellas and two pairs of wellies she never could quite fathom, but they were ditched in favour of space. She was heading to Lancaster to recover her eldest, Evan, who was due home for the summer. She was in no doubt that the car would be jam-packed with boxes and cases and bags of dirty washing typical of a student with limited though exclusive priorities. She guessed that he wouldn't have made it to the on-campus launderette for at least three weeks, but the car would cope; she knew that.

She retained that confidence even though she'd loaded a box of her own in the freshly cleared space which looked enormous once the rear seats had been flattened. In that small wooden crate she'd collected some elementary gardening tools, rubber-coated gardening gloves, a tray of bright, perky marigolds and a small bag of planting compost. She'd also added a few discoloured Lego figures, and finally made sure that she had a fairly robust plastic bag into which she might place similar items that were due to return home for a good clean-up. At the last minute she remembered a bucket, scouring pad, scrubbing brush and plenty of absorbent but hard-wearing cleaning cloths.

As she sped past the Lancaster University buildings which stood adjacent to the M6 she looked in on the campus and calculated that she would have a good three hours to get to Manchester and then return in time for her allotted rendezvous with Evan. That should be enough barring any stop-start congestion on the motorway system around Manchester's periphery.

She reached the cemetery in good time, decanted her requisite graveside refreshment kit and walked resolutely round to her daughter's plot. The gravestone looked stained and dirty, but the gold lettering shone through the mould and etched Alice's name clearly for any passing onlooker. The spring flowers were well past their best, but Gilly knew the routine and she'd soon transform the site appropriately. She knelt on her plastic bag to spare her knees from grass stains, and set about removing the old plants and weeding the plot. She chatted to her daughter absentmindedly, and to any passer-by it would have sounded like a coherent though naturally one-sided exchange. Having cleared the bed in front of the stone she then excused herself and walked across to the standpipe and filled her bucket with cold water. The trick was always to mop up any detergents with a cloth as they tumbled down the face of the stone before they reached the soil. However, scrubbing off the green-tarnished marble demanded a smart balancing act between scouring and mopping if the earth was to be protected prior to digging in the new plants. Throughout she chattered away as if in explanation of every aspect of the task to her lost little one.

The tears gathered quickly. She knew it would happen; how could it not? She sat back on her heels and wept quietly at one stage as the futility of it all overwhelmed her, but then she rediscovered her purpose and pushed on vigorously. Twenty minutes later the scene looked at least tended and cared for. She admonished herself for her long absence and begged Alice for forgiveness. She told the little mite just how much she was missed and just how often she featured in their daily lives, but then she trailed off, forlorn at the prospect of her daughter's unreachable solitude. Was there indeed life after death? Would she find and gather up her lovely little girl again one day? Would she still be a little girl, still playing with her Lego people? Could Alice see and know and understand her mother's heartbreak? And then Gilly froze momentarily at the disturbing notion that Alice could indeed see not just her mother's anguish and eternal love, but also her reprehensible behaviour, her disloyalty to her daddy, her frivolous lifestyle that brooked only censure in lieu of admiration. A wave of self-loathing coursed through Gilly's frame; the weakness of the living exposed before the honour of the dead.

Gilly cleaned her trowel and hand-fork. She deposited the wasted plants in the nearby dumpster. The marigolds did look impressive and she smiled and sighed in relief. She carefully placed the My Little Pony models in her plastic bag – they would soak in soapy water for several days at home and then be scrubbed up in readiness for their next shift in months to come. The Lego toys looked resplendent against the pale clean marble. Gilly gave her daughter a quick review of the family, and especially of her big brothers who were set to come home for the summer. How Gilly wished that Alice could be there to greet them. The distress overpowered her again and she held her hand up to her face as if to contain her emotions, but it was hopeless and she wailed out loud, looking left and right to check that other mourners were not disturbed by her sorrow. She was alone, and she felt truly alone in her isolation.

Driving back north she made reasonable time and found herself draining her cappuccino in the university coffee shop just as Evan dropped into the chair beside her. He looked a little hung over she thought. When she leaned over to embrace him the stale stench of booze washed over her and she rebuked him half-heartedly for his previous late night. He just laughed. He looked content…well, apart from the thumping headache, and he looked bigger somehow, broader, more grown up. He said it was down to his rugby training, and when they stood to leave she gasped as she realised he must have added another stone at least, and mainly across the shoulders. She hugged him again. She was proud of her boy. He, on the other hand, thought that two maternal clutches in two minutes in the public forum of the uni café were more than enough. They went out to the car and Evan directed his mother round the internal road system so as to be able to park the car right up against the main door to his on-site flat. He did the heavy lifting down three flights of stairs. An hour later they were back at Rowan House. Half an hour after that the washing machine was already bashing through its cycle.

The very next day Gilly almost repeated the uni run for her younger son, Will. This time it was a much easier project chiefly because the lad had taken the Stirling train via Edinburgh to Oxenholme (Lake District). Being on the main line south to London Euston, the service was usually fairly quick and reliable. It also meant that he could only bring what he could carry, leaving a lot of clobber in the box room of his flat for the summer recess. Stirling needed the accommodation for summer course students. The drive across to the other side of Kendal took only twenty minutes via the village of Sedgwick. The route avoided Kendal's tedious one-way system altogether. Will hadn't put much weight on, but he did sport a fulsome beard which camouflaged him from his mother's anxious gaze on the station platform. He grinned at the successful charade, but lacking his elder brother's social scruples, he picked her up in a great bear hug and whizzed her round and round in front of all the other disembarking travellers; some grumbled, but some smiled in appreciation of his mother's obvious pride.

Back home the boys settled in quickly, but they discovered new and unexpected boundaries just as quickly. No sooner had Will's limited luggage hit the flagstones in the hall, the brothers set out for the outhouse and their rusting old mountain bikes. But no, apparently that wasn't a good idea. Mum explained that they were banned from the fells for the duration of their stay, at least on wheels anyway! They gawped at her without the slightest inclination of her true intent.

"Don't argue with me," she pleaded. "You've just got home and I don't want to spoil the mood for you, but unless you've been keeping track of the news you'll not be aware of the no-go zone up there on the tops."

"Aw, Mum, c'mon, what the hell is that supposed to mean?" whinged Evan.

"Cut the language for starters, young man. I'm your mother, not some uni drinking buddy. Have you really not heard about the gunman out there?"

"Gunman? What on earth…?"

"A young lad not much older than you two was shot dead on the fells recently only a few miles from here," she intoned severely.

"Shit…no way, I mean…"

"Oi, language! Don't ignore me! He was a young farmer. He was out on his trail bike and some nutter shot him from a long way off with pinpoint accuracy apparently."

"Bloody hell… Sorry, Mum, but that's awful. Why, what are they saying?"

"That's the worrying bit," she offered. "They just don't know. It's all very quiet in Kendal and we're beginning to think the police have no leads at all."

"But they've closed off the hills?"

"Well, erm…not really, but I don't want you up there."

"Aw, Mum, c'mon, you're not serious?"

"Yes, I am bloody serious, to use your vernacular. I suspect there is something going on which involves a lone wolf who thinks he can protect the countryside from all that wear and tear by scaring off the main culprits."

"You mean the bikers?"

"Yes, the bikers. It's not something I'm close to. I mean… I'm not a tree-hugger of any kind, but I can see the green lobby's point of view. It's just a scary level of response in my view."

"But we're going mountain biking, Mum. It's people power. We're not at risk in the same way if the bloke is anti-trail bikes."

"You don't know that. None of us know that for sure," she insisted.

"Mum this is daft," Evan asserted. "What does Ben say?"

"I've no idea," she responded defensively. "What has that got to do with anything?"

"He's a trail bike rider, Mum, c'mon. He'll know the score, surely."

"I've no idea," she repeated, "but you're not going up there on those bikes and that's it. You're grounded. Boots or cross-country runners, but no wheels and that's final."

She didn't wait to see their disgusted faces. Turning away she made for the back door and the sanctuary of the kitchen.

For the ensuing weeks Ben stayed away just as she had anticipated. She expected her boys to tap into the older boy's network pretty quickly, if only to pursue the murder on the fell a little more keenly, but Ben kept his distance from the house. She saw him periodically working hard out on the land. Once he even waved to her as he passed by the end of the garden beyond the drystone wall on his quad bike and trailer set. But if she missed his physical attentions she simply got on with life knowing that their next assignation would be well worth the wait.

Henrietta also kept clear. That really did surprise Gilly, but she put that particular absence down to a wish, perhaps on Henri's part, to give them all a little more family time now that the boys were back. Whatever the cause, Gilly took it as a stroke of good luck, and she hardly gave the girl a second thought for weeks.

Two weeks later Keith overheard a most bizarre tale in the works canteen at the quarry. One of the contract haulage drivers was in taking a very sweet tea before heading off south with another low-loader of weighty slabs. Keith sat in the corner. He didn't like to mix too often with the work crews believing their free time and space to be important to them. Who needed to make small talk with the boss during break time?

"So tell me again, what did they say they were after?" asked one of the forklift drivers.

"Explosives!" the driver replied. "I think it's code for weapons… Semtex…you know…terrorist stuff."

"Christ, you havin' me on or what?"

"No, no, straight up. They even had sniffer dogs all over the rig. It was an *artic*, like, you know…a freezer van actually, but they went through it with a fine-toothed comb I can tell you."

"Sniffer dogs? Really? I thought that was more the drugs scene, if you follow."

"Well I thought that too, right enough, but maybe they train them up in the same way but for different substances, like?"

"Yeah, maybe," the fork-lifter considered, as he peeked inside his sandwich, "and where was this again?"

"On the M6 – first services after joining the motorway."

"Was it just you, or just a few lorries at random, or what?"

"It looked pretty organised to be honest. They did pick out a random selection, but I could see other teams sniffing around all the parked-up trucks too. Maybe they're working on a tip-off."

"Bloody hope so, otherwise they're just shooting in the dark, aren't they?"

The HGV man stood and moved over to the open bin where he jettisoned his plastic tea cup. He turned back to his lunch mate and as he made for the exit he said, "No change there then," and pushed through the door.

Keith had neither moved nor flinched, but he hadn't turned a single page of his newspaper either. He hastily did so. Then he bolted down a tasteless pie and chips, swilled back with tepid tea. He tried to behave as casually as he could while taking his leave, with a few nods and smiles, before heading out to find Morgan.

17

insider dealing

"Look, Austen, I'm the chief constable, not God Almighty! I can't guarantee you anything. This is turning out to be a very lucrative little earner, and the scale of the, er...benefits, shall we say, is enough to compensate for the risks. But in agreeing that the risk factor has suddenly spiked, I would just point out that it's a lot more threatening to me in my position than it will ever be to you."

"Hey, Lou, I can still go to gaol too you know," Austen Smiley retorted with apparent nonchalance.

"You hardly need me to acknowledge that, Austen, but your anxiety is recognised and understood. Our circumstances clearly have changed, and not for the better, but the situation remains manageable. Our little scheme was running along very smoothly with very few wrinkles until some crackpot decided to take out a young man on a motorbike. Even that hasn't yet come close to upsetting the practicalities of our process, but the interference of the Met has narrowed our contingencies considerably.

"Tell me again how your reliable little lap dog, er...what's his name, Keith, yeah Keith...how he came across the truck search operation."

"By accident, and that's one of the aspects of this that really bothers me. We should have been informed. We should have known about it."

"And done what exactly, Austen?"

"Put in place some alternative distribution plans, of course."

"Like what? Come on, Austen, you know that your routes south for the merchandise have relied exclusively on heavy haulage. Okay, the transfer of the packages has taken the trail bike route more often than not, but only as far as the major arteries and then it's been transferred to trucks. Operation Trucker hasn't been in place for very long, but already it appears that my instructions to ignore all vehicles evidently coming out of the Lakes area have been beneficial."

"Yes, but the guy who spooked Keith has already undergone a search down at the Lancaster services on the M6. To answer your question, that's what brought Keith to Morgan in a bit of a flap."

"Ah yes, that was it, and correct me if I'm wrong, Austen, but wasn't the driver pulled over while contract driving for a Scottish firm?"

"Maybe, I'm not sure."

"I think you'll find that the Lakeland trucks are being allowed through. Anything that looks like it's from somewhere west of the motorway is getting straight through. So anything like your corporate quarry livery will passport a vehicle due south with minimum fuss. After all, the various forces up and down the main routes simply cannot stop every vehicle. They don't have the resources to do it, and so far, though it's early days, the logic of choosing a selective approach has been readily accepted."

"But for how long, Lou?"

"Like I said, I don't play God, especially over the decision-making process in London, but this'll run for some time, trust me."

"I'd like to, but I think we need another option, and quickly."

"I don't disagree. If we're sticking to the timeframe, we have another two years to work this production line good and hard. My gut feeling is that the biking delivery routes are just as good now as they were before this crazy tree hugger got his gun out and went completely over the top. In fact it's arguable that the extra attention in the press and even among the general public works in our favour."

"You think so?" Austen probed with a hint of incredulity.

"I do! It seems to me that willingly taking to the fells when there is an armed lunatic at large with a death wish on two-wheeled joy-riders equates to a calculated risk executed behind a certain camouflage. I mean…who would take that on in normal circumstances?"

"Doesn't it put our two lads in greater jeopardy because there will be fewer bikers out there?"

"Possibly, I'll grant you that, but if our despatch riders can tag themselves somewhat expediently onto some of the groups out there, presumably they would be less vulnerable."

"You mean strength in numbers?"

"Yeah, something like that."

"But young Morgan favours the lone rider approach to avoid any potential recognition within any group of bandits."

"Austen, you're beginning to sound like some of those campaigners who spend their lives observing traffic movements on the highways and by-roads just so that they can submit Excel spreadsheets to the local parish council – as if they're ever going to do anything with that sort of information. Half of them are there just for a cup of tea and a chat. I'm sure most of them live so remotely that they just need some company every so often. Ask them to get out and fight for something and I think we could all prepare to see nothing much of anything."

"That's a cynical view, Lou. I have some sympathy for them. I'm not a rambler or hiker. In truth, I spend very little time in the great outdoors, well...since I was a teenager I suppose, and that's a very long time ago. But when you can see the devastation out there even from the car, when you drive along some of the minor roads and single-track routes, you realise that it must be really bad close up."

"Oh let's not get all melancholy, Austen, please. It's just a bunch of lads and blokes who live mundane lives by our standards. So they want to leave behind the likes of Whitehaven or Barrow and have a bit of fun out in the sticks – what's wrong with that? Some of these liberal do-gooders need to get a life, I'm telling you. They're stuck out there in the rain and the mist most of the time. They've got nothing better to do than complain about a section of society that they feel is well beneath them and should stay there. Perish the idea that half a dozen lads from Ulverston might take a trip round Woodstone Fell on a Sunday morning, only to have fingers wagged and walking sticks waved in their direction by social elitists wallowing in their own green credentials."

"Lou, far be it from me to bring us back to the point in hand, but I should perhaps remind you that what they do is illegal, and you are the most senior police officer in the county!"

"Yes, well...point taken, of course, but solitude engenders loneliness in my opinion, and lots of these retired well-off liberal types only join these action groups for the social, if you ask me."

"Lou, let's hope nobody asks you. If they get that close we might be in serious trouble. Don't kid yourself about rural seclusion. People are well connected these days – you know, Internet and all that – and they remain in touch and are usually well informed. Look at our little trooper Keith."

"What about him?"

"He lives next to a farm on a hilltop some miles from any recognisable civilisation. You might recall that I helped finance the purchase of the place just to encourage him to take over at the quarry. He's our fall guy if the brown stuff should hit the proverbial fan."

"That much I haven't forgotten," the chief constable reaffirmed.

"Some of your bods have already been up his two-mile drive to check out another trail bike incident which apparently occurred not long after the shooting."

"Really! What did Canny Keith make of it all?"

"It wasn't so much his take on it, but his wife's. Apparently some of their immediate neighbours had lodged a complaint about rogue biking up on the escarpment just above the farm. In fact it was the farmer's son, I believe, a young bloke who would fit the profile of your poor victim almost to the mud-splattered leathers."

"Don't tell me, poor old Keith is surrounded by rainbow warriors..."

"Hardly surrounded," Austen responded. "There's a mere handful of people up there, but the message is clear. An eclectic bunch of people living on a hill in the wide open space, far away from anywhere, is not only aware of what's happening out there, but they're also directly engaged in these events in their own different ways."

"I think we can dispense with the philosophy, Austen, and I think you'll discover in time that any complaints of that calibre that seek to undermine the farming community will be quietly ignored. My chief superintendent is under strict instructions not to ruffle those feathers. We have the farmers and most of the landowners onside, and that's the way it will stay. In terms of your man Keith, how are you managing his expectations?"

"In what sense?"

"Well...his reactions seem to be a little edgy from what he's been telling you and young Morgan."

"No, no, hang on...Keith doesn't talk to me. Keith doesn't know I'm in on this, remember?"

"Sorry, Austen," the chief constable blanched in embarrassment, "I need another coffee to wake me up. Fear not, I've got it. Keith remains entirely in the dark about our involvement. He deals with Morgan and the other lad only, yes?"

"Not quite, Chief Constable," Austen replied with maximum sarcasm. "Keith doesn't even talk to the other boy, Stevie. In fact, Stevie is unaware of Keith's clandestine role and of ours, of course. Stevie thinks that he and his mate Morgan are making a fortune secretively. That it's just the two of them. Keith is cognisant of Stevie's commitment to the scam, but there is no overlap. Equally, Keith talks to Morgan, but certainly not to me. Keith does not know about either of us. I'm not sure how he'd react if he knew, but to be brutally honest he must never find out. If things go belly up, he's our sacrificial lamb."

"As are the two boys," the senior police officer confirmed, and Austen Smiley nodded his acceptance.

"A question though, Lou," Smiley continued. "If your man is suppressing complaints directed at the farming community, how come you sent a couple of bobbies up to Keith's place and to the farm next door?"

"I don't know the details of that particular incident, Austen, but naturally we have to be seen to take complaints seriously. I imagine that a statement was taken, that sort of thing, but it's either been left in the in-tray already or it's about to be. We have one other minor complication to keep an eye on, and I've already lined up my chief super accordingly."

"And?"

"It's a new detective we've just adopted from down south. He's come up from East Anglia I believe. It wasn't an appointment I wanted, but our recruitment board outflanked and outnumbered me, so he's with us."

"Why's that a problem?"

"Well it shouldn't be if we keep tabs on him, but he has some excellent though harrowing experiences from London to rely on and he appears to have an impressive record in disrupting organised crime syndicates – people and drug trafficking through the ports, that kind of thing."

"Great, just what we need," Austen Smiley added, with a rueful grin.

"Yes, I share your reticence, and we're going to have to be doubly careful because he also comes fresh from one of the few parts of the country in which the biker bandit problem, as you call it, has been successfully dealt with. That would have remained largely irrelevant, but for our hot-shot nutcase who has now presented our rather keen new man, DCI Lehrer, with a brand new entry ticket to the trail bike off-road show. I think we could have redirected him away from Operation Trucker – he has better things to do – but an open homicide of this very public nature demands that we put our newest and most accomplished detective on the job. You will relay that information to our Welsh wizard, will you not?"

"Sure, no problem – the boys are going to have to be very careful."

"I'd expect nothing less, but it's worth reminding ourselves that we are wading into ever more dangerous territory."

"Because of the gunman, you mean?"

"No, no, I still think that's a tenuous risk, statistically speaking, and our new detective may unearth him sooner rather than later. That would get the press off my back and quickly restore the status quo. The drop in biker numbers would surge back up, and Morgan and Stevie would be able to blend into that scrum much more easily. No, I was thinking about the Met. If they're pushing out from London, that means their intel is good. Also DCI Lehrer will probably still retain some good connections in the Met and we must try to keep him busy to prevent him from chatting to any old muckers in the big city. If we get two more years out of this scheme I'd be surprised, but Morgan must be ready to shut the whole thing down at a moment's notice."

"That's okay, Lou – it was always part of the plan, as you know. What we haven't got is that alternative option I mentioned earlier."

"You're right, Austen, but before we throw that around a bit, I do need that extra coffee."

With that, the chief constable of Cumberland Police, dressed in an open-necked casual shirt, pale jeans and a pair of well-worn loafers, rose from their small table in the corner of the secluded open-air garden behind the cutest coffee shop in Grange-over-Sands. He padded towards the rear door, ducked inside and disappeared.

Austen Smiley stretched his arms back over his head and struggled to control a tired Sunday morning yawn. A little old dear looked over the top of her *Sunday Telegraph* from the far side of the enclosed courtyard and smiled warmly in his direction. She looked elegantly turned out and he guessed she must have been to church. He too looked rather smart with his navy blue blazer, confident tie, fawn chinos and expensive brown leather shoes. He too had been to church; she knew that. He was that wealthy chap who had paid for their new church roof. She knew that too, but although the other chap had looked vaguely familiar she hadn't been able to place him; not yet at least.

Louis Minton soon returned with two creamy lattes. He settled back into his chair and carefully stirred up the shot of coffee in the bottom of the tall glass with a long stainless-steel spoon.

Austen Smiley ran his fingers through his grey-peppered thatch and leaned in close to his confidante. "I think I may have been recognised," he whispered, "but don't worry, it's my Church connections, that's all," and he nodded discreetly in the direction of the *Sunday Telegraph* broadsheet which entirely blanked its owner from view.

The chief constable smiled, and then he edged his chair around a little so as to present less of a profile to his potential observer. He was about to make an observation of his own, but Austen chimed in first.

"I had another question, my friend."

"Uh oh, that sounds ominous," Louis replied, as he carefully replaced his glass on its somewhat challenging oval saucer.

"There has been a rumour knocking about among the biker boys that your lot nabbed a rather prestigious miscreant some months ago. Apparently he was a very well-known professional rider who was dim enough to be using the Lakeland fells as a bit of an off-duty playground."

"Oh yes," offered the senior officer, "and where is this heading I wonder?"

"I was hoping you could tell me, Lou. It is said that the young man's ego was so out of control that he even wore his corporate leathers, complete with his main sponsors splashed all over bike, limb, torso and crash hat, just for the bragging rights."

"Yes?"

"Well…is it true?"

"Can you tell me a bit more, Austen?"

"Eh? I was hoping that you might do that for me."

"I just want to know how much you know."

"Ah ha, so it's true then?"

"Carry on, Austen."

"Well, er…as if that weren't mind-blowingly stupid enough, this joker got nicked trying to breeze straight through your blue line at the bottom of Grizedale Forest, and then got arsy with your boys, thereby guaranteeing a somewhat more public exposure than perhaps he might have bargained for. It is said that he was taken to Bowness nick and that he was cautioned. Then a serious case was put together by your legal people for the Crown Prosecution Service." Austen halted his account and waited for his accomplice to react.

"So far, my good man," he whispered acerbically, "ten out of ten and a gold star. However, I can stop you there. The CPS file wasn't nearly robust enough and we had to drop it."

"As they say in Glasgow, Lou, ma heed disnae button up the back, man."

"Come again?"

"You don't really think I'm that gullible, do you, Louis?"

"What are you getting at?"

"My sources tell me that the case against him was very robust, but as you say, it was dropped nevertheless. But those lonely hearts who live in miserable isolation up above the snowline, as you described it earlier, decided to pick up the baton just to see how far they could run with it." Louis' eyes narrowed with suspicion, but Austen continued. "Two of them started hawking the idea round the UK head offices of some of the major moto-manufacturers, especially the global Japanese firms, to try to pin down and identify the reprobate in question and his host sponsor. Trust me, Lou, when you research big global companies from the investment perspective, as indeed I have many times over in my inglorious past, it doesn't take long to reveal the extent to which these hugely successful enterprises have gone to promote their green credentials. It's a farcical notion I know, petrol-driven firms so huge that as household names with logos recognisable in every corner of the planet, they actively sell the concept that their thirsty polluting machines are in some way good for the environment. Apparently it's all to do with the new green technology they have developed back in Japan."

Louis Minton bowed his head and took a slow sip of his coffee.

Austen continued with gathering momentum.

"It is said that our two men out in the wilderness were successful in tracking the culprit down and discovering his host sponsor. The intrusion reached Tokyo and Osaka within hours of the facts being established, the UK management team having realised the potential for significant reputational damage on a global basis."

"Stop!" Louis insisted. "How the hell did you get hold of this? Who knows about it? How far has it already gone?"

"Never mind how it came my way, Lou. The impact of this clever bit of secret squirreling could be catastrophic, and not just for the reputation of certain Japanese engineering firms. The interesting aspect at this juncture is that the process of anticipated exposure has stalled. We don't know what's happening at this point. We believe that some form of injunction was taken out by the firm in question so as to protect themselves and their man from any damaging revelations. It may be that some form of negotiation is underway, but I'd be astonished if these fresh air zealots are open to bribery, at least not in its usual format. What worries me is that yet again we have the potential for a seismic shift in attention towards the biking menace, as the media would describe it, and there could very easily be some super-sensitive questions asked about your contribution to the apparent smothering of the facts."

"Fuck it!" was all his partner could say.

"So I'm still on top marks am I then, Lou?"

"Oh yes, Austen, you smug bastard, top marks with every gold star in the teacher's sodding book."

"Any bright ideas?"

"Not right now, off the top of my head. I really had thought that the case had died a death. We shut that one down so quickly. I don't even think we have the file any more, that's how confident we were."

"Oops, perhaps a little ambitious then," Austen joked.

"Okay, smart arse, what do we do next? We need some cover on this one."

"Well, I dare not venture to suggest that you may have to refund them their pay-off," Austen quipped, "so my suggestion would be to get your chief super to rope in that new detective. He needs to get in amongst some of these action groups and lobbyists and find out who's been quick-witted enough to unearth this gem. I just can't imagine why this information would stay secret for much longer. It's just too valuable to the eco-warriors to let it lie for very long at all."

"But sod it, man, the original leak can only have come from some very obvious sources: my people, not just those who were involved with the arrest but others on the inside; the biking yobs involved on the day, or the villain himself via his own big mouth."

"If I were you, Louis, I'd start with those who link up regularly with the many disaffected groups that make up the anti-bike lobby."

"You mean the liaison officers?"

"That looks like a good first base to me," Austen offered pointedly.

"Okay, Austen, I will, and thanks for the tip. For both our sakes, we need to put this lethal little genie back in the bottle."

18

new directions?

Ruby inserted the key and pushed her head around the door. "My, my," she said audibly. She was alone. Nobody was remotely within earshot. She stepped inside the apartment. It looked like the show-photo on their holiday cottage website. The last time she'd witnessed Ben's own quarters looking quite so impressive had been after Katarina's pre-season clean out. She wondered what it meant.

Returning across the yard she spied the Polish girl lugging two buckets through the yard gate and out towards the fixed caravans. She headed off after her and caught her up in the first of the vans.

"Katarina, hello, how are you getting along?" she asked.

"Yez, good, Mrs M. I am on target, I sink," the girl answered, her blonde ponytail swishing about as she tried to carry on with the cleaning and talk to Ruby at the same time.

"I was just wondering, Katarina, has the boy asked you to do any cleaning for him?"

"Mrs M, er...you mean Ben?"

"Yes, Ben. It's just that his apartment looks amazing, and, well... I haven't asked you to do that, have I? Or maybe I did and just forgot," Ruby added, in an agile attempt to relieve her cleaner of any sense of penitence.

"No, no, Mrs M...you did not ask me to, but I am sorry. Ben ask me to," she explained.

"Oh I see," Ruby responded, wide-eyed but hardly surprised. "I thought that would be it. It's far too neat for it to have been his handiwork."

"Yez, yez...but please forgive me. He ask and I don't say no! I should say no! He knows I work for his mama, but he is so kind, such a nice boy.

I stay a little after shift, I clean up the mess – you know what it's like, Mrs M."

"Oh I know alright. I just hope he paid you."

"Yez, no problem. He is a kind boy. You did a good job, Mrs M," she smiled nervously.

"I just wish he'd tell me when he borrows you, that's all."

"Borrows? Zorry, Mrs M, but what do you mean?"

"Oh no, don't worry, Katarina. I just meant that if he gets you to do some cleaning I need to know about it so that I can manage your time here, you know...your shifts."

"Ah yez, of course. I tell him next time, er...no vorries."

"Don't you worry, Katarina, I will have a little word with him." With that she stepped back down from the caravan doorway and made to return to the farmhouse, but as she turned away another question loomed in her mind. Turning back she stuck her head in through the door again and said, "Why did he want the place cleaning anyway?"

"Oh I don't sink I know dat, Mrs M. Maybe he has girlfriend coming," the cleaner suggested with a cheeky grin.

"Oh...really?" Ruby questioned, unable to hide her surprise.

"Maybe. I not sure," replied the Polish girl lamely.

"Have you seen him with a girl up there? You know, Katarina, have you seen any visitors when you have been here?"

"No, Mrs M, but I only get here in ze morning time." Then she laughed a little and raised her hand to her mouth to stifle her embarrassment as the implications of what she'd just said sank in.

Ruby ignored the slip. "I'll have to keep my beady eye on that boy," she promised. Then she turned away again and walked off towards the gate. An uneasy shroud of anxiety descended upon her briefly. What if Ben had taken a shine to Katarina? She might be five or six years older than him, but a more attractive girl in the vicinity simply didn't exist. But then Ruby chastised herself. Katarina was a sensible young woman. She had parental responsibilities. She wouldn't be messing about with the young son of one of her clients, and anyway, she couldn't be staying over on the quiet. She had her daughter to attend to every night, and what a lovely little thing she was too. No, that's not it, she surmised, but something's going on.

She determined to keep a watching brief. She didn't feel comfortable with the idea of spying on her own son, but then she reasoned with herself that such were the potential skirmishes for close family living on top of one another in a remote spot. At least he had his own pad to escape to. It wasn't going to be embarrassing for any of them, with a bit of luck.

As the next few days and weeks turned over she casually scrutinised his movements whenever she could without appearing furtive or going out of her way. She asked her husband, Eric, if he had noticed anything untoward, but he just shook his head and muttered something undecipherable. She decided that he wouldn't have noticed even if Nicole Kidman had been bedding down in Ben's flat.

She even tried confiding in Gilly one day when she bumped into her out in the lane. It took a bit of circuitous construction to bring the conversation around to her own son's comings and goings, but she had hoped that Gilly might have been a little better informed since she was mobile every day taking her own boys, or at least one of them, up and down the lane twice a day. Gilly had claimed abject ignorance and shown apparent disinterest. In fact Ruby thought her neighbour's reaction was a little terse bordering on rude. It was as if she had found the question simply too intrusive. In any event, Ruby had come away none the wiser.

Gilly had quickly rallied to support her own sons when their summer jobs popped up on the agenda just ten days after they'd returned from university. The three of them had convened a domestic pow-wow to formulate the best daily travel arrangements from the options open to them. Shift work made it difficult for the two boys to drive out to work together in the spare motor. Convenient overlaps in their two different schedules did occur, but infrequently, and their working locations were not easily joined in a round trip. So they decided that Evan would take the car. Two reasons swung the decision in his favour: his was the longest commute to Ulverston, and he would likely be travelling home filthy from the cattle auctions and Gilly didn't want her car to stink of cows or bullocks.

Gilly was committed therefore to driving Will to and from the Farm Store in Grange. It wasn't too far – twenty minutes or thereabouts – and she liked the cafes and the few shops that Grange sported down by the seafront. She also relished the idea of getting to chat to at least one of her sons regularly for the next several weeks. She already felt anxious about their travel plans, but she handled that reluctance with the loving understanding of a mother learning how to let go. The only short-term disappointment was that their girlfriends were not coming to stay before they all went off on their travels, thus denying her the opportunity to thoroughly vet their suitability. Perhaps she'd meet them at Christmas.

Her regular taxi service gave Gilly the random chance to see Ben on occasions as she traversed the stony lane down to the main road or up to the house. Sometimes she would see him from afar and she'd see that he was engrossed in one of the tasks of the day. Other times he'd pass by on the quad and give a gentle wave, and Will would enthusiastically return the salute. She rarely saw him when she was alone. She missed him terribly. She missed the young man's physical prowess; more so of late because of his daft mother's silly chattering in the lane one day when she appeared to be hinting that she might know of the secret love affair being pursued by the two of them. Gilly hadn't been entirely sure of what Ruby had been trying to say, but it took some time later and not a little analysis for Gilly to conclude that perhaps Ben had found a younger girlfriend. Gilly herself had seen no evidence of such a person, and indeed neither had Ruby, but that seemed to be at least a safer result than the prospect of Ruby warning Gilly off, without having the courage to say quite as much. In her confusion, Gilly found herself slipping into a quiet melancholy as the time for her lads' departure abroad drew ever nearer and her enforced separation from Ben stretched on and on.

The only silver lining to her rather moody, short-tempered cloud was that Henrietta's visits remained infrequent. Whenever she did appear the girl invariably seemed much more relaxed and happier than she had for some time.

19

early birds…

The black Mercedes van took the last corner smoothly, and almost silently, before coming to rest in a secluded lay-by at the side of the narrow road. The three young men inside the vehicle unbuckled their seat belts and leaned forward from their bench seat up front to get a look at the sky above. There were very promising broad patches of blue sky in contrast to the heavy grey cloud cover that had cloaked their departure from Skelmersdale just over an hour earlier. It was still early. They'd left the Merseyside conurbation well before most Saturday morning shoppers were on the move, and they'd hoped that their commitment would pay dividends once they'd barrelled up the M58 to connect with the M6 heading north. Now, after an uneventful drive, they sat close to the foot of Grizedale Forest, just above Low Nibthwaite, and the buzz of anticipation electrified their nervous excitement. In twenty minutes they'd be flying through the woods and burning up the forest tracks high above Coniston Water to the west and Windermere a little further over to the east. They'd planned their route meticulously, but some of it was well known and involved some of their favourite high-speed stretches. This was familiar territory, as was their leafy covert parking spot.

After a last desperate draw on their cigarette stubs they threw the doors open and jettisoned their fag ends into the bushes and onto the road beside the vehicle. They clambered out, stretched, yawned, and then moved slowly towards the back of the van where the driver yanked hard on the pull-handle and eased both rear doors wide open. The different members of the group fell silently into a practised routine. One grabbed a light metal-alloy ramp and clipped it into place toward the middle of the door space. Another copied him at the other side and soon a metre-wide ramp, two metres in length, reached down from the tailgate to the tarmac. The third stepped up into the carrying space and eased his way between two of the three trail bikes and started to unclip the strops and ties with which the bikes had been secured in transit. The first bike, a Husqvarna, was manoeuvred clear of those adjacent and rolled down the ramp by supportive, caring hands. The bike was wheeled back and quickly raised up onto its retractable stand. Before the second machine was released, a flurry of helmets, boots, gloves and leathers spewed out from within the van, all being caught in mid-air and laid down quickly at the roadside.

As the two lads looked in on their driver who struggled to release the front end of a Honda, they started in shock as a tremendous crash accosted them from behind and they turned expecting to see the first bike collapsed on its side for want of a parking stanchion properly applied. They were not disappointed, but that wasn't the issue.

A phalanx of burly blokes stood facing them on the road. Dressed uniformly in dark clothing, wearing heavy boots and balaclava masks, they stood in two neatly staggered lines. They each carried the same crude but terrifying weapon – a heavy pick-axe handle, each one held firmly in the one hand while being slapped audibly and very threateningly into the palm of the other.

Without warning one of them, a chiselled muscular specimen, stepped forward. Wielding his weighty club through a great arc in the air he crashed it down on the blameless Husqvarna as it lay before him, and with a rapid series of devastating blows he destroyed the machine as its petrified owner stood riveted to the spot gaping in horror. As the petrol seeped out from burst lines and fractured tank, another masked figure moved forward, rolled a fat thumb across a cheap cigarette lighter, and threw the incendiary onto the evaporating pool of liquid on the tarmac. The flame erupted immediately with that muffled surge of petrol drawing in the necessary air for combustion, and bike components began to fizz and buckle under the intense blaze that ensued.

Not a word had been spoken. The young bikers had frozen, desperately trying to gauge just exactly what was happening to them. The back line of balaclavas moved quickly, with military precision, towards their victims who immediately tried to squeeze around the edges of the open rear doors before making a hasty escape. It was not to be. For the van driver, crouching in the back of the vehicle with nowhere to run, there was simply no escape. As for his mates, one risked a fatal blow by rolling under an open door and scrambling away down the side of the unmarked van only to be lifted off his feet by another masked monster, one of two unseen sentries standing at the front corners of the Merc for just such an eventuality. The three of them were manhandled with such overpowering physical strength that they abandoned the instinctive determination to fight back. One screamed and yelled, firstly for help in the forlorn hope that somebody, anybody might hear his cries, and then in a tirade of abuse directed at his attackers until the fat end of a pick-axe shaft was rammed into his face. It broke his nose immediately and smashed a mouthful of teeth into the soft tissue of his tongue and left cheek. He collapsed in shock and was left lying by the side of the road whereupon his friends and co-conspirators were heavily beaten by several assailants and left with broken bones, crushed joints, huge welts all over their bodies and a variety of split and bleeding wounds. Back in the lay-by, not twenty metres from where they lay in a moaning, whimpering, crumpled heap, both Honda and Kawasaki were dragged out onto the road to suffer the same fate as the first machine. Their impressive and not inexpensive German carrier was then bludgeoned to a wreck. Panels were bashed in, doors ripped off, glass windows and windscreen cleared through with effortless ease. Tyres were slashed and outlying engine components were trashed where possible within the tight confines of the engine compartment.

The last thing the van driver saw before slipping into unconsciousness was the apparent leader of the group pulling a spray paint can out of a bum-bag which he wore clipped to his belt. He shook the can vigorously. His incapacitated victim and witness recognised the rhythmical clicking of the nodule inside the canister, and then he passed out.

DCI Lehrer was heading into the office on the same Saturday morning. He'd promised himself and his eager wife that today would be a day to get the boots on and get out into some of those wide open spaces. In truth his ambitions had been twofold: to take a breather on the hoof with Janice, and also to keep a wary eye out for some of the dreadful landscape degradation he'd seen some weeks earlier at the quarterly meeting of the National Park action group. However, the murder investigation had stalled. They'd managed, through adjoining regional police forces, to rattle a few cages among over-zealous online combatants from either side of the 'countryside access' divide, but in his heart he knew they were grinding to a stop. On that basis he felt compelled to go in just to review their data again and to try to pull out the faintest clue they may have passed over and missed. Janice had been understanding, but visibly disappointed.

The drive across to Kendal from Windermere had been fairly quick. He noticed that opposing traffic heading into the Lakes was much heavier and sported a number of boats on trailers. It was still fairly early, but midsummer weekends on the water were clearly very popular. As he dropped down into Kendal and slipped into the one-way drag his phone bleeped. He tapped his hands-free responder on the steering wheel and took the call.

"DCI Lehrer!"

"Boss, it's me, Caroline. Where are you?"

"Five minutes from the office."

"Blast! I was hoping to head you off while you were still close to Windermere."

"Why? What's happened?"

"Oh, it's not good," she said, and then paused. The silence irritated him and he assumed he'd lost the connection, but then she burst into life again. "There's been a very nasty incident over by Low Nibthwaite. Do you know where that is, Chief?"

"Er, yeah, I think so, er...bottom end of Coniston, isn't it?"

"Yes, but that's Coniston Water not Coniston village," she pressed.

"Yes, yes, that's what I thought."

"I think you should get over there pronto, Chief. It would help if one of us could get to the scene quickly."

"Fill me in – what have we got?"

"Three bikers attacked by what sounds like an organised mob of heavies. All in grave conditions, one of them fighting for his life, Chief."

"Bloody hell, what are you saying? It's barely ten o'clock on a Saturday morning!"

"I know, but these guys must have scoped this out over several weeks."

"Serious casualties, you say?"

"I know, I know…sounds hard to believe, but that's what we've got. I think our evasive marksman has stretched the spectrum of appropriate responses to a completely new bandwidth."

"Sod that, Caroline," Lehrer grunted, "it sounds like open warfare to me. I think we might need those UN troops with their light-blue helmets out there patrolling the patch." He sighed in frustration. Escalation was the last thing they needed. He felt sure the top brass would want an external task force thrown at the problem. "Look, Caroline, I'm over the river now. I'll come in and collect you. Is the chief super about?"

"Pull the other one, Chief. It is Saturday," she snorted down the phone.

"Thank God for that – last thing I need right now. See you at the main door in about two or three minutes."

"Roger that, out."

When they reached the crime scene they were instantly taken aback at the apparent scale of the devastation. Beyond the tapes a couple of forensic chaps deftly stepped around the charred and wrecked subjects of their close attention. Camera flashes sporadically illuminated the area.

DS Caroline Sutton just gasped as she got closer. She thought it not unlike a news reel image from Beirut or West Belfast on a bad day in a bygone time. The remnants of three motorbikes lay randomly strewn about the narrow lane, each one tortured and twisted as it lay in the middle of a scorched patch of blackened road. Ahead of them stood the wrecked hulk of what had once been a Mercedes van. Every aspect of the vehicle revealed a frenzied offensive, all except the offside main body panel. There in unmistakable metallic silver aerosol paint, etched against the stark black background of the vehicle's side, read the simple message: YOUR JOB MINTON.

DS Sutton wheeled round and was about to draw the DCI's attention to the slogan when she found him at her shoulder staring at the same lettering and cursing under his breath. Neither of them needed to ask who Minton might be. It could only be Chief Constable Louis Minton, and that, in turn, could only mean that this had certainly been a calculated act based on careful preparation and deliberate execution.

The two detectives crossed to the forensic team. They were shown two other sectioned areas which exhibited patches of blood and possibly urine on the surface of the road, but the scientists were adamant that the whole area should be meticulously combed in an attempt to collect any extraneous evidence that may have been deposited in the heat of the confrontation.

One of the uniformed officers explained that he and his shift mate were first on the scene after a local farmer had raised the alarm. Amazingly, they were beaten to it by an ambulance from Barrow-in-Furness, but they were just quick enough to catch a single sentence from one of the injured before he again lost consciousness. The lad had simply reported that there had been possibly ten assailants with bloody big sticks, as the copper paraphrased for the detectives. The injured were in a very bad way and had been taken to Lancaster General, not to Barrow. Lehrer thanked him for his input and prompted him that a statement would be very helpful at the end of his shift. He then turned back to the white overalls and double checked that they would get photos of the spray-painted message, however embarrassing it may prove to their head man, and also that they would get a sample of the paint. It would also be imperative to check for boot prints or wheel tracks in the thicket at the side of the road. With responses in the affirmative, the detectives then took a short stroll round the approach bend in the road and down to the nearby junction just to get the lie of the land and to examine grass verges for fresh wheel tracks – nothing! Then, with the local farmer's details taken from the uniformed officer, the two detectives sped off to the farm in the fond hope that other movements in the area may have been noticed early that morning. They would put out a call for information to all local dwellings and settlements, but with their luck it seemed like they were clutching at straws.

As they pulled into the farmyard, Lehrer left his younger colleague and headed for the noise of a tractor round the corner of an old barn. Caroline Sutton barked a series of instructions over the phone: an alert for any vehicle in Cumbria carrying a sizeable group of males (she questioned the apparent futility of such an poorly defined alert, but wanted it released anyway); an urgent instruction to Traffic for monitored CCTV facilities on the M6 and A590 to look closely at vans or minibuses, or even two or three heavily laden cars travelling in convoy; an administrative search via holiday rental companies to see if any properties could be identified as accommodating all male groups either last week or for the coming week, and finally a command to have a press briefing set up at their Kendal HQ in two hours. It was all desperate stuff, she knew that, but their luck had to break some time. Perhaps today was destined to be that lucky day.

20

Trojan horse?

Chief Superintendent John Campbell remained aloof and unreachable to many of those around him. His reluctance to engage in the humdrum existence of the lower ranks had created within those echelons of the force the belief that the man harboured a misplaced sense of superiority. Clearly he was a very senior officer, but his overbearing and rather condescending attitude tended to hold his underlings at arm's length, an uncomfortable position for those who attributed his distance to an assumed intellectual and not just authoritarian supremacy. When managing up the chain of command to his chief constable, Louis Minton, he was servility itself, despite his ingrained envy of the man's elevated success. Dropping down the food chain into the murky waters of the wider team was not his most reliable aptitude, and it showed.

David Lehrer had garnered sufficient gossip among the ranks to be wary of the chief super. He realised of course that it would always be easier for a DCI to hobnob with senior officers than those in his own team, but during his settling-in period he had felt the necessity to maintain his guard in skirmishes with both the chief super and the chief constable. It appeared, at least, that he could rely on little interference or intrusion from his direct line report, and it therefore pricked a sense of intrigue when the chief super approached him early on the Monday morning with an interest in a specific recent event.

It had, at best, only a tenuous link to the unprecedented attack on the three biker boys which had taken place only two days before. Moreover, the approach took place in the open office in the midst of a swarming throng of task force personnel who hurried back and forth as they installed an entirely new operational office facility in double quick time. Despite the din of technical chat, the chief super had sidled up to Lehrer and impressed upon him the urgent need to unravel the incremental details of a particular arrest and caution of a professional GP motorbike rider, something which had occurred some weeks or even months ago. The detective took some time to grasp the basics of the order, and was mildly shocked to uncover the essential drive of the instruction: namely to isolate the source of indiscretion which had leaked the nature of the event to interested public parties. The grass was assumed to be one of their own. Lehrer was denied the option of further discussion in the relative calm of his own office by his superior's hasty withdrawal. Standing there in the mayhem of a 'rapid reaction' technical build he found himself unsettled and inquisitive about the real drivers behind such a tangential directive delivered at such a demanding juncture. Despite a sense of mild instability, Lehrer did at least remember reference to the same incident being made at the earlier national park meeting, which he'd attended with PC Mitch Mitchell.

Once they'd got the communications and data systems up and running Lehrer convened a general meeting at which he reviewed their current investigation in its entirety for his sizeable new squad. Taking on board an entire task force had not been his keenest wish, not least for the potential embarrassment it might cause if even these impressive resources could not make the required breakthrough and begin to bring their collective efforts to a successful conclusion. On the other hand, he'd been delighted to learn that the chief constable had insisted that their new man should be given the prestigious opportunity to lead the whole team. In reality, the chief constable had insisted that the chief superintendent should cede control to Lehrer with the hollow encouragement that the DCI, "Should at least be given enough rope with which to hang himself," but of that dubious recommendation Lehrer remained mercifully ignorant.

Few promising results had materialised during their weekend endeavours. The three young victims of the mob attack were still in a serious condition, all sedated, and one in a deliberately induced coma through which the medics hoped to transition him gently off the critical register. With no further input from them, the task force had no more to work with than the mumbled, potentially garbled message he had left with his rescuers.

A bunch of blokes with sticks was not the most precise description the hastily gathered crime unit could have hoped for, but there it was.

It transpired that DS Sutton had located a CCTV traffic recording of a minibus heading down the A590 south of Kendal towards the M6 junction. The video had pinpointed a mid-morning time on Saturday last. It had looked like a travelling rugby team or something of that order. At first she had dismissed it, but then overriding her own suspicions of hyper-sensitivity she had chased it up through the bus hire company and found herself disappointed to discover that it had indeed been a rugby team from Keswick. The timings and relevant locations just didn't fit, not unless the vehicle possessed instantaneous time travel capability.

They picked their way through any references to small groups of men perhaps on holiday or visiting the region and ran off with a number of holiday cottages to be paid an urgent visit. They extended that thought process by imagining that small groups of men need not necessarily be holidaying without partners, wives or sweethearts – perhaps a bunch of committed environmentalists had left their ladies early on Saturday with a specific and very clandestine project in mind – but that philosophy fell away quickly when the problems of maintaining secrecy across a larger mixed group like that were acknowledged.

Young farmers or even just farmers in general were discounted almost immediately. This band were among the least likely to react negatively to the growing surge of motorbike abuse. Many of them, especially the younger ones, saw themselves as part of the biker bandit brigade, and most of those were happy to wear that badge with pride.

The relatively new and as yet largely untried social media outlets (that was to say untried by most of the task force) continued to throw up some juicy exchanges, but the recent disappointments suffered by the Cumbria force were already beginning to cajole their now more numerous contingent down different avenues of investigation. DS Sutton remained anxious to keep the social media screens scrolling over. So far it had been the only font of new potential leads, even though the quality of those prompts had not yet justified her attention.

Above all, and in the absence of any apparent traffic movements that might have conveyed a bunch of rough diamonds into and then out of a precise and quite remote Lakeland location, they simply could not determine how the gang had evaporated so easily if not for some sort of reabsorption into the local community. There had been no events of any note, no forestry gangs on a Saturday, no roadwork crews, nothing to excite the ferreting task force.

"Hey, what's this at the bottom end of Coniston?" one young officer chirped, prodding a stiff finger at the map so recently pinned to the wall of the information centre.

"What? What've you got?" queried DCI Lehrer.

"It's a great big place within its own grounds. Lots of trees by the looks of it, and the gardens appear to run down to the lakeshore. It looks like it has its own jetty, and boats and what not."

"Yeah…and what do you make of it?"

"Well, you know…I think it's one of those outward bound centres, you know, hiking, sailing, night-time orienteering, that sort of thing. It's just that I did a development course at a similar place further north, up by Ullswater. It was at Watermillock I think, and, er…well, I nearly got sent to this one here on the map instead. I'm pretty sure that's what it was then, and maybe still is."

"And what's the idea?"

"Well, bunches of blokes!"

"You mean people who go to the activity courses? They're mainly male. Is that what you're suggesting?"

"Well, yeah, actually. The corporate management courses are a bit more mixed I'd say, but I reckon it's still a very masculine environment."

"Is it possible that the in-house trainers are mainly blokes too?" Lehrer asked, with a glint in his eye.

"Oh yes, I'd say so, but there aren't that many. The team I met at Ullswater was a four-man team, emphasis on the male element."

"Okay," mused the detective, "so wouldn't you agree that the outdoor types might be extremely anti-bike, at least in the off-road context?"

"I would. The guys we worked with just lived and breathed the natural world. They were constantly on about ecological issues, environmental protection…you know…the exact opposite from these firms that take company execs and managers out in Land Rovers into a mud bath or a boulder-ridden, dry river bed just to drive over the rocks at precipitous angles at about two miles per hour. It's a freebie for the visitors – the company's paying after all – but most of them end up disappointed."

"How come?"

"They always expect to be flying around the countryside and crashing through rivers that wash over the bonnet, with lots of ooohs and aaahs about the breather pipe running up the side of the jeep, you know, petrol-heady stuff. But after an hour they'd rather sit on a grassy bank and have a fag."

"Speaking from experience then?"

"Yes, unfortunately – used to be in an office job before the force."

"But you think the outward bounders might be worth a look?" Lehrer pressed, as he tried to keep the discussion on track.

"Well, yes, sure. I mean...Saturday mornings are usually changeover days when one set of clients is leaving after a week (or a few days) of abseiling, canoeing, or raft building. The next group is travelling in and probably checks in any time after two-ish in the afternoon. If you've got a bunch of blokes who have had it up to the neck with these trail bike morons wrecking their very own natural world, well...maybe, just maybe, they might take a pop at some of them if they know their regular parking spot."

"It's only just up the road from the crime scene to that place on the map after all," Lehrer agreed.

"Yeah, that's what I mean. They'd see regular offenders and perhaps track them back to their start point. They'll have spotted the van parked up during the day on previous Saturdays – who knows? I reckon it's worth a rummage through that team there at the end of Coniston. High Nibthwaite, isn't it? Yes," he assured a gathering posse of officers who were leaning in on the discussion. "Let's check their website to see what sort of activities they do these days. It'll give us an idea of the size of the team."

"But if it's only three or four, as you suggested earlier," Lehrer probed, "they'll just not represent a big enough mob."

"But hang on, DCI. There are lots of these groups dotted about the region. There's another up at Graythwaite – not a million miles away from our crime scene. What if they'd coordinated some like-minded reinforcements to assist on the day? Then, after the action, the mercenaries high-tailed it back to their own shops immediately?"

"How far is it, realistically?"

"Oh, I'd guess no more than eight kilometres, five miles. These guys are super-fit. They could jog that in half an hour, especially if they took the commercial forestry tracks which offer an easier running surface than a true cross-country course. Even better, they could drive from Low Nibthwaite to Graythwaite on the same tracks through Grizedale and be back home for a coffee in about ten minutes – no risk of passing one of our cars on the main road or getting caught on CCTV providing they avoid current felling sites which are usually set up with cameras and lights to protect working sites from theft."

"Time we put this to the test. Come on, let's saddle up and take a trip out there," Lehrer proposed. Turning to his colleague DS Sutton he asked, "Caroline, can you take one of these lads with you and drop into Graythwaite Lodge at the same time? We can see from their websites here that they have similar schedules of activities and teams of probably about the same size. Two sets of heavies working together would fit the sketchy description we have from one of our victims, so let's see if we can rattle their cages and check what bits and pieces fall out. If in doubt, don't hesitate to call for backup, and don't forget to nab their mobile phone numbers."

Lehrer had approached PC Mitchell about the supposed arrest and later cover-up of a professional rider. Mitch's reaction was enough. There was something in this, no doubt, but the constable wouldn't be drawn and feigned ignorance as to just how something quite so potentially damaging could have been eased gently out into public circulation.

Lehrer took a drive over towards Broughton and fought his way up a narrow rough track to a remote and beautifully situated farmhouse not too far from the route of the Cumbrian Way path. Patrick Lawner had noticed the car inching its way up from Blaythwaite and had stood at the gate to welcome the unknown and unannounced but not entirely unexpected visitor. He recognised the detective as soon as his greying blond head popped up from behind the car. The two shook hands and one followed the other into the house.

An hour and a half later, and only after two pots of tea and a plate of sliced Madeira cake had been consumed, Lehrer emerged into the afternoon sun now fully cognisant of the true passions at play within the community. He had witnessed Patrick Lawner's own operations room and spent some time scrolling through the man's action group website.

The extensive range of evidential photographs had been both enlightening and thoroughly disheartening. Had he thought some of those exchanges on Twitter left little to the imagination, so too did some of the abuse that the older man had suffered at the hands of aggressive bloggers who had dumped their venomous bile all over his screen with worrying regularity, and for many years to boot.

He had even picked up on the bizarre tale of local residents on one side of the motorbike divide threatening others in their immediate locale. One crazy old girl, with delusions seemingly well beyond her true status in life, had taken it upon herself to badger local residents and parish council members with intrusive, threatening telephone calls during which she would shriek down the line, "We can make it difficult for you in the community you know!" It turned out that her grandson was one of the offending riders who would travel out from Kirston village to see her in her remote and rather dilapidated cottage via a complex network of illegal routes across the Briary and Woodstone Fells. In essence it had been a cry for help in the face of potential calamity. The spectre of loneliness had driven her to combat directly those determined to rid the fells of the mechanised vandals; such an outcome would curtail her grandson's trips considerably.

Had he doubted the gravity of Lakeland society's behavioural challenges, or of its dire financial position after years of dwindling recreational revenues, Lehrer came away with an even sharper focus on the urgent need to tackle the problem, even if that demanded radical solutions.

He also headed back to base, down that same rough track, with clarity on the subject of information spillage from within. Mitch hadn't been protecting himself when dodging the DCI's earlier interrogation, but he had clearly known the source of the leak, and he had certainly known of its deliberate and calculated nature. The conundrum the DCI was left to chew over rested on the inquisitive line back to his own superiors. He could readily appreciate that negative publicity in the business world may very easily equate to glorification of a superstar sportsman in the eyes of the less discerning trail bike community. Keeping the star's arrest quiet could have prevented a wave of copycat misdemeanours. On the other hand, the value of exposing a global brand to legal censure and vilifying criticism could so easily have been used to turn the tide against the culprits *en bloc* while simultaneously getting the supportive elements of the public onside. Lehrer felt bemused and uneasy. Was there something else going on in the background? Could it really be that his senior ranks had been bought off with corporate money? Didn't the injunction do the trick in the end, or was there more to it? Had local politics or even national and international politics, come to think of it, facilitated or even enjoyed the greasing of palms? As he reached tarmac again, Lehrer wondered just what he'd got himself into with his move north. It looked like time for hard hats and sandbags, and maybe even a mine-detector for the office.

Before the end of the week, both Chief Superintendent Campbell and Chief Constable Minton felt compelled to face the media together. It was a prosaic, lacklustre performance at best. The two looked distinctly uncomfortable, appeared to lack a real grasp of the task force investigation underway, and took fright when questions were prompted by journalists from the national news networks.

Fortunately they were at least able to promise a degree of imminent success following the terrible display of mob violence which had marred the previous weekend. It got them off the hook. They gave away no meaningful details, but they reported with honesty and relief that progress was indeed being made. It proved a useful distraction from the earlier shooting. The infinitely more serious crime still retained its own secrets, much to the evident frustration of the entire team.

DI Young and DS Sutton had returned from their respective calls to the activity centres at High Nibthwaite and Graythwaite with almost identical reactions. Each outdoor pursuit team had consisted of five male trainers, all in their late twenties or early thirties. All had grudgingly admitted that they were aware of their counterparts at the opposing school, but everyone had denied any form of familiarity or close working relationship. They all had reasonable alibis, but all of those appeared to be the same; namely that they were cleaning and tidying up their equipment and tackle, but they couldn't put forward any third-party witnesses to validate their claims. Such activities on a weekend changeover day were entirely credible, but for nobody else at each centre to have seen any of them doing their chores at the specified times had seemed a little odd. With domestic cleaners, office administrators and kitchen staff hustling to and fro, surely someone would have clocked at least one of their outdoor trainers, but no. More than anything, the visiting police teams had been struck by the feeling that the tale was too simplistic and too tight, and, more to the point, the lads had seemed undeniably defensive in their exchanges with their inquisitors.

When pushed a little further it had also transpired that due to withering demand, redundancies were on the cards. If, as was believed, the impact of the biker plague really was beginning to deplete active participation in this and so many other forms of outdoor pursuit, then surely the detectives had uncovered a potential motivation for the violent attack of the previous Saturday. That too seemed a bit of a stretch, but a justifiable one. Revenge was always a powerful inspiration.

The force would be returning the very next day with adequate warrants. They felt sure that phone records would link the two groups, but in addition the forensic team had come up trumps with two unexpected traces: one strand of coarse dark hair which they had located on the wrecked Mercedes van where it had snagged on the edge of the shattered windscreen, and a mucus sample on the road surface close to where the badly beaten victims had been recovered. The casualties were still in no fit state to assist the police further, but their own DNA had been eliminated from the two samples recovered at the crime scene. Young and Sutton reported a growing confidence that the young PC's hunch about the High Nibthwaite training centre was about to prove invaluable. DCI Lehrer had of course passed this on to his senior rankers just before they faced the press. It probably did the trick. They had scraped through, only just, on the basis of the upbeat mood they were able to project towards the end of their difficult session.

21

stalked by the stork

By the end of July Gilly suspected that she might be pregnant. Her periods had always been irregular, but she really was quite late, and she didn't feel right in herself. She'd been pregnant enough times, albeit some time ago, to believe that her slight sense of disorientation and morning queasiness were vaguely symptomatic of something rather serious. She simply didn't know who the father might be and she cursed herself for not having been more careful. Initially she suspected that she only had a choice of two, neither of them being her husband. However, after pegging back through her diary she was hugely relieved to discover that Keith might in fact be the father. Their last physical encounter may not have been up to much, but it did, after all, fit neatly into the prospective timeframe.

Reflecting on that educative analysis she realised with complete surprise that she was delighted. It wasn't that her husband's potential paternity actually got her off the hook, no, it was that she was thrilled with the prospect of having a baby after all these years. She wondered how Keith would react. It certainly wasn't something they, or she more to the point, had planned. Surely her time for family making had passed. She fretted momentarily about the boys and their reactions, but then quickly counselled herself that they would be delighted for her. For them, in a practical day-to-day sense, it would impinge only rarely on their independent lifestyles. Then she allowed herself the potentially troubling melancholy of Alice's perceived opinion. As her eyes glazed and she fought back the tears, she could only hope that Alice would understand, that she'd be pleased for her mother, and that she wouldn't be jealous of a new baby who would naturally absorb all of her mother's attention.

But she sat back with a smile and thought, well, why not? She acknowledged the near perfect family environment around her, putting aside her own extra-curricular activities which of course would cease. She conceded that she certainly had the free time to commit to such an important and exciting new development. Then she thought she should go to the pharmacy and get a tester kit before she got carried away with it all.

Her sons had done their working stints and scraped some money together for their trekking exploits. They had been gone less than a week. Ben hadn't reappeared, as had been their original plan two months earlier. She hadn't really noticed, and now, well, somehow it just didn't appear all that important. She wondered how she'd react if he appeared at the back door one morning.

Then she remembered Henrietta and speculated as to her reaction to the good news, if indeed it turned out to be more than just a phantom pregnancy. She hadn't seen Henrietta for a few weeks, but she knew Keith had been to see his sister once or twice at her flat in Ambleside. Perhaps it was better that way round, although to be fair, the girl did appear to be more optimistic these days and was certainly easier to be with.

By the end of August Gilly Salcombe knew that not only was she pregnant, but also that she was close to her critical twelve-week term. Her pregnancy test kit had been very positive, but she'd then taken herself off to her GP and confirmation had followed very quickly thereafter.

She knew she'd have to tell her husband, Keith, before very much longer. She'd have to hide a growing bump fairly soon, so that wouldn't do. Overall she felt happy and relaxed about it. She'd even driven down to the cemetery again to kneel at Alice's grave and pour out her innermost thoughts to the marble headstone, and of course, to reassure her spiritual daughter that she could never be replaced in her mother's heart, not even by a new infant.

She had worked out something of a revelation plan for Keith one Sunday morning. They sat in the kitchen supping coffee and chatting over the Sunday papers. Gilly waited for the most comfortable break in their thread before dropping down from one of the high stools and crossing to sit down next to Keith on the new kitchen sofa. She placed her hand on his and gently assisted him in closing the broadsheet in which he was immersed. He looked at her quizzically. It was mid-morning. He wondered what was going on.

She wasted no time in asking him how he might feel about having another baby. After nearly choking on his coffee he turned towards her and looked at her more intently. He tried to gauge any apparently mischievous humour in her eyes, but quickly decided there was none in evidence. He then took her steady gaze to signify something more earnest and he looked up at the kitchen clock while assessing the likelihood of sex before a Sunday lunch. That would be rare indeed. He questioned her about her motives; another baby at her age? Was that what she really wanted? He agreed with her that perhaps she needed more to do with her time, but that was hardly adequate justification for bringing a newborn into the world, a child, he pointed out, who would only reach the current ages of their boys and therefore a degree of independence when she herself would be sixty and close to drawing her pension. She slipped smoothly round some of these counters and tried hard not to show any irritation at his negative posturing.

She talked about the boys, one now revelling in the heady cosmopolitan atmosphere of Toulouse, the other hitching rides through Patagonia, and she expressed her joy at the exciting futures that lay before them. But they were close to living their own independent lives and she was being left behind. He sympathised of course, but he acknowledged that perhaps the paternal bond was something of a looser affair than the limpet philosophy of some loving mothers, and he cautioned her for the need to give the young lads, fast becoming men, space in which to mature. In saying as much he had, involuntarily of course, helped to bolster her claim that she had the emotional capacity and the physical resources about her to commit herself to motherhood afresh.

He tiptoed metaphorically into the realm of their loved and lost little girl, wanting merely to check on the relevant drivers in that particularly sensitive chamber of her obviously broken heart, but he quickly ascertained that there was no substitution theory at play. That, he had always feared, would be a disastrous psychology to pursue.

When she reached the point at which she thought the notion was beginning to find a place to settle in his own mind, she then leaned forward, took both his hands in hers, and kissed him gently. He looked a little perplexed, but then she declared the truth as simply and as sincerely as she could manage. She didn't take her eyes from his for the duration of her confession. He huffed and sighed, and leaned back into the corner of the sofa as if capitulating to the inevitable. As he did so tears welled in his eyes and he looked down at their hands in embarrassment. Gilly pulled him up and hugged him tightly as the two of them wept quietly, each wondering what lay in store as such a momentous new chapter in their lives was about to unfold.

A harsh knock on the back kitchen door arrested their emotional clutch, and they each looked up, bleary-eyed, to see young Ben from next door clearly visible through the glass.

A surge of anxiety immediately rushed up from her feet and she felt the blood pressure pulsing in her neck. She hadn't seen him for three months – well, not like this, not at the back door. And Keith was right here next to her and not at the quarry; so many Sunday mornings had been lost to that gaping great pit, but not this Sunday morning. Oh my God, she thought. What will I say? She leapt up from the sofa visibly agitated. She moved quickly towards the door muttering something of a perplexed question; whatever could he want, or words to that effect. As she neared the door however, she realised that Ben was not alone. There, just a little to one side, stood Henrietta sporting a relaxed and beaming smile. When Gilly commented over her shoulder that her sister-in-law was also outside with Ben, it prompted a similarly fitful response as Keith jumped up out of the deep comfy chair and made haste to catch up with his wife.

They opened the door together, their faces adorned with the most comically bemused frowns that their visitors immediately laughed and asked them what on earth was wrong.

"Nothing, no," Gilly stammered, "nothing at all. What gives you that idea?"

"You look like you've just been caught with your hand in the biscuit tin, Gilly," Henrietta grinned.

"Sorry?" she responded, even more confused.

"You know...that diet you were telling me about?"

"Oh that, yes," she faltered, "I mean...no, no I haven't," and then she realised that she was taking the wheeze far too seriously.

"Oh dear," Henrietta mocked in commiseration at her sister-in-law's misplaced gravity. "We haven't come at a bad time?" she asked plaintively of her brother, whose face peered over his wife's shoulder with a matching look of mild consternation.

"Er, no, not at all," he threw back in an attempt to dispel his visitors' apparent hesitancy. "Come on in, come in," he urged, stepping back into the room and tugging on Gilly's elbow to clear the doorway. "This is a surprise, and er, well...to what do we owe this unexpected pleasure?"

Henrietta looked a little coy and turned to Ben, by her side. She smiled up at him, but she looked uncertain, as if waiting for his lead, or maybe just a prompt. He returned her gaze with a warm smile, but then folded his arms across his chest and looked down to the floor, a clear sign that this was her call and her lead. Gilly's eyes flicked frantically from Henrietta to Ben and back again as a welling instinct told her that something momentous was about to spill out into her very own kitchen. Keith looked increasingly confused, and he looked at his little sister with a soft affectionate smile, just hoping that nothing too serious was about to unfold.

"We have news," Henrietta began.

"Ah, right," Gilly mumbled, still trying to engage with Ben, but he avoided eye contact.

"Well, don't sound so excited, whatever you do," Henrietta teased.

"Sorry, Hen. Sorry, love," Gilly effused apologetically. "What is it? Come on, do tell," she urged with rising incentive. Henrietta paused as she tried to order her practised delivery.

"We are getting married," she said quickly, and then looked at her listeners with a wide grin. "Isn't it fantastic?" she suggested gleefully, flicking back a strand of hair, eyes darting from one to the other.

The older couple looked truly speechless. A crashing silence descended upon them and for a couple of seconds they stood mute before the younger pair. Suddenly Keith clapped his hands together in mock celebration, declared his obvious shock and pleasant surprise, and stepped forward to engulf his sister in a warm heartfelt embrace. As he clung to her, the two siblings missed the telegraphy of betrayal which leapt from Gilly to her young lover as his sheepish, guilty smile met her bewildered searching gaze.

Gilly quickly commandeered her own confused expression, as her husband released his own sister from his enveloping arms, transferred her to an arm's length appreciation and then kissed her gently on both cheeks. Then he stepped to the side and clasped the younger man's hand firmly, offering the warmest of congratulations. He slapped the lad on the shoulder with his free hand and applauded him for his romantic agility. Gilly and Henrietta hugged each other too, as a trickle of teardrops were smeared together cheek to cheek in fond celebration.

The questions gushed forth: how long had they been seeing each other? What had they planned? When was the big day to be? What sort of wedding, and where? Where would they live? Keith invited them over to the soft chairs, and then he scuttled off to get some champagne from the cellar.

As they toasted the happy new couple, Gilly began to settle into the new order. Had she not already made such a critical decision, this news would only have tipped her into the right frame of mind to accept her husband as the father of the new and growing foetus inside her. No one would ever know for certain, but of course, it was the most natural fit, a solution which worked from every perspective. She began to relax. She began to understand why Ben hadn't been knocking on the back door of late. Yes, she thought, it had been an understandable distraction, this pretty younger woman whose sulking depression had been magically banished over recent weeks. Now it all made sense. She sipped only tentatively at her glass of bubbly.

They learned that the wedding would be a very quiet affair; just Ben's family, the two of them of course, and their lads if they wanted to attend, and a few close friends. But they learned also that the civic ceremony would take place very soon. It was the end of August and the soon-to-be newlyweds wanted to be hitched before the end of September. Raised eyebrows and commensurate sarcasm was rebuffed when Ben put the urgency down to the demands of the farm during the autumn period. They wanted to get moved into his modest but comfortable quarters on-site before the new season's workload ramped with fencing, walling, worming and putting the rams to the ewes across his extensive flock. Gilly cracked the obvious joke about the tupping season for young farmers too, all the while fixing Ben with a steely stare, but he brushed off the sarcasm and continued to outline their short-term plans. Henrietta also sipped modestly at her glass of golden fizz.

They confessed that they hadn't yet found the courage to inform his parents of their new and exciting prospects, and in fact, they were due round to the farm next. Henri would continue with her job in Ambleside, and one of her first tasks would be to balance the sale of her small flat there against its use as a holiday rental property. She wasn't looking forward to the regular commute, but she hadn't doubted for a second that all of it would be so very worth it, and at this girlish admission she leaned over to her hunky younger man and kissed him. Ben flushed a full crimson and looked shyly away.

The close gathering began to turn up the volume as they laughed and chatted through the excitement of new domestic circumstances. In the end, and despite Keith's tactical introduction of coffee, Henrietta simply couldn't contain herself for a minute longer.

"There is more news, actually," she blurted out with adolescent excitement.

"Go on," her brother encouraged warily.

"No surprises really," she grinned, "but you were right about those young farmers," and she poked Ben hard in the ribs. "September wedding because we are, of course, pregnant," she announced dramatically.

Keith just stared blankly. Gilly literally choked and only just managed to contain her coffee as she spewed it back into her wide cup. Now it was Ben's turn to examine the truth in her eyes, but she flashed a forgiving smile back to him before leaning forward with kisses and hugs for each of them.

"Do you know," she started, and she glanced at Keith who nodded his advocacy in return, "you're not the only ones with very important news this morning." She patted her tummy with the flat of her hand and offered a conspiratorial grin to her sister-in-law.

"No, you're kidding?" screeched Henrietta, as Ben's quizzical expression could have frozen his face for all eternity. "Are you really? Are you pregnant as well?" Henrietta pressed.

"Yes," Gilly nodded excitedly. "I'm still short of twelve weeks, but I think it's going to be okay." She welled up. Keith held her hands tightly on her knees. Henrietta kneeled forward by the coffee table and wrapped her arms around Gilly's shoulders. She squeezed hard and the two girls cried some more. Ben sat back in his chair and made a conscious decision to take these new arrangements precisely as they were. Life had been running along pretty well of late. Now it was simply getting better.

22

outwardly bound

Also by the end of August Lehrer's task force had begun to make in-roads to their many problems. The two sets of 'outward bounders' had succumbed to the unerring accuracy of modern forensic analysis; one member of each group relinquished a direct match to the unavoidable mark of DNA chemistry. Phone records dragged others into the violent conspiracy and before they knew it the entire group was in custody and facing much more serious charges than any of them had ever imagined. It may have been the case that the three victims of their shameful attack were now well on the way to good recoveries – only the worst-off remained in hospital – but Lehrer cleverly let it be known that he favoured an attempted murder plea and released as much to the press. Within the offensive mob there reigned an atmosphere of remorseful panic as they were left to stew in the prospect of a very public trial and very lengthy sentences. In such intimidating circumstances their unity began to crumble, kept as they were on remand and scattered across three different secure centres. Finding it impossible to maintain uniform stories the truth leached out in such a way as to incriminate three leading individuals for the more egregious aspects of the assaults. Lehrer hadn't thought for a realistic second that such a charge would be approved via the CPS, but, as ideas went, its flotation not only dissolved the solidarity of the defendants, but it also began to erode the confidence with which other self-professed countryside vigilantes had begun to take the law into their own hands.

The Low Nibthwaite attack had encouraged a rash of similar skirmishes throughout the August summer holiday period. Fortunately for Lehrer and the task force, many of these were easily and quickly dealt with. The DCI could at least point to a growing number of positive scores when grilled by his ethereal chief super, who drifted around the edges of the squad rarely offering insight or support, but often emanating the critical rancour of a man under career pressure.

The incidence of confrontations began to slide. The force was beginning to feel that it might be winning. However, the murder investigation continued to frustrate them.

Police work may rely on repetitive research processes and much attention to detail, but the results of such work often adhere to the philosophy of swings and roundabouts; no sooner had the attacks on motorbikers (provoking some equally violent retaliations, it had to be said) begun to ease off, the numbers of two-wheeled invaders surged again. As investigations continued into the early autumn it began to appear as if the scourge of rural vandalism had rebounded to its previously antagonistic levels.

23

trial by trail

Morgan had only taken the job after rooting around in those old warehouses on more than one occasion. He'd reasoned that the risks associated with breaking and entering the premises, through the ropy old chain-link fence, were minimal. If he got caught he'd probably only get a warning from a local copper about the inherent dangers of quarries in general. The fact that he'd discovered the place quite literally by accident when out on his beloved Kawasaki had convinced him that secluded access via the old railway track would be just about perfect. Getting the job hadn't been difficult. It may have been a bit of a step down in status, but he was earning ordinary money at the time despite his long hours in more conventional employment. He'd long ago assimilated the knowledge and practical skills required to make the *White Magic*. His search for suitable premises in which to build his simple but effective production laboratory had come to an end on that fortuitous day.

Once on the inside it hadn't taken him long to measure the lax security arrangements and to fathom the necessary routines and protocols to get supply, production and delivery underway. His London contact had taken some convincing. He'd won him over in the end when he allowed him to try the product in the men's toilets of the Killington Lake Services high on the Shap Fell section of the M6. The deal had been struck there and then, but Morgan had recognised the necessity of tying in some influential though hopefully protective guardians who could smooth his passage along the delivery routes as required. The chairman, Austen, had been startled by his approach but bought in quickly. He promised to get a fixer high up in the local constabulary, and until quite recently that had worked well. The Feds had stayed well clear of the open fells despite the growing number of illegal bands of visiting bikers. Christ, he could have done without that escalation. On the other hand, it offered a natural camouflage for his supply routes through the countryside.

It had always appeared prudent to him to keep distribution away from the main roads. Quarry trucks offered an enticing mule train out to civilisation from the Lakes, and he knew he'd have to use that outlet to some extent as production grew. But there would come a time, if output matched expectations, when external parties would come sniffing around; law enforcement or dangerous competitors on the other side of his London fence. Two-wheeled transport in difficult terrain allowed him, and his able sidekick Stevie, to retain personal control.

Stevie too had been a walkover – nothing to lose. Keith, the boss of the place, had been very shaky from the start, but Morgan had assessed some form of high-level control on-site as an important characteristic of the plan. He'd kept the two senior men in the dark for some time about the other's involvement. However, when Austen Smiley had advised the need for a bit of clout at ground level, only then did Morgan confess that Keith had already been deployed. Keith still knew nothing about the scale of the overall team beyond Morgan himself and Stevie, the latter still naively believing that the scam was just for the two bikers themselves.

In recent weeks the frequency of their drops had begun to slide. Keith's stress levels had reached permanent overflow and Morgan had been avoiding the man whenever possible.

Together Morgan and Stevie had watched the recent news reports with mounting apprehension. The changes taking place across the countryside were obvious to them. The shooting earlier in the summer had been a real shock, but they'd judged it to be an isolated revenge attack of some sort. But when gangs of thugs had started ambushing bikers with growing regularity, and seemingly beyond the reach of the law, they had begun to worry. It wasn't the risk of suffering such an assault, no, that wasn't their concern. They believed themselves nimble enough to be able to stay clear of such rampant aggression. It was the reaction from the police. Their increased presence across the region was undeniable. They'd even introduced trail bike pursuit teams. Both Morgan and his accomplice had witnessed racing police bikes on several occasions. They'd only just been smart enough to peel off from the bigger groups they'd been riding with to avoid the potentially messy business of being hunted down and probably arrested while loaded with small compact packs of their extremely valuable cargo. Still, despite the evidently increasing peril attached to their cross-country endeavours, they had at least maintained some form of supply stream. Their customers had let it be known through their carefully groomed pickups that production quotas were below their agreed targets. They understood the issues, but they expected fulfilment. Tensions had been rising steadily, and Keith Salcombe's histrionics had not proven helpful. The size of the prize maintained keen focus. They were raking it in. If only Keith Salcombe had understood the true scale of the scheme overall. But he hadn't, and still didn't, and that was almost certainly a good thing.

Young Stevie had discovered an audacious route eastward skirting Grizedale and dropping down close to the Sawreys, and then directly onto the Windermere ferry. He'd been out on a Sunday morning blast with a bunch of local mates. Racing round the tight bend in the road and straight up the flat ramp of the Windermere ferry, as one of a roaring band of nine riders, had just been fabulous. Of course they got the usual snooty stares from drivers and foot passengers alike, but they'd taken over the flat deck of the hawser-drawn craft and fended off critical glances with bold abandon.

Half way across the water it dawned on him – what perfect camouflage. Make sure the number plate is attached and visible before the final approach on the tarmac, and who could raise any objection? If asked about the heavy mud coating on the machines, just bluff it out. Who could be in a position to gainsay any fabricated claim about where they'd been, or what they'd been up to? For a lone biker, perhaps on a weekday ride – even one who had taken the trouble to clean his bike up before returning to the legal highway – well, what could go wrong? So he'd decided to include the crossing in his next delivery run.

Morgan had checked the weather reports carefully and the two of them agreed the dates and times of their next two drops. Collection was coordinated. Everything was in place and Morgan took the first run.

The old ring-fenced gate arrangement to the rear of the site led out into an overgrown screening thicket, and from there a narrow cinder track quickly found the flat ballast bed of the former mine railway line. After he'd secured the gate with the old rusty chain and pressed home the weighty padlock through the links, Morgan threw a leg over the idling Kawasaki KX450 and took a quick scan of the site perimeter before throttling gently away into the bushes. He wore a shallow rucksack firmly bound over his shoulders and tightly clipped across chest and waist.

The backpack comprised two separate compartments in which he usually carried an inoffensive mix of odds and ends which would pass muster if his bag were ever searched. Close to his back and in a cleverly concealed lining to the bag he'd carefully inserted eight vacuum sealed plastic bags, six down the back and two under the base of the rucksack. Each contained an off-white crystalline powder of enviable purity. As the poor man's heroin, this quality of synthetic amphetamine or crystal meth was highly sought after by dealing syndicates up and down the country. In the bigger cities where sophisticated networks thrived on mass distribution, the quality of his product had channelled Morgan's supply lines into some of the most avaricious and sickeningly violent drug gangs in London. His price was high, but demand just continued to rise.

As he put some distance between himself and the quarry he steadily began to increase his pace. His drop would take place in a lay-by just off the Carnforth junction of the M6. The merchandise would be taken south from there by minibus on this occasion. He knew his contact from experience. He foresaw no problems, but he knew he'd have to be alert at all times, especially with the increased police numbers in the area.

He headed south, skirted the village of Abbots Reading and cut up through the woods to approach the River Leven crossing at Backbarrow from the north. Climbing again he tugged on the throttle and powered up and over Bigland Barrow and veered in the direction of Lindale, employing a testing mix of muddy tracks and minor roads. It was early, not even breakfast time for most folk, and he estimated that steady speeds and low engine noise were his safest bets when on level ground and near habitation. The autumn mists clung to the contours of the land and helped to hide his progress. The stunning autumn colours swathing the awakening countryside were entirely lost on him as he concentrated hard on his route. His chunky Bridgestone tyres ripped up the soft ground beneath him as he pushed anxiously onward.

From the outskirts of Lindale he took a cross-country stretch to Low Meathop village and then rounded Meathop Hall and accelerated out to the open marshland by the Kent estuary. His judgement of the Morecambe Bay tides had been perfect. With the waters out and the great sandy reach beckoning, he crossed the flats directly to Sandside and Arnside. He stuck closely to the coastal paths around Silverdale before yielding to the Warton Marshes which he circumnavigated inland and then pushed on towards Carnforth.

The drop took just a couple of minutes, as the packages were secreted into a purpose-built cavity in the driver's door of the bus. Barely a word was spoken. The bus drove off and headed directly to the M6. Morgan headed north and thought he might try a slightly more circuitous and certainly more challenging course home.

Two days later it was Stevie's turn, but this time the drop-off point was further north, back at Killington Lake Services. He was determined to try the Windermere ferry crossing, and he set off on familiar tracks for Finsthwaite, past the waters at High Dam, and turning north on the minor road towards High Stott Park. He dipped off-road again into Bark House Wood and Bishop Wood towards the ferry ramp on Windermere's western shore. These were familiar trails indeed, with some racy stretches, and he hit the gas and shouted for joy inside his visor as the chill morning air rushed past his leather-clad form. The entire run was thrilling. Not once did he feel threatened, and he encountered no difficulties in entering the services lorry park via a hopelessly inadequate security barrier from the narrow country lane beyond. The drop was simplicity itself – the goods were quickly transferred from one rucksack to another. His only exchange with his counterpart revealed an expectation for two identical runs on the same two days of the following week, at the same times and in precisely the same places. This was not unusual in terms of previous delivery schedules, but Stevie swallowed his irritation and pointed out that there were unpredictable obstacles to be overcome in the current, sensitive climate. They would do their best, but nothing could be guaranteed. His contact had merely offered to pass his comment up the chain of command, and then he'd sloped off to a waiting express coach to London – perfect cover.

The following week brought with it a shift in the weather as the rains returned with some persistency. The two riders knew instinctively that bad weather only enhanced their vulnerability. It wasn't that their Yamaha and

Kawasaki machines couldn't cope. On the contrary, that dynamic blend of high-tech power and skilful daring embraced the deteriorating weather with glee. The bigger the test, the more fun was to be had. However, many riders avoided the wet. Those without suitably weather-proof kit just got soaked very early in the day, leaving the remainder as an uncomfortable experience. Wet weather days tended to reduce numbers drastically. Morgan and Stevie knew they would be more noticeable as rare, lone bikers out there in the drizzle. Their peripheral radar would have to be carefully attuned.

Morgan's delivery run took longer, mainly because of the poor visibility, but he'd factored that in, and everything worked smoothly.

Stevie knew he'd have to take it a little more slowly on his favoured speed runs, but he set off early, as had Morgan two days earlier. The water on the tarmac seemed to flow like a seething brook as he tanked it up from Finsthwaite. When he turned off into woodland he had to drop a gear or two to maintain traction in the sopping dead leaves and churning mud. Descending into a hollow in Bishop Wood he almost sank to a sludgy stop as his front forks compressed forward at the bottom of the incline, but he just managed to throttle back, shift down again and then chug up to the top of the ridge and to firmer ground.

The unseen projectile smashed through his visor, blasted most of his cranium through the back of his helmet and projected his vanquished frame clear from the moving Yamaha almost instantaneously. The overwhelming power of the assault dumped his lifeless form out of sight on the slippery slope beyond the ridge he'd just crested. The trail bike grumbled on for a few metres, was held up by the dense and waning ferns, and then simply keeled over and was engulfed by the greenery. Shortly thereafter a dark figure emerged from the trees further down the track and walked silently towards the scene of young Stevie's horrible demise.

Two days of unremitting desperation for Morgan drove him eventually up the metal steps to Keith Salcombe's office. He bashed a flat hand on the managing director's door and walked straight in, much to the surprise of Keith, his junior assistant Jason, and his secretary, engrossed as they were in a review of transport expenses. It took just one annoyed glance up from the paperwork for Keith to immediately appreciate that something was terribly wrong. The auxiliaries needed no second bidding and left the two men to their obviously pressing agenda. Morgan closed the door firmly behind them, but suspected that the secretary remained within earshot just down the corridor.

He turned hastily to the senior man and whispered forcefully, "Big problems, boss – I think they might be on to us."

"What?" Keith exploded, and Morgan urged him to hush just in case they were being ear-wigged by the girl beyond the door. "What's happened?" Keith whispered, real panic flashing across his features.

"It's Stevie. He's either gone AWOL or he's missing in action. Either way I just can't reach him."

"What?" Keith asked again. "Since when – how long's he been missing?"

"Two days. He made an early morning drop over in Shap. Well, I should say that he set out to make that drop, but my contacts tell me he never made it. I haven't seen him since the previous evening when I gave him the cargo. I haven't been able to raise him by phone or even by text."

"Jesus Christ," Keith sighed, his sense of trepidation rising quickly inside. "What could have happened? I mean…where could he be? Has he been missing before…you know, when you just haven't told me?"

"No, don't be daft!"

"Well I don't know, Morgan, for fuck's sake. He could be anywhere. What about his mates, his family, anybody like that?"

"That's just it, boss. I've put in a few calls but got blanks at every turn. Nobody's seen him for a bit. More to the point…" and he waited for the impact he knew it would have, "his mum is just about crawling up the walls."

"Oh, of course, he lives at home doesn't he?"

"Yeah, and his mum is going to call the police in the next twenty-four hours, I'd say. I've managed to get her to hold off for these last two days, but she won't hold out much longer."

"Shit, Morg, if she does that we are well and truly stiffed."

"You don't say, man. The thought had crossed my mind, you know."

"Okay, okay, sorry, but what the hell are we gonna do? What options do we have?"

"Not many, to be frank. But the good news…"

"Good news," Keith erupted again, "good news," he sneered. "Do please tell me the good news. I do so need cheering up."

"Well think about it, for fuck's sake, and get a hold of yourself," Morgan spat back with venom. "If he'd been arrested I think we could guarantee that the boys in blue would have been round here already, and that clearly hasn't happened."

"That's true enough," the older man conceded, "but that almost asks more questions than we have answers for. If he hasn't been arrested, where the hell is he?"

"We shouldn't discount the idea of a bad crash, especially in the conditions he had to deal with the other day. He might be lying injured out there, or even worse…" and he let the awful conclusion hang in the air.

"Do you know the route he was going to take?" Keith pleaded.

"Yes, but I took a quick skim over the early section to Windermere ferry this morning, and there was nothing. I think most of his intended route from the ferry was on minor roads and I can't help thinking that someone would have spotted him by now if he'd taken a slide."

"Has he missed any shifts here, at work?"

"Oh bloody hell, boss, is that all you're bothered about?"

"No, just shut it, Morg. I didn't mean it like that. I was wondering who else might have missed him apart from you and his mother."

"Ah, righto, that's fair enough, yes," Morgan admitted. "He missed a full shift yesterday and he'll miss another later today. The lads know he wasn't in yesterday, but I said he had the old Delhi belly and would surely be back in today."

"So, tongues are going to wag soon enough then."

"No doubt about that, boss."

"And if we don't do something soon, we may well look pretty suspect if the police get ahead of us and we haven't reported him missing from work."

"Yeah, good point," Morgan agreed.

"Hey, have you tried checking the local hospitals, you know, accident and emergency intakes, that sort of thing?" Keith prompted with some optimism.

"No dice – checked 'em all, nothing relevant."

"Damn it! Is he on any of these new messaging services...er, what do you call them...er, social networks or something?"

"You mean social media?"

"That's it. What do you think?"

"We're both on Facebook, but no, there's been no sign of him on there either. He certainly hasn't contacted me or responded to my messages."

"Fuck it, Morgan. I think we have to go to the rozzers, but first we have to clear that lab of yours."

"What? No way! That's not the deal. That's not how we planned events like this. We just have to keep them well away from those old sheds."

They heard the clacking footsteps outside as someone mounted the metal stairway. Then they heard a muffled exchange in the secretary's office next door, followed by bold steps along the corridor behind them. She knocked on the door and slowly opened it. She looked disparagingly at Morgan and then beyond him to the managing director.

"Mr Salcombe, I have a special delivery package here for you which must be signed for. It's DHL, but they won't accept my signature for some reason. It has to be yours. It's addressed to you personally."

"Bit odd," Keith replied. "Pass it over then."

She handed it to Morgan who stalled momentarily with the package in hand, and then reached over to Keith with the jiffy bag between finger and thumb. Keith signed the delivery note and the girl left to get it straight back to the courier.

Keith unzipped the bag with a deft pull of its red plastic cord. He pulled out a flat rectangular package in blue plastic with an air-tight seal. Morgan gasped as he recognised his own merchandise. Keith looked up at his petrified accomplice. Turning anxiously back to the empty bag, he ripped open the attached delivery notice and then flattened the folded note openly on the desk with the palm of his hand.

NO MORE OF THIS STUFF
FIRST AND LAST WARNING
REMEMBER – YOUR LITTLE YAMAHA FRIEND
HAD NO SUCH WARNING

"No, no, Jesus Christ no," whimpered Keith Salcombe.

"Is he dead? Is Stevie dead do you think?" Morgan spluttered miserably.

"I don't know, I mean…how the hell should I know, for fuck's sake? Maybe they've got him."

"Who, who's they?"

"Sod it, Morgan, how would I know?" Keith seethed. "I know one thing – we're done. It's all over. We clear that warehouse tonight – everything, not a trace left, the lot. Christ, they even know my name!"

"Shut it, you mug. It'll take more than one night to clear that kit out of there, and anyway that's not gonna happen. That's not the agreed plan, and you know it."

"Fuck you, Morgan, you mad bastard. It's too late. The police will be here in a day or so whatever we do. We can't take the risk."

"If you're right, then we need to control it from here. If we try operation wipe down we'll never get through it in time, and all the activity will leave too many signs that something's going on down there. We need to prepare for them coming here, and to control that process," Morgan insisted with increasing confidence. "We encourage Stevie's mum to make that missing person call, and we, meaning you of course, make that missing employee call. Then we sit and wait. They'll come. We'll handle it."

"How the hell are we gonna pull that off, Morgan, just tell me that?"

"Very calmly, boss, very calmly indeed. I'll trigger his poor old mum. You await my signal and then you make that call. Destroy this note and let me deal with the package."

He stretched his hand over the desk and picked up his own sealed packet. Then he turned and left, closing the door gently behind him.

24

Eric sees red

Eric chugged into the yard and parked the John Deere buggy close to the farmhouse kitchen door so that he could nip in for a warm-up beyond the reach of a robust and gusting autumn wind.

"Why them?" he pleaded over his brooding, mid-morning coffee. He turned the mug round and round in his big, dirty farmer's hands and stared hopelessly into the dark brew.

"What do you mean, love?" Ruby asked as she turned towards him, hands immersed in the warm water of the washing-up bowl.

"Them!" he grunted as he flicked a nod in the direction of the big house next door. "Why the bloody Salcombes, of all people?" he complained. "He could have married into a decent farming family from round here, couldn't he?" he opined plaintively.

"Oh come on, love. She's not a bad lass, I'd say. Pretty enough too."

"Pretty enough? For our lad? Do you really think so? I mean…she's alright, I suppose, but there must be nicer girls at Young Farmers I'd've thought."

"Eric Meaner, you know every farming family within ten miles of here. Most of them you don't like, you treat them all with suspicion, and you go out of your way to avoid having to socialise with them. So don't give me all that claptrap about pretty farmer's daughters just hanging off trees waiting for our Ben to come along. You know they don't exist. The best-looking girl anywhere near here is our shift cleaner, Katarina," she insisted with some confidence.

"What, the Polish girl?" he threw back at his wife with a quizzical frown.

"Yes, the Polish girl," Ruby retorted, fixing her husband with a dismissive stare. "The Polish girl," she repeated deliberately, "who works as hard as anyone I know. She does us proud every day she comes up here. She's a big-hearted lass that one, but she comes with her own, er... baggage, if you could call it that."

"How d'you mean?"

"Well, she has that little one of hers, doesn't she? Cute little thing," she added. "But that would have been too much responsibility for a lad like Ben. He's got enough on his plate here with the farm and all the other businesses."

"Dead right there, and what the bloody hell is little Miss Fancy Pants gonna be doing to help him out with all that then? Nothing, that's what," he hissed with derision. "Maybe you're right, maybe Katarina would have been a better bet."

"Eric, love, just listen to yourself. You make it sound like Ben had the pick of the fillies; all in his own time, whenever he was ready, like... well you know, like they were just lining up for his personal inspection or something."

"What do you mean? What's wrong with our boy then? You'd think a ready-made home and a business like this would be just what a young lass wanted, but oh no, not these days. It's all too much like hard work."

"Now just you stop it. There's nothing wrong with our Ben, and you know that's not what I'm saying, but he's still young. He was always shy with the girls. He'd barely even had a steady girlfriend. He just needed a bit more time."

"Aye well," he grumbled back into his coffee, "bit late for that now. She's here, moved in, and putting her nose in where it's not wanted."

"Enough!" Ruby insisted. "It must have been quite a challenge for her, rolling in here, an older woman – still young I know, but older than Ben – having to face the lad's parents to deliver a bolt from the blue like that."

"Yeah, a shotgun – great bloody start that was."

"Oh come on now, Eric, you know what she said. They were already planning to get married and things just, you know...got out of hand. It can happen to any young couple. I don't think it changed their plans at all."

"She trapped him, Ruby. Can't you see that?"

"That's rubbish," she said abruptly.

"Just because you can't see it doesn't mean it isn't the truth," he contested. "You were just selling him down the river a moment ago – too shy, needs to grow up, all that crap! Now look at him."

"You be quiet, Eric Meaner, or I'll take my rolling pin to you. They're happy together. You can see it. Even Katarina says so."

"Oh does she now? Well, that makes it okay then," he quipped.

"Don't be so damned cynical. He's our son. He needs our help, just like any lad would at this stage in his life." She looked over at him where he sat on the other side of the big farmhouse kitchen table. He seemed to have lost some of his confidence; he appeared perhaps diminished in some unfathomable way, and she smiled ruefully. "Look, love, it's different for us all now. We have to adopt a different approach, a fresher outlook, you know…think about them rather than us, that sort of thing. Don't you see?"

"Dead right," he grimaced. "And you can bet your boots she'll be round here more and more often," he muttered. "Just look at the way she's started. She's in here to see you every evening when you're trying to get the dinner on. Ben might expect her to be getting his dinner on while he's out on the quad tending to the ewes. And don't forget about *her*," he warned, casting another nod in the direction of their immediate neighbours. "She won't be able to keep her neb out, mark my words."

"Who, Gilly?"

"Yes, bloody Gilly, Mrs bloody Hob Nob," he alluded, sticking his nose in the air with a flick of a forefinger. "She'll be jamming her spanner into the works and wanting to know all our business. She'll be trying to push Ben around just like she used to try it on with me when they first got up here."

"Don't be daft, love," Ruby soothed.

"Oh it's daft, is it? D'you know, Ruby, I'd swear she thinks it's all a big game. She's got bugger all to do all day, and she's always chipping in with her bright ideas and her very important points of view. She sits there watching what we're all doing, trying to push us and pull us around to get things done the way she wants them to be done. She has no idea of seasonal priorities; it's all about how things look. You do realise she had another pop at me a couple of days ago about the forestry section? It's just too messy apparently. When friends or committee members come up to visit her in the big house she expects the land either side of the lane to look neater. Neater! Bloody hell, I mean what is she on?" he asked with evident irritation. "She's got no idea, not a clue, and that's why she'll be into our business through the back door."

"Give it a rest, love, please. You're sounding paranoid."

"That's just because you're blind to that woman's controlling tendencies," he asserted. "I swear she thinks the work ethic up here is for her to manage. Even when her own lads come back you can see a different phase of the managerial machine kick into action. She sits there pulling the strings to suit her own needs: builders, farmers, students, quarry owners and managers...you name it, she thinks we're all hers – her men on the hill, at her beck and call."

"I've heard enough of this, Eric..."

"I'm not bloody well kidding, Ruby. Mark my words. She'll have a finger in every pie before you know it – sodding Salcombes!"

"Eric, for goodness' sake, just wrap up. Gilly's not even a Salcombe. Think about it. She married Keith, that's all that makes her a Salcombe."

"Yes I realise that, but she'll be playing Ben through this lass... Henrietta, and you can't deny that *she's* definitely a bloody Salcombe. I wouldn't trust any of 'em, I'm telling you."

"Okay, okay, stop going on. You sound like a tape recorder...on and on and on with the same nonsense. Look," she commanded, "Henrietta is now our daughter-in-law. We must make her welcome and do our best for her and for Ben. I think she's trying really hard. You never know, she might turn out to be lovely even in your eyes. She might be just what he needs."

"Well don't hold your breath, that's all I would say. She's not going to be helping on the farm – almost certainly because she hasn't a clue about farming. She's heading off every day to Ambleside for that cushy estate agency job. I don't suppose she'll be mucking in during the long nights in the snow at lambing time, will she?" he posed defiantly.

"I don't know, Eric. As you say, she seems to like to come in here to see me when she gets home in the evening, but that's no bad thing. At least she's not spending her evenings alone in that flat or with Gilly and her brother, so you can't have it all ways. What's more, as you were once very good at sums, you might have worked out that by lambing time she'll be like a balloon and close to lambing herself! And as if that's not enough, she can't be around the sheep at that time. It's too dangerous. The risk of infection is too great – have you forgotten all of that from my time?"

"Sod it! Right again," he sighed in resignation.

"Hoy, don't you be so selfish. You're supposed to be glad that you're about to become a granddad – not much indication that our Rhona is going to beat her little brother to it after all."

"Well that's true enough, but when Henrietta stops working she'll either be in here getting under your feet or she'll be spending days at a time with Her Ladyship. If she's not getting her instructions from Mrs Lah-dee-dah, she'll be getting them from her big brother instead – Mr Corporate bloody Heavyweight. You can just see him tittle-tattling to his mate Austen Smiley about some of those development grants, or about that knackered septic tank."

"But didn't we fix the septic tank?" she implored.

"That was the old one," he replied in frustration. "The newer one's been seeping out for ages too – you know, the one for the caravans? Ben's trying to get some more cash out of Smiley's mates on the council."

"Oh, right," she said with some hesitation. "Maybe Henrietta can help with the paperwork," she suggested.

"Oh yeah, spot on, love. That'll pull a few strings," he replied sarcastically.

"Right, that's enough, you miserable old bugger. I was going to offer you more coffee, but that's forfeited now. Out you go, go on, out," she harried. "You have better things to do with your time, and if you come back later with the same face on it'll be dinner on an old tin plate in the barn for you...if you get any dinner at all."

He sighed as he stood and flipped his flat cap into place. Then he pushed his arms through the holes in his quilted sleeveless jacket – body protection against the colder seasonal temperatures – and then shuffled towards the door. As he lifted the latch and stepped out into the yard, Gilly's elderly tenants passed by with a wave and a cheery hello as they forged their way out onto the fells above the farm. He nodded and grunted something indecipherable as he climbed into his covered ranger, and then motored away down the lane.

Near the bottom of the track close to the road he rounded the last bend and immediately spotted Gilly's brawny Volvo loitering to one side of the gravel strip, with its offside tyres on the grass verge. Wisps of exhaust feathering into the cold air under the car declared that the engine was still ticking over. Eric could tell that Gilly was looking out and slightly down from the open driver's window, obviously in conversation with someone out of sight and below the level of the lane. He guessed it would be Ben. He'd expected to find him in the lower reaches as he'd had reports from those girls at the lodge about a couple of wayward ewes running loose among the trees in the plantation.

As he approached, Gilly looked skittishly in his direction. She turned back and forth erratically as she tried to make ready to continue up the hill to her home, but also to finish off the discourse with her counterpart below. She looked a little flustered, Eric surmised, as he squeezed his rock-hopper past the bulky frame of the car. As he drew to a halt behind it and looked back over his shoulder, he noted Ben and the dogs by his quad bike at the edge of the roadside wood. Gilly pressed hard on the accelerator and the Volvo lurched away homeward bound with a scourge of gravel and stones. Eric shook his head in quiet dismay. His demeanour needed little translation in her rear-view mirror.

He lumbered down the steep short bank to the stone wall below and looked across to his lad.

"What the bloody hell did Her Ladyship want?" he shouted into the trees.

"Oh nothing much, Dad, just chatting," Ben replied, bending down and making an exaggerated fuss of one of the Border Collies.

Father sensed his son's discomfort. "What d'you mean, just chatting? Since when did she ever give us the time of day other than when she wants something doing? Anyone would think she owned Rowan Tree Farm instead of Rowan House," he snorted with derision.

"Oh she's alright really, Dad," Ben retorted, desperately trying to think on his feet.

"Oh yeah? *Since when* is what I'd like to know." A statement rather than a question.

"Aw c'mon, Dad, she's probably just trying to be nice, you know, with me and Henri and all that."

"Aye well, maybe you're right," the older man huffed in disaffection. "That would fit, I suppose."

"How d'you mean?"

"Well, son, I can't imagine that an interfering cow like her sees her sister-in-law as anything other than a direct line of access to us and our business. That's what I mean."

"Eh? What are you getting at?" the son challenged with a hint of indignation.

"Hey, don't go all bloody dim on me now, lad. If you expect that lass of yours not to be put under pressure by that bloody awful woman, you can think again."

"Give over will you? Henri has married into our family not Gilly's. Why should it be a problem?"

"Huh…eh, lad," Eric shrugged, with another slow shake of his head. "You've done some great things here…some grand new ideas for the business, and I take my hat off to you. But you've got a lot to learn about women, if I'm any judge. You take care. I don't want to sow any seeds of doubt between you and your new wife. She's a nice enough lass, that's for sure, but if you think she's not close to her brother, and therefore her brother's other half, then think again."

"Give it a rest, Dad. I know you've been going on and on at Mum over this in recent weeks, and it isn't helpful, believe me. We've all got a lot on our plates right now, and that isn't going to change as we go through the winter. Henri is trying her best. You need to cut her some slack and give her a bit more trust and a lot more support."

"Oh do I indeed, really?" Eric blustered, embarrassed by a ticking off from his own son.

"Yeah, I'm serious."

"And there was I thinking a bit more support out here from my new daughter-in-law might be the least of my expectations," he muttered.

"Oh c'mon, Dad, she's got her own job to do, and she's pregnant," Ben objected.

"Yeah, and whose bloody stupid fault is that, I wonder?"

Ben bit his lip and quelled a rattling tirade just before it achieved the *comments to be regretted later* category – he was addressing his father after all. "Dad, you have to give her a chance. If you condemn her even by association, what chance will she have of ever getting things right with you?"

"Eh? What are you driving at?"

"Well, I mean...if her family connections to Gilly and Keith are enough to bar her from our inner circle she will never find a real home with us. Don't you see that?"

"What I do see is Mrs bloody Bossy Knickers sticking her oar in, that's what I see. I mean answer me truthfully, what did she want to talk to you about just now?"

Ben coloured a little and turned to the dogs to hide his reaction from his father. He stumbled through a couple of hasty options in his mind as he brought the three animals to heel. The charade wasn't lost on his father.

"She was just asking about the timber business, that's all," he offered, lamely.

"You see!" exploded the old man. "I knew it."

"No, no, nothing like that," the boy deflected. "She wasn't asking about the business itself, you know...facts and figures, profit and loss, that sort of stuff. She was just asking about the mess down here alongside the main entrance to the drive."

"Sorry? Are you pulling my wire, son? She was complaining about the mess? Did you tell her that this is a working bloody livestock farm? Did you mention the range of businesses we're running here? Did she give any indication that she has the faintest fucking notion of just how hard we're working on this fucking countryside titivation project?" He turned away, visibly fuming, and he struggled back up the grassy bank towards his mini-jeep. At the top he looked back down to Ben, pulled a wagging finger out of his jacket pocket and shouted, "Just be damned careful with that woman, that's all I'm saying. She'll have your lass ferreting through all sorts of stuff before you know it. We don't need our finances spread all over the county. There are too many nosy bastards round here who will be straight off to the grants office or even the sodding police if they ever get wind of just how and where we've used some of that funding."

"Dad, for God's sake, calm down," Ben shouted up to him.

"No, I won't calm down," father bellowed to son. "You don't know the half of it yet. I won't sit back and let that manipulating bitch get the better of us, and if you don't keep that girl of yours in order then I will."

"Oh, bloody marvellous – thanks for all your support, Dad," Ben yelled back. "I can always do this kind of work on my own farm you know. That way you won't have to worry about the business financials attached to all the different outlets we run nowadays. It's not just bloody sheep farming now, is it? You're not just dependent on a decent price for lamb or a few quid for a bag full of fleeces. Maybe we should up sticks and try our own place. You could always revert to sheep – think you could manage that now, at your age?"

Ben knew he'd gone too far. The old man turned away and threw a dismissive hand in his son's direction as he climbed into the buggy and slammed the lightweight door so hard that it cracked the lock mounting. He could hear his father's curse from twenty paces. As the engine fired up the dogs sprang up and made for the wall. They cleared it in a single leap until their young master screamed at them to return and they scuttled to heel with the same agility.

Ben stood there pondering his last two human exchanges as his father raced off toward the cattle grid and the main road beyond. The woodland floor was strewn with felled logs and all manner of off-cuts. Sorry stumps protruded from a confusion of trimmed branches. Upturned tree root clusters punctuated the agitated landscape. It was true, he thought. It looked a godawful mess. It could have passed as a battle scene from *Gladiator* – that opening sketch where what's-his-face is lining up the Romans to face the Hun – and it hardly smacked of scenic perfection right next to the main entrance to their property. Obviously it had been a mistake to pick on the timber patch as a decoy for his father. Yes, he had long been aware that Gilly was irritated by the woodland carnage, but that hadn't been the point of her stopping by the roadside. If only he could have conjured something less emotive for the old man – too late now.

He thought about Gilly. In fact, he thought about their often riotous sexual encounters in months gone by. He found himself repulsed by the memories. Perhaps he really had moved on.

He checked the metal pegs securing the trailer ramp. They were firmly wedged, holding the board in its closed vertical position. The tetchy ewes imprisoned behind it returned his examining gaze, and then he threw a leg over the quad bike seat and turned the ignition key. As he moved away into the trees on a temporary working track, he whistled the dogs into line and they followed obediently.

25

rumour and fact

Janice gave her man a sideways look as she poured the morning coffee. She'd been talking to herself for the last two minutes. He was lost in thought, fretful, uneasy at best. She'd known for some time that the motorbike saga was gnawing away at him inside. He wasn't used to this; that was the problem, she thought. But she felt utterly helpless. She understood the issues – she could hardly avoid them with tourist numbers plummeting, even accounting for seasonal adjustments – but she simply couldn't solve a murder mystery for him, though she'd love to try, if only to release him from the torment.

She placed the steaming cups on the breakfast bar and offered the hot milk up for him to pour. He blinked and appeared to re-engage, and he apologised immediately as the delayed discussion resurfaced in his conscious mind. She took his hands in hers, softly rubbing her thumbs across his knuckles. She asked how he was. He seemed to hesitate, but then he assured her he was alright – a bit tense perhaps but...well, that was to be expected after several months without progress, and an entire task force at his disposal. She tried to reflate some sense of optimism by reminding him of the many successful arrests they'd made amongst the vigilante brigades who had, for a time, held sway over their leather-clad adversaries, but he quickly fended off her efforts and she knew he was right. Having a skilled assassin still roaming the fells, potentially at least, was the real nub of his very serious predicament. He did concede, however, that the time which had elapsed since that unsolved heinous crime was beginning to give him hope that the incident would indeed prove to be an isolated act of retribution for some unknown, unseen grievance. The only problem with that of course was that they had exhausted those limited avenues of enquiry very quickly.

Just as he was beginning to conclude that they should probably go back to the start and rake through everything just one more time, his attention was stolen by the insistent buzz of his mobile phone. He swallowed a mouthful of rich dark roast as he picked up the device. He recognised the number immediately. Raising his eyebrows to his wife to indicate mock surprise, he stabbed at the green button.

"Hello, Chief. This is an unexpected pleasure. To what do I owe this privilege?"

Janice knew precisely who was on the other end of that conversation and he didn't belong to the Cumberland Police. She motioned that she'd slip into the sun room and take her coffee with fabulous early morning views of Windermere before her. David Lehrer nodded his understanding and smiled to her as his former chief superintendent replied with, "Ah ha, David, you recognised the secure number in a flash, obviously. How are you, my friend?"

"Fine, Chief, just fine, thanks. What about you?"

"Yes, not bad, not bad at all, and please, David, you must call me Charlie. We're old colleagues I know, but old friends too I trust. I can't tell you how much you're missed down here in the flatlands, but I suppose that wonderful Lakeland landscape has captured you forever, and I can't say I'd blame you either."

"Well…er, Charlie…you could say that, although there are few places in my heart like Suffolk. I do miss the coastal stretches down there, those big skies, a good pint of Adnams…you know the sort of thing."

"What? You haven't discovered a drop of Coniston Bluebird or a mellow pint of Yates bitter yet?"

"Oh yes, Chief…sorry, Charlie…yes, yes indeed, but not all that often. In fact, to be frank, it's been hectic since my backside first hit my office chair."

"Yes, so I understand," offered Charlie Carlingford, Chief Superintendent of the Suffolk Constabulary.

"Ah," ventured Lehrer, "so you know the form then?"

"Not exactly, David, but I heard things were somewhat frenetic."

"You can say that again, Chief. No sooner did I get to know the team than boom! We had a homicide on our hands, and open warfare out there in the greenery of the national park. I don't think we've come to terms with it yet, and we've been at task force alert for a couple of months now."

"Warfare, what do you mean exactly?" asked his former superior with evident concern.

"Oh it's a ludicrous situation, one which has been mismanaged long-term to the extent that it's now way out of control."

"What is? What are you referring to?"

"Do you remember the trail bike problem we used to have not so long ago, down there I mean, in East Anglia?"

"Yes, of course."

"It was more of a menace than anything else, just something that irked too many people and lots of land owners with different vested interests."

"Yes, yes, I remember."

"Well try to magnify that a hundredfold. Picture, if you can, hordes of petrol-heads careering about the fens and the reed beds in huge numbers and usually in large travelling bands, you know...ten or a dozen bikers in a posse, and swarms of them. That's the scale of the invasion we're suffering here. They come from all over the northern half of the country and they are just ruining the natural beauty of the region with devastating consequences on the local business community."

"Really, how come?"

"Sorry, Chief, how come we let them in, or how come the region is losing money?"

"Well, both I suppose," the chief replied sheepishly.

"It's actually remarkably straightforward. The force up here has sat back for too long and has allowed the problem to escalate. All the carefully coordinated action plans we worked through with Norfolk, Cambridge and Essex have passed them by up here. The destruction of the landscape just on the eye has been enough to deter tourists in large numbers. There are areas here within the national park looking like vast scrambling courses for yobs in leather. It is genuinely ugly, in fact so disappointing that revenue streams to all manner of holiday businesses have been slipping away for years. I think we're at crisis point..."

"And people have started taking the law into their own hands, I'm guessing?"

"Precisely! One shooting, as yet unsolved, and a wave of ambushes of regular bikers by strong-arm gangs of green warriors and locals who are finding themselves short of a bob or two at the end of the week, if you understand me."

"I do, David, and it sounds very messy. But what on earth is up with the Cumberland Constabulary? What we did down here wasn't exactly astrophysics, let's face it, but it did the job."

"I know, and I've been ramming home some of those lessons, but I can only get traction amongst the local action groups. Our lot appear to be, well…I mean, I'm not really sure…not disinterested exactly, but lacking a bit of backbone. It's very odd. They have all the same tools, but no apparent willingness to use them."

"But surely the terrain is a major obstacle in itself," the chief prompted, defensively.

"It's not that, Chief. I really don't think the practical difficulties are any greater – they're just different. Chasing a bunch of rogue bikers from one valley to another is very much like skirting around fens and broads to achieve the same goal. No, it's not that, it's something else," Lehrer said with a sigh of exasperation.

"And the National Park Authority? What's their input?"

"Zilch frankly – they put up a few signs and make leaflet drops. They try to organise action days, but it's all half-hearted, and with no active pursuits and no arrests to speak of, you end up just asking why they bother."

"County council?"

"Just the same. Actually it's like the Bermuda triangle Cumbrian style. The county council blames the park, the park says the police are not supporting them, and the police blame the county council for not doing more to help the park."

Both men took a breather and Lehrer quietly downed a little more of that wonderful coffee. Just then Janice reappeared with a stern look on her face, tapping her wristwatch to warn him of the time. He'd promised to drop her off in Windermere before heading over to Kendal.

"But, Chief, you surely didn't call to talk about biking bandits and spineless local authorities, did you?" Lehrer continued in a vain attempt to speed things up.

"No, but it's all very interesting. I wonder if I should have a word with Louis Minton. I knew him when he was still at my level, before he got the top job."

Lehrer felt immediately uncomfortable. "I think you'd need to know more before you could do that, Chief," he stated cautiously.

"Yes, yes, of course, don't worry, and I'd have to square it all with you first. We'd need to get our ducks in a row so that it wouldn't reflect badly on you, naturally. No, no…" he trailed off, deep in thought, "no, it was something else. A preliminary tip-off if you like."

"Uh oh, sounds ominous," Lehrer joked rather lamely.

"And it is, I'm sorry to say." Lehrer sat forward in close attention. Janice could see the shift in his demeanour. The chief carried on. "I had a little whisper directed my way last week from a good reliable old mucker of mine in the Essex squad. He's well connected in the Smoke, as you'd expect."

Lehrer's eyes narrowed and his brow creased a little in concentration.

"Apparently there is growing interest in the northern reaches from within a particular drug cartel in South London."

"Wow, really, do you know where in the north exactly?"

"No, David, not yet – apparently north of Manchester and sounding much more like Glasgow or even Edinburgh, but we must be devilishly careful because we have a plant in there and we dare not put that source at risk. I know you understand these things," Charlie Carlingford asserted intentionally.

"Yes, sir, of course, but you wouldn't be calling me if this thing was passing me by on the way up to Scotland, so what do you feel able to reveal?" he urged, as gently as he could.

"Finger on the pulse, as ever, David," jibed the chief.

"Just trying to pay attention, Chief," he laughed.

"Indeed, and quite right too. What I'm about to tell you is so damned secret that if I got any kind of inkling that this was out and about I'd be up there on a trail bike myself to sort you out. Now, I don't want you to fret unduly," encouraged his old boss, knowing that it was a truly futile introduction, "but there is the whiff of an insider up to no good somewhere up there. I really can't tell you where, and you might question this indiscretion in light of so little information, but I want you to be very careful and to watch your own back. How well do you get on with your immediate team? Are they shaping up?"

The questions threw Lehrer completely, lost as he was in thoughts of relatively mundane leaks about pro-bikers at the police constable level. Then he remembered the strange approach he'd had from his new chief super which had pushed him in that direction.

"Er, pretty well so far, I'd say, but you can send me Adders from Ipswich if you like," he joshed.

"Dream on, Detective Chief Inspector – that will not be happening! DS Addison is too valuable to us here in Suffolk, I can assure you of that. But listen, there is the earliest tick of a warning coming out of the Met that there is some kind of connection between a senior officer somewhere up there, rank as yet unknown, location as yet unidentified, with one of the capital's least pleasant criminal syndicates. Lives are at risk. Large amounts of money are swilling around in the wrong channels, if you follow?"

"I do, Chief, but I've had no sign of anything like that up to now. There is something drifting around about drug trafficking north to south, but it has seemed distant, and frankly the least of my worries right now."

"David, be on your guard, and keep your ear to the ground. That's all I'm saying. When I know more I'll let you know through the same means."

"Pay-as-you-go SIM card? Unrelated old mobile?"

"Indeed."

"Chief, I'm grateful of course, and if anything starts to smell like a Lowestoft kipper I'll return the favour."

"Excellent. Oh and, David, just one last thing – next time, do please call me Charlie."

The hard December frost had cast the tyre ruts in rigid lines of crystalline mud. The girls could easily make out the previous passage of several motorbikes as well as some mountain bikes, not unlike theirs. The same gnarled treads had been pressed into the dirt and then captured in an overnight sub-zero timeframe, which continued well into the morning courtesy of a clinging white mist. Poor visibility hampered their best efforts. They had been working steadily since taking an early breakfast, intent as they were on mapping a number of optional new training routes for their off-road endeavours.

As they paused at the top of the ridge, Lucy called out grid references from the weather-proof map she'd pulled out from the inside of her garishly pink Altura jacket. Helen jabbed a cold stiff index finger at her mobile phone as she collected the relevant notes and coordinates. These would be reassembled later and downloaded into their mobile training planner. The entire route was being recorded by an on-board chip for the same purpose, but they wanted belt and braces backup just in case it suffered a technical glitch. Despite the air-chill and the hanging greyness, they were still making good progress and already looking forward to that hot bath, a late lunch and an afternoon curled up by the open fire with a good book. They'd been forced to take a little more time than expected because of the treacherously icy surfaces they'd encountered on raised and exposed sections of their chosen route. The obvious conclusion went unstated; that it was pointless getting injured when pushing hard in difficult conditions.

They rolled delicately out of the copse, crunched through the frozen surface of a trickling stream and then swooped down a small incline towards a narrow road. Crossing the tarmac with a quick and cautious look both ways, they entered the dormant deciduous wood and joined a truly ancient stretch of drovers' road, once solidly replete with keyed stonework that had long since given way to the ravages of time and severe weather. Soon the lane turned gently to the left and joined with another track, one obviously quite popular with motorbikers by the looks of it. The girls looked at each other with a grimace and a shake of the head – not much good as a cross-country running track – but they pedalled onward, rolling up and over a series of undulating mounds, enjoying the surging momentum of the downward chutes.

Helen worked hard up what looked like the last hillock before a line of trees ahead. However, as her rear wheel bit into the unresponsive hardened turf she skewed to the right, slurred across the face of the slope and then, in trying to correct her course, lost her back end completely. She yelped as her right hip met the hard ground with force, and she slid off to the left and into the crispy bracken. In a second Lucy was at her side having negotiated the same preceding descent with one foot flat on the ground, skidding to a stop alongside her fallen partner. She lowered her robust Cube mountain bike into the frost and took a few quick steps to tend to Helen. She was alright; a little shaken and immediately worried about the injury risk to her right side, but relieved that she could pull herself up on Lucy's arm. Lucy held her for a moment's reassurance. Then she helped to dust off the frost and leaves and to take a closer look at Helen's stricken Bianchi, which had embedded itself in the dense bracken.

Helen spotted it at once. Lucy's line of sight had shifted slightly and had locked on to something of apparent concern. The girl's anxiety was etched in her face.

"What is it, love?"

"Not sure – look, over there, down below, just there in the bracken," Lucy said.

Helen turned in the direction of her pointing finger, but couldn't pick out the same disturbing feature. She rubbed her sore hip and pushed up onto her toes to try to catch a glimpse of whatever was unsettling her girlfriend.

"Here," Lucy urged, "let me show you," and she set off down the slope crunching the russet brown stems underfoot. The quizzical look only deserted her when a cry of wide-eyed despair rang out into the wooded apron around them. Helen hurried as best she could to catch up.

There before them, half hidden in the rusty winter ferns, lay the unmistakable form of a near-skeletal cadaver. It appeared as if the corpse still wore the remains of motorbiking leathers, certainly to his lower torso. The words 'Yamaha Moto-Cross' stretched down his leather-clad right leg. He – they assumed it to be the body of a man – still wore his robust clip-down boots and even his crash helmet, but his right arm lay exposed to the bones and his chest cavity gaped grotesquely where scavenging animals had pulled and picked at his innards. The corporeal void continued up beyond the collarbone, through the neckline and into the rounded dome of the helmet. Only then, on closer inspection, did they realise that the back of the headgear was missing and the shattered skull had been violated and meticulously cleaned out.

Helen turned away and spewed into the undergrowth. Lucy stood transfixed by the monstrous image in view.

26

a lone wolf?

Detective Inspector Young recognised the girl's voice immediately as he picked up the connection via the Penrith switchboard. She sounded strangely clipped, abrupt almost, but in his mind's eye he could see her slim languid figure with shapely pins encased in dark leggings. For an uncomfortable second he thought she might be calling to ask about the progress of her partner's formal complaint lodged a few months earlier, but she quickly put him out of his misery.

She had his attention as soon as he'd registered her first sentence. It was a body. She'd found a body. No, *they* had found a body in a wooded clearing not too far from the western shore of Windermere. It had been there for some time and was badly decomposed. The wild animals had been at it, and there was a motorbike lying in close attendance. When he asked her to describe the location in more detail, she simply fired a six-digit ordnance survey grid reference to him down the phone. He asked her to hold on while he hurried across the office, with the cordless phone pressed to his ear, to get a closer look at their enormous regional map which was pinned to the wall of the operations room. There, she repeated the reference coordinates for him again and his forefinger raced across and then down the topographic contours before settling on Bishop Wood near Graythwaite.

It was only when he and the CSI squad arrived an hour later that he understood the mapping exercise the girls had embarked upon. They looked frozen stiff, having waited out in the cold for him to get there, and he quickly got them wrapped up in blankets as the investigators began to tackle the gruesome particulars. The girls gave him as much information as they could as they stood by the police van on the narrow lane just through the trees. Young nudged them around the side of the vehicle to protect them from the gentle but chilling breeze that had now cleared the early freezing fog. When he felt they had given all they could, he offered them a lift home, bikes and all, but they insisted that the best way for them to combat the cold, and to overcome the initial trauma of discovery, was just to get back in the saddle and pedal on to the next stage of their test run. He advised them to head for home directly, but they assured him that they would manage.

It didn't take long for science to match the mangled remains with the first name on their priority missing persons list. Stevie Simms had been reported missing several weeks ago by both his mother and his employer. When Young reported in to Lehrer the two men concurred almost immediately: they had a shooter out there – a lone wolf, a man (almost certainly a man) intent on picking off his victims at leisure, and most definitely at his convenience. He embodied one of their worst nightmares in a protracted investigation so challenging. Assuming this to be a second kill, with some considerable time between the two despatches, should they expect another very soon? Or should they simply expect to find another body, or more, now that the winter frosts had begun to reduce the density of foliage alongside tracks and pathways? When DI Young formally briefed the entire operational squad about the nature of the find, he could see the frustration within the group and almost feel the tension building as the details emerged.

Lehrer's primary concern was to keep the lid on this potentially explosive development. They all instinctively knew that if the press were to get hold of their latest news they would see a free-for-all in the media. The detectives knew that the perpetrator would be more vulnerable for as long as he believed that this particular kill remained undiscovered. He would be far more likely to make mistakes, to perhaps reveal some small chink in his armour, if he continued to feel untouchable. Lehrer was so eager to maintain secrecy that he even considered not going to his new chief super with the update. He put it off for several hours while he chewed over his own misgivings and fretted about the implications of the tip-off he'd received from his ex-boss down south. It was his anxiety over any public reaction to an undesirable leak that forced his hand. He knew, and readily understood, that his seniors would not thank him if a public outcry were to greet a media jamboree.

Lehrer and Young took off for Rusland Quarry. DS Caroline Sutton drew the short straw and drove out, together with a WPC liaison officer, to visit the dead boy's fraught mother.

Their first port of call was up the alloy stairs to the managing director's office, but there they only learned through Keith Salcombe's secretary that Mr Salcombe was actually working from home. Apparently his wife, who was nearly six months pregnant, was having a tough time of it, and her husband had wanted to be close to home just as a precaution lest anything go wrong. The secretary felt sure that it would be appropriate for the detectives to drive over to Rowan House since their need to speak to him appeared so urgent. Lehrer knew that she'd telephone him as soon as they headed back down the noisy steps, but it didn't matter. The place wasn't far. They'd go there, but only after talking to the lad Morgan Dyer who was, by chance, on shift and at work.

Morgan's earlier statement, shortly after his boss had notified the force about their missing worker, had been routine enough in the circumstances. However, as a close friend of the deceased, he would surely want to help in any way possible. They couldn't have underestimated the young man any more even if they'd set out to do so deliberately. Morgan Dyer rose to the challenge with a maturity neither of them had anticipated. While DI Young approached three others in the quarry team, but only under the guise of furthering their enquiries about Stevie Simms' disappearance, Lehrer grilled Morgan Dyer in some detail about their exploits as lads out in the sticks on those prized machines. The impromptu interview revealed little of note – if anything it only helped to reinforce the notion that the key to their growing mystery lay out there in the greenery among bands of bandit bikers and countryside activists. Somewhere hidden in either or both of those haystacks lay that all-important needle that would thread their search through the right loopholes. But just as Lehrer brought the exchange to a close, with a stern instruction for Morgan not to reveal to any of his colleagues that Stevie's body had in fact been recovered, the young man propelled himself into the limelight with the insistence that he should assist poor old Mrs Simms in identifying her son's remains at the police morgue. That would be the following day most probably, and he asked to be kept informed about the practicalities.

One of the two policemen was taken aback at the condition of the lane up to the Rowan Tree settlement. The other had been there once before. As his boss gripped the moulded hand rest on the inside of the passenger door to steady himself against the gyrations of the car, DI Young casually and almost subconsciously extended his developing erotic fantasies about the strikingly beautiful lesbian girl who, he knew, resided at Rowan Lodge. The long track tested their vehicle to the limit, not in terms of speed or resilience, but in scraping its front spoiler and low hanging exhaust silencer over several ridges of displaced gravel and stones. As they passed over the small cattle grid at the gates to Rowan House, Young looked in through the adjacent gates of the lodge and there he saw the Lucy girl standing in the driveway. She smiled and waved with a hint of self-conscious embarrassment, but before he could respond, the confused and intrigued detective slipped beyond their mutual line of sight and carried on up the small incline to park by the fountain in front of the big house.

Keith Salcombe appeared almost at once, thereby confirming, in Lehrer's mind at least, that he had indeed received prior warning of their impending arrival. The man was fretful and ill at ease. As he ushered them into the property, Lehrer found himself disappointed at the narrowness of the hallway. He had assumed something much grander. However, as they continued through to the library, where Salcombe apparently ran a modest home-office facility, they encountered the man's wife, Gilly, who looked pale and drawn at first encounter. She apologised needlessly for feeling a little under the weather – her visitors could see that she was proudly pregnant and they dismissed her self-critical appraisal immediately and kindly. She would bring them coffee and then she must sit down and take a rest.

The library was a simplistic affair, modern and functional, but it lacked sufficient daylight through the old sash windows. They sat there in the gloom for some time discussing the dreadful news of their recent discovery in the woods. Salcombe expressed real surprise bordering on shock to learn that his own neighbours, the two professional female athletes in the adjacent property, had been responsible for the discovery. Lehrer took the opportunity to reinforce the message that the police were very anxious to suppress the news for as long as possible, and that all relevant parties, including even the dead man's mother, should do their level best to guard this knowledge assiduously. Lehrer had known that such an imposition was almost certainly beyond realistic, but the woman had apparently agreed steadfastly with DS Sutton that if it would help to track down her son's murderer then she was ready and willing to play the game. Anyway, she had pointed out, who would she tell? With no close family after her husband had died, and only one really good friend around the doors, surely she could string her along that her boy was still just missing.

Secrecy of this kind didn't seem to trouble Keith Salcombe at all, and yet the cause of his obvious discomfort plagued Lehrer throughout their discussions. Perhaps the man was fitful about his wife's worrying state of health in her delicate condition. But no, it was something else, but Lehrer just couldn't pin him down. At one stage in their exchange, as DI Young confided that he'd interviewed three shift workers at the quarry earlier, Salcombe looked very agitated. He appeared anxious to know exactly who and where, on a site as dangerous as a huge industrial quarry. However, the detectives put the man at ease. The three of them concluded that there was little more to be gleaned than had been gathered from their first interview with Salcombe not long after he had filed his missing person report some weeks ago. They did agree, nevertheless, that somewhere out there in the motorbiking community there must be at least a handful of blokes who would surely be able to furnish the detectives with a more meaningful understanding of the dead man's activities and lifestyle. Salcombe appeared to share that view. Yet at the same time, he cast doubt on the perceived helpfulness of Morgan Dyer beyond the feedback he'd already given. They mulled the idea that if some bikers had shared their favourite outdoor pursuit with young Stevie, then surely Morgan would have been in on the act as well. Salcombe seemed unconvinced, and his reaction left his visitors perplexed over such an inconsistency.

Finally, as Salcombe was clearly making ready to end the discussion, DI Young asked about the farm lad next door at Rowan Tree Farm. He was a trail biker wasn't he? Was it too far-fetched to expect him to be moving in the same circles as Stevie and Morgan? Again Salcombe looked edgy at the suggestion, and his interviewers began to sniff the odour of animosity there perhaps. It was only when they needled him a bit more that Salcombe revealed his family ties by marriage to the farming clan next door. Raised eyebrows from the coppers elicited an unprompted and outwardly unnecessary explanation from their host that his own sister had married Ben Meaner, the young farmer next door.

They said to one another later, as they bumped their way back down the treacherous track, that the man had been less than delighted with that recently declared union. They could only put it down to the usual family squabbles of a typical domestic situation, one which could only be exacerbated by the close proximity of the two families in question on top of that hill in the middle of nowhere. At that juncture in the proceedings Mrs Salcombe had returned to clear the coffee cups away and, uninvited, she had chipped in freely to the discussion about the still-newlyweds next door. She had appeared quite defensive of the young man and had spoken in almost maternal tones about him. In stark contrast, her brief interjection about her sister-in-law coveted much by way of diplomacy.

Hitting the tarmac and gunning the car forward, the two of them exchanged views and attempted to arrange their next steps in their blind-alley investigation. Forensics had returned little beyond a standard ballistics report based on remnant entry wound traces. They gave nothing exceptional to look out for in that respect. Lehrer, on the other hand, did have an exceptional marksman on the loose, very cleverly killing at will without depositing a single clue to his identity.

Their conversation tailed off as they approached Kendal. DI Young had backtracked to the Lucy girl and the tantalising wave she had given him as they'd driven in through the gates to Rowan House.

DCI Lehrer knew they had to make more of Stevie's biking mates, including the enigmatic Morgan Dyer. In that summation of their position, Lehrer recognised that they had not progressed at all since Simms' reported disappearance several weeks earlier.

And so it was that a rough-looking, unshaven young man in considerable distress accompanied an elderly woman as she shuffled into the dimly lit cold room at the Kendal Police Pathology Laboratory. Lehrer had earlier insisted that Morgan Dyer should arrive before the victim's mother, so that he could make the identification first and thereafter prepare himself as best he could to help his late friend's distraught parent. Caroline Sutton later swore that the woman had aged ten years in two days as she watched her struggle out of the police car and look up at the characterless building which, she knew, contained her only child.

Morgan drifted alongside her and put his arm around the woman's shoulders in a supportive embrace. She looked up and sideways into his eyes as hers filled with tears, and he hooked her left hand through the crook of his right arm and pressed it against his ribs as they set off slowly towards the main doors.

Down in the lift to the second-level basement, and Morgan's sense of dread welled inside his chest. He knew what to expect, and it still frightened him nevertheless. Lehrer patted him softly on the back in an attempt to show support and admiration. As the unlikely couple stepped into the sterile yellowish light of the chamber, the woman gasped quietly at the sight of a single corpse lying monumentally still in near-silhouette form on a stainless-steel table. There were several such tables, but only one occupant, and for that Morgan was perversely grateful. He hoped that she would find the lack of others lying alongside her boy somehow reassuring, distinctly personal and therefore not an environment which might somehow dilute her own son's significance.

After her initial hesitation they approached the bench. She was quickly disconcerted by the apparent profile beneath the white sheet – it lacked a nose, or so it appeared. She again looked up at her escort, anxiety boring into him as he tried to maintain a modicum of control. He patted her hand and then released it temporarily.

"Let me, Mrs Simms," he said softly to her. "But be strong," he advised. "This will stay with you forever." Then he stepped forward and heard her stifle an emotional sniffle behind him. He drew the cloth back to reveal the head, and then he retreated to take up her hand again. As she registered the reality before her she cried out and gagged into her free hand. Lehrer, standing nearer the door, just couldn't look any more. He knew of course that he had to achieve that positive ID, but he'd already heard Morgan's unequivocal confirmation, and he just couldn't watch this poor woman's trauma take hold.

Much of the face was still intact, protected over time by the victim's crash helmet. However, the hideous aperture blasted through the skull between the boy's eyebrows was unmistakable. His mother stood stock still, hand to mouth, a gentle weeping seeping out through her fingers. She stared at her boy as a thousand pictures from yesteryear tore through her mind, and the heady concoction of reminiscence and motherly love consumed her completely. Why this? Why now, just…why? Then her examination took her a little closer and she realised in abject horror that half of his neck was missing, as was the back of his head as it lay on what looked like a hard plastic board. She started in shock and gripped Morgan's arm with renewed force, and then the anger began to rise. She disentangled her hand from his crooked arm and made to pull the cloth further back, but her minder seized her tiny coarse hands immediately and simply said, "No, Mrs Simms, please, no. You won't want to see that. We've seen enough, haven't we?"

The woman again looked intently at him and answered, "Morgan, I know that you two were such good friends. You know…I often wondered how things might have been if the two of you had grown up together, you know…as little lads like…together. I think you would have had great fun – two little tykes running about the place," and her eyes drifted off momentarily as she pictured their imaginary games in her back yard in Ulverston. "I can only imagine how upsetting this is for you. I'm grateful to you for just being here to help me. This can't be easy for you either. But I can see that my boy is in a terrible mess. I remember when he was born and they laid him on my tummy and he was all warm and sticky. That was a terrible mess too, but lovely in every way for a mother. I just want to see him for the last time, son. You understand, don't you?" And he nodded, holding back his tears as she drew the cloth down to the boy's waist and revealed the cavernous ribcage and the extended skeletal arm. She wailed in grief and indignation, and all he could do was to stand there with her and wait for her anguish to relent just a little. Then the two of them turned to leave. As they passed the detective standing by the door they both nodded with grave affirmation that indeed Stevie Simms had been found after all.

27

more men!

The Christmas period had left Gilly Salcombe maudlin. It wasn't just that she'd been struggling with her pregnancy all the way through, and her problems hadn't let go of her for that all-important few days when her sons were home. Was it necessary for fate to be quite so cruel? The constant trips backwards and forwards to hospital in recent weeks had worn her down, and a number of confrontations on the lane with that grumpy old bastard next door hadn't made those trips any easier.

On top of that she'd been disappointed and quite depressed by the boys' girlfriends, each of whom had visited just before and during the New Year celebrations. She chided herself at the recollection – it hadn't been Kira, Evan's girl; no, she had been very approachable, and a pretty little thing too. She could readily understand why her young man had crept along the corridor to the girl's room in the early hours, although the climactic moaning could have been suppressed with a little more discipline and a little less abandon. No, it was the other girl, Shelley, Will's new lass. She had proven likable enough, but Gilly had immediately seen herself in the opposing form when they'd first met, and from that moment she'd worried about any Oedipus tendencies that may be lurking within his moody chemistry. Shelley was a buxom heifer in the making, with already heavy breasts and a broad beam, and not the cutest look. Will had appeared so obviously obsessed by those heavy swingers that Gilly had almost taken fright at the sight of a young man's longing, and she'd seen that very same look in the eyes of another young man not so many months ago. Gilly had found the physical expression of their togetherness a little distasteful, but she thought she'd hidden her true feelings well enough. The very image of them having sex just turned her cold. She could only hope that the crush would pass for each of them and that they'd move on soon enough. Uni life was like that she supposed. Kira would be welcome again; she knew that.

Keith had been detached throughout. It hadn't been the quarry; the Christmas closure had spanned several days and reached right into the New Year. He'd spent a whole day messing around on the parking drive with his Range Rover. She couldn't imagine what he was up to; something about new speakers for the round-sound system, but it had been a bitterly cold grey day and she'd left him to his own devices.

Austen Smiley had called round the day before New Year's Eve. He'd been his usual effervescent self, full of festive chat and frivolity mainly for the benefit of the two new girls on show. Again Gilly had espied the gentle inclination towards that girl's boobs, and the more he drank after lunch the more charming and leery he became. Will had coped pretty well Gilly had thought, but she heard him cracking a few sarcastic remarks in her direction later in the day, and his mother hoped that those little nuggets might signify the beginning of the end of that relationship. She knew he could do better, even accounting for her own maternal bias; she just wanted his next girl to be slim and attractive and nothing remotely like his mother.

The greyness that had descended upon them at Christmas maintained its grip right into mid-January. Gilly had to work hard to find those uplifting moments of happiness, joy even, in the dour, sky-less world of their hilltop retreat. Again she clashed with Eric Meaner, but this time out in the lane while talking to the two girls at the lodge. He shouted at her as he roared past in that nifty rock-hopper; something about standing clear and letting a man get on with a day's work. The girls just grinned and shrugged their shoulders at the peculiarities of an anti-social old git like Meaner – aptly named they suggested – and they all laughed.

Henrietta had shown a marked increase in the frequency of her visits running up to the holiday break. Thereafter, moving into January, she came round just about daily and the two pregnant women shared a good old cackle about all sorts of amusing politics amongst the men on that hill. Keith had remained distant, disengaged maybe, but then he was back to his usual long hours at work. Eric appeared to be wrestling with a growing sense of anger and frustration with the two bumpy ladies on-site. Henri reported to her sister-in-law that his constant slights and criticisms had become more voluble and less tolerable. Apparently Ruby had taken up the role of watchdog and regularly gave her old man a caustic jibe or two in Henrietta's defence. However, the continually negative, even toxic atmosphere had not only created a serious rift between the two old curmudgeons, but also between them and their son, Ben. Henri also relayed her own misgivings about her husband's inner turmoil – trying to balance the physical and emotional needs of an ever more heavily pregnant wife alongside the demands of an important parental relationship had been taxing Ben to new levels of patience. All the same, Henri had confided, Ben had proven the most wonderful lover, and they still managed fairly regular encounters, much to her delight. Apparently he'd developed a rewarding taste for her straddling him, on top so to speak, so that she was comfortable despite the bump. He seemed fixated with her enlarged breasts, and she giggled at her own indiscretion.

Gilly must have looked thoroughly crestfallen. Henri's home truths had rendered her immediately envious and, despite her best efforts, Gilly instinctively knew that she had failed to mask her own disappointment. She was floored by Henri's next direct question about her own physical frolics with Keith. Presence of mind came to her rescue at once. She was able to trade her own persistent discomfort and general ill-health during pregnancy against the very thought of Keith's unwanted attentions. Keith had succumbed to that overwrought excuse, and that was something at least, but the image of him going at her in her present condition turned her stomach. Ben, on the other hand, well...on reflection, that would be an altogether more manageable prospect, but she could hardly share that with the boy's pregnant wife, now could she?

According to Henri, Ben had taken to getting out on the fells on his motorbike a little more often of late. She imagined that it relieved the tension in those difficult farmhouse relationships, and she also conveyed the belief that it made him more vigorous with her in bed too, in a gentle but manly fashion. Again Gilly silently demurred. She would have to come up with a strategy with which to deflect Henri's penchant for sharing such emotive gems, but for now it didn't rate as a priority.

She recognised, nevertheless, that since Henri had now stopped working in Ambleside and formally taken maternity leave, the girl would likely be round to see her very often. That would need to be moderated too by some means, or perhaps their maturing terms would give them both different ways to spend their time in preparing for the arrivals of new little people. Through experience, and ten years more on the clock, Gilly knew more of what to expect. She would try to help Henrietta as best she might without instilling the fear of God into her about some of the unpleasantries. It would all be worth it in time, and their newborn babes would, of course, grow up together – two more men on the hill, according to the scans and tests.

At that point in her considerations, Gilly grew tearful, but also determined. Naturally she had wanted a girl, not to replace dear little Alice, that would be impossible, but to balance up the masculine imbalance at home. She really had craved a little girl, but when the notable appendage had been pointed out to her on one of the later scans she knew that she should simply be grateful for the apparent good health of her baby. As for Alice, well, perhaps that had been another cause of Gilly's often morose outlook over Christmas; the fact that she hadn't been well enough to take the trip down to the cemetery. She had wanted, as she did every year, to place some festive toys and bunting on the grave, but she'd failed. A deep-rooted sense of guilt plagued her, and now she accepted in her heart and mind that such a trip wouldn't take place for many months, probably not until the autumn. A mantel of great sadness pressed down on her. She could only hope that Alice would understand and forgive her, again.

28

dereliction of duty

It was rare for the chief constable of Cumberland Police to visit the Head Office of the Cumbrian Lakes National Park Authority, but the leading lights of the two pivotal regional organisations knew each other quite well and spoke regularly if infrequently on the phone.

Louis Minton had earned promotion to the top policing job in the area some three years ago, in 2005. Oswald Page had held the chief executive post at the CLNPA for nearly eight years, having succeeded in a rather tense political in-house rivalry that had erupted when his predecessor had effectively, and unexpectedly, transferred to the Snowdonia National Park in North Wales. Page had guarded his cherished position ever since, and against several potential usurpers.

Their meetings were for the most part convivial affairs. They usually touched on key areas of overlap between their two institutions, and Ozzie Page had come to learn that Louis Minton focused most particularly on the success or otherwise of any specific joint ventures or projects that their operatives beneath them were engaged in. These were not too numerous, and sometimes involved other regional organisations like the Forestry Trust or the Nation Trust.

Page was a short, thick-set man who wore expensive suits and cared not to venture into the wide open spaces all that often. Around his middle he probably carried an extra stone and a half, and his short-cropped hair, unusually dark and complemented by a spurious moustache, gave him something of a comical air. However, he commanded sensitive political radar inside a fast-moving brain that missed little. As an advertisement for healthy outdoor living, in the fresh damp air of the Lake District, sadly Ozzie had been poorly cast.

Louis Minton, by way of contrast, looked the part and tried to walk the walk too. He usually pulled it off, but not always. As a hard-bitten ambitious copper he'd seen some sights and been in some scrapes, but the higher he had risen in the police hierarchy, the less comfortable he had felt about the required mental agility in the cut-throat office environment of an important Home Office department.

Putting all that aside, Louis was on a mission; a buck-passing mission which needed to employ a decoy of the simplest kind. In short, he needed to assuage public concerns about the growing levels of violence and vandalism on the fells. He needed to raise visibility, but he didn't have endless resources nor did he want to raise the risks for a certain rider who regularly took to the great outdoors with a specific purpose in mind. More visibility through the deployment of park rangers appeared to be a toothless solution to his problem.

Page's personal assistant, a leggy redhead by the name of Belinda, had expected to hear the two old geezers rumbling on for anything up to an hour through the glass partition behind her chair, where she sat as sentry to the little fat man's domain. She showed their visitor in and then returned quickly to deposit a coffee tray on the low table, knowing all the while that her boss was staring at her cleavage as she bent forward and also that the uniformed chap was assessing her long legs and shapely bottom from behind. She had withdrawn to her own barricade outside the door for no more than ten minutes before she perceived a degree of disaffection from within.

"So what you're trying to say, Louis, is that my people on the ground are not doing their bit, is that it?"

"In part, Ozzie, yes, and I think that's a reasonable assessment."

"Oh, you do? Based on what, exactly?"

"Based on numbers and results…or lack of them."

"That's interesting coming from you, and what's it supposed to mean?"

"Meaning where the hell do your rangers spend their time and what do they do all day?"

"Back off, Louis! We've been here before and I'm sure neither of us wants to do this again."

"Oswald, stay calm for God's sake. A lot is hanging on this, including your job and mine. In my humble opinion we really haven't been here before, and we need to take some radical steps if we are to recover our credibility in the immediate term."

"Credibility – what are you getting at?"

"Ozzie, what would you rank as your single biggest achievement here in your time as chief exec?"

"What is this, a job interview?"

"No, come on, Ozzie, what are you most proud of, seriously?"

Page looked at his oppressor warily. "The size of the organisation, its structure, its efficiency, how we get things done with limited numbers, that sort of thing – the place was a tangled mess when I got here. There was so much on the periphery and little at the core getting the key objectives lined up and ticked off."

"That's interesting," the policeman replied.

"Is it, why?" Page asked, sensing that he'd been outflanked.

"What are or were those key objectives, then?"

"Oh, getting the finances in order was very important. We needed more staff, better systems and much more, but we had to be able to show financial prudence first. Now, the Authority is nearly three times bigger than when I first arrived. We're moving towards a plan to link up with the Yorkshire Dales National Park in a few years' time, and there is even distant talk of us putting in a bid as a UNESCO World Heritage site," he beamed half-heartedly, still feeling uneasy.

"But isn't the Authority's primary objective, always and at all times, the protection of the landscape and all the flora and fauna within the park? I mean…wasn't that the first basic principle of the park's establishment, way back?"

"Well, er…yes, of course, but…"

"But you didn't mention it once in that very nice little Lakeland promo you just gave me. How on earth you expect to extend the park across the M6 into the Dales and manage an even bigger space when so many onlookers would question your ability to manage this one, well, I have no idea."

"I'll take that one on the chin, thank you, Louis."

"Ozzie, don't you read the papers, listen to the news, get out on the patch, that sort of thing?"

"Cut the sarcasm, Chief Constable, it's hardly becoming."

"We have a serious outdoor crisis on our hands and you need to ditch the pinstripes and get some green wellies from somewhere and get out there for a week of sight-seeing."

Page snorted with derision and was about to respond to the implied criticism when Minton carried on at a gathering pace. "Tell me, Ozzie, how many rangers do you have now? Is it still twelve to fifteen or thereabouts?"

Page snorted again in disbelief. "I've got eight, and you should know that from our regular reports, Chief Inspector," he answered with a level gaze.

"And how much of their time do they spend uphill and down dale?"

"If you mean how much time is spent out of the office, I'd say about three and a half days a week, but not all of that time is on the land. They do advisory classes and talks, seminars, leaflet drops, photographic assignments, all sorts."

"That explains why my lot never see them, or only very rarely, to be fair."

"But that's always been the way, Louis," the chief executive pleaded.

"But that's my point – our circumstances haven't always been like this. Christ, Ozzie, how long have you been in this job, five or six years perhaps?"

"Nearer ten, actually."

"And for four or five of those years the entire economy of the Lake District has been steadily sliding into the lake, and we are to blame for it."

"Speak for yourself, Louis."

"Wake up, Ozzie," Louis Minton spat across the desk at his opposite number. "This fucking biking plague has been allowed to grow by your inactivity. The lefty liberal politically correct approach to marauding rural yobs has long since expired. These morons need a stiffer response..."

"Which is presumably why your boys and girls in blue have made so many arrests of late, Louis?"

"Now who's being sarcastic? You know my people can't act after the event, and despite considerable upgrades in manpower recently, we still can't be everywhere at any one time. Your guys have got to drop everything else – I hear that putting no-entry signs out on the fells is especially effective. What we need is an all-out surveillance campaign, yours in tandem with ours, but more eyes and ears. It might be something we can take to the press, you know, at the next press conference."

"But I've got nothing much else to give."

"Oh come off it, Oswald. One of my DCIs tells us that the quarterly action group meetings your people run here, with all the active participants from across the Lakes, is instructive only to the extent that your people are the most reluctant to get out there and man up to the task."

"Oh is that right?"

"Yes, actually. Maybe you should sit in on the next one. I reckon there is more determination in some of the spotters out there in the sticks who put their necks on the block every time they confront a violent band tearing up the country paths. Those guys are private individuals, often middle-aged or elderly, who have nerves of steel and real courage. Your people are taking them for granted."

"I'm sorry, Louis, but that's just derogatory claptrap. You don't know any more than I do about the workings of that group."

"But it's your group, man!" Minton quipped in desperation. "Look, it's nearly two months now since we discovered that poor lad's body. We managed to keep it out of the *Gazette* right through into the New Year. We've only been partially let off the hook by suffering no new fatal shootings in what now looks like a four- or five-month timeframe. Who knows when that amnesty might be broken by this nutter with a deadly eye for the moving target?"

"You still think the two murders are connected?"

"We do, just by relying on the similarity of the attacks, but we've got nothing to work with."

"It sounds macabre I know, but it almost sounds like you need another one just to help you pick up some leads." Minton stared at the man blankly.

"Oswald, despite your apparent reticence we're having considerable success in tackling the vigilante groups that mushroomed late last year. There have been quite a number of convictions, and some of them have produced serious long-term sentences. But it's created new difficulties. The local community is militating against us. Yes we are seen as successfully cracking down on a violent wave of tit-for-tat reprisals, but in the same frame we are seen as defending the original and ongoing perpetrators of extreme rural vandalism right across the region. We can't talk to the farmers any more – they see us as being on the wrong side – and many of the younger farmers are keen bikers. But the business community is on its last legs and the countryside warriors are clamouring for even more arrests and public demonstrations of bikes being crushed."

"You're not serious?"

"I am. I know it sounds crazy, but the landscape is a slimy muddy mess for mile after mile, and outwardly decent, mature, balanced people want some action."

"And what good would it do for me to go out in a jeep for a few days to see this muddy mess?"

"Fuck it, Ozzie, you're just not getting the message! I can see now why your troops appear to outside observers to be lacking in any sense of urgency or determination. Listen up, my friend. Whether you like it or not, you are seen as presiding over a soft-touch organisation which has naively allowed this calamity to befall our region. I've heard it said several times in mixed group meetings that all of this only started to happen when you took charge."

Page looked aggrieved and lifted the wagging finger in response, but Minton bashed on.

"I know that's unfair, but it may not be if you want to examine just the last half of your tenure. Put another way, Ozzie, if you were to take that drive over the high passes and around the remote lakes you simply wouldn't recognise the area from the lush green contours of your early days here in Cumbria. I can't do much more, not least because I've a got a double murder to unravel and I'm struggling even with all the resources of a task force. I need your chaps to get out there and to be seen to be out there as often as possible. We can bring these biking bandits to heel, and I do accept that a few arrests and convictions will soothe the locals quite quickly, but you have to take this problem much more seriously. I'd even support you at government level in trying to get you more resources, but I need you out there making a proper fist of playing the Lake District ranger. Can I count on you, Ozzie?"

"I'll take that drive, Louis, that's all I'm saying."

29

risk and reward

"You're still doing it, aren't you, Morgan?" Keith Salcombe sneered, incredulous. "After all that's happened, and all that we've discussed, bugger me…you're still running the risk, aren't you?"

Morgan Dyer looked over his shoulder and scanned the empty vehicle repair shop. Then he took a single step and poked his head beyond the frame of the gaping sliding door just to check that no one was approaching. Then he turned to the senior man. Pulling a fat fist from inside his donkey jacket, he thrust a thick envelope into the man's hand, instructing him to hide it immediately. Salcombe quickly looked up and surveyed the yard beyond as he buried the packet in his on-site all-weather coat. He felt utterly and instantly compromised, but the need for evasive action stole the opportunity to object.

"That's a lot of money in there, Mr Managing Director, so don't go spending it all at once. That might be something of a giveaway, you might say," and he grinned mischievously.

"You are unbelievable, you know that, un-fucking-believable! Your best mate has not long been put in the ground, shot between the eyes by some clinical hitman on a contract, and yet you're still running the risk. You saw that note – sent back to us with our own merchandise – I mean… what do you want? What do you need to understand before you pack this thing up once and for all?"

"Relax, big man, you're always on edge, always seeing the downside, never the positives," the younger guy retorted.

"The downside? Bloody hell, Morgan, the downside in this case is death. It really is that simple. There's nothing to debate. However you've managed to pull this off, you have, inadvertently, courted the attentions of some ruthless people from a world you and I just don't know or understand. These guys will kill you. We've had that warning."

"Hey, boss, they might get you as well, or even you before me," Morgan teased.

"Fuck you, Morgan. Wise cracks are not really helpful just now."

"Oh, do give it a rest, man. I've got this covered."

"What with, a set of cross-wires in a telescopic sight, and a luminous red dot on the bridge of your nose?"

"Oh yes, very quick, I'll give you that."

"Morgan, I'm not joking. These people are playing in the big league and they have been for some time. You've just got your pissy little second division team promoted. They're already watching you. We know that they have you measured up. To them you're about coffin size. If they could find one of Stevie's cross-country routes, even one of his newest tracks, they must have all of yours down on a map with a highlighter pen. It's just a question of time, son."

"Which is why I've changed my modus operandi," he smirked. "Big words there for a Welsh boy like me."

"Cut the crap, Morg, what d'you mean?"

"Oh no you don't, not that easily anyway."

"What?"

"Didn't you always tell me never to reveal my methods, just to keep you in the clear in case you get nicked?"

"Well, yeah...but, we're beyond that now by some distance, so level with me, what's been happening in recent months that allows you to chuck a fistful of notes at me like this when we should be keeping our heads down?"

"We are keeping our heads down, don't you worry about that. Obviously losing Stevie has drastically cut the number of bike runs available to us. I'm still doing mine, but I've deliberately worked out several new routes, and I've forced my pickup contacts to regularly change their collection points. More importantly..." and he took a steadying breath before looking Salcombe in the eye, "I've been using our trucks for about sixty or seventy per cent of our deliveries." He waited for the explosion, and he wasn't disappointed.

"You're doing what? Say that again...you're stashing narcotics on our quarry wagons, is that right?"

"That's it, and it's working."

"Working! Fucking working! Are you totally insane?"

"Chill, boss, for Chrissakes, it's the perfect strategy," Morgan asserted.

"You are mad, completely mad – didn't you get the message about random haulage checks some months ago? Isn't that why we stuck to the trail bike approach?"

"Ah yes, boss, that's true, but I am reliably informed that anything with a Lake District plate or company name is being let through the net. I have been using that route all along, but just with less dependence on it. Just recently I've ramped it up as a back-fill for Stevie's workload."

"Reliably informed – by whom? What the hell are you up to, Morg?"

"That's for me to know, and not something for you to fret about. Let's stick with the old idea of you not knowing enough to be incriminated, shall we?"

"So when a tipper or flat-loader comes in here with a local ID you slap a few bags of magic dust in packs under the wheel arch or behind the spare wheel or up the driver's arse or somewhere, is that it?"

"Well yeah, something like that. Actually, it's a lot cleverer than that, but yeah, that's the gist."

"As I said before, Morg...you are just un-fucking-believable."

"Hey listen, Keith, the stuff is vacuum-packed and thoroughly sealed against the sniffer dogs and anything of that type, and it's working, as I say."

"Oh great, that makes me feel so much more comfortable. Now every time I see a sub-contract wagon from Scotland or Newcastle I can relax and put the kettle on, but if I spot a low-loader from Barrow I should pull on the brown corduroys and cycle clips just in case."

"Keith, as you just so eloquently pointed out, I think the punishment, if caught, would rank just a little higher than soiled trousers for the laundry basket. Anyway, you could always give me that forty-five grand back and pretend you know nothing about all of this."

"How much?" Salcombe whispered in genuine amazement, quickly patting the bulging wad in his coat pocket.

"The right reaction, boss, if I may say so. Like I said, it's going well, and of course we have Stevie's minor share to...how shall I put this...to accommodate, yes, that's it."

Keith Salcombe looked utterly resigned to his horribly compromised position. He was still in this trap and had been from day one. If he couldn't stop this outrageous character from risking their lives, well, he might as well take the payback. God, how could he, through his own movements and behaviours which were surely being observed, hope to convince an unseen assassin that he wanted nothing more to do with Morgan's money-making machine? To get it right might conceivably save his own life. To get it wrong, he was sure, would simply add an extra body to the death toll. Hell's teeth, why not just go down there tonight and smash Morgan's illicit production plant? Answer – because Morgan would fit him up with the police for sure...and probably even get away with it himself. Shit...Keith was screwed – completely screwed!

He looked at the younger man and smiled ruefully. Then he patted him on the shoulder, shook his head whimsically, and set out across the slimy grey yard back to the office as a snow flurry breezed in from the north.

30

old man of Coniston

Lehrer cursed as he pulled in to his own drive. Looking up to the house, illuminated from within in stark contrast to the dark February evening all around, he spotted a heavy-set, grey-haired man standing next to Janice. They both looked momentarily down at him and then raised their lines of sight to scan the wintry scene over Windermere with its twinkling lights punctuating the nearer shore. He remembered: it was Oliver Stanton, the quick-witted chap from the action group meeting many months ago, who had known Janice from years long gone. Janice had arranged dinner, and her husband had promised to be home a good hour ago.

As he climbed the outside steps to approach the front door, it was opened from within to reveal a testy woman pointing at her wristwatch. He apologised profusely, kissed her warmly on the lips and gave her a gentle hug with his free arm before pushing through to the kitchen and offloading his briefcase. He stepped quickly through to the lounge.

"Oliver, what can I say? I'm so sorry. Have you been here long?"

"Yes I have actually, David, and I am delighted to have had your lovely wife all to myself for more than an hour," he answered with a beguiling smile. "We were just reminiscing about the old days and how she and I first met through her late husband Jeff. It had seemed so long ago until now, and as if by magic, it seems like last week."

"Good times then?" Lehrer ventured.

"Oh the very best, David, I can assure you. Jeff was a good man, very steady, dependable, solid...if you know what I mean, and Janice was, well...Janice I suppose. I'd never seen so much energy in one person ever before, and she was exactly and precisely what Jeff needed to bring the best of himself to the fore, so to speak. He was a very shy man in so many ways, with something of your own modesty, David, if I may put it like that."

"Maybe she has a natural affinity for modest men?" Lehrer suggested with an impish grin.

"Well, you know, David, I was just thinking the very same, but this wonderful woman," he said, nodding to Janice in the doorway, "has just been reminding me of her interim encounter with the now infamous Lee Phillipson."

"Ah yes, and I think infamy is about right. Did you ever meet him, Oliver?"

"Yes, yes indeed, here in the Lakes. You may not know," he continued, looking questioningly at Janice for clarity, "that Janice and Jeff had indulged in a frightfully demanding restoration project over in Coniston village. Of course they made a terrific job of the whole thing as you might expect, but the indolent Mr Phillipson appeared less than keen to help maintain the good works after poor Jeff passed away." He paused, suddenly suspecting that he had trespassed on sensitive ground, but Janice came to his rescue.

"Don't worry, Oliver. David has had the inside story probably several times too many, but I often think that Lee Phillipson may simply have been the catalyst that brought the two of us together." She moved closer to her husband and threaded an arm around his waist, smiling into his eyes as she did so. "The price was high you could say, more so for Lee than anyone else, but there can't be many men so loved, like David Lehrer here, who qualify as a woman's fourth husband. That's bravery of the highest order if you ask me," she joked.

"Nonsense, my dear," Oliver quipped. "A luckier man anywhere on the planet would be very hard to find, and as you were saying earlier, two out of four isn't a bad percentage," and they laughed. "And you two look good together, you should know that…if it hasn't been pointed out already."

"D'you know," Janice cut in, "Josh was saying that to me on the phone just the other day. You remember Josh, my son?"

"Of course, mischievous little beggar, if memory serves," Oliver reflected.

"Not so little nowadays, naturally," Janice added, "and in some ways the real driver behind our relationship, eh, love?"

"I hope there's a bit more to it than that, but I'm happy to run with it," Lehrer offered with an affectionate glance.

"There we have it, Janice, that modesty again," Oliver asserted. "The way I heard it, David, young Josh would be staring at an old brick wall in some poky Victorian cell by now if you hadn't plucked him from the jaws of injustice."

Janice nodded, and moved away to collect a wine glass from the cabinet. Returning to the bottle on the coffee table, she said, "And that, at the very least, deserves a very immodest bowl of merlot for my knight in shining armour."

"Sounds good to me," Lehrer sighed, the day's tiredness threatening a yawn from somewhere down in his shoes, "but I'm a long way from celebration in my current, rather onerous task."

"Oh, love, you must stop fretting. The break will come," she soothed. "Look at him, Oliver. Two stones lost in the last three or four months from pure anxiety."

"She's right, David. I know it will be of no comfort at all, but you do look a little drawn, and certainly lighter on the feet than when we met at the action group session late last summer."

Lehrer absorbed the observation without flinching, but inside he registered their care and concern.

"How is it all going, if I may be permitted to ask?" Oliver said.

Another sigh and a gentle shake of the head greeted his enquiry. "On the rogue biking front we can claim some success, so the members of your committee and all of those unseen activists spread thinly across the county can take some succour from that. There have been negative results too in that sphere, in particular the souring of relations with the farming community. But on the flip side we're winning the battle of the vigilantes, which you will have read about, I'm sure."

"Some terrible confrontations," Oliver agreed.

"Yes, but we've nailed some of the worst offenders and also begun to bag some of the bikers as well. I do believe the reported incidents of illegal riding are beginning to subside. I'm sure that the publicity surrounding bike crushing and heavy penalties on driving licences is having the right effect."

"I can second that," Oliver confirmed. "Our figures, from the tracking devices we have on some of the more popular routes, are showing a definite decline. I also think that there is more ranger activity out in the wilds now, and that can only help your chaps at ground level."

"As for the more serious stuff, well…what can I say? Obviously I can't tell you anything in detail and I know you'll understand that, but we have little to work with despite two publicised fatal shootings. It really isn't looking good."

"Is there a chance that the maniac who is responsible may have melted away now that the wave of biker abuse is being turned back?"

"It's distinctly possible, Oliver, but my instincts on these things are usually reliable, and right now I don't feel at all comfortable. Apart from anything else, we have a duty to catch this animal even though he may have hung up his camouflage jacket for good. Whoever he is, it looks almost certain that he's a double murderer – I'd like to ensure he doesn't make his hat-trick – and there are other aspects floating around on the periphery that I simply can't discuss with you that leave me unsettled and unsure of our position."

"That's not a place you like to visit very often, I'd suggest."

"That's right," Lehrer replied meekly.

Janice interrupted them. "Dinner in five minutes, gentlemen! Please move through to the dining room and make sure you take that bottle through with you. And, David, please also make sure that the two of you have changed the subject by the time the starters arrive."

Feeling suitably chastised the men wandered through, lingering for a while at the mysterious lake view and the pitch darkness beyond.

Just then Lehrer's mobile buzzed in his back pocket.

"Damn and blast, Oliver – so sorry, but I must take this."

Oliver raised his hand and wafted the intrusion away casually. Lehrer stepped back into the lounge. Janice looked through from the open kitchen, eyebrows raised, head thrown back to emphasise her disappointment.

"Hello, Caroline, what have you got?"

"Some progress I think, Chief."

"Go on," he urged.

"I managed to get to three more lads this afternoon and this evening…Oh, sorry for the late call, Chief, just realised the time."

"Don't you so much as think about it. Carry on."

"Yes, well…three lads who were willing to talk about their daft bloody biking escapades and make it sound like they're stealing the crown jewels every time they take to the hills. I mean they know it's wrong, and it doesn't sound like they'll ever stop doing it – you know, Chief, taking the risk – but they know the stakes are much higher now after the death of Stevie Simms. They want his killer taken off the fells as soon as possible, naturally, but the majority of these lads just can't bring themselves to help us because it incriminates them and they know it."

"But this time?"

"This time I have some boys who knew Stevie Simms and know Morgan Dyer too. Morg is a bit of a cult figure in their group I'd say."

"Why's that?"

"Oh, it's just his character, his style, his manner, that kind of thing, and also that he's usually pretty flush, if you follow – always happy to buy the beers on a night out, or the teas and buns at the biking cafes in Broughton or Grasmere, that sort of thing. He's also got a lot of high-end kit for the sport, and these lads know how much some of this stuff can cost."

"Interesting!"

"Yes, but not as interesting as their behaviours, or should I say biking trends."

"What d'you mean by that?"

"It's something and nothing, but it's odd, that's all. The lads seemed disgruntled about a few things relating to Stevie and Morgan – just little background niggles that had been irritating the wider group for some time. Oh, and that's another thing, Chief. The Meaner boy, up at Rowan Tree Farm, was a casual member of the same unit. He's probably worth a thirty-minute chat just to see if he can shed any light on our two guys. But where was I? Oh yeah, a little bit of animosity knocking around the group I'd say."

"Such as?"

"Well it's odd really, but they described how either Stevie or Morgan, or both on occasions, would agree to ride out with the gang on a given day and either leave halfway through the day, or not join until halfway through the day."

"Maybe they were on shifts at the quarry," Lehrer said, thinking out loud.

"They'd tend not to commit on working days, which made sense to me. But sometimes they'd all gather – we're talking up to a dozen in their regular group, mainly out of Ulverston and villages around the town – at a chosen meeting point, like the Internet café in Coniston, and set out from there. Sometimes one or both of our boys would be there on time as agreed. Sometimes the group would be hanging around waiting for them for an hour before getting hacked off and just leaving without them. On occasions they'd ride with the group and then just disappear at an undisclosed juncture and not be seen again for the rest of the day – no announcements or earlier warnings, just vroom, gone! Other times quite the opposite – no sign all morning and then come mid-afternoon they'd appear and tag along for the rest of the day's jaunt."

"Did nobody ever try following them?"

"No! That was my first question too, but it appears that Morgan isn't the sort of bloke you'd want to get on the wrong side of, and anyway, he and Stevie are...were, oh shit...you know what I mean, Chief, but among the very best riders in the team. Nobody could keep up with them for long."

"Wherever they were going to, or indeed coming from," Lehrer contemplated.

"What's more, our two would sometimes – only sometimes – wear small close-fitting rucksacks of the type designed for biking generally – not too bulky, so no problems of side-swing on a tight bend."

"Carrying what?"

"Oh, just biking kit really, you know...some tools, a spare pair of gloves, maps, visor wipes, energy gels, that sort of thing."

"But they'd carry that sort of stuff as standard on every trip, surely?"

"Bloody hell, Chief, I'll be getting your job next. That's exactly what I thought. Why travel with a small rucksack of backup supplies only sporadically?"

"There was no such rucksack recovered from Stevie Simms, was there?"

"No, Chief, but that could just have been a *no rucksack* day, whatever that means."

"Okay, Caroline, this is the plan. I'll get Iain Young up to see the Meaner boy, er, Ben Meaner, that's right. Iain knows the layout up there. Tomorrow morning sharp I want you to gather a couple of vans of uniforms, plus dogs, and get down to that quarry. I'll have the warrant waiting for you after my next call. Give that place the full treatment. I know you and I are thinking exactly the same thoughts."

"Aye aye, Skip, I'll be on it. Out!"

Lehrer killed the call. Good girl that Caroline Sutton, and not just as bright as a button either – bet those lads opened right up just to prolong their time with an attractive girl like her. There were still some good tactical calls coming out of the old dog yet, he thought, with a wry smile to himself.

He made a quick call and then punched in a text message to DI Young. Then he sloped off back to his wife and guest with a renewed air of optimism.

31

stairway to heaven

DI Iain Young crunched his way up the long stony driveway to Rowan Tree Farm. It was becoming familiar. He even knew to watch out for the deep ruts at the two hair-pins. All the way up all he could think of was Lucy – those legs, the pert arse, the long auburn hair. As he drove round the last bend by the Lodge House he looked in through the ornamental metal gates. He didn't see anyone, but he could have sworn that a curtain shifted in the nearest window. The girls' four-wheel drive wasn't in its familiar parking spot in front of the house.

He drove on up the slight incline to the farmyard and parked up where he thought his car wouldn't get in the way. Old Mr Meaner was hardly the most welcoming farmer in the area, but his wife soon interceded in a potentially fractious exchange. As soon as she realised the purpose of the visit she despatched her grumpy hubby up to the top field to fetch their son.

Ben Meaner was not best pleased to be interrupted in his work. Lambing time was imminent and, as he pointed out very early in their brief discussion, his wife was eight months pregnant and in need of regular attendance. His hands were full, he thought.

As soon as their chat turned to rogue bikers on the fells Ben Meaner nearly lost any modicum of self-control. He explained very pointedly that he had no time for such bullshit and he couldn't see any problems with farm lads having the odd blast along the tops on a clear day. When DI Young alerted him to the real-life statistics, which suggested young farmers represented only two per cent of the problem of illegal motorbiking in protected areas of the national park, Ben just shrugged his shoulders and visibly detached himself from the conversation. Young brought him round with the simple, though fairly aggressive suggestion that if he didn't stop being such a prick he might just unearth a hitherto buried complaint about Ben's own illegal activities up on the fells. The official statement – complainant anonymous at this stage – still festered in his slow-burn pending tray. It could so very easily find itself on the top of the pile.

It was all to no avail. Ben knew little of the celebrated Morgan Dyer, except to say that he had believed the bloke to be employed at the quarry over yonder owned by his brother-in-law, Keith Salcombe. DI Young doubted the technical veracity of Salcombe's ownership, but yes, Ben had seen Morgan out on the fells. Even so, the riding group DI Young continually referred to retained little significance for Ben. He'd ridden with them a few times in the last year, but by and large he was just too busy to take a whole day out with a bunch of lads in the countryside. He had known the dead guy, Stevie Simms, but only through those same few outings with the same bunch. He looked completely blank when the detective asked him about their unusual behaviours and rucksacks and all sorts of wacky stuff. The lad had constantly looked at his watch and DI Young decided it had been another wasted trip up that bloody awful lane.

As they parted Young thanked Ben Meaner for his time. Ben scowled a reluctant goodbye and headed back to his quad bike where the dogs lay quietly in the short trailer attached.

"Good luck with the baby, in fact with all the babies," Young shouted across the yard.

The lad turned and almost relented before conceding a muttered, "Thanks." Then he revved the quad away out of the top end of the yard and onto the high field. DI Young watched him go, wondering what sort of life it was to be out there in late February with a light dusting of snow on the ground. He shivered as he climbed back into his car.

He executed a simple three-point turn and then set off down the first slope of the track toward the first bend at the Lodge House. There, to his surprise, stood Lucy in all her slim, sexy, athletic glory. She had some small firewood logs crooked in one arm and she looked up as if to check who was approaching. She smiled and waved at him and he slowed to chat through the descending nearside window. Again that moment of doubt took hold as he feared she might raise the issue of her partner

Helen's earlier complaint, but no, she was just being friendly. It was small talk, pleasantries and nothing more, but when she leaned in through the window to hear what he was saying a brisk hilltop gust blew her hair across her face and he smelled her freshness as it wafted over him. God, she was truly breathtaking. He felt a stirring in his groin, and as she drew her hair back with a delicate finger she locked her eyes onto his. She said she'd just popped out to the wood store by the gate to replenish her supply for the wood burner, and hell wasn't it freezing. But she was wearing only those signature leggings and flimsy top; definitely not winter attire by any means. She looked back to the house momentarily and gestured with her free hand saying that he should come in for some tea. As she did so the wind flattened the fabric against her body and he almost started at her proud, hard nipples as they pushed through the cloth. She recognised his lust immediately. He looked away as her eyes challenged him once again. He agreed, hopefully not too eagerly, to join her, and she advised him to drive the car into the gateway and just park it before the gates.

By the time he'd stopped the car, she had dipped back into the front door leaving it slightly ajar for him to follow. He hurried across the drive and ducked his tall frame under the low lintel, stepping into the warmth of a small porch. He closed the outer door and pushed on the inner. It creaked a little as it swung open into the next room, and then he saw her.

She stood just in front of him at the bottom of a narrow carpeted staircase. She looked up into his eyes again and smiled nervously. Then, to his astonishment, she lifted her skimpy top over her head, baring her firm round breasts and a rippling athletic abdomen. She threw the top to one side as her lustrous shining auburn hair, shot with streaks of chestnut and copper, cascaded over her shoulders. He stood stock still. His breathing quickened and he stared at her perfect form. She allowed her eyes to drop to the rude bulge in his trousers. Then she surprised him again. She sat down on the stairs behind her and deftly wriggled her firm bottom free from her leggings, which she quickly jettisoned with a casual flick. She lay there on the stairs completely naked, elbows resting on a higher step behind her; a bewitching natural beauty, her alluring softness challenging any last vestiges of discipline left within him. He stepped towards her while releasing his tie and discarding it. She sat forward, pulled on the belt around his waist and unzipped his fly. In an instant she had his liberated penis in both hands, a magnificent specimen, gorged, pulsating, demanding, and he bent low, taking his own weight with a supportive arm planted on a stair tread behind her, and he pushed it into her with not a moment's care.

She literally cried out as he penetrated her, and then gasped in panted breaths as she met his thrusts with her own pelvic responses. With his free arm he lifted her slight frame off the stairs as he lunged into her with an increasing rhythm, and she moaned loudly and swore profusely at their crazed abandon. It didn't last long. He felt her stiffen slightly as her back arched away from him and she gasped again just before he erupted into her with a series of shuddering convulsions, and it was over.

Not a word had been said. They lay there for less than a minute in their ridiculously tangled pose, before he pushed himself up and away and stood above her looking down, searching her eyes for some form of understanding or explanation. He zipped up quickly and bent to retrieve her clothing so that she might cover herself, and she sat forward with forearms parked modestly over her drawn-together knees. He shook his head in abstract confusion. She smiled, and then a girlish giggle escaped from her soft full lips.

"Why?" he pleaded.

She looked at him earnestly as if to suggest that such a simple question could only prompt a very complicated and lengthy reply. She looked down, shifted slightly on her carpeted perch, and said, "I don't know, I mean...I'm not sure. It was something that happened when you came up to interview us, you know, last year, about that little spat on the fell with the young bloke up at the farm."

"What? What do you mean?"

"Oh shit, if only I knew...if only I could explain it, but I don't know myself. I just thought it might be nice, you know...just special in some way. You're a good-looking guy and, well, I somehow imagined that you'd be good at it."

"What?" he snorted. "Good at it? Christ, that's a first...I think."

"For me too, actually."

"What, on the stairs, you mean?"

"No, no, I mean...my first time." She searched his handsome face again for signs of understanding.

"Oh God no, you don't mean to say that this is the first time you've had sex with…?"

"Er, yes, that's what I'm saying." She looked away, not out of embarrassment, but merely to gather her thoughts.

"But you didn't feel as if, well, I mean… It didn't feel as if…"

"Well there are ways for us girls too, you know," she interjected.

"So why this…why me…why now? You live with…er, Helen isn't it? I mean…what does all this mean? I'm very confused."

"How d'you think I feel? I love Helen, and we're great together… and we have great sex, let me tell you, but I've just been getting these odd feelings. I find myself quite often wondering what it would be like with a bloke. When you came up here something just pinged in my head. I can't fathom it out, but something changed, and I just started to question my own sexuality. I began to think that the limits to my sexual preferences and appetite might be much more flexible than I'd realised. I've been attracted to girls all my life…well, for as long as I can remember. My earliest boyfriends just left me cold. I never knew why, until an older girl, a woman really I suppose, seduced me and it was truly wonderful."

"But now?"

"Oh boy," she laughed. "Now I'm all over the place. Now…well, let me just put it like this – you certainly know how to use that thing," and they both shared a good laugh.

Then she appeared to sit up with a jolt, and she threw a quick glance at the large clock above a door to her left.

"Oh my God, quick – you must go, and quickly. Helen is due back any time now. Please, please, you must go." They both hurriedly rearranged their clothing.

"What will you say to her?" he asked, as they completed the task.

"What?"

"To Helen – what will you tell her?"

"Nothing! No, nothing at all just yet, if ever! I have to get my head around this."

He nodded and turned to the door. He peeked out to check that the coast was clear, and then turned back to her as she stood in the porch.

"Er, Lucy…can we do this again sometime?"

"What, on the stairs? Are you some sort of pervert?" she joked.

"No, no...I mean, can I see you again?"

"Oh yes, you can see all of me, and hopefully for much, much longer next time. No idea how we'll manage that, but I want more, that's for sure. And hey, are you...er, attached?"

"No. No I'm not. I'm divorced."

"Can only be the job then – nothing wrong with that thing in your pants," she grinned.

He smiled to himself as he walked back to the car. As he got there and opened the driver's door he heard her shout, "Next time, Detective Inspector Young, you might want to tell me your name," and with an affectionate wave she disappeared and closed the door against the cold.

Bumping back down that infernal track DI Young had to ride the verge at one point so as to let an approaching vehicle pass as it battled uphill. As she passed, Helen gave the detective a frosty stare – could be worse, he thought with a smile.

Young's colleague DS Sutton had endured a much more frustrating trip to the great chasm in the ground. The team had gone through every building including, and especially, the semi-permanent Portakabin offices. They'd even called for the chief engineer on-site to shut down operations just long enough for a unit to cruise every level down the peripheral roads which wound their way inexorably to the deepest area of the great void. They found nothing unusual. The dogs took something of a skittish turn in an open area by the cutting sheds, a patch used for casual vehicle parking for cars, vans and trucks, but they simply couldn't isolate anything of substance and by late morning they simply had to abandon their search empty-handed.

The managing director, Keith Salcombe, hadn't been on-site at the time of the search. His wife was nearing the end of her confinement at home and he had been spending increasingly lengthy periods working from his home office in order to remain on-hand should his wife require urgent help. When the news of the search-warranted invasion of the quarry had been phoned through, he had reacted in an extremely agitated fashion, but his compromised position allowed him only the dubious luxury of sitting there and waiting for an update when the police eventually finished their task. The interim period was purgatory for him, but the relief – a lifting emotional safety valve which blew several hours later – almost reduced him to tears. He decided there and then that he couldn't keep the charade going any longer. He resolved to break the deadlock.

32

new men on the hill?

March appeared destined to be the month for babies. During the first week the earliest lambs appeared; little white specks with spindly legs out on the frozen green hillsides. They tottered about and did their utmost to stay close to their mothers at all times. Ewe's milk was of course a powerful motivator for them, as were a couple of vixens that had been chased off more than once by Ben Meaner on his roaring quad bike. The protective warmth of a mother's heavy winter fleece quickly became another key feature as the north wind cut into the frail creatures. By the second week the Meaners were hard at it right round the clock, ferrying the apparently weaker arrivals, or the odd ones rejected through faltering maternal instincts, back to the farm and the warmth of the straw-laden pens in the main barn. The birth rate accelerated through the middle of the month and then began to taper towards week four, but then the ewes' human counterparts stole centre stage.

Both Gilly and Henrietta gave birth just before the end of March, their rushed trips to hospital separated by only two days. Gilly had suffered a difficult gestation throughout, but perhaps it was her body's own experience, a physiological memory of sorts, that rendered the culmination of her term relatively straightforward. She had felt the twinges at breakfast time, but declared herself still a fraction too early, until her waters broke all over the kitchen floor as she dropped some fresh toast into the rack. Keith had her in the car in a jiffy, and in Lancaster General Infirmary within thirty minutes – no mean achievement in itself – and his wife gave birth to a strapping eight-pound two-ounce baby boy less than three hours later. Mum and baby were declared fit and well, and little Joe Salcombe took to the breast in double quick time, such that the medical staff quickly began to focus on other priorities in their surprisingly heaving ward. Father, Keith, really did cry at the sight of his suckling son, but he assessed his circumstances as only partially rehabilitated from the months of anxiety he had recently grappled with.

Forty-eight hours later Henrietta found herself ambulanced to the same hospital as a blue-light emergency with all sirens blaring. Her exhausted husband was somewhere out in the high country when his presence had been most urgently required. Despatching his father in the rock-hopper to recall the lad had, in his mother's mind soon after, appeared a waste of time. She'd called the emergency services. With no sign of her menfolk, she'd climbed into the ambulance with her troubled daughter-in-law and set off cautiously down the unhelpful lane before winding up the pace as soon as smoother roads were reached.

Henrietta had hitherto enjoyed a fairly normal pregnancy. As she lay in the speeding ambulance holding her distended bump against the unnatural pain, she wondered if her enforced isolation from all the birthing around her on the farm had been worthwhile. She would have much preferred sitting in the hay of the lambing barn bottle-feeding the orphans. Ruby did her best not to advertise her escalating anxiety. She could tell from the forwarded radio messages from the crew to the hospital that Henrietta and her unborn child were in some considerable danger. All Ruby felt able to do was to hold the girl's hand and try to maintain an admirable state of calm. Ruby wished the girl's own mother were still alive, but that was a fruitless line of escape, and she knew the poor thing had only Ruby herself to rely on.

By the time Ben arrived at the hospital, his mother looked very disconcerted. The expectant father quickly adopted his mother's angst when he saw the size of the medical workforce attending his wife – even the registrar was there. Henrietta drifted in and out of semi-consciousness. Her deathly pallor did nothing to encourage those around her and through her torpor she tried to maintain a vigilant line of sight to the monitor displaying her baby's heartbeat.

After several hours little had changed. It took Ben nearly thirty minutes of determined argument with his mother to get her to agree to take his car keys and head off home. She had been reluctant to leave him in such fraught and unpredictable circumstances, but she knew her husband, Eric, would be battling an intense workload and in serious need of help with the flock.

Thirty-six hours later Henrietta was relieved of her baby son by Caesarean section. Utterly exhausted she slept for twenty-four hours. Little Jamie Meaner troubled the scales at just six pounds and two ounces, but of course that had been pre-assessed. However, his distressed condition, which had given cause for alarm throughout the protracted, intended natural delivery process, showed no signs of improving as he lay curled and defensive in his incubator. Ben too was out on his feet and slept fitfully in an armchair at his wife's side, punctuating his sentry duty with regular trips to the intensive care ward for updates on the son he was yet to hold in his own hands. Little Jamie's difficulties continued for days, although his mother gradually clawed her way back to the land of the fully conscious, only to absorb the debilitating mood around her and to adopt it for herself.

Gilly had paid a visit on her way home with her new baby, but Henrietta had been in no fit state to recognise her, let alone engage. Gilly had left truly perturbed and urged Ben to call as often as he could with hopefully improving news, but those calls never came and their collective trepidation reached out into the days ahead.

A week later and Gilly had envisaged two new little men on that hill, but the depth of her disappointment had left her morose and forlorn, and her mithering mood seemed to transfer to everyone around her. She had been in the maternity ward for such a short stay that even her eldest son Evan, on campus at the university, had missed her before her rapid departure back to South Cumbria. Evan's girlfriend Kira, of whom Gilly most certainly approved, had insisted they drive up to see the newest member of the family. Their beaming faces had lifted Gilly temporarily, and Joe had been a gurgling guzzling bundle of energy who was already putting on weight. He was certainly not sleeping for more than two or three hours at a time in any given twenty-four-hour period. Later, as they headed back down the lane, the two of them concurred that Evan's mother was deeply concerned about her new nephew's predicament. Even Keith had appeared unsettled or distracted at a time when he could have been expected to be focused only on his own new addition to the family.

Gilly could tell that the Meaner household had tipped into disarray as the heavy burden of frequent hospital visits sandwiched between the seemingly endless demands of the sheep, not to mention many other important obligations about the farm, stretched them all to the limit.

Ruby became terse and less forgiving as she and her husband struggled to get through their arduous daily duties supported by very little sleep indeed. She knew they were just too old for this caper, but what choices did they have? She noted that her husband became equally unforgiving of his closest farming neighbours for their lack of assistance in their hour of need. However, during one of a growing number of fractious exchanges and wearing arguments, she felt the need to point out that his lifelong evasion of anything approaching endearing, neighbourly behaviour was now bearing fruit. But, when she moaned about Keith Salcombe's effective disappearance as far as any offers of help might be concerned, he laughed out loud and told her not to be so damned stupid. Hadn't she been told enough? Keith was a feckless lightweight, and one day he'd get his just desserts. After another week had gone by, the local agricultural college reacted to their plight and despatched a couple of lads to help for a few mornings a week. It proved a godsend, and probably rescued them from complete implosion.

Austen Smiley paid his duty call when little Joe was three weeks old. His bachelor credentials leapt to the fore as he politely declined Gilly's offer to hold the wee mite, and she chuckled at his boyish reluctance. In truth, she conceded, the boy's father hadn't been any more forthcoming. But then Austen and his old friend and work colleague Keith had slipped away into the home office for a business catch-up. Austen emerged later with a very serious frown to his harrowed brow, and Gilly could only guess at what had impressed him so negatively. Keith later feigned ignorance about any perceived disaffections and he brushed aside her interest with a hitherto unusual fuss over the smallest member of the Salcombe tribe.

Jamie Meaner's very first ordeal in life had shifted from Lancaster to the Manchester Children's Hospital in Pendlebury, an additional two-hour round trip for worried family and relatives. Little Jamie was seriously ill and fighting for survival. His parents were in pieces. His grandparents, bereft of any means to alleviate their grandson's suffering, grew more apprehensive and more sullen. Anger bubbled just below the surface.

*

David Lehrer's extensive team had harboured great hopes of the surprise search at Rusland Quarry. Their nil return dashed those hopes severely and left the entire unit frustrated beyond description.

They pulled in Morgan Dyer again, but he bluffed his way superbly through an interview that gave him more information about their lacklustre investigation than he gave them. However, while he was putting on the nonchalant performance of his life, for that's how Lehrer and Sutton saw it, the drug squad turned over his small terraced house in Ulverston and discovered some small quantities of cocaine used, by the looks of it, for personal consumption. The raid produced nothing else and Morgan left police HQ knowing that a charge was pending. As he rode out of the police station car park he smiled beneath his visor. Clearly they were onto him, but they'd come so close from various angles that he began to believe that they'd write him off now and concentrate on other lines of enquiry.

33

rope or chair?

When Keith had confessed to him in his home office, Austen had, in his own judgement thereafter, eked out an Oscar-winning show of shock and rising anger. In a way it hadn't been an act – how could the spineless fool have been so stupid? Actually, he considered, it did fit a pattern. Keith had been a huge disappointment since he'd returned to his home patch. He'd done nothing but belly-ache and whinge for years, despite his comfortable surroundings and his relatively undemanding role at the quarry. Christ, that damned hole in the ground would last long enough to give the idle waster a pretty decent pension – what more could he want? Okay, so he'd been duped by the lad Morgan, so what? In fact he'd been dim enough to have missed the structure and dynamics of the entire scam despite his own very reasonable and fairly regular cash-in-hand profits.

Austen had known for some time why the two ex-school mates had not quite followed the same stratospheric voyage to success: Keith was just not intuitive; he was only a fucking accountant after all. And his crazy wife had been playing him for years – fair enough; not a bad shag on a weekend trip away. Those tits, Jesus, how could you not have a bit of fun with those mamas?

But now Keith had stepped over a very dangerous and perfectly invisible line in the sand. His suggestion that he, Austen, should somehow go begging to his friends high up in the police in order to negotiate some form of plea bargain – which fucking planet did the prat think he was on? A confession about extensive and sustained narcotics production and distribution would not roll over quietly. The game was worth very substantial assets. It involved equally enormous risks and linked them all to heinous and very casually violent criminals the likes of which Keith fucking Salcombe couldn't even imagine. What a prick! To think that he honestly believed his old school chum could randomly open up the biggest can of worms the sleepy county of Cumbria had seen for many a year, and then almost indifferently pull a few strings and make it all go away. Then what, back to happy families, back to bringing up the nipper in their subsidised manor on the top of that ridiculous fucking hill in the back end of beyond?

Well, Austen hadn't given it a second thought. There was simply too much at risk; not just lots of money, but status and lifestyle, comfort, excitement and, of course, total independence, not forgetting basic liberty. No, Keith was right. Something would have to go away – that would be Keith. The only question would be method: industrial mishap perhaps, or shooting accident? The latter could be easily engineered up on the hill. The former surely couldn't be too difficult with a bloody great commercial quarry to play with.

Would he need to tell Louis? No, don't be daft. That would be a disaster worthy of Keith himself. What about Morgan? Nah, he'd get the message without a word spoken, and besides, he's not the one shitting his pants at every turn.

34

vein of truth

The horrors crept up on them and the desperate anguish in their hearts consumed them from the inside as they sat listening to the paediatric oncologist. The poor man had been here before, but his own heartstrings were pulled taut and, as a father himself, he could barely make the first thrust into the earth-shattering dissertation no parent ever wanted to hear.

He started talking about blood analysis, blood groups, DNA and a range of specific medical details that almost, but not quite, camouflaged the devastating impact of the word *cancer*. It drifted across to them in mid-sentence, as they held hands tightly and tried to sift out the salient points. At first there was doubt, stark incredulity, a flash of alarm in startled glances exchanged while trying to keep up with the pace. Had he really said that? Wait…wait, had he just told them that their little Jamie had been born with cancer? How could that be? How could that not have shown itself before now? Hadn't the pregnancy been plain sailing…well, in relative terms?

In ten minutes they learned more than they had ever wanted to know about infant cancers. The rarity of such a terrible diagnosis did not make them feel any better; they felt more cheated and angry, if anything. Their gathering understanding of statistics – suggesting that babies afflicted in this way represented a mere fraction of one per cent of all children with cancer – further robbed them of hope. Moreover, they discovered that of the very few cancers having the temerity to attack little children, their new baby had developed the rapacious form of leukaemia known as AML or acute myeloid leukaemia, for which survival rates appeared extremely challenging.

As the distillation process continued, and they fought doggedly to assimilate and to analyse every scrap of essential information, they descended deeper and deeper into a wretched emotional darkness from which they feared they might never return. Any realistic assessment would have convinced them that little Jamie's predicament was indeed severe and almost certainly inescapable. In any event, the hideous road to the baby's recovery and to their own psychological salvation appeared long and dangerous, a journey they were already embarked upon, equipped only with their burgeoning love for each other and for the child of that love. They had neither the time nor the capacity to question or rationalise the direction they were being taken in. They committed themselves, by default, to a harrowing odyssey stalked all the while by trepidation and woe.

Jamie's condition had been diagnosed through a relatively simple blood test. A bone marrow sample had already been extracted from his tiny frame in order to confirm their assessment. No, there was no chance that they might have erred.

Something had happened to him late in gestation in the womb, a genetic mutation from what the paediatrician called a genetic predisposition. It meant nothing to them, but they knew to fear for this new life they had brought into the world. Apparently the problem centred on his creation of white blood cells and the failure of that production system hidden away within his tiny quantities of bone marrow. Too many white blood cells, although essential to his immunity against infection, were clogging up his bone marrow such that the cells themselves were not maturing properly. This, in turn, prevented the manufacture of healthy red cells and something called platelets. When, bemused and shocked, the parents of the patient looked askance at the unusual term, the specialist explained that platelets were responsible for the clotting mechanism inherent in blood. They nodded vaguely and tried to maintain keen concentration as the unfolding nightmare swirled around them.

Once some of his own bone marrow stem cells had been collected, Jamie would then be subjected to intense chemotherapy – at which point Henrietta cried out in despair and the doctor had to pause simply to allow Ben to steady their collective resolve. Of course the treatment would be severe in order to hopefully kill off the myeloid cells in their little boy's body. But it would kill some healthy cells too, and a depletion of white cells would make him vulnerable at his very tender age. A few days later, when hopefully his system would be cleansed, they would reintroduce his own stem cells through a drip and hopefully normal blood cell production would begin again.

At the risk of drowning them in more technical jargon, the nervous paediatrician completed the particulars of the proposed regimen with an explanation of the two different types of bone marrow or stem cell transfer available. There was method in his insistence. The first, autologous, they would try first, naturally, as it was less invasive using only the patient's own cells. The second, allogeneic, would be a backup or second stage infusion. The mute acceptance in their faces told him immediately that they realised that this would be something of a last resort. He explained that something called matching proteins were very important in these circumstances. Donated blood components had to match the recipient's profile if they were not to be rejected.

Did they understand? They nodded on autopilot.

Humans acquire their matching proteins half from their mothers and half from their fathers. So the requirements for a good match with Jamie's profile at this second stage transfusion would almost certainly come from one or other parent. Any siblings, brothers or sisters to little Jamie, would have a one in four chance of possessing the same matching proteins, but of course Jamie was the first born so that was irrelevant.

Similar matches further along the family chain were extremely rare, but the medical team would want to examine the potential for just such a match with other family members just in case they were required.

He enquired as to their immediate and extended family structures. They looked momentarily disconcerted, as if any reference to the outside world beyond their own horrific ordeal was somehow offensive in its intrusion. He pressed them nevertheless.

On Ben's side there were parents, but no grandparents left to call upon, and just his older sister besides himself. No, she didn't have any children.

On Henrietta's side she lamented the relatively recent loss of both her parents and declared her brother Keith to be her only blood relative. But then she threw out her two nephews, no, three nephews now…and she slumped at the incursion of Gilly's new addition and wept quietly into her husband's shoulder. But the specialist looked delighted – despite the rare incidence at these extremes, the longer the bloodline, the better the chance of finding some useful donors. They didn't want to have to go out to the Anthony Nolan donor service unless it became absolutely necessary. With the best will in the world, anywhere in the world, respondents may not come back immediately.

And so, they would be required to give a blood sample immediately, and possibly a bone marrow sample too in the very near future. In addition they would naturally be expected to coral the entire family to follow suit irrespective of their random locations. The hospital would urgently coordinate the collection of blood samples initially via local GP practices as necessary. Ben and Henrietta quickly pointed out that Ben's sister Rhona was in Newcastle, while Henrietta's three nephews were at home, in Stirling and in Lancaster respectively. All other named family members were at home living cheek by jowl on the top of a hill in Cumbria.

With a new sense of purpose to distract them from fear and dread, the anxious parents first went to give their own blood samples. Then they set about contacting the entire clan to organise their commitments and to establish the when and the where in each case. Within just a few hours they had the essentials in place.

Although Gilly had initially objected to the idea that her bouncing baby Joseph should have to suffer a pin-prick in his heel, she had relented almost immediately and felt thoroughly ashamed of her selfish stupidity in such dire circumstances.

Ruby had wept uncontrollably at the awful news and declared her intention to leave for Manchester at once, but her distressed reaction helped to position their logistical arrangements in the forefront of their minds. The hospital had limited capacity for parent lodgings, especially over an extended period of weeks or even months. Initially both Ben and Henrietta would be able to stay, but sleeping in chairs in corridors wouldn't work in the long run and wouldn't be recommended. The very notion that they should go home, and leave Jamie all alone, even accounting for the very attentive and caring staff, seemed somehow abhorrent to the little lad's shattered parents. However, his mother was now formally discharged and had effectively crossed into post-natal care, so she could take a break if they, together, felt it might help. Failing that, she could stay and Ben might go home if only to relieve the pressure on the farm between trips up and down from the Lakes to Manchester and back again.

These were onerous, emotional and difficult decisions for two traumatised young people new to parenthood. They were adamant that at least one of them should be in attendance for the little mite at all times. They sat there looking into the incubator just watching his subdued little frame, which offered the slightest twitch of reassurance every so often. Hours ticked by, and only Ruby's arrival in a flood of tears persuaded them that Ben should probably head home. Hopefully he could get some sleep and put in a few hours on the farm before heading south again the following evening. Perhaps Ruby would complete the exchange so that Eric wouldn't feel abandoned, and to ensure that he had indeed delivered his blood sample to the local GP for express delivery to the hospital.

It appeared obvious to them that Henrietta would not be leaving that hospital any time soon. What sort of mother would do such a thing? She would need a lot of practical and emotional support, but first of all they really did need to concentrate on getting all the samples in.

Ben set off for home. He held it together as he gave the two girls in his life a huge three-way bear hug, but as he progressed down the corridor the tears tumbled down his cheeks and his blurred vision robbed him of the observation that many people there that day gave him their hearts.

Time slowed. Everything developed a languid, slow-motion pace to it that only inflated the pressures under which the family group laboured in their tense co-existence. Frictions between neighbours on the hill accrued a renewed agitation. Eric at first grew sullen and took to himself even when not left alone on the farm. The first flush of holiday cottagers and caravanners had flooded in for the recent Easter holiday period. Then the intake had relented a little, but still each new visitor was demanding, and Eric had never been the most amenable host.

Then an explosive confrontation took place between Eric and Gilly. Ben had let it slip that Keith Salcombe had not yet submitted his blood sample. Eric had reacted furiously and marched round to the house and banged loudly on the front door. When Gilly came to the door, in all innocence, with baby Joe resting on her shoulder, she faced an abusive tirade from the old farmer fit to wake the snoozing cherub. When she then explained that Keith had gone away for a three-day business trip to a quarry in Dorset, Eric was apoplectic with rage and she hastily slammed the door in his face as the baby bawled in shock. Eric returned to the yard, muttering to himself and cursing the outright selfishness of a no-good waster who could easily have nipped down to the quacks in Newby Bridge before he'd gone off on his jaunt. Ben noticed from about twenty yards or so that his father was crying as he climbed back into his mini-jeep and blasted out to the open fields. Ben had also drawn the same conclusion about his feckless brother-in-law. He was beginning to detest that man. How his wife failed to see her brother's true character defied Ben's version of common sense.

Katarina promised Ruby that she would keep an eye on the farm's menfolk and holidaying visitors alike whenever she could during Ruby's anticipated absences in Manchester. She realised that Ben would be away just as much if not more than Ruby, and that Ruby's real concern in the domestic context was for Eric. Ruby had grown to love that girl for their mutual solidarity, and here she was again, giving of herself in their time of need. It would not be forgotten.

Then Rhona appeared quite unexpectedly and quite late one afternoon. She reported that she'd driven from Newcastle to Manchester first, before rebounding back up to Cumbria. She had just wanted to give the exhausted new parents some form of support, and then perhaps to bring some good news back home with her. Alas, that wasn't possible, and she chided her mother gently for not having made sure that new baby clothes had been made a priority. In all the chaos and wretchedness no one had thought to buy something for the baby that might just help poor Henrietta to believe that her first born did indeed have a viable future. The new mum had been completely overcome and had clung to Ben's big sister like a limpet as she'd poured her heart out.

Ten agonising days ticked slowly by. Keith had buckled under pressure from his wife and submitted his samples at the local surgery for urgent despatch to Manchester.

Ben and Henrietta shuffled into the paediatric oncology ward and went immediately to check on their son. His scrawny arms lay splayed to both sides and his pale, bowed legs poked helplessly from the two large holes in his disposable nappy. It was as if he was being held down by the weight of tubes and monitors attached to his ravaged little body, but there was nothing they could do. They couldn't even hold him to let him absorb that primeval sensation of parental warmth and physical proximity. He was indeed exactly as he looked, alone in the world and fighting for his life.

The consultant oncologist took them into his office just a little way down the corridor. He appeared nervous once again, just like the first occasion when he'd had to spill the most dreadful news to them. Henrietta grew tense in anticipation of more punishing feedback. She had seen for herself that Jamie was not progressing and certainly not putting on any weight despite his nourishing drip. The specialist sat them down and then curiously buzzed through to an adjacent office and asked a female colleague to come through. When she arrived she was introduced as a blood specialist and the anxious parents braced themselves for more devastating technicalities.

She delivered the details as sympathetically as possible, but there was simply no hiding the failure of Jamie's autologous stem cell transfer. The patient's parents seemed to crumple at the news, however expected it may have been. The doctors pushed on. They would now move quickly to stage two, just as had been outlined during the very first assessment briefing. However, they had a problem, one of ethical rather than medical considerations, and they needed to seek acceptance from their immediate audience that they could discuss their difficulties candidly. The urgency of the situation demanded total complicity.

Ben and his wife appeared lost and confused in all the apparent complexity.

"What exactly do you need?" he pleaded in tired desperation.

"Right now we need your understanding," the oncologist replied. "Then we will need a decision from you," and he looked pointedly at Ben and then Henrietta.

"Okay," said Ben, "I'm sure we're not going to object, so what is it?"

"Mr and Mrs Meaner, what I'm about to do is highly unorthodox and arguably well beyond the normal rules of ethics governing patient confidentiality. Our patient obviously can't speak for himself, and in circumstances such as these some observers would suggest that I really should have this conversation with each of you separately, such is its sensitivity." Ben glanced askew at Henrietta only to register that the two of them were equally bewildered. The good doctor pressed forward.

"You will of course readily understand that we must not delay, for Jamie's sake. You will also remember that the next phase involves a stem cell transfusion from a donor, usually one of the parents."

"Yes, yes, of course," Henrietta confirmed with a flash of irritation.

"We have identified the best protein match for this next step in the process," the doctor continued. "It is with the boy's father," he added, but in saying this he looked not at Ben, but at Henrietta, who recoiled and sat upright in the back of her chair, a glint of recognition in her eye.

"What is it? What's the matter?" Ben quizzed, with mounting confusion. He looked at the medics and then at his wife and then back to the medics again.

"Mr Meaner, there is no other way to tell you this than just to say it outright." Time stopped. Ben shuffled on his seat, perplexed, uncomfortable. "Mr Meaner, I'm sorry to have to inform you that you are not the father of this child."

35

next in line

If Ben Meaner's world had been knocked sideways by his son's potentially fatal illness, then it was rent clean asunder to discover the heartbreaking bitter truth that his son wasn't his at all, and that the woman he loved beyond measure had dealt him the cruellest blow imaginable.

The flight mechanism had kicked in immediately. He'd jumped up and out of his chair like a jack-in-the-box as his subconscious reaction drove him away from those who had heaped savage disappointment upon him. He took several steps into the corner of the room as his wife, convulsing with guilt, wailed into her hands, bending forward to her knees, instinctively trying to minimise her own culpable presence in the midst of the maelstrom thrashing around her. Ben stood facing the wall with his head in his hands. He fought to constrain the tears, but his erratic sobs punctuated the heavy atmosphere as the medics looked on, knowing that their revelations were not yet complete.

Suddenly Ben span on his heel. He took two quick strides across to his stricken wife, leaned closely over her and bellowed, "Why? There is nothing I wouldn't have done for you, and you reward me with this. How could you?" With that, he picked up his plastic hospital chair with one strong hand and cast it against the wall with an enormous crash. The oncologist's colleague reached for the phone intending to call security, but her senior stayed her hand and motioned that all would settle very soon. Ben headed for the door, which he threw back against its hinges, and stepped out into the corridor beyond. He stood there for just a moment, his head bowed, shaking gently from side to side in sheer disbelief. Then, as if he'd made a crucial decision right there on the spot, he turned quickly and walked directly back in through the open door which he closed softly in its frame. He picked up the forlorn chair and righted it noisily in front of the desk. He sat down heavily, placed his hands on his knees and looked at the medics, but not at his distraught wife.

"What does all this mean for my so…er…for Jamie?" he asked.

"We have a match, Mr Meaner."

"You do…really?"

They looked at him blankly. Then they looked at Henrietta.

"It's Keith… Oh Christ, it's bloody Keith!" Henrietta shrieked, as she writhed with remorse and regret.

Ben just gaped at her. He turned slowly to the consultant who nodded his slow affirmation of the claim at stake. Ben rose from his chair, slowly this time, and made for the door. There he looked back at the professionals behind the desk and simply said, "Just do it. Get him down here and take what you need, and then just do it." Then he was gone.

The doctors knew that it wasn't Ben's approval they needed – he wasn't the father after all. However, with Henrietta's snivelling agreement provided through a vigorous nodding of the head, they at least felt confident that either she or they might summon the real father forthwith.

As Ben drove north he tried to work through the practical aspects of what he should do next. As the miles clicked onto the dashboard register the acid in his gut gnawed at him continuously. The swelling fermenting anger in his heart helped him to focus. He had so many questions and the answers to all of them impinged in some way on his own life and his own future up on the hill. More important to him, however, were the answers to those questions that might dictate whether or not little Jamie would have any kind of future at all. He bit his lip as he thought of that tiny bundle of flesh, tapes and tubes and he just hoped that the lad could survive and thrive.

He determined not to tell his parents anything about the day's sickening revelations. How could he? What would he say? How would they react? Above all, how would his father react? Now, there was a consideration he'd rather not have to wrestle with until he'd got his head back together. He'd leave Rhona, his sister, well out of it too. What would be the point? What would she say? What could she say – the next-door neighbour has been shagging his own sister, despite her being married to my little brother, and now look what's happened? Hell, in the middle-term it could get very, very messy at home, but just now it was essential that Keith, that useless bastard Keith, got himself down to the hospital and did his duty. Shit, if Keith were still there by the time he made it back, he'd go round there and kick his arse into that sodding Range Rover and send him down the M6 with a few bruises for company. Then he thought about the police – wasn't incest illegal? How the friggin' hell could he grass up his own wife? Putting her worthless brother in the frame was one thing, but his own wife?

When he reached the lower gates and the start of the rough old lane up the hill he saw Gilly's Volvo descending towards the road so he waited to let her exit over the cattle grid. As soon as she had cleared the grid he accelerated forward without looking into her passing vehicle. As Gilly passed his waiting SUV just beyond the rattling old cattle grid she smiled sympathetically and tried to flag Ben down with a waft of a hand out of the window. He roared right past her, but she'd seen the tears cascading down his stubbly face and she'd instantly feared the worst in Manchester.

Keith Salcombe had been summoned south by his tearful, distressed sister. When he'd queried the medical results over the phone and asked Henrietta if she was sure they were right, she'd exploded down the phone and demanded he get his sorry arse underway immediately, and certainly before Ben got home – she couldn't vouch for her brother's safety in that regard.

When he reached the hospital two hours later he parked up and rushed inside in search not of his son, but of his sister. He found her resting in the visitors' day room with a plastic cup of tea in her hand. As he hurried towards her with open arms intending to comfort her, she threw the tea in his face and angrily told him not to come anywhere near her. The ward sister witnessed the incident, as did two other attending parents, and she whisked him off to the consultant's office to keep him out of harm's way. Henrietta was asked to join him there in five minutes or thereabouts; in fact, as soon as the consultant himself reappeared.

Keith sat there alone and in a fitful mood. He was in turmoil. He guessed it must have been their very last time together, immediately before Henri had apparently met Ben when he'd called at the house. God Almighty – how was he going to get out of this jam? He believed he could always wend Henri round to his own way of thinking, but Ben, well…

that was another challenge altogether. Then he remembered the simple but important appreciation that Ben was his sister's husband. Incest was bad enough, and something he'd fretted about throughout his adult relationship with her, but adultery too, and now this…a desperately sick child. Shit, what was he going to do? How could he even hope to keep this from Gilly? And what about his own grown-up sons? Oh, no, he just couldn't contemplate any sort of outcome there, not yet.

He stood and began pacing backwards and forwards. Then his mind switched the points and he ran off down an arguably more dangerous track, if that were possible. The drugs – and his confession to Austen! Shit, he thought, had that been just a massive mistake? Up and down, up and down the clean washed floor he went, and at every second turn he looked out of the window and into the trees beyond the car park with the earliest hint of springtime greenery. The movement helped him to concentrate as he chewed his problems over in manic search of workable solutions.

As he drifted across the front of the desk something caught his eye – a manila file with a name tag protruding from beneath the cover. He thought it read BABY MEANER, and when he leaned over for a closer look that's exactly what it said. He looked back to the frosted glass in the door of the office. He noticed that the frame of the door had been split at both hinges, but the door appeared to have closed perfectly well nevertheless. He stepped over to it and eased it open. Peering through the crack both ways, up and down the corridor, he could see nobody in close attendance so he quickly made his way back to the desk and flipped the file open. Little Jamie's blood analysis stared back at him from the facing page, but there, in the lower margin, a hand-scribbled note took his breath away.

36

rough justice

Keith returned home very late that night. The procedure had been painful and he'd been advised to stay in overnight, but he'd rejected that option. He hadn't been prepared for that and he had a gathering clutch of important things to do that might just save his neck both domestically and in a judicial sense. He just had to see Austen again. He hadn't seen his bastard son at all.

It had rained all day and as the Range Rover bounded over the cattle grid and up the hill it splashed and dashed its way through torrents of hilltop drainage which washed yet more loose material from the track and into the ditches either side. In his headlights he could see the torrents tumbling towards him, and in his festering anger he almost lost control at one point, skewing the rear offside of the vehicle close to a short stretch of steep bank which could so easily have rolled him over.

He pulled up abruptly outside the main door having given up on the idea of parking alongside the other cars round the side. To do that would have exposed him to the belting rain on his short walk back to the house. He pushed on the front door, but it appeared to be locked. He cursed as he fumbled for his keys realising that he'd left them in his coat pocket in the back of the car. He got soaked retrieving them, and that certainly did nothing for his mood. Stumbling into the hall he saw his wife, Gilly, coming down the stairs in her dressing gown.

"Where the hell have you been?" she challenged.

"What?" he said, taking off his jacket and shaking the raindrops free before hanging it on the coat stand.

"I said, where have you been? Do you know what time it is?"

"What the fuck is that to you?" he shouted back. He took two steps towards her and she shifted uneasily, sensing an unusual threat.

"What's the matter?" she asked. "I haven't been able to reach you all day."

"I've been with my sister in hospital, if that's okay with you?"

"What? Till this late in the day? Is there a problem? Are they alright…I mean, is there any improvement?"

"No, no, there isn't any improvement…thanks for asking," he spat back at her.

"Sorry? What do you mean? What's going on?"

"What's going on? Well, what an interesting question. What d'you think's the matter? What could possibly be wrong – my sister being marooned in hospital with a terminally sick baby – what could possibly be the matter, I wonder?"

"Eh, love…what are you saying? Why are you being like this?" and she moved towards him, placing a gentle hand on his shoulder. He brushed it off, scowling at her with such disdain that for the first time ever in his presence she felt as if she were in physical danger. He turned away and walked through to the kitchen. She followed him reluctantly, drawn in, hypnotised almost by his arcane, agitated state. She watched him open a cupboard and reach up for the cognac bottle on the top shelf.

"Love, it's nearly one o'clock in the morning. You don't normally drink at this time of night."

He barked at her, "Leave me alone, alright, just leave it."

"What's happening, love? What's this all about?"

"What, is it not enough to see my own sister at the end of her tether, miserable, desolate, hanging on for her son's dear life? Should there be more, Gilly, is there more?"

"What? What is this obtuse crap? Why are you talking in riddles?"

"Oh, riddles now, is it? That's rich coming from you."

"Look, just stop it! Stop this right now!" she shouted.

"Stop what, Gilly? What am I supposed to stop? Shouldn't you have been the one to put some things on hold, Gilly? Wasn't that your responsibility, Gilly – you fucking hypocrite!"

Her tears greeted his snarling aggression. He glared at her, expectant, waiting for her to respond. She was adrift, floundering in confusion. What was he getting at? What could he possibly be referring to? She tore off a piece of kitchen roll, wiped her eyes and blew her nose. She cleared her throat and said, "Like it or not, Keith, you're just gonna have to tell me. You're not getting out of this kitchen until we sort this out."

Keith broke down. He sobbed uncontrollably, his hands covering his face as if ashamed of his apparent weakness. He stood there shaking, his staccato sniffles accentuating her alarm. She moved around the breakfast bar and approached him. He turned back to his late-night warmer, grasped the glass and swallowed the golden nectar in one go with a backward throw of his head. He planted the empty glass loudly on the bench top and pushed it away as the burning spirit descended in his chest. Then he turned to her and looked directly into her eyes, his own seething with a hatred he simply couldn't mask.

"Sort this out?" he queried in softer tones that belied his inner fury. "Sort this out? And how the hell are we supposed to sort this out? What shall we try first – is it the fact that you and your very own young farmer have been fucking the brains out of each other, or perhaps we should somehow try to tackle the rather uncomfortable reality that the little bastard lying in the cot upstairs isn't my son?"

Wide-eyed, she gasped in disbelief. "Fucking bitch!" he yelled, and his right-hand haymaker caught her high on the left cheek just below the eye and on the side of the nose. The impact of the blow sprawled her backwards across the kitchen floor, the back of her head catching the edge of a tall stool at the breakfast bar as she fell. She retained a dizzy consciousness, just, and her arms flailed about as she tried to get up from the floor. She saw that she was bleeding and she felt sure that she'd suffered a broken nose and possibly a fractured cheekbone. Pushing herself up to a sitting position she looked about in search of her husband fearing that another attack may be imminent, but he'd gone. She was alone. She burst into tears.

The following morning Ben was hurrying through his chores knowing that he had to set off for the M6 just after a no doubt hasty lunch break. As he skirted the perimeter of the garden at Rowan House, and moving at pace on his quad bike, he glanced up towards the house and suddenly braked hard. There in the upstairs bedroom window he saw Gilly standing completely still and simply staring out into the fields around them. It was at some range, but he could see that she was in her dressing gown – not unusual in the morning – but he felt sure that there was something odd, something wrong with her facial appearance. He couldn't quite see enough, but then she turned slightly and looked directly at him and he identified an ugly swelling to the left side of her face. He stopped the quad, climbed down and walked over to the drystone wall to get a slightly closer look. He realised that she was in distress, and then, just for a moment she stepped away from the window and he thought she had moved away quite deliberately. But then she reappeared and began to wave to him frantically, beckoning him to come to the house.

He slipped in through the back gate and passed the garden shed – scene of many physical exploits for the two of them in the past. He walked quickly up to the back kitchen door and was about to knock when a grotesquely disfigured countenance appeared at the window. He swallowed hard as she unlocked the door for him. As he stepped inside she clung to him and cried and cried. He held her close and let her emotions run their natural course. Then he looked down at her and gently brushed her hair back from her wounded features.

"Was this Keith's doing?" he asked in sombre judgement. She nodded lamely. "My God," he sighed, "what sort of creature does this kind of thing to his own wife?" and at that instant he thought about his own wife and he knew without reservation that he loved her with every fibre of his being. Gilly looked up into the warmth of his caring eyes and she began to speculate as to the nature of this quietly indignant young man's reaction to the disfigurement before him. She felt disconcerted. She knew that they, the two of them, had offended her husband in such a fundamental fashion that he would probably never recover from the hurt they had inflicted upon him. However, she was acutely aware, how could she not be, that the young man in her arms, her former lover, was not only the father of her own child, but the husband to her own husband's sister with whom he had a terribly sick child languishing in hospital. She wished only the best for them all, but how on earth could she navigate her own way through this emotional labyrinth, let alone help those around her to do the same?

"Ben, you must sit down," she mumbled through her swollen lips.

"Not before I've smashed his face in," he responded defiantly.

"No, no, Ben, that's not going to help, really... It just isn't going to sort out any of our problems. Anyway," she continued, "he's not here. He left early this morning."

"So where is he? Up at that sodding quarry, I suppose?"

"I don't know, but I guess so, yes. It would make sense."

He looked fondly at her again. "How many times did he hit you?"

"Just once...only once," she offered. "It looks bad, doesn't it?" she asked.

"You can say that again," he said with a wry smile, and he stretched across to her and kissed her lightly on her good side. A tear ran down her smooth cheek, but she checked it with the back of her hand. "Why?" he asked. "Why did he do it?"

She looked down, twisted her fingers together, and tried to get her next few statements in the right order in her head. This was going to be a shock to Ben, she knew that, and she so desperately wanted to protect him from the heartache. He'd had enough of that already, and she couldn't possibly imagine how he was going to survive this next emotional bomb-blast.

"Look, Ben, I think the hospital situation has really got to him. He seems to have been under great pressure at work for some months and now, with your baby's grave difficulties, and Henri's appalling anxiety of course, and well...I just think it's pushed him over the edge in some way."

"You're defending him, Gilly. He doesn't deserve it," Ben insisted. "Nobody has the right to do this kind of thing to another person, least of all to his own wife."

"I know, I know, Ben, but he had some more bad news yesterday... er, at the hospital I mean."

"Oh, I bet he did," Ben smiled with apparent sarcasm.

"Ben," she prompted, "I just have to tell you this as it is. Please try not to overreact. I don't think I could stand another commotion like last night." He looked immediately wary. "Ben, you need to know...that Joseph is your son, not Keith's. Joe is our son," she added for emphasis.

The shock stunned him into silence. His lips opened and closed twice, but emitted no sound. He leaned back into the chair and not once did he take his eyes from her. He saw the truth in her statements in her own eyes. She smiled at him sympathetically, warmly, lovingly, he thought. And then he simply cried, softly, head bowed, overwhelmed by the tragic complexity of the convoluted maze their intertwined lives had come to represent. She sat forward and took his hands in hers and let his torment wash itself away.

Then he adjusted his seat and wiped a crude sleeve across his face to dry his tears. "So this is why he assaulted you?" he asked. "This is what good men do who have been wronged by their loved ones, is that it?"

"Yes, I suppose that would be his defence."

"And before he punched you, did he have the courage to tell you anything else that he'd discovered in hospital yesterday?"

"Just that Jamie was still showing little sign of responding to his treatment," she replied.

"Interesting," Ben retorted.

"What is?" she asked, intrigue jostling to the front of her focus.

"That he had nothing else to say to you last night."

"What are you getting at?" she queried, now getting worried.

He sighed with disappointment and shook his head just once. "Gilly, it's your turn now I'm afraid."

"What? What are you talking about?"

"You know it's almost a relief just to share this with someone I trust. I can't even tell my folks."

"Share what, Ben, what?"

"Joseph might be my son, Gilly," his voice breaking just like his heart, "but Jamie isn't." Her eyes again searched his for any hint of an explanation, but then he simply stammered, "Jamie is Keith's son, not mine."

She gasped and gagged, and a line of spittle leaked out from the swollen corner of her mouth. The sickening truth ripped through her, pillaging every last morsel of tolerance she may have saved for her pathetic husband. Her prejudices for and against her sister-in-law, Henrietta, dissolved in the angry bile of her cramped gut. That corrosive bitch had sweet-talked her way into all of their lives and this was their collective reward.

Ben stood and looked down upon her as she wrestled with the myriad implications of this latest reveal. He bent over her and kissed her softly again, and then he left via the same back door and strode out along the garden path.

37

hope springs…

Two weeks had passed and Ben was constantly close to exhaustion. The endless travelling up and down to see the bairn, combined with the normal, exacting demands of the farm were giving him no respite to speak of. He'd maintained his attentive vigil by the lad's incubator not just out of a sense of responsibility, but also from a sense of love. He argued with Henrietta, who he still held at arm's length, that he had committed to the child in good faith and that he, Jamie, had so very few people he could rely on – a point amplified by Keith's consistent absence.

Henrietta had remained in a state of mild shock, a condition nurtured by her own gratuitous self-loathing. She dared not think about the reality of her circumstances. She wished only that her son might get better and from there they would take each day as it came. Her love for Ben had never wavered, but she fully appreciated his hurtful reluctance to maintain merely a close caring bond for the baby and nothing more.

They were rewarded when wee Jamie's blood counts began to show a definitive improvement, and shortly thereafter they began to witness an increase in his twitching movements among the web of plastic tubes around him. Then he acquired a few grams of extra weight and for the first time in weeks they began to believe that he might just pull through after all.

To the nursing staff who understood the tragedy and complexity of the Meaner case, Henrietta remained the subject of silent ridicule and off-hand procedural comment. Her husband, on the other hand, had been granted near superhero status, especially among the younger girls for whom he presented all of the desirable characteristics of an imagined partner and lover. Not only was he gorgeously handsome, but he had the morals of a saint and the stamina of an ox. They fussed around him whenever he was there, and later, much later, Henrietta would assure him that his halo effect had most certainly rubbed off on the little one in the form of near constant attention and observation. Henrietta could see the way the cards were being dealt and she suffered their unspoken criticism stoically.

The news of Jamie's upward progress was greeted rapturously and with many tears of joy back on the hill. Keith had been seen only rarely in weeks, and Ruby had expressed her disappointment at his lack of attention to his own sister, not to mention his sickly new nephew. Ben had let the comment pass – there would be a time, and it wasn't too far off. Eric had maintained his distance. Secretly he had suspected for some weeks that all was not well between the cantankerous woman next door and her less than impressive husband, but he'd kept his thoughts to himself. Besides, he was flat out with sheep, holiday lets and pheasant feeding, so it wasn't as if he had time to gossip.

Katarina had made sure that Ben's apartment was always spotless and fully stocked with all the extras: beer in the fridge, snacks and eats of various kinds, clean towels and even some ironed shirts. Ruby had told her to ditch the ironing – he was a farmer after all – but no, she had insisted that he should look his best when going to see his wife and son in hospital.

Gilly had kept to herself, certainly while her great welt had been so prominent immediately after her beating. But even after her recovery she had received few visitors and had stayed indoors with her healthy boisterous baby. She had confronted Keith with the other half of the story as soon as she had felt well enough and strong enough to hold her own. There had been no histrionics, no blazing row and no violence. She had balanced the books; it was as simple as that, and he had no more room in which to manoeuvre. She had instructed him to give some thought to how they might manage together, both families, when Henrietta returned from Manchester. From that point in time they had lived rather separate lives and tolerated one another on the periphery.

Ben had spoken to Gilly only once since that awful exchange of mind-blowing home truths. He knew she would support him in whatever awaited them shortly at another looming crossroads in their lives. That support was mutual; she knew that too.

38

trailer tale

"Hey, boss," DS Sutton called to Lehrer as he stood on the other side of the operations room, "I've got Iain Young on the line here," and she beckoned him with an urgent wave.

"Put him on speaker," Lehrer instructed.

"Iain," she said, "I've got the chief here on speaker – can you just rewind and give us that first bit again."

"Gotcha, Caroline! I'm over at the Lancaster service station on the M6. I've been looking at some of these lorry checks, as you know, Chief."

"Yes, and what've you got?" asked the DCI.

"A breakthrough, I think, Chief." Others close by in the office began to listen in and Lehrer instantly regretted the squawk box indiscretion. He knew he couldn't turn it off now. That would give too many negative signals about trust and team work.

"We are all ears, Iain," he said, smiling to the team members gathering round.

"We stopped a truck half an hour ago. Its livery suggests a Barrow firm and Traffic have confirmed a Barrow area plate." An expectant silence reigned in the office. "The dogs went berserk round the end of the trailer. When we yanked the weather caps off the ends of the tailgate crossbars, you know, right at the aft end of the trailer, we found eight vacuum-packed plastic-wrapped bags which had been carefully inserted into the hollow section of one crossbar."

"Bloody hell!" Caroline Sutton exclaimed.

"My reaction exactly, Caroline," Young added. "One of them had perforated inside the frame, probably through vibration of the vehicle."

"Any accurate assessment of what the stuff is – cocaine, crystal meth, what?" Lehrer enquired.

"Oh, it's crystal meth, Chief, no doubt about it."

"What did the driver have to say for himself?" Lehrer asked.

"Heh…d'you know…he looked a bit sheepish, I can tell you, but I'm sure that he's just a contract driver. He knew nothing about this. He looked bloody terrified, frankly…once he realised what we'd found."

"And where was he heading?"

"Croydon apparently, guv. Handy for South London I'd have thought."

"So are the drug squad offering any ideas?"

"Well, Chief, I really don't think they need to." Quizzical looks crisscrossed the office.

"Why so?"

"Apparently these random checks have let a lot of Cumbrian wagons simply drive through. It's all about some regional protocol to do with being selective and targeting carriers from Scotland, well…all points further north I'd say. But it's not this one's destination that's the giveaway – he's carrying building slate from Rusland Quarry."

39

if at first...

They descended on the quarry like drones, uniformed officers in short sleeves fanning out across the site in the warm May sunshine. The dogs pulled hard on their leads at first, but were then released and followed eagerly.

The chief engineer had looked a little crestfallen, not when he saw the vans roll up, but when Lehrer asked him to shut everything down to allow machinery and machine spaces to be carefully checked in safety. He complained that it hadn't been all that long ago since the last visit, and he wondered what they hoped to find this time that they didn't locate last time.

When he made a sarcastic quip about police harassment Lehrer had rounded on him and asked what he'd meant.

"Well, I had your chief constable on the phone not ten minutes ago looking for my chairman, who doesn't spend a lot of time on-site, I have to say. Then five minutes later he's on again, I mean...how often do you get two calls from the senior policeman in the district within just a few minutes? And then you lot appear up the main drive and close me down for the second time in just a few weeks."

"That is unusual, I'll grant you that. That's more calls than I get from the big chief in two months never mind five minutes – what on earth did he want?"

"Like I said, he was looking for the chairman, Austen Smiley, but he's rarely here."

"Yes, but why the follow-up call so quickly after the first?"

"I think it was just an afterthought. He asked me where my managing director was."

"By name?"

"Well, er...yes actually. It struck me as odd in that he didn't ask to speak to Keith directly –Keith Salcombe, that's our MD – he just wanted to know where he might be."

"Does seem odd, I must say, but I take it Keith Salcombe isn't on-site otherwise he'd be right here with us?"

"Yes, that's right. Keith is working from home again today," he said wearily, as if it had become customary.

Lehrer took his leave temporarily and headed out to check on progress. He was unnerved, certainly curious, and he knew of the Smiley character by reputation. He was also disappointed to discover that Morgan Dyer wasn't on shift. He called on reinforcements to pay Morgan a visit and to drag him out of bed as soon as possible.

After an hour they had nothing. The dogs had again acted excitedly in the loading and parking areas. They wondered about the possibilities of particle traces in these spaces born out of delicate and discreet stashing of narcotics on a variety of vehicles, but it seemed unrealistic. Perhaps those trucks that were regularly used as supply vehicles carried some form of microscopic contamination, but again, it was a stretch to expect traceable spores at ground level. Lehrer had asked the elderly foreman about their precise loading methods, but there was nothing alarming about those procedures and nothing to point them in an alternative direction.

As before, they drew a complete blank. The frustration was palpable as the small groups of searchers slowly regathered at the quarry head and were left kicking their heels while detectives from the task force and the drug squad convened an impromptu review meeting. It was only as they broke and Lehrer commented to the foreman that it was as if there was another section of the site that was somehow invisible, that the elder statesman shot back, "Well...I don't know what you lot are looking for, but I take it your lads have been down to the old rail head and those derelict warehouses down there?"

They all stopped and just looked at him like a bunch of Easter Island statues.

"Come again?" asked DS Sutton.

"The old warehouses – round the back o' that spoil heap over yonder," he said, pointing with a craggy finger. "I must be the only bloke here who remembers when we used to ship out so much slate and stone that we had to use the railway down to the old docks at Port Haverigg, y'know...over by Millom."

Lehrer looked like he might explode. The old boy continued.

"The railway got ripped up years ago and it's all fenced off and overgrown now. The old road down there from here is impassable now, just overgrown with hawthorn and dense thicket, but I bet you can get through on foot. It's only ten minutes at worst."

Lehrer's phone buzzed in his pocket as DS Sutton led the troop in search of their holy grail.

"DCI Lehrer!"

"Detective Chief Inspector, it's Chief Superintendent Campbell here."

"Oh, Chief, hello...er, how can I help you? You seem to have called at a very opportune moment."

"I see, and why's that, Detective Chief Inspector?"

"I suspect we are just about to make a breakthrough at long last."

"Ah, I see. Allow me to postulate that it may have something to do with the narcotics end of our investigations."

Lehrer remembered his former chief superintendent's warning and was instantly wary.

"And why do you say that, Chief? Has someone been gossiping in the ops room?"

"No, because the chief constable just rang me and instructed me to get you, with some urgency, out to a place called Rowan House. Do you know it?"

"I know of it, but DI Young has visited the place more than once. He's standing right beside me. I'm sure he could have us there in no time."

"Just as well – I suspect you have no time to lose. The chief constable wants you to apprehend a certain Austen Smiley on the grounds that he may be intending to commit a serious offence." Lehrer's eyebrows arched in surprise, and he looked in alarm at his colleague.

"Isn't that where Keith Salcombe resides, Chief?"

"Precisely, Detective Chief Inspector, and I must urge you to get there just as quickly as you can. Go now!"

"We're on it, Chief," and they were indeed racing towards Young's car.

"Oh, and, DCI Lehrer…?"

"Yes, Chief," Lehrer panted.

"Smiley is believed to be armed."

As Lehrer and Young spliced through the main road traffic under a silently screaming blue light, DS Caroline Sutton and her search teams broke cover from the dense undergrowth behind the quarry spoil tip. There they stood: a short series of rusty, dilapidated industrial sheds which fronted to a long straight line of concrete and beyond that a lower level thick with bushes. At first sight they took it to be a loading platform that once had enjoyed railway service right alongside.

As the bolt croppers tore away two obviously modern padlocks, the dogs yelped in excitement and anticipation. They weren't needed. Walking through into the second bay of the old warehouse the entire production facility of bottles and jars, pipes and tubes lay rudely there for all to see. Outside the team easily picked up trail-bike tyre tracks which threaded their way through more dense foliage to another stretch of old rail bed and a padlocked perimeter gate. Beyond that they recognised pickup and trail-bike tracks in the dirt which disappeared into thin green scrub.

Earlier that same morning Ben Meaner had returned reluctantly from his tour of duty of the many ewes and lambs scattered around the lush green fields. He'd been dreading this day and this moment for some time. He knew that relationships within their tight hilltop society would be extremely difficult after Henrietta's return from hospital with baby Jamie. That day was still some way off, but the confidence and optimism on display among the medics in Manchester had encouraged Ben to believe that the little one would survive and prosper. They couldn't predict a middle-term or long-term outcome, but it was enough for Ben to plan constructively for the little boy's future.

He hadn't discussed any of his ideas with his wife, Henrietta. Her deceit had wounded him severely. It all felt so very raw. He knew he had his own confession to make at the right time, but he saw his pre-marital liaison with Gilly as an indiscretion to offend Keith, not so much Henrietta. In any event, and for all Ben knew, Keith may have already enlightened his sister on the subject of Gilly's misdemeanours and about the paternity of her child, Joseph. Ben had decided that he'd cross those bridges when he came to them. For Keith he cared not a jot. For Gilly he found his affection growing not receding, and for Henrietta he knew only an abiding love that he hoped she would accept and reflect. However, for his own parents Ben retained only fear and anxiety. He knew instinctively that they might take the convoluted truth badly, but just how badly? He could only assume negative fall-out; he just hoped it would remain within his compass to manage the situation.

When he drove back into the yard he saw his father heading into the kitchen for breakfast and Ben knew that the time was upon him. He swallowed hard, climbed off the quad bike and lumbered over to the heavy kitchen door. Two full-English plates, with acres of toast and marmalade, were devoured by two very hungry farmers, and when the tea mugs were reaching empty Ben called for some refills and then asked his mother to come and sit down at the table – he had something important to say.

His father had grunted something about having to get back to the bird feeders and his mother had wanted to get some cleaning materials together for Katarina before she rolled up for work, but he insisted in a quiet, authoritative manner and both began to think something was wrong in Manchester despite all the good news of late.

He tried to prepare them for difficult tidings of a very different kind, and he opted for a plea for their help and understanding in coming to terms, practical terms, with their changing circumstances. He just about lost his father's interest right there, but he soon recovered the old boy's attention when he admitted that the first disjoint in the story was undoubtedly his, Ben's, own error and his alone.

When he confided that he had been having a sexual relationship with Gilly Salcombe his mother had taken a sharp intake of breath and tears pricked behind her eyes. When he quickly reassured them that their secret tryst had certainly been terminated as soon as Henrietta had entered his life, his father snorted with derision as if to question why he was even troubling his mother with such trivial nonsense. His mother, however, visibly unsettled and already angrily simmering, asked how long they had been...seeing each other. When he surprised her honestly she recognised instantly that her own son could have barely broken into his early twenties when that damned woman had first seduced him.

She considered that for no more than a second or two before launching a blistering verbal assault on her next-door neighbour, impugning every aspect of her character and her abject lack of responsibility. Eric listened to his wife's impassioned tirade and began to adopt much of her fierce animosity towards the conniving, interfering bitch he had always struggled to tolerate.

When Ben delivered his first depth-charge, that little Joseph was in fact his own son, Eric had reached over the table and slapped a fat palm across his son's face before Ruby had been able to pull him back into his seat. She had roared at him to get a grip, suggesting that if anyone needed a beating it was her next door. A lull in the storm allowed their brains to race forward in disparate directions as they crunched through a series of very distasteful questions. As those questions began to formulate Ben then told them that there was more.

The silence was overpowering. He looked at each of them, recognising the pain he had inflicted upon them and he wished with all his heart that he could dismantle the truth and wipe this very sticky slate spotlessly clean, but no. He reminded them of some of the finer technical details of Jamie's illness, and they nodded meekly when he re-emphasised the vital need for a matching donor to supply the bairn with his life-saving transfusion. They began to look a bit vague, clearly wondering where this could possibly be going, and then he simply revealed that the closest match had been not with Ben himself, but with Keith. Then he'd looked at them, seeing them through blurred vision, and realising that they hadn't grasped the essential significance of his statement. He pointed out that most matches came via a child's parents. Still they didn't lock onto his blunt message. Keith was Jamie's natural father. Eric and Ruby had looked at each other momentarily for mutual confirmation of their worst possible fears. Their daughter-in-law...their own son's wife...had been pregnant all along with her brother's child. The disgust, the revulsion, the unbridled loathing for those bastards next door just ripped through the two of them from head to heart. Ruby had slumped forward onto the table and wailed her heart out not for those atrocious creeps through the wall, and not even for her own son who had clearly been gravely wronged in this hellish tale, but for the two little boys who had been born into such a vile sub-human scandal. Eric had erupted with all manner of expletives and vowed to wreak revenge on those inbreds, and Ben, in his desperation to present some moderating ideas on how the dreadful state of affairs might be handled, lost his father's engagement completely.

Eric made for the door, grabbed his cap, picked up his shotgun and shouted that he would be with the birds in the copse if they needed him. He opened the door and then turned back as if to say something, but then burst into tears and withdrew, slamming the door loudly behind him.

Ruby cried herself into exhaustion in five minutes, shaking her head and offering unfinished sentences between the sniffles. Finally Ben was able to instil some sort of calm, and he outlined to his mother the parameters within which he thought he and Henrietta could still make a go of things on the farm. She had looked at her son with renewed pride for his decency and for the sacrifices he was proposing, but she was less than convinced. She foresaw the enmity with which the two families would each hold the other, and she could see no reasonable hope for harmony on the hill with the incredibly divisive nature of crossed paternity to negotiate on a daily basis. She voiced one of her greatest concerns; that of simply being unable to welcome Henrietta back into their side of the family. She projected that time would not be the fabled healer in a toxic set of relationships of this complexity. In truth, she wished the Salcombes would just bugger off and let the Meaners carry on farming, but she knew that such an unlikely outcome would not solve Ben's own challenges as a parent.

His mum had then simply risen from the table and walked out. She'd muttered something about Katarina, and was gone.

Ben sat there sipping the remains of his cold tea. He just didn't know what to do next. As a default option, or was it pure escapism, he hurriedly got changed and then drove off down the lane en route to Manchester Children's Hospital.

Eric prowled his way through the woods arguing with himself and cursing out loud as he weighed the facts. The outwardly impossible scenarios for congruence between hostile parties prevented him from drawing any kind of optimistic outlook for the months and years ahead. His visceral loathing of his neighbours ran unconstrained through his head, and he lamented the destructive impact that the two of them, that sour-faced bitch and her feeble husband, had visited upon his own son's hitherto promising prospects. As he proceeded from one bird feeder to another, his twelve-bore strapped across his back, he scuffed and kicked his way through chicks and juvenile birds as they gathered around him in search of any spillage at the feeders. He bellowed at them in blind rage as the harrowing reality of his son's situation settled in his mind. Through the copse he went, along the fairly well-worn path, talking out loud and swearing like a sailor, and with every step his hatred for those good-for-nothing incomers ratcheted ever upward in his heart.

After filling the last bin, he slumped onto his favourite seat, a bare chunk of granite that afforded a reasonably clear view of a shallow dell in the middle of the trees. He stood his gun on the ground and leaned it casually against the nearest trunk. He gnawed at his knuckles as he tossed the potential outcomes around in his head. The tension pulled at his gut and his shoulders and neck ached. His hands shook and he wiped his tears away periodically with his sleeved forearm. The birds dispersed, and calm fell over the glade, but Eric Meaner's mind was far from at peace. He sat there for fully ten minutes as he churned his way backwards and forwards, mulling every sorry detail, feeling every piercing slight his poor lad had endured.

Then a commotion broke out to his right, not thirty yards away and down by a crumbling old wall. The birds scattered, adults and some of the younger ones taking to the air, the chicks scurrying for their lives as panic ensued. Bleary-eyed he may have been, but the old farmer started in his crude seat as he caught the unmistakable outline of a fox's brush just disappearing behind the stones. He grabbed his gun and immediately flicked off the safety catch. He aimed at the next gap along the wall in the anticipated direction of the fox's movement, but he was too slow as the reddish blur skipped through the target area and he let go with both barrels only to pepper the wall with six-shot. A moment later and looking up from his reload, Eric saw the predator bounding away between the trees with a young bird clamped between its jaws. He yelled at the invader, pure anger and frustration consuming him, and then he snapped the gun shut, applied the safety, and set off through the glade back towards the farm.

40

rally cross

Lehrer was impressed. He had to hand it to the younger detective; the man could certainly drive. The senior man had hung on tightly as their emergency tactics had carried them quickly towards their goal. In truth he'd been miles away in his head. He still couldn't quite decide where to place his notional bet: Chief Superintendent Campbell, or Chief Constable Minton. Charlie Carlingford back in Ipswich had been right all along, but had Louis Minton really telephoned the quarry earlier in search of the man Smiley, or had someone merely impersonated the chief constable? The answer to that question would surely surface very quickly so long as they caught up with Smiley before he had the opportunity to do anything stupid.

DS Sutton had radioed through with the news of her successful discovery in the unused warehouses down at the quarry's old railhead. The reported wheel tracks at the perimeter of the old site surely accounted for the murder of Stevie Simms – he must have been shipping crystal meth when he died. The same proposition would certainly explain Morgan Dyer's confounding behaviour – they needed to locate him quickly.

The car flew over the cattle grid and raced towards the first bend in the gravel track. Young checked the turn of the steering wheel counter-intuitively as the back end of the Mercedes was allowed to drift wide around the curve. Then the rear wheel power pulsed into the dirt as soon as he'd straightened up, and the vehicle lurched forward and bolted up to the top of the next rise. He took the extensive course like a rally driver blasting through Kielder, and as soon as they reached the final approach to the house and lodge, just before the last bend to the farm, they saw a car parked askew in front of the house. A lone figure with what looked like a weapon of some sort appeared to be banging aggressively on the heavy front door. Young didn't hold back. He knew despite Lehrer's earlier call for uniformed assistance that it was down to the two of them. Backup just wouldn't get up there in time. The Merc left the lane at speed in a straight line tangent to the developing bend and roared up the driveway to Rowan House where it skidded to a stop with a raucous drag of granite stone chippings.

Lehrer was out and around the passenger door in a flash.

"Mr Smiley? Austen Smiley? My name is Detective Chief Inspector Lehrer from the Cumberland Police. Can we have a word, Mr Smiley, please?"

DI Young had leapt out at the other side of the car and moved smartly off to one side so as to mitigate the risks associated with two police officers standing side by side before an armed and potentially volatile suspect. The shotgun was clear for them to see at such short range. Indeed it looked like a splendid specimen of craftsmanship; an Over and Under, twelve-bore, with an elegant swirling engraving visible on the side of the receiver and an ornate carving on the wooden stock. Smiley took a sideways glance at one officer and then the other, a hint of frustration – or was it disdain? – pursing his lips before he turned to face them. The detectives froze.

"Mr Smiley…it is Austen Smiley, is it not?" Lehrer demanded in level tone. The man gave one barely perceptible nod. "Mr Smiley, can we start by putting the gun down?"

"Are you mad, Inspector?" he retorted, much to their surprise. Each detective looked confused.

"Mr Smiley, I can see that you are holding the gun in just one hand and that you are not threatening us, but would you like to put the gun down, sir?"

"Inspector, have you any idea how much this beautiful piece is worth? If you expect me to put it down on these coarse chippings then you must have another thing coming," and he chuckled dismissively at the apparent stupidity of the request. "Do you know anything about weapons such as this, Inspector?" he demanded.

"Enough to know that in public places, where the weapon may be a danger to others, it should be in its slip or at the very least broken and therefore safe from accidental firing," Lehrer replied. "Clearly neither of those conditions is met currently. You'll be telling me that it's loaded next."

"That's right, Inspector, it is."

"For what purpose, if I may ask, Mr Smiley?"

"No purpose – the safety catch is applied. It's perfectly safe."

"So what is your business here today?"

"I am visiting my friend and colleague, Mr Keith Salcombe, to show him this fine piece of hardware. He is thinking of taking up shooting and so I promised to let him have a few pops with this remarkable thoroughbred before he decides whether it really is his cup of tea or not." With that he quickly drew up the shotgun in both hands and snapped the breech open. He deftly picked out two bright red, brass-topped cartridges and stuffed them in his trouser pocket. Then he snapped it shut again and held it out to Lehrer at arm's length. Lehrer stepped forward with great relief and took the gun from its owner.

"So how was it supposed to go then, Mr Smiley? The two of you would step out into the fields behind the house and fire off a few shells at nothing in particular?"

"Exactly, Inspector, just so that he could get a feel for the dynamics of the thing, you know…the recoil, stepping into the aiming stance, that sort of thing."

"But, Mr Smiley, you have only two cartridges on your person right now – the two you've just put in your pocket. I can see them from here inside the lining of your trousers and I don't have to search you to see that there are no more cartridges available to you."

"Ah, yes…however, Inspector, I do have more in the car, of course," Smiley suggested.

"Perhaps, Mr Smiley, but when we approached just now in the car, DI Young and I saw very clearly that you were banging ferociously on this door with a primed weapon in your hand. Frankly it doesn't look like a social call. The fact that the residents here have not responded to your outwardly aggressive approach suggests to me that they would rather not admit you or even acknowledge your presence here. Would you like to start again and tell us just exactly what you are doing here?"

At that moment the rasping sound of hurried footsteps broke to their right. Turning to the source of the intervention, all three men witnessed a fit, wiry elderly man running from the side of the big house towards the main gates at the end of the short drive leading to the lane. Instinctively he looked to his right and quickly ground to a halt. He appeared to be about to say something when his line of sight locked onto the shotgun in DCI Lehrer's hand. He held up a remonstrative hand and began to back away as if in some sort of alarm. DI Young whipped out his ID card and assured the man in simplistic language that he need not be afraid.

Just then a distant siren peeled through the trees and reached the four men as they stood there on the drive.

"Don't worry," DI Young impressed upon the man, "that's just our backup."

He looked at them all with a rather bemused expression, and then simply said, "Well you're too late. You're all too late."

"What do you mean? What are you trying to say?" Young pressed.

"Let me show you," he replied, and he headed back whence he'd come. "It's not pretty mind, I should warn you of that."

As the entire group circled round the house to the back garden, their new ally gave a reassuring wave to an elderly woman in a little cottage which nestled in a rear corner plot. They could tell immediately that she was in some distress, and their guide explained that it was his wife. They were tenants in the cottage, and they had made the discovery together.

"What discovery?" Young asked as they neared the rear door, a kitchen door they supposed.

The man simply pointed in through the glass in the door.

The carnage left them aghast. They could make out the essential elements of the kitchen layout with breakfast bar, wood stove and dining area. In the middle of the room, close to a doorway leading most probably out to the hallway, lay the remains of a man whose body appeared to have exploded across the wall behind him. In the foreground a woman's body lay crumpled at the base of the breakfast bar. Two wooden stools appeared to have disintegrated under the force of a blast that had blown away much of her torso and the left side of her head. They could see her spine clearly exposed even from their position beyond the back door. The entire scene seemed to have been splattered with blood, bone fragments and bits of soft human tissue.

The look on Austen Smiley's face told the detectives that here was a man who may have harboured ill will towards one or both of the people lying inside that room, but he'd not been the perpetrator of such a brutal double murder. In fact, the unguarded terror written across his face probably suggested that he had neither the courage to do such a deplorable thing, nor had he ever been anywhere near such barbarity ever before. Lehrer absorbed that truth in a moment, and at the same time reminded himself that Smiley was almost certainly linked to an illegal narcotics scam that would engulf at least one and possibly two high-ranking officers in the Cumbrian force – he sincerely hoped there wouldn't be more.

DI Young slipped on a single forensic glove and gingerly tried the back door to the kitchen. It opened quite normally and they immediately heard the sound of a baby crying somewhere beyond the kitchen deep inside the house and possibly above them in a first-floor bedroom.

Back at the quarry, the techies from the CIS were just arriving and beginning to set out their forensic stall. Neither DS Sutton's team nor the company's off-shift employee, Morgan Dyer, had realised just how close they had each come to running into the other in those old secluded warehouses. As Morgan was making his exit through the rickety perimeter gate and making sure that the padlocked chain was securely back in place, the police vans were racing up the main drive and DCI Lehrer was presenting the senior man on site with his approved search warrant.

Morgan wore a shallow tight-fitting rucksack, this time carrying twelve sealed packs of crystal meth. He'd decided to use the Kent estuary run again as he hadn't been that way for some weeks. He'd arranged his dropping point accordingly, this time in the village of Milnthorpe, south of Kendal and not far from two motorway junctions. As he edged through the trees and away from the stone-hewing chasm behind him, he remained pleasantly unaware that a separate despatch of merchandise hidden in the trailer of a Barrow truck had in fact been detected at the Lancaster motorway services just a few hours earlier.

41

epilogue

Three weeks later a teenage couple walking hand-in-hand on the sands at Silverdale turned to call their two golden retrievers to heel. The young lovers had been dawdling along, stopping often to kiss and to hold each other tightly while trying to keep the wayward pets within reasonable whistling distance. The bay tide was so far out that they could just about make out the thin shimmering ribbon of ocean on the far horizon. For a change the midsummer sun shone down relentlessly and warmed the pale bare skin of the scantily clad, youthful figures otherwise alone on the vast expanse of open sand and silt.

But patience was wearing thin. The dogs must have stumbled across a live crab in a rock pool by the shore and they would not be persuaded to leave the poor thing. The girl jogged over to get them on their leads, leaving her boyfriend to admire her slender shapely form from the rear as she rather athletically distanced herself from him. Then, as she approached the four-legged reprobates, she gave a sharp shrill scream and appeared to stop dead in her tracks. She stared intently dead ahead and her young man bolted across the flats to be at her side.

There was no mistaking it. It was a badly decomposed body lying jammed between two small boulders. Little was left of the head and it appeared as if much of the skull had been repeatedly smashed against the rocks by the fierce tidal flows typical of the estuary. The body appeared to be clad in some sort of all-in-one body suit although it was difficult to identify any distinguishing features beyond that. However, a black backpack remained tightly clipped to the torso. One leg remained intact and in fact wore a robust leather boot. The other had lost its foot at the ankle and bare bones protruded from the gaping hole in the suit.

Morgan, just like his mate Stevie many months before, hadn't known the moment of his death. He'd made good progress that morning and had again timed the low tide to perfection. He'd been plugging away at a steady but inconspicuous pace. Just as he splashed through the broad wash of the river's outflow to the sea, at the lowest point of his crossing, the silent supersonic bullet had smashed into his visor, evacuated most of his crash helmet's contents out into the warm summer air, and hurled him backwards onto the silt. Within a few hours the rushing tides had soon buried the evidence, piling Morecambe Bay mud over the Kawasaki such that it would never be seen again. Morgan's body, however, was picked up and dragged for long distances by the ebb and flow of successive tides until eventually it was captured on the shoreline by a heavy collection of rocks. Dental records and ballistic forensics attested to the true fate of Morgan Dyer.

David Lehrer's task force was soon disbanded and his immediate team reverted to a slightly more predictable mix of cases as they came and went in the general scheme of things. The Cumbria force was left without a chief constable, and following Louis Minton's arrest John Campbell had stepped up a level to keep a steady hand on the wheel pending a new appointment. He was hopeful that his own application had some realistic merit.

Through direct contact with the Metropolitan Police in London, and relying heavily on their inside information feed from South London, Lehrer was forced to concede that the Cumbria shootings were almost certainly down to an exemplary professional hitman who had been sent north to staunch the intrusive supplies of crystal meth to the organised syndicates south of the river. What plagued the DCI for years thereafter was the disorientating juxtaposition of the clinical assassination of two targets, both accurately identified and efficiently despatched, compared with an apparent case of mistaken identity which had cost a young farmer his life.

The Rusland Quarry Company continued to work its gigantic excavation. Despite the loss of two lads in the cutting shed, a chairman and a managing director, it appeared to rumble on with hardly a step out of line. Austen Smiley, like his accomplice Louis Minton, was remanded for a variety of charges relating to the manufacture and distribution of class A drugs; Smiley also for conspiracy to murder.

It hadn't taken them long to uncover the brutal killer of Keith and Gilly Salcombe. His wife Ruby had discovered the sorry remains of Eric Meaner in the barn at Rowan Tree Farm. He'd sneaked away from the gruesome murder scene and doubled back behind the perimeter wall entering the farmyard unseen. He'd slipped in through the sliding back door of the barn, sat himself down on a hay bale, stuck the murder weapon in his own mouth and pressed the thumb of his outstretched hand hard against the trigger.

Ruby had spent a month in psychiatric care, but she had returned home to the farm only after securing the agreed condition that Ben and his wife Henrietta would move into the farmhouse and that she, Ruby, would move into Ben's former apartment. She had learned not just to love her son as indeed she always had, but also to respect and admire him. She didn't think she could ever love her daughter-in-law, but she recognised that Henrietta was mourning a loss too, and that she remained vulnerable. Moreover she realised that her son truly loved that girl with all his heart. Just as importantly, he loved each of their two little boys in equal measure and Ruby acknowledged that those little ones were indeed their parents' natural offspring.

Ruby knew that Ben had shown weakness over his liaison with Gilly, but he'd been just a boy finding his way in the world of testosterone-driven opportunity, and she deemed the dead woman culpable in that specific context. How long ago it now all seemed, and how quickly her son had grown up. There was nothing left but anger and hatred for the late Keith Salcombe, but together, Ruby considered, Gilly and Keith had been just as responsible for poor Eric's demise as he had been for theirs. Ruby thought her prospects grim without the long-term love of her life, but when she saw those two little lads crawling about the farmhouse kitchen floor her heart melted every time. She could tell that Ben's boy, Joseph, would take control – he was so much bigger than his brother – but just to see Henrietta's son, Jamie, there at all warmed Ruby to the core, not least because she knew her own son felt the same way.